Awakening
of an
Alien God

Awakening
of an
Alien God

an occult sci-fi novel by
R. Douglas Burns

Magic Hat Books
14066 Creekview Trail
Tyler, Texas 75707
http://magichatbooks.com

MagicHat Books
http://magichatbooks.com/

ISBN-13:
978-0615703657

ISBN-10:
06157036587

Library of Congress Control Number: 2012917822

Searchers after horror haunt strange, far

places. -- H. P. Lovecraft

Preface

Welcome to the third novel of the Messengers trilogy, a series inspired by a reoccurring lucid dream I had while living with my wife and small children on an isolated Missouri farm. I've attempted to craft Awakening of an Alien God so it will stand alone on its own merit, but you might want to read the first and second novels first for a number of reasons.

One reason is that in the preface to the first novel of the series, Messengers of an Alien God, I discuss how I, whom many would term an atheist, came to write a novel about what are at first observation supernatural creatures. I explain that I'm not exactly an atheist, but that doesn't mean I believe the dogma of any of the dualistic religions. I do believe human consciousness is more than just an "epiphenomenon" of the chemical dance of atoms in the brain, as Amit Goswami writes in "The Self-Aware Universe."

This backstory shouldn't distract from the story, but I have to admit this line of thought, as well as my own attempts at astral projection, did greatly corrupt what I originally meant to be a purely Lovecraftian theme spanning a single novel. However, if the backstory interests you, I recommend you obtain the first Messengers novel.

As it turns out, in all three novels, the archangels and their human hybrids, are not so much supernatural as preternatural. This is an important distinction, I think, for some may argue that quantum mechanics, as is currently understood by 21st Century physicists, casts almost a preternatural light on reality. Is the universe(s) a shared dream? Is there such things as time and space, or is everything, including ourselves, and our consciousness, merely projections of the quantum vacuum?

That these questions may be explained by quantum mechanics and super-collider experiments rather than supernatural forces seems a fine point – at least for people like myself who can understand the concepts but not do the higher math of Schrödinger's probability wave-collapse equations.

But rest assured; I'm not trying to craft a new religion, but just tell a good story based on a thought-experiment spanning some twenty years.

R. Douglas Burns
October 2012

A Caveat and Request for Contributors

My alpha-editor, Linda Anderson, and I have worked hard to provide you with clean, grammatical copy, but with only two editors working on 300,000 words of fiction, I'm sure you will find a few typos. If you'd like, and you think the novels worthy of your time, you can help me further clean up the copy by going to my website at http://magichatbooks.com and making comments. I promise to give each and every comment consideration. If you make substantial contributions – even if you only find a typo or two – I will add your name to a list of contributors in the back of the respective novel in the next edition.

Alternately, you may always email me at robertnovel2002@gmail.com with comments and corrections.

If you're reading this on a Kindle, perhaps an easier way for me to find and incorporate your suggested changes, will be for you to turn on the Public Note feature.

For more information on Public Notes go to https://kindle.amazon.com/faq#PublicNotes.

By the way, you'll have to turn on "make reading status and rating public" before you can make your notes public.

If you have the hard copy of any of the novels you'll need send me the page number and a few words of the phrase or paragraph you where you found an error.

1.

Truth and Illusion

Marguerite.

Something had changed. Something fundamental to the nature of the world and for a human angel living in it.

Marguerite's flying companion, the angel who had once been the human May Tyre, gave no sign of noticing the change. She was intently studying something small and white moving through the hay meadow several hundred feet below them. The white speck kept pace with the angels' slow, languid flight path. To see better, Marguerite blinked, but only with her inner eyelids, which were whitish, transparent membranes. The blink wetted her wind-dried eyes, and the white blot resolved into familiar form and sharp detail. From the remnants of her human mind, she dredged up a word.

"Dog!"

She said as much – shouted it, really – to May over the soughing sound of wind passing over their fully extended wings: "Dog!"

May pointed at it. "Dog? My child?" she asked, and then screeched. She screamed often, for no apparent reason, like someone waking from night terrors. Maybe she was.

Marguerite didn't answer the question and gave no heed to the scream. There was no point. May was different from most of the other angels. As with Tommy and a few others, the implantation of the homunculus seed and its associated consciousness had been done before the archangels had realized just how fragile the human mind was.

Angel May was sometimes lucid, sometimes not, sometimes violent as well, and always on the verge of panic. She reminded Marguerite of a severely disturbed child she had once taken care of – when she was human, of course.

She had once been human, hadn't she?

She concentrated. *Yes, she had been human, but that was a lifetime ago, before she had been reborn as an angel.*

If she flew closer to May, perhaps she could snatch her attention away from the dog. The problem was that in flight, hers and May's fully extended wingspans were twenty feet tip-to-tip.

She dropped below May, folded her wings back and turned over with her back to the ground, then re-extended them. She didn't need to flap the wings, and they worked as well as when she flew upside down as right-side-up. Somewhere in the back of her mind, she knew her wings didn't keep her in the air, but some aspect of her angel mind compelled to use the appendages anyway. May banked to the right for no apparent reason, but May did many things that were senseless. Marguerite mirrored her turn, hoping to get May to look in her eyes. Sometimes she could coach her into semi-lucidity if she could make eye contact. As she turned, she was tempted to see if the dog had made a hard right too, to see if it really was pacing them on the ground as she had first thought. Why the dog was so important was hard to fathom, but it had something to do with the shift in reality she had felt moments before.

She gradually closed the distance between her and May until they were flying almost face-to-face. May smiled at her, a good portent. The breeze of their flight made a muted *whoosh* as it funnelled between their wings and tousled May's shoulder-length blond hair.

"Hello, Marguerite," she said as if they were seeing each other after a long separation.

May kept looking over Marguerite's shoulder, still obsessed with the dog. Marguerite hoped May would not eat the dog. May had been eating many inappropriate things lately. Marguerite remembered liking dogs – slobbering, furry mortal things – when she had been mortal herself, but she had not liked them for breakfast.

"Hello, May," Marguerite said. "Something has changed. Have you noticed?"

"Something is always changing," May said. "That's the way this world works. Not like the saucer world."

"Yes, May. But . . ." She stopped talking for she had lost her companion's attention again. May was darting her head right and left, desperate to look past her.

"Where did it go?" May said in a panicky voice.

Marguerite became aware of another sound beyond the whoosh of her and her sister's flight – a *whump-whump* sound, quickly growing louder. *Whump-whump*; she could feel it vibrate the human-like skin that stretched drum-tight over the bones of her wings. *Whump-whump.* Louder now, it was a familiar sound, but one she couldn't name.

WHUMP-WHUMP!

She folded her wings back so she could return to normal flight without slapping against May. She rolled as she fell, enjoying the sensation, letting herself drop a good dozen feet, and then she caught a glimpse of a huge, dingy, dark green thing – the whump-whump thing.

May's shriek shattered the morning sky as Marguerite collided with the body of the whump-whump thing and bounced under its curved nose. She caught a glimpse of a shocked human face through the Plexiglas window. His mouth was agape, which along with the black lenses of his wrap-around sunglasses, gave him a death's head appearance. Then she was rolling underneath the craft to be spat out behind.

Helicopter, she thought, that was it: a helicopter, pleased with herself that she could remember such a trivial word from her past life.

She spread her wings and flew backwards, her feet down and kicking as if she were treading water, and watched the helicopter pass. It was a huge thing, sausage-shaped. Twin rotors, one forward and the other aft, both spun so fast they blurred. Something was wrong with the front rotor, though. The *whump-whump* sound was now a sort of *whump-thump, whump-thump.* The craft lost altitude and fell below her, then leveled out. As its flight stabilized, a huge gossamer leaf rolled off the top of the fuselage.

It was a wing, Marguerite realized. A wing. May's wing, but May was not attached to it. Far to her left, another wing fluttered down to Earth. No May was attached to it either. Marguerite looked down and saw the other pieces of May falling to the ground. Was that a torso? There a leg?

May must have collided with the helicopter's blades. Only Marguerite's little indulgence of free-falling had saved her from the same slice-and-dice fate.

The *whump-thump, whump-thump* faded as the helicopter headed toward Lost Lake with a machine's indifference to May's fate. But what about her feelings? Was she a machine, too? She had just lost the only friend she had, and she felt nothing. Then she hadn't felt remorse or love or hate since her metamorphism. She still had words for such feelings, but they had become archaic terms. Now she was overwhelmed by unfamiliar feelings, and she struggled to find the right words to match them. Something was changing, and it was bigger than May's death. With the exception of May, Marguerite had mostly avoided the other angels. Somehow she and May had been bonded through one of the humans, though the details of that bond were vague. Maybe one of the humans would know. She would find one and force it to tell her.

At once, she missed May. She missed May despite her craziness – maybe because of her craziness. A staggering loneliness threatened to overwhelm her as the realization sank in that helicopter blade had chopped her only companion into a dozen pieces.

She did have feelings after all!

Below, the white dog had found one of May's legs and was dragging it by its toes into the underbrush.

Should she follow the dog or the helicopter?

Stupid thought. Of course she should retrieve May's parts before doing anything else.

Bryan.

Shortly after dawn, Bryan woke from a disturbing dream to find Suzanne sitting in the Shaker rocking chair near the fireplace.

She was sobbing ever so softly, staring at her lap, looking at ... what? He couldn't tell because the chair's arm blocked his line of sight. His senses were addled by the heavy weight of the dream, and he hadn't noticed at first that she was semi-transparent.

First she was undead, now a ghost. Or was he still dreaming?

He didn't care.

His heart rose in his chest to see her, dead or undead, hallucination or apparition.

He had been sleeping on the couch since burning her body and those of John Wright, Laura' undead lover, and Frank Marshall.

He and Laura had set the funeral pyre ablaze the day after entombing the archangel Samiazaz in concrete. How long ago had that been? It felt like countless lifetimes, but it was only a few weeks ago.

Still bundled in his grandmother's quilt, he swung his legs off the couch and sat up, expecting the vision to dissipate. But the Suzanne ghost remained. She let out another barely audible sob and began to rock slowly back and forth, never taking her eyes off whatever was in her lap. She was barefoot, her toenails painted black and dressed in an all-white, ankle-length gauzy gown. A thin, cherry-red twist of a ribbon served as a belt, cinched the dress just under her breasts. Thin filigrees of lace framed the bodice and neckline. There was something classically nineteenth century about the outfit.

She looked up, and her face was diaphanous as the white gown. He could see the stonework of the fireplace through her, but otherwise she looked the same as he had known her in life – or rather as he had known her when she was merely undead, not a stone-cold, rotting, dead thing, not the thing he had burned at Lost Lake.

He just sat on the edge of the couch, happy to watch her rock in the chair, feeling more at peace than he had since losing her. He saw nothing horrible about her, nothing frightening. Quite the contrary; she was as unconventionally pretty as he remembered, but of course, she wasn't beautiful the way a fashion model was beautiful. True, her skin was transparent, and her Irish redhead complexion was apparent from the faint scattering of freckles on the blush of her cheeks and neck. But he though he was fully aware of her flaws – of her chin being perhaps a bit too large, of the premature crow's feet at the corners of her eyes, even of her tendency to slump – yet the parts fit together in a whole that he found beautiful. If he thought about her face, she might even be a little plain, but if he let himself feel her, she was shrouded in perfection.

She continued sobbing.

Could he touch her, comfort her somehow? He desperately wanted to. His heart tore to hear her cry, but the apparition appeared as delicate as a soap bubble, and he feared to even breathe in her direction. The desire to close the distance between them overcame this fear. He started to stand up, but his legs were wadded up in his grandmother's quilt, and he nearly fell on his face.

Waving his arms for balance, he plopped back down on the couch. Suzanne stopped sobbing but continued rocking, still intent upon whatever was in her lap.

He began untangling the wadded quilt as he would untie a difficult knot, stealing a glance at Suzanne while he did so. The quilt, like everything associated with her, had taken on a transcendental aspect, an encrypted map of an unseen world, a hand-sewn object that less than a month ago had been swathed in portent when he had used it to wrap Suzanne's undead body. Now, with her gone, it was just a mundane and musty rag. The quilt's patchwork lizard no longer scurried magically from panel to panel; the colors of the leaves and vines, those maps of faded green and red threads that had glowed with colors beyond the ordinary, were now just faded scraps and deserving only of the trash bin.

He hadn't realized it at the time, but the quilt had taken its magic from the undead Suzanne, who had been both in this world and in another astral plane. It also occurred to him now that more than anything, more than the fantastic sex, it had been this mix of meaning and mystique surrounding Suzanne that had bonded him to her, perhaps forever.

But Suzanne was not merely *undead* now. She was really *dead*. He found the idea of her "translating to another plane of existence" was just so much crap. He had seen her body; when her spirit left it, the body had become merely a hunk of rotting meat. He and Laura had waited overnight, hoping the undead would rise again. But when they returned the next day and found Suzanne's, Sheriff John Wright's and Frank Marshall's bodies already decomposing, they had burned them. Nearly a month later, he could still remember the smell of the black, greasy smoke the bodies made as they burned.

Bryan hadn't just seen and smelled the proof of Suzanne's departure. He felt the loss so deeply and fundamentally that he couldn't describe it.

He finally got his legs out of the quilt.

"Things feel dull and lifeless since you died; died for real, I mean," he said, knowing how insufficient this sounded, knowing he would not have been able to confess such a dependence on her if she had been really here with him, either alive or undead.

She looked up from her lap – startling him. Had she seen him? Had she heard? But her ghostly eyes stared right through him, making him feel as though he was the ghost, not her.

Maybe I am the ghost. Maybe it is really me who's dead. I feel dead inside since she left.

Somehow this was a not a nihilistic thought but a reassuring one.

He stood up to see her better. She held a large red book the size of an unabridged library dictionary. Hints of gold sparkled in the edges of the fine leather binding. It was a bit worn at the corners, and the pages were semi-transparent as she was, but the text upon the pages was opaque and glowed faintly. She traced a finger down the text, and where she touched, the text glowed brighter, then dimmed as her finger moved on.

"I was dreaming – not of you, I think, but of thousands of you, millions of you in a foamy sea," he said to the apparition. With this proclamation, he surprised himself, for memory of the dream had faded until he tried to explain it to her. "I honestly don't know if I'm still dreaming, if this is truth or illusion."

Only one way to find out.

He took a step toward her. She stopped crying and looked up from her book, her eyes wide open in what was either amazement or shock. The vision rippled momentary as if a wall of heat separated them and then winked out, leaving him staring at an empty rocking chair.

The chair continued rocking as if of its own accord.

He took another step to touch the chair and stop it rocking. All at once, he was shivering. The room was cold. The fire had died down to embers long ago, but this spot, though closer to the residual heat of the stonework was frigid. But the wood of the chair's arm felt warm.

Draping the quilt over his shoulders toga-fashion, he padded toward the kitchen. He had been sleeping almost fully dressed, in jeans and a T-shirt. He had lost a sock in his sleep, and the kitchen's tiled floor was cold on his one bare foot. He turned and looked back into the living room, hoping that Suzanne's ghost had reappeared.

The rocking chair remained empty.

He shouldn't feel this bad over losing a woman he had known so briefly; that was neither logical nor reasonable. But then neither logic nor reason ever had anything to do with love. It would have been different, he imagined, if the love had been one-way, if he had loved Suzanne but she had not loved him, the way it had been with Laura. The breakup with Laura had hurt, but in a way it had been a release from a kind of bondage. But Suzanne had said she loved him, and though her love was just as unreasonable and unlikely as his, he had believed in it. He hated to admit it to himself, but such unconditional love was what he'd always been looking for. A psychologist would probably tie it his fears of abandonment as a child, but it didn't feel like some artifact of his screwed-up childhood. It felt real.

To be so dependent, so needy, wasn't manly, but so what? Now all he felt was an inconsolable grief as devastating as if he and Suzanne had been together for decades. He had never been able to believe in a Big Kahuna-type god, a supernatural alpha male who arbitrarily dealt out eternal reward and punishment. As early as age twelve, he had thought the whole concept belonged in a comic book or a graphic novel. But now he wished he could believe in such a being, for then he would at least have somewhere to direct his anger.

He had no appetite, but knew he should eat. He hadn't left the house for a week – had hardly left the couch – and the cupboard was bare except for a single quart-sized mason jar of green beans his grandmother had canned. She had died two years ago, and the beans were at least that old. Would they poison him? Kill him?

Did he give a shit?

He unscrewed the ring holding on the lid. As he pried off the edge of the lid with a knife, he heard a hiss. Was the hiss a good sign or a bad sign? He sniffed. The beans smelled okay, sort of salty, but maybe he should boil them anyway. He dumped them in a pan and found there was enough propane was left in the tank to light the stove, a small favor of the gods. He tried to raise up some gratitude but failed.

As he waited for the beans to boil, he sat at the kitchen table, studying its faded Formica top, feeling like a complete loser.

Now what?

His moment of self-pity was interrupted by the unmistakable sound of helicopter blades. Any kind of aircraft flying over Creedance County had been rare since the fall of the archangels' saucer. He rushed to the back door and swung it open, and was in time to catch sight of a huge double-bladed helicopter flying toward Lost Lake. The thing was built like a bent sausage, painted Army green, with a single red blinking light on its belly. Something looked askew with one of its blades. A white kite-shaped thing sailed off the top of the fuselage and began seesawing its way to earth. Then the helicopter dropped behind the loblolly pines and out of his sight.

He watched the white kite-shaped thing fall, not sure what it was. The sighting had been so brief that he first suspected it to be a vision. But the *whump-whump* sound of the blades persisted though the helicopter was out of sight.

Creedance, Missouri, and Harmon County had been for all practical purposes isolated from the rest of the world for nearly a year. Were things going to be returning to normal now?

He wasn't sure if he cared. The pan of beans on the stove was making bubbling sounds, and he stepped back into the kitchen long enough to dump the boiling mess in a bowl and retrieve a spoon. Stepping back outside, he squatted on the cracked three-foot-square slab of concrete that constituted the back porch.

He had sat there for several minutes, waiting for the beans to cool, before he noticed the dog. It was mostly white, but had a black band across its eyes that made it look like wearing a bandit's mask. It sat on its haunches near the rusted fifty-gallon drum where Bryan burned trash. He was wary of approaching the dog, even though it looked friendly. Since the fall of the archangel saucer, many families, especially those living in town and the trailer parks, had been unable to feed themselves and their families, much less their pets. Many had allowed their dogs to go feral.

But the feral dogs usually traveled in packs, and this dog – he guessed it to be a Border Collie mix – was just sitting and watching him, showing no signs of hostility. Moreover, he could swear the dog was smiling at him.

"Woof," the dog said.

"*Woof* means *hungry*, right girl?"

The dog perked up its ears but didn't wag its tail. *What did that mean in dog-speak?*

Bryan's parents hadn't permitted him to have a dog when he was a child, and he was unsure of how to interpret the dog's body language. Shouldn't it be wagging its tail?

As if reading his mind, the dog began wagging its tail.

A friendly dog-sign if there ever was one. Or was it? If he were wise, he'd go back in house and wait for the dog to leave.

An old empty stainless steel bowl was still sitting by the porch, He used to put out food for stray cats. As it turned out, he hadn't been feeding cats as much as he'd been feeding coyotes. A pack had come through in the middle of the night, and he woken to an unholy howling and scrawling. The next morning all the stray cats were gone. Even weeks later, he would still occasionally find a bit of orange fur or a gray paw, but no whole cats. If any of the cats had survived, they had gone to someplace were there was more cover.

He tentatively tasted the green beans and found them still steaming but not too hot to eat. He spooned about half the beans into the cat bowl and set it about arm's reach from where he sat.

"Hungry, girl?" Bryan wondered what he was doing. He couldn't feed himself today, and here he was sharing with a stray dog. Was he that desperate for companionship?

The dog gave a little yip and stood up on all four legs, its tail still wagging, and gave a big yawn, but didn't come forward.

"It's all right," he said. "It's not much, but it's warm."

The dog trotted over to the bowl, hesitantly sniffed the beans, looked him, but did not eat.

"What's the matter? Not good enough for you?" Bryan scooped a spoonful of beans into his mouth. They didn't have much flavor, but they were salty and warm.

The dog began noisily scarfing up the beans in great, gobbling mouthfuls. In a second the bowl was clean.

"Woof," the dog said, but in a different intonation.

"If that was a 'thank-you,' then you're welcome," Bryan said. "If that's asking for more, then you're dog-out-of-luck. The cupboard is bare."

Again, Bryan could swear the dog smiled at him. Then it trotted across the backyard and into the undergrowth. Evidently, now that dinner was over, the dog had better things to do. Bryan finished his beans in lonely silence. As he got up to go back in the house, the dog returned. It ran in an easy lope across the little back yard, carrying a rabbit in its mouth and wagging its tail. It dropped the dead rabbit at the edge of the concrete pad and backed away, head lowered, hunkered down on its stomach with its front legs extended, whining submissively.

Obviously, the rabbit was a gift to him, the god of green beans.

Moving slowly, Bryan knelt and picked up the rabbit. There was no blood and the body was still warm. Its head lolled loosely, neck broken.

Bryan went back into the house but left the back door open, no longer worried about the dog. He put on some old rubber kitchen gloves, and skinned and gutted the rabbit over the sink, a skill he learned from his grandfather, who had been missing since the fall of the saucer. He thought about throwing the skin to the dog, but somehow that seemed an insult. He turned to the door and found the dog was now sitting on the concrete stoop but making no move to come inside.

"Would you like your share of the rabbit cooked or raw?" Byran said.

"Woof."

"Okay, cooked it is."

He heated a skillet and found a bit of cooking oil in a bottle. Not really enough, and what he really wanted was some flour to bread the meat, but that was just wishful thinking. He did find salt and pepper and made do. He disjointed the rabbit, and in a few minutes, it was sizzling in an iron skillet.

The dog disappeared before the rabbit was finished cooking. Nevertheless, Bryan divided the pieces on two plates and took them back out to the stoop. The meat was greasy and gamey, but more filling than the green beans. The single rabbit provided barely enough for one, but as he ate, Bryan wished the dog would return for its share. He was just finishing the last piece from his plate when the dog returned.

"Here, girl," Bryan called and set the other plate on the ground.

Had she brought him another rabbit?

But as the dog came closer, Bryan could see that whatever it carried in its jaws was too white and smooth to be wild game. Bolder now, the dog dropped the thing at Bryan's feet, then went immediately to the plate of cooked rabbit.

For a moment the nature of the new gift didn't register; his mind simply refused to accept the idea that the friendly dog had brought him a human hand.

The hand had been neatly severed at the wrist as if by a very sharp knife. There was no blood, and the mother-of-pearl skin told him that it was not really the hand of a human but the hand of an angel.

❋ ❋ ❋

2.

Fly Above My Reach

Major Minor.

All the soldiers in the Chinook helicopter jumped at the bang.

"An angel! Unbelievable! An angel just rolled over windscreen!"

The pilot shouted this over the intercom so loud it made Major Karl Minor's ears ring. The other soldiers jumped harder against their safety harnesses at the pilot's anouncement than they had at the bang.

It took a second for the word *angel* to register with Minor. He had heard rumors of flying alien creatures in this little backwater Missouri county, but Minor suspected the pilot, Chief Warrant Officer Tim Scalzi, was messing with their minds.

Stuck back here in the cargo bay with the antique Jeep and shoulder-to-shoulder with the ten-man squad, Minor wondered what really happened. These were strange times, what with the power grid and most electronic devices still down. The situation was common throughout the United States, and as far as anyone knew, the rest of the planet too. Without modern communications, the world had once again become a place where misinformation and superstition ruled.

Had it ever been different?

But angels? What a load of crap. Minor knew from experience that Scalzi was something of a joker, but he made a mental note to have Scalzi pee in a cup on a regular basis when they got back to Fort Leonard Wood. That would cure him of making such pranks.

His thoughts were interrupted as the rotor started making a noise like a tire blown out at sixty miles per hour. Then the entire airframe began shaking, threatening to fall apart in midflight. Minor's butt bounced on the unpadded metal bench, and his teeth rattled. He could feel as well as hear the shuddering groans of the aluminum airframe increased.

The grunt soilders rocked on the benches. One grunt had neglected to correctly fasten his safety harness, and on one of the jolts ejected him from the fold-down bench. He fell face-first onto the twelve-foot-long wooden crate strapped to the deck in the middle of the cargo bay.

The private pushed himself back on the bench, wiped blood from his mouth, and fumbled back into his safety harness. He pointed to a new gap in his front teeth to the soldier sitting next to him, apparently trying to rouse some sympathy. His buddy just nodded toward the forward bulkhead where crudely painted big red letters proclaimed.

<u>Standard Brief:</u>
Get in
Strap in
Shut the Fuck Up
And Don't Touch Nothing

The Chinook rocked to the other side and Minor and the grunts were again thrown against their harnesses. The refitted World War II Jeep strained against its moorings. Minor was glad that none of the Humvees on the base had been running. The antique Jeep was a lot lighter. He certainly didn't need a six-thousand-pound Hummer crammed up his ass. Besides, with a Humvee, the helicopter wouldn't have had room for what the Major thought of as *Plan B*, the contents of the skinny wooden crate that the private had just tried to take bite of.

"Shit!" Scalzi shouted over the intercom again, and the helicopter's nose jerked down, causing Minor to slam against the man sitting next to him.

"Feathering front rotor," Scalzi shouted, and the helicopter leveled out.

"A little dicey there for a moment, as we were so low," Scalzi reported. "But this bird will fly on one rotor. It won't hover. But it will fly. We're almost to the objective. As soon as we clear these trees, I'm setting the beast down before something else falls off. Who knows if the damned angel hit the back rotor too."

The "beast" was a CH-47 Chinook helicopter, an aircraft that had been the workhorse of the United States Army since the Vietnam War. A heavy lifter, the Chinook was designed to carry ten tons or more of troops and equipment. Minor didn't know much else about Chinooks, but he had seen one make an emergency landing in Iraq. Because of the massiveness of the rotors, the aircraft wouldn't come down fast even if the pilot had wanted it to. It was a fifty-foot-long, manure-green, sausage-shaped glider. But if the second rotor failed, Scalzi would need a long stretch without trees or structures to land on. In the Iraq War, a lot of open desert was available if an emergency landing was needed. Here in central Missouri, among pine and blackjack oak forests, with cow ponds every hundred yards, an emergency landing might be a different story. The second rotor had better be okay. If the crash didn't kill them on impact, then what was in the wooden crate might do the job.

The airframe's convulsions settled to a steady shuddering. The helicopter continued losing altitude, and Scalzi was still talking at motor-mouth speed – but about his angel vision, not about their chances of surviving the landing: "She was beautiful! Full breasts, skin like ivory. Red hair. Irish red. But those eyes – they looked right at me through the bubble. I saw the other go up and over through the eyebrows. But I don't think she was the one who must have hit the rotor! That was the honey-blonde one."

Major Minor knew a little Chinook jargon: The "bubble" was the chin bubble, the Plexiglass window below the main windscreen. The "eyebrows" were smaller windows above the front-facing windscreen.

Scalzi's voice calmed. "We've cleared the trees. I don't think the beach is long enough on this side of the lake. I've got to bring her down on the beach anyway. We may hit sort of hard. If we're lucky, it won't do much more than tear off a rear landing gear."

Minor shook his head. Scalzi had been excited talking about his hallucination, then was as cool as a fish when discussing their possible deaths. But what had they really hit? Another aircraft? This had once been an alternate flight-path into the Columbia Regional Airport, but so few planes were flying anymore, that scenario didn't seem likely.

"I'm going to try to lose a few knots by skimming the lake before we hit the beach. It's going to sound rough, but we'll be okay, I think." Scalzi said matter-of-factly. "Better strap yourselves in and hold onto your balls, anyway."

The thought occurred to Major Minor, who was a veteran of two failed wars and a failed marriage, that Scalzi's warning applied to life in general, not just this landing. *Hold onto your balls, it's going to be rough. Too bad no one had given him that heads-up before he got married.*

Minor became very calm, as he always did in any life-threatening situation. Did he really care if he lived through this? At forty-five, he often found himself waking up bitter in the morning and staying that way until he drank himself to sleep at night. Worse, he often spent the rest of the day perpetually pissed-off.

In fact, his mood was more than pissed off. On some days his anger rose from his gut and threatened to totally consume him. This had been happening more and more often since two years ago when Marge, aka, The Bitch, his wife of fourteen years, had left him. The last few years of their marriage had been miserable for both of them. And truth be told, he had been relieved to be out of it. He missed the half his retirement benefits that she had taken with her, but he wasn't sure what he would have done with himself if he had retired, anyway. Relieved or not, she had taken more from him than his government benefits. Gradually, so slowly he hadn't been aware of it happening, the world had become a dead place, and everyone in it, including himself, was just stumbling through life robotically, like walking dead. It was as if some living and vital though unseen part of himself had changed into a clockwork machine. That machine-like soul now ticked off life in bitter, discrete moments. *Tick, I might die. Tock, big fucking deal. Tick, asshole pilot, he should have dodged whatever we hit. Tock, I can't even get angry. Tick, if we crash it'll hurt like hell.*

Tock. What an asshole I've become.

"We've cleared the pines," Scalzi reported over the intercom. "I see clear water, and I'm taking her down!"

Minor's stomach rose as the helicopter dropped rapidly. The feeling of falling lasted for an indeterminable time, then there was a bump came in rear. The Jeep shook hard in its tie-downs. There came the sound of water, like whooshing waves against the hull of a boat, then another bump, this one hard enough to make the airframe vibrate like a steel drum hit with a sledge hammer. Major Minor was thrown against his safety harness and his balls bounced on the bench – just as promised. The *whoosh* ended and was replaced by a rasping sound, and his rear end bounced on the bench again, and he nearly bit off the tip of his tongue. Then, anticlimactically, the helicopter came to a rest.

Major Minor unsnapped his safety harness. He didn't have to order the ten-man patrol to do the same. They were way ahead of him. The rear cargo ramp dropped with a bang, and they all piled out on a sandy beach. Amazingly, no one got trampled or shot themselves or their buddy in their panic. Minor wondered if he could get away with shooting one or two of the effing idiots, maybe just in the leg or butt, as a matter of tough love. Probably not, he decided.

He checked out the helicopter as he stepped onto the beach. Though the engines had shut down, the rear rotor was still idling. The front rotor was motionless. There was no smoke, but the Chinook smelt of scorched oil and hot metal.

Minor ordered the unruly soldiers to go back in the Chinook and unload the Jeep and the rest of the gear off the craft before anything else happened. He was at a loss on how to deal with the Plan-B crate as it weighed more than two thousand pounds and would take a special operation to unload it. He'd have to hope a fire didn't break out on board.

"Where, sir?" asked Sergeant Smith, the only regular military member of the patrol besides the major and Scalzi.

"Where what?" He spat and it came out bloody. Smith looked at the bloody spittle but didn't inquire if the major was all right. And Minor didn't volunteer that the blood was only from biting his own tongue on the first jolt.

"Where do we put it?"

"Anywhere, just get it off the rotorcraft," Minor said. "If you see smoke, get your ass out of there."

About a half mile from the Plan-B crate should be safe – but he didn't say this.

"Yes, sir," Smith said. He looked around. "How about over there in that clearing in the woods?"

"That'll serve," Minor said. If he squinted he could almost make out a large open space about a hundred yards into the forest. A break in the brush seemed to lead to it.

He didn't return Smith's salute – he just wasn't in the mood – and walked around to the front of the helicopter where he found the right front landing strut was bent at an odd angle.

Scalzi and the co-pilot –Minor couldn't remember his name – had exited through the forward side hatch, and now both were staring at the front rotor. They stopped talking as Major Minor approached.

"Well?" Minor asked.

"We're lucky to be alive," Scalzi said. He had removed his flight helmet and was scratching his balding head. Some previous injury caused Scalzi's right eyebrow to be permanently arched. It gave him a permanent supercilious expression.

"Good thing we didn't put the Jeep on the triple-hook, or we'd all have pine trees up our asses," the co-pilot said. Scalzi said nothing, but Minor saw him do a little sideways kick on the co-pilot's shins.

The triple-hook system was used to carry heavy loads externally, suspended on cables beneath the belly of the Chinook. Major Minor had argued for it so they could carry more supplies in the cargo hold. Scalzi had argued against it because of "all the fucking pine trees." Major Minor had relented, making a note to let Scalzi be the first one to eat pinecones when they ran out of rations.

Everyone liked Scalzi.

I detest him.

Why didn't he like him, other than the fact he didn't like anyone very much these days? He suspected he despised Scalzi because the men liked him. Women probably liked Scalzi too. They probably cheated on their husbands with him. Scalzi was a natural-born leader, someone who men will follow unquestionably, but also someone who didn't want to be a leader of men. That enough was enough for Major Minor to wish the goddamn rotor had spun off and gone up Scalzi's butt.

"Like I said, maybe you're just lucky, Major," Scalzi said.

"Luck had nothing to do with it," the co-pilot said. "It was skill."

Skill? You little pissant! How could anything about my life be called lucky?

Before Minor could ask for an explanation, the co-pilot pointed up the rotor. "See that blade there, to the left?"

"Yeah, I see it."

What's wrong with me? Am I getting senile now? He was talking about the landing. Of course, he was talking about the luck of the landing.

"Notice its tip is turned up about a foot?"

"So what?" Minor said.

"It's not only bent," Scalzi said. "I think about six inches of the tip is missing."

Intentional or not, that raised eyebrow said to the major: I think something is missing from you, too.

"I repeat," Minor said. "So what?"

"If as little as a pound of blade is lost, the vibration can shake the craft apart in minutes – or even seconds," the co-pilot said. "If Warrant Officer Scalzi hadn't feathered the blade as quickly as he did, none of us would be standing here now."

"I'm not sure about the second part," Scalzi said. "But I am about the lucky part. If the angel . . . " He gave Major Minor a glance.

The lifted eyebrow made him look disrespectful, and Minor felt his temper rising again. ". . . if the angel or whatever," Scalzi continued, "had struck the blades further in, then we really would all be picking those pinecones out of our assholes." He pointed to the ground. It was littered with pinecones larger than a man's fist.

"*Asshole* must be the word of the day," the major said. The two men just looked at him blankly, and he remembered he hadn't said anything out loud about the rotor passing up through the warrant officer's rear passageway.

"Those angels must be made out tough stuff," the co-pilot said matter-of-factly, changing the subject.

"That's enough talk about angels," Minor said. "I've heard the rumors the same as you. But our mission is a fact-finding one – as well as strategic – and until we capture an angel – or at least photograph one – then we're treating them as unsubstantiated rumors. Is that clear?"

"Yes, sir," the pilots chorused.

"But that's no rumor, sir," the co-pilot said and pointed toward the middle of the lake.

Across the still water, a wedge of metal jutted hundreds of feet into the air. Jammed into the lake at an oblique angle, it looked a sinking Titanic. Its dimensions and massiveness above water suggested much more lay beneath. Though he had seen the aerial reconnaissance photos, Minor's brain still needed a few seconds to process the dimensions to understand that he was looking at a huge saucer-shaped structure from edge on. It was too large and too precisely constructed to be a fabrication made from galvanized roofing and pine two-by-fours. It looked like the saucer in that 1950s black-and-white science fiction movie. What was its name? The one where the saucer lands on the White House lawn and a huge robot emerges? Like that one, except many times larger. A real, live flying saucer. Or perhaps a real, *dead* and *not*-flying saucer, for a blackened gash stretched at least half the length of the exposed object and appeared to extend beneath the water. The edges of the gash were folded out like lips and lined with black. A shiver ran up Minor's back. This was why they were here; this thing was the whole reason for their mission, but his orders said to investigate the *artifact*. The words *flying saucer* were not to be used. That was the official policy, and until this moment, he had bought into it. *Artifact*. Aerial reconnaissance via film wasn't very reliable, but with most of world's satellites out of order, spy satellites included, film photography was the best the U.S. military had, best anyone had – maybe. But this was no fucking artifact. This was a huge saucer-shaped craft that had no business being stuck in the middle of a lake in the Missouri backwoods.

Major Minor checked his watch, an ancient Timex, another reminder that most of the world's digital electronics were dead.

Minor avoided looking directly at Scalzi or the co-pilot. He nodded at the Chinook instead. "Will it fly again?" he asked.

The Chinook's airframe was modern, but its electronic cockpit instruments and engine controls had been retrofitted with hardware from a Vietnam-era museum display.

"The air frame and engines are good. And I think I feathered the blade before the front transmission was damaged," Scalzi said. "But we're not lifting again without a new rotor,"

"And we need another landing gear," the co-pilot said, kicking at the flat tire, its axle bent and twisted. "If we want to land as well as fly."

Looking at the ruined landing gear, Minor asked, "What did it hit?"

Scalzi shrugged, but only with his left shoulder, which balanced out the permanently raised eyebrow on the right. "There was a rock outcropping in the middle of the lake. Who knew? And before you ask, the nearest parts are at The Wood."

The Wood was Fort Leonard Wood, the shittiest Army basic training base where the major had ever been privileged to be stationed. The area was always ten degrees hotter in the summer and ten degrees colder in the winter than anywhere else in the state. If skies were blue anywhere else in the county, they would be gray and overcast over the base. On base, the rain might fall on a summer morning and drive the local humidity up to miserable levels, but only thirty miles away the weather would be cool and comfortable.

"There are a half-dozen Chinooks at The Wood, all with dead electronics, of course," the co-pilot said. "There are Apaches that are running, but nothing big enough still flying to transport a rotor. It'll have to come by ground."

Minor shook his head. Electronic communications were down. Unless they could find a working phone to use, he would have to send men to the military base and back with parts and a mechanic, a three-hundred mile round trip. They might make it with the 1960s jeep still in the cargo hold – if they could find enough gasoline.

Major Minor barked at the two pilots. "Help the grunts set up the base camp; we'll need every man for that. Then we'll deal with getting spare parts."

"Yes, sir," they chorused again.

"You two would be fucking Tweedle-dee and Tweedle-dum, except for that pot gut of yours, Scalzi, and you . . ." Minor still couldn't think of the co-pilot's name ". . . you're as skinny as a peckerwood meth head."

The two men shrugged and grinned. They'd both been in the Army for a while, and though the new Army was a lot kinder and gentler than the one the major had entered decades ago, they took such verbal abuse as a matter of stride. It was to be expected. They saluted and walked toward the rear of the Chinook, slowly, not in a hurry to help with the heavy lifting. There was a sense of déjà vu – more than déjà vu, of an infinite rerun of just this mundane moment, and at that instance, Minor was nearly paralyzed by depression. He wanted to move, to climb out the abyss he felt stranded in, but he could only stand there, watching the piggish men in their unkempt uniforms, with their disordered minds, awkwardly move crates that had corners that had not quite right angles. His hand moved to the pistol in its side holster. The coolness of the gunmetal was comforting.

In the brush to the east, a blur of white and black caught his attention. His paralysis broke, and he turned slowly, his hand, claw-like, on the pistol. As soon as he faced away from the Chinook and the men, he was able to let out a breath. He hadn't realized he'd been holding it, but apparently his breathing had been immobilized along with his mind, body, and soul. The white-and-black shape resolved itself into a dog, but not just any dog. It was surrounded in a kind of mist that sparkled in the morning sunlight. It hopped over a section of dilapidated fence and sat on its haunches looking at him. The mist of sparkling particles disappeared – Minor was reminded of those old, old Star Trek transporter effects.

Though not all that clean-looking itself, the dog seemed a stranger to this world of mud and disorder. Minor wanted to check with his men (*his men, hah!*) to see if they saw it too, but he feared that if he looked away, the morass utterly devoid of order and hope might swallow him up whole.

The dog gave a single yap and headed toward the lake. Minor followed, not daring to look behind. Somewhere along the way he lost sight of the animal. His feelings were mixed, part despair, part missing the irritation offered by the broken machines and men that would take his mind off his chronically pissed-off mood.

He tried to concentrate on the fresh air, the cleanliness of the park. He told himself – lied to himself – that this was enough. He paused and surveyed the area, trying to fill the emptiness by absorbing the sensations of the landscape.

A morning fog still lay over the water and crept up onto the beach where he stood. He could see the helicopter had made a gouge in the sandy gravel way into the shallows and beyond.

The sun crept up over the pines; the fog began to clear. Minor could see the shallows were stirred up and muddy. Where the muddy trail in the water ended, the wide smudged track in the gravel began. It ran straight for a while, then hooked around, barely missing a three-foot-high concrete obelisk that looked like a miniature Washington monument in the middle of the beach.

A warped brass plaque on the concrete pedestal boasted mossy letters that read: "Welcome to Lost Lake."

He didn't bother to read the rest of the inscription; it probably went on about public funds at work or some such bullshit, like on a monument in every other public park in the world. Minor was just glad Scalzi had been able to see the monument in the fog and avoid it. From the ruts in the gravel, it looked as if the left front landing gear had already been trashed before it hit the beach.

It was a good thing, a very good thing, that Scalzi had been able to swerve in time. This Chinook had been fitted with oversized fuel tanks: large cylinders that extended from sides of the airframe and lay right behind the front landing gears. If Scalzi hadn't managed to put the crippled Chinook into a tail spin, and if one of those big fuel tanks had hit the obelisk, it would have been like a fish gutted by a dull knife. The landing would have then been not a landing at all, but a crash-and-burn.

But now Minor was inclined to agree with Scalzi about the luck factor. That fishtail spin could have had totally different results.

He walked further down the beach. Now that the fog was clearing, he got a better look at the saucer. Seen from edge-on, the object could be mistaken for an impossibly large wing. The object's reflection told Major Minor it really was what the aerial photographs suggested: a disk-shaped craft right out of some 1950s sci-fi movie.

If the rest of the saucer was intact underwater, then extrapolating from what he could see, then entire craft must be nearly a thousand feet in diameter, a regular flying battleship. How deep was Lost Lake? Was it deep enough farther out to accommodate a craft of such size? As the mud settled he could see the bottom here at the beach. Shallows. The bottom must drop off sharply farther out.

His superiors had suggested the locals could have erected a fake saucer as some sort of prank or tourist attraction, which had supported his innate suspicion.

But his suspicion had evaporated with the morning fog. The sun had broke completely free of the towering pines, and light glinted off the polished metal. This was no collection of inflatable weather balloons, no riveted-together hodgepodge of tin roofing. Wonderment caught him and carried him back to a place he hadn't visited since he was a child. He clamped down on the feeling, fighting to gain control of his emotions.

No! I refuse to believe this thing is from another world.

From his twenties to his thirties, he had been stricken with the UFO bug. Like many in the military, he had heard pilot reports of strange sightings, of huge objects moving at impossibly fast speeds, of reports being politically suppressed, of a conspiracy to hide the truth. He'd never seen a UFO himself and so doubted their existence, but damn it, he had wanted –

badly needed – to believe in something more noble than the human race.

We all believe in what we need to in order to get through the long, dark night of the soul.

Eventually, his belief and his sense of wonderment went the same way as his belief in Santa Claus and the Tooth Fairy. Or his Christian faith, for that matter, which he had lost at as a teenager. In retrospect, he had needed to believe in something mysterious and more powerful than himself and humans, just as his fundamentalist family needed to believe in a big invisible man in the sky despite all evidence to the contrary. He had looked to the sky and imagined it populated by a multitude of UFOs staring back at him, instead of the eyes of God.

Now that sense of wonderment had returned, but it scared him. Like a jilted man who dared not love again, he was afraid to wonder once more.

Minor shook his head. He was being an idiot. Some part of his mind would always look for something beyond reality, something that transcended this shithole swamp of life. It was an obsolete response. He was a living fossil, like an armadillo.

He'd read somewhere that when startled, the armadillo's programmed response was to jump about a foot in the air and roll into an armored ball. Such a response might work if the armadillo's enemies were all toothed and clawed and bent on eating them. But the armadillo's biggest threat in the modern world was the automobile. When a moving vehicle passed over it, an armadillo would still leap a foot up into the air – only to collide with the undercarriage. The highways of the U.S. Southwest were littered with their bodies, a kind of Darwin award for the four-footed.

He was like one of those stupid armadillos. He had instinctively thrown himself into the machinery of marriage and family and career. Now the marriage was dead. The family was gone. His career was history. He was road kill. He was dead. He just hadn't lain down and accepted it yet.

It would have been so much simpler if the rotor had shaken us apart, if Scalzi – damn him and his fucking eyebrow too – hadn't been so quick to swerve.

Behind him, he could hear the men's muffled voices as they struggled to unload the cargo. They were probably cursing him for not helping. But he was an officer after all, and they were noncoms and enlisted men. Beyond that, he just couldn't stand to be around his fellow humans right now.

A muddy trail through the deeper water marked helicopter's route as it skimmed across the lake. The mud was settling as he watched. A few hundred yards out, there was a block of something gray and amorphous.

More concrete? Another monument?

He squinted, and the form resolved into a block. Its surface lurked just below the surface of the water. It didn't make sense. Squatting there like a big gray toad, mostly hidden, it would pose a serious hazard for boating. So what was it doing in a recreational lake? Whether the gray thing was made of granite or limestone, or was another frigging concrete obelisk, he couldn't tell, but he could see a wide black streak across its top, nearly a foot wide: the skid mark of the helicopter's landing gear tire. Whatever it was, it had obviously been the undoing of the landing gear.

Was something moving in the shallows? Was it just the sunlight on the water? Or his imagination? He did still have an imagination, didn't he?

He walked on down to the edge of the water. Here at the shallows, the mud had completely settled and the water was preternaturally clear with a green tint. Small dead fish floated nose-up in the shallows. Even without the dead fish, Minor knew such clearness in a natural body of water was not good. Clear, colorless water was a sign that its pH was too high for anything – algae, weeds, fish, even bacteria – to grow. Something must have happened recently to drain the lake, thereby further raising the water acidity. Probably all the fish in the lake were dead, not just these in the shallows. But it might not have been a recent thing. The fish could have been dead for a long time, preserved in water too acid for even bacteria to live.

Lost Lake? It should be called *Dead Lake.* Maybe this was a good place for him to die. His hand found the holster of his standard Army issue 9mm Beretta M-9. His fingers toyed with the Velcro holster strap. He could walk out in the water, put a bullet through his head, and like the fish, lie there preserved for months.

A thin wave swept toward him and lapped at his feet. The wind had died, so whatever triggered the wave must be underwater. But all the fish were dead. *Was there a leviathan-like ancient catfish that still lived in the sterile water?* There! He saw the source now, about ten feet out from the shore. As the swirl settled, he caught a glimpse of a long, pale white form just under the surface.

Awakening of an Alien God

The morning sunlight reflected off the lake, blinding him for a moment. He waded into the water, its coolness soaking his trouser legs to mid-calf. Another step and the water rose above his knees. Some trick of the light or perspective made the lake look shallower than it really was. He took another cautious step, but the water did not deepen. He must be standing on a sort of shelf. But he still couldn't see clearly. He might drop in over his head if he went farther.

A cloud crossed the sun, and the reflections were muted. He could see clearly now. The swirling object was larger than he first thought. It was mostly white and roundish, with a glob of swirling black – of what? Filaments? Tendrils? It almost looked like human hair. Unseen current stirred other parts that looked like lace curtains. The currents parted the coal black tendrils for a moment and disclosed what appeared to be a face. He gasped, then calmed himself. The mind plays tricks. That was all it was; his mind was showing him what he wanted to see – or feared to see.

A jellyfish? He knew freshwater jellyfish existed, but they were only a few inches in diameter. Whatever was out there was the size of a Portuguese Man of War.

Bigger.

He drew his pistol and thumbed off the safety, not quite knowing what he was going to do with it – shoot a bunch of submerged dead pondweed?

He took another step and another and another, and then he was standing right over a corpse. And not just any corpse, but that of an incredibly beautiful and naked woman. The water was so clear, it was like looking into a crystal coffin. She was perfectly preserved, her skin was pale as marble. A yard or more of long fine, black hair swirled about his ankles.

She lay on her back with her legs together, one hand modestly covering her crotch, the other draped casually on her breasts. Her cheeks had a rosy blush, and just a hint of fine blue veins traced under the curving flesh of her breasts. Her nipples were bluish-green. She lay on what looked like a bed of white lace curtains. Her eyes were closed, peacefully, as if she were sleeping.

He realized he had absent mindedly brought the barrel of the pistol to the side of his mouth. There was a bullet chambered and the safety was off. *Am I really prepared to bail out?* He lowered the weapon, pushing the thought of suicide out of his mind to make room for the fantastic mystery lying beneath the green water.

Except for the extremely pale skin – not cyanotic like a corpse's, just extremely pale – and the bluish areolae, she might be lying there alive and only holding her breath.

Shit! He had been so enthralled with scoping out her body he had let the pistol dip into the water. No problem, it would still fire. Was he ready? Did he have the balls to do it? He could hold his breath and lie right down beside her. His blood would swirl around her, mix its red tentacles with the strands of her ebon hair.

He found this thought poetically satisfying. A good, pretty death at the end of a bad, ugly life. But he wanted to touch her first. What would her skin feel like? As cold as the water he now stood in? Holding up the gun out of the water, he bent over with one leg in front of the other for balance. If he twisted to one side and stretched he could touch her face, her shoulders, her breasts. Why? He'd seen plenty of dead bodies before, some of them of once beautiful women, true *spoils of war*, and after the first few, his reaction had always been something between mild revulsion and indifference. And in truth, this wasn't a sexual attraction; it was more like being drawn to touch a work of art. The water felt cool. He stretched, not quite reaching her, his hand inches from her forehead. If he brought down his face until the water rose to his shoulder . . . there! His fingertips found her face.

Surprisingly, her skin felt warm, much warmer than the chilly water. How long had she been submerged? Less than an hour? Now fully aroused but not really thinking what he was doing, he leaned down further and slowly stretched a hand toward her breasts. He couldn't quite reach them, not without dunking his face. Was the water safe? He laughed at this. A minute ago he was ready to blow out his brains, and now he was worried about E. coli in the water?

He took a deep breath and dunked in his face, and feeling like a naughty schoolboy, he groped a breast. He closed his eyes on reflex. His erection grew painfully hard. He raised his head out of the water, gasping for breath.

When he looked back to this lady of the lake, she was staring back at him with eyes the color of jade! Before he could move, she grabbed his wrist. He tried to pull free, staggering backward, nearly falling on his butt as his heels dug into the soft sand of the lakebed. Holding his wrist with a grip of steel, the Lady of the Lake slid through the muddy shallows. He fell back, in ankle-deep water now, and backpedaled, pushing his feet against the sandy bottom, dragging her with him. He still held his pistol and drew down on her, but she was entangled with his legs now and he couldn't fire without shooting himself in the bargain.

And he didn't want to shoot her. Couldn't imagine shooting her even to save his own putrid soul.

Her head came out of the water, and she smiled at him, and he lost all impulse to shoot her.

"Help me," she said. *Was it a question, a plea, or an order?*

He managed to get back on his feet and pull her all the way to the beach. Out of the water, she weighed a ton. He leaned forward and put his back into it. It was like trying to move a car. His boots sank deep into the gritty sand.

He fell forward, breathless, his heart pounding. After a minute, when his breath returned, he rolled over on his back. She was standing above him, smiling, beautiful, invincible. What he had mistaken for curtains or elfin burial shrouds were in fact huge diaphanous sheaths of skin attached to her back. She spread these sheaths now, like a moth drying its wings in the sun.

That's what they are, he realized slowly. *Wings. She has wings!* He felt stupid, an earthbound slug, which should have depressed him further, but he found the abyss he had been staring into only minutes ago had been filled with enthrallment.

"You have to be careful with suicide," said the six-foot tall, naked, beautiful entity standing over him. "It doesn't always take in these parts."

She was beautiful and horrible all at once, and there was no other word for her but *angel*.

✳ ✳ ✳

3.

Byzantine Shadows

Laura Jacobsen.

Laura Jacobsen slumped on the littered, sagging sofa in her living room, smoking a bit of locally grown bud, revisiting the echoes of a recent dream-laden sleep, wondering what the hell she was supposed to do with her life now.

For the last two weeks she had been waiting for Bryan to come around. She had given him every reason to never talk to her again, but he was extremely codependent, and she had expected him to come knocking on her door by now.

Laura knew Bryan was suffering from the loss of Suzanne, his undead lover, as much as she was suffering from the loss of the undead John Wright. She also knew neither she nor Bryan could ever hope to have the charismatically erotic attraction for one another that they had with their undead lovers. Nonetheless, she had expected him to come to her for comfort of one sort or another. Maybe it was his compulsion to look after her. And what did she want from him? Well, if he was co-dependent, then what did that make her? An addict?

She would have found succor in his attentions if at some level, she could have have assured herself it was all right to be dysfunctional. But she was more than merely mildly messed up. She was obsessing over the loss of a lover who had been twenty-some years her senior and dead, or at least dead-ish.

She guessed Bryan would have found release in some perverse masochistic way by putting up with her fucked-up obsessions and her crap. She felt a twinge of guilt: He would have found relief from the inherent, often unnamed guilt that all co-dependent personalities suffered from, and which people like her unconsciously manipulated.

She felt she and Bryan had been programmed, destined by some schizophrenic cosmic mind, to feed upon each other. Not exactly soul mates, but karmically connected. Or was she deceiving herself? A twinge of guilt, numbed to the point of self-parody, assaulted her.

She was not a parasitic bitch. She was not!

She mentally batted away the thought. Did she give a flying fuck about such things anymore? Bryan had obviously, finally, wisely, given up on her. Who could blame him? Even when they had been in a relationship – and he had been a kind and considerate partner – she had acted the schizoid, often abusive, controlling lover.

Maybe she was a parasite and a loser on top of that.

But though Bryan's avoidance of her was understandable, how to proceed? Nothing was left for her here. Only a few weeks ago, she, Bryan, and the undead but still animated John Wright, Suzanne Zimmerman, and Frank Marshall had entombed Samiazaz, the last archangel, in concrete. Upon Samiazaz's entombment, some spell had been broken. (She hated the word spell but didn't know what else to call it.) The undead had become simply dead, perhaps translated to some other dimension, into another type of body. Whatever the reality, she and Bryan had been left behind and, in mourning, had made a pact to make a joint expedition into the saucer. Their plan had been to explore the saucer, to see what kind of world it enclosed. Now that all the archangels were out of the picture, the saucer was the home of nearly a hundred angel/human hybrids, including May and Marguerite. They sometimes entered it through the great gash in the skin that had been caused by the vigilante fertilizer bomb, but more often would just roost in large numbers on its outer surface like huge pigeons.

She and Bryan had made a pact in a *why-the-hell-not* state of mind. An exact word for this existed, but in her semi-dazed and confused state, Laura couldn't remember it. She had hoped to find a way to locate John in the alternate universe that could be accessed through the saucer. Though Bryan didn't speak of it, she was sure he had the same, slim hope of finding Suzanne. So in a way, they were supporting each other's dysfunctional love obsessions.

But did that make it all right for her to try to pull his strings?

She felt incompetent to deliberate on such ethically fine lines. Her head hurt when trying to untangle the metaphysics of reincarnation and destiny on other astral planes. After his death but before his translation to another plane, Uncle Robert had tried to explain it to her. But his exegesis sounded like a muddled collection of modern physics, Buddhism,

Brahmanism, and New-Age spiritualism. She loved the old man whether he was dead or alive, but knew that his explanations were often just so much bullshit. In fact, he would be the first to admit so, but would probably use a word like *balderdash* instead.

Memories of Uncle Robert made her smile, and she took another toke, a big one, holding in the smoke for a small eternities until it escaped in a cough. Her eyes watered. Her mind buzzed, and the world vibrated in harmony.

One advantage of Creedance being technologically thrown back into the early twentieth century was that the local pot growers couldn't really market their crops beyond the county line. Nor were they were hampered by fly-overs by narcotics agents because few aircraft remained operational. As a result, the citizens of Creedance enjoyed a cheap, plentiful supply of marijuana with no worry of prosecution. She suspected half the town was getting stoned on a regular basis now. Most modern distractions had disappeared after the Fall. There were no broadcast or cable television shows, few consumer goods, even no electricity at times. Local stocks of prescription drugs such as a Valium, Prozac, and Xanax had been depleted, as had the stores of narcotic pain relievers such as Vicodin and Percocet, so both legitimate sufferers and 'respectable' junkies had gone cold turkey. Everyone was searching for alternatives to their addictions. Moonshine was still plentiful, but as the commonly used condensers were old car radiators, there was a high chance of it being contaminated with glycol from antifreeze or lead from soldered joints. As a result, Creedance's citizens, even those more conservative – housewives, one-time bankers, even ministers – were buying tickets for the Marrakesh Express.

As for her, she used to be able to take or leave such things, but to numb the loss of John Wright, she had started smoking pot regularly, every day, sometimes several times a day. Life had become a long, sleepy journey with a few weird rest stops along the way.

She giggled out loud. If *Sheriff* John Wright were here now he would have to arrest her. Her eyes moistened, and she felt a dull pain in her chest. Who would have thought that she would find meaning and mystery in life loving a man his age? He was a cop, for crying out loud – and a right-wing conservative. Not exactly a Rush Limbaugh, but a bird of a feather, for Christ's sake! And, oh, there was also that little matter of him being undead, of having blown out all of his gray matter through the top of his head with a .357 magnum.

She took another toke. The world stilled, and she became simultaneousl content and excited like a child on Christmas morning.

Now what had she been thinking? Whatever, if it had been important, it would eventually come back to her. At this moment, she found herself happy to stare into the darkened open doorway that led to the basement.

A thunk sounded from that stairwell, startling her. Did something move there? It had been a faint, dull knock like knuckles rapping on wood. She stared into the complex shadows of the stairwell, and the small hairs on the back of her neck tingled. Was that a face lurking in the shadows? Bright glittering eyes, framed by cascading Rasputin-like hair, coalesced in the darkness.

Who? How did he get in?

Where was her aluminum baseball bat? Under the bed in the basement, the most useless place to keep it, of course. The air became heavy and thick. Dust motes stopped dancing upon the stray rays of bleached-out light leaking through the narrow gap between the living room's drawn curtains. The sun chose that moment to rise above the loblolly pines surrounding her house, and a new beam of yellowish bright light lasered through the air to illuminate the first step of the stairwell. She avoided looking into the fading shadows, afraid to see the face that held those metallic, glittering eyes. Her heart seemed to stop.

"Who are you?" she wanted to ask but dared not speak or look up. More than anything, she wanted to get up and run, but her body was immobilized as if she were in a nightmare.

She saw a movement at the base of the doorway. Her head swam and she forced herself to breathe, which reassured her with its sound, and her black cat, Isis, stepped from the shadows into the muted light of the living room and scurried across the dirty carpet to the front door, where she whined, "Leett mew-ou-t, mmm, mew-ou-t."

Laura let out the breath she had been holding. *It was only the cat!* Calm returned, then departed as Laura slowly realized the eyes she had seen had been too high to be the cat's. With wavering will, she forced herself to look back into the stairwell.

The sunlight penetrated further as the sun broke over the treetops, dissolving the shadows. Nothing was in the stairwell except her Navy surplus pea coat. She took another breath, and her heart began beating hard in her chest. *But what about the eyes?* The jacket lacked buttons. That's why she had stored it in the stairwell.

She suspiciously eyed the smoldering joint in her fingers. *What was in this stuff?* The local growers had obviously been experimenting with selective breeding and cross-pollinating. She dropped the doobie in a cup of water on the coffee table. It sizzled briefly and went out. Maybe getting stoned several times a day wasn't such a good idea.

She showered in the downstairs stall – cold water only because her propane tank was empty. As she dressed, passages of a dream from last night before returned like a faded, lost letter. She remembered something about a huge, recumbent blue giant moving across a moonlit sky. Like a constellation figure, his frame was outlined by bright stars, like a connect-the-dots monster. His eyes, though closed, were defined by two brilliant white stars. Bryan had been with her in the dream, but the clock had been turned back so he was only a recently pubescent Bryan. Other shapes –clowns of all things –had been pursuing the giant across the sky. Maybe *pursuing* was not the word; *attending* was better.

Clowns, though, was right word. They had looked like clowns, though a bit on the orange side, and were definitely in attendance to the giant, an entourage trailing at his heels. Like him, they were ghostly images anchored by stars.

Though all the sky-figures possessed unseen power, the clowns disturbed her most. She hated clowns, had actually been terrified of them when she was a child. The dream also had another constellation outline that reminded her of a Winnebago camper. What did it all mean? She had no idea. Like most dreams it had a logic all its own.

She shook her head to dispel the dream and again regretted that last doobie.

But the damned clowns had seemed so real!

The effects of the marijuana somewhat wore off with the cold shower, but the sense of unreality persisted, whether from the dream or from the fright of looking into the complex shadows of the basement, she didn't know. It reminded her of the time she spent in the alien saucer. Life had a dreamlike quality there, a sense that reality was irrational, with no clear line between what was real and what was not. It both unsettled and intrigued her. Though disturbing, the feeling of disorientation was an improvement over the sense of emptiness and lack of purpose that earlier threatened to suck her soul into a dark pit.

Slacker time was over. It was time to take action. If Bryan wouldn't come to her, she'd go to him.

Ignoring her earlier moral quandary, she considered using Bryan's love for her to spur him into action. That was the core of his thing with the Zimmerman woman; Bryan needed to feel loved. All men needed to feel loved to a degree. They were all lost boys. For some, the need translated to feeling admired, adored. Others, threatened by their own need, always wanted to be in control. Their egos had to be constantly boosted, which made her an accomplice to attempted self-aggrandizement. With Bryan it was different. He was a true lost little boy. He needed regular reminding that he was loved. His was really a sweet neurosis, but it invited abuse.

She once had a cat who had been taken away from his mother too soon. He wasn't like other cats. He wasn't independent. He wanted to be cuddled, even when he was a grown-up tom. Bryan was like that cat. Was that what Suzanne had given him? Or had it been so physical with her as to be spiritual, as her love for John Wright had been? She looked inward for this answer, but drew back as the pain returned.

She would not find this answer within herself. She couldn't analyze herself as she could others. As for Bryan, she could easily sink into the role of the idealized mother figure, at once loving and authoritative, close and intimate, but ultimately unattainable. She could be a manipulative bitch, and he'd follow her back into the alien saucer, follow her to hell.

Could she do that and still live with herself?

She was all to aware of her own weaknesses, flaws of character that her past affair with Bryan had allowed her to see clearly. The more Bryan had loved her, the more she had trusted him. Yet the very trust she felt spurred fear of violence. She knew Bryan would never hurt her, that her conflicted feelings and fears of abandonment came from being abused by her father, someone she should have been able to trust implicitly. But that knowledge didn't matter. The fear, the aversion to a trusting, loving relationship was rooted right down in her muscle memory.

She had run headlong into this emotional wall not just with Bryan, but with anyone else she had become romantically involved with before, male or female. Bryan had just been able to intellectualize it more, and be patient with her as a result. But her feeling of being damaged goods had never gone away. She had learned to recognize it, but was unable to reach down to where it lived and get rid of it, like carrying a big ugly, dead toad her pocket. It was there, it was disgusting, but she couldn't bring herself to touch it, much less accept ownership.

The only love relationship in her life that hadn't dead-ended had been with John Wright. Why him? Why then? The toad had still been there, but it hadn't mattered. She would have taken it out her pocket and kissed its slimy warts if he had asked her to – and laughed as she did so.

Momentarily she was overwhelmed by the smell, taste and feel of John Wright's skin. Dizzy, she had to brace herself against the couch as memories washed through her. She could feel the need there, between her legs, but it was more than just physical, more than hormones and pheromones, wasn't it?

Wasn't it?

As powerful as any addiction, a bottomless hunger consumed her. For the sake of her very soul she had to find him. This was the love that poets had written about, a love she had believed to be pure bullshit – until she fell in love with the reanimated John Wright.

So should she manipulate Bryan? Let him fuck her if he wanted, and afterward tell him that she loved him? No, that just didn't feel right and probably wouldn't work anyway. Bryan wasn't stupid. He was really quite intelligent. He had just the one emotional Achilles heel. Besides, they had been through too much together. It was like they belonged to some dysfunctional family now. She had been able to trust him as much as her screwed-up soul had let her. She owed him better treatment. However, he was tortured by losing his undead lover too and admitted it, so reminding him of Suzanne was probably actually a straight-forward ploy.

Outside, the morning was clear and warm with slight puffs of clouds. It wouldn't be a bad day for a walk, but Bryan's house was six or seven miles away, and she had a sense of urgency now. She decided that seven miles without engine failure was too much to ask of her ancient Volkswagen Beetle. She went back in the house and changed from sandals to grungy Nike cross trainers. Once mauve with pink laces, they were now mostly ecru from toe to heel. Her hands trembled from the memory of John Wright as she tied the laces. When they first made love, his untying these very shoes had been a first step in undressing her.

She tossed a few unread novels, *To a Lighthouse* among them, out of the VW's passenger' seat into the back. The Beetle was a true Beetle, a '60s relic with an oversized metal button on the floorboard that she had to push with her toe to engage the starter. The battery was weak, barely strong enough to turn over the engine. On the second push of the floor button, the engine popped, coughed and stuttered. The car had a manual choke, a pull-knob on the dashboard. As the engine warmed up, she gradually pushed in the knob, and the stuttering smoothed out – sort of.

There was a miss at normal idle, and she had to pump the gas pedal to keep the car from dying. She nearly stalled it as she put it in gear and let out the clutch, but she jammed it into second gear, and she lurched was out of the driveway, the rear tires slinging gravel and dust behind her. The engine noise smoothed out to a deafening din, and her presence of mind returned. Did she really need Bryan or any man? Did she need a Sancho Panza to join her on her quixotic quest? Why couldn't she just return to the saucer on her own? The answer was she needed Bryan to help her find John Wright because he was essential in some way that she could only intuit. She tried to analyze this intuition, but there was no logic to it. She was not one of those weak-willed women who needed a man to give her life purpose – was she? But she did need a friend, a compatriot, and Bryan was the closest thing to either of those she had. Maybe that was all there was to it.

A shadow engulfed the car, and she hunched in the driver's seat to peer up into the sky, half-expecting to see another angel saucer. Instead a huge blue man stretching across half the sky had blotted out the morning sun. She screamed and drove into the ditch.

Bryan.

"Hello? Anyone home?"

Bryan was still sitting on his back porch with his new dog when he heard Laura call out. "Out back," he yelled back.

As she came around to the back, he said, "I didn't hear you drive up."

"I had a little accident about four miles back," she said. "The Beetle is in the ditch."

"Accident? Are you hurt?"

"Only my self-esteem."

She looked dusty and tired. Sweat stained her gray hoodie, and dark circles were under her eyes. She still looked good though.

"Who's your friend?" she asked.

"You mean the dog?"

"Who else? Do you have an invisible friend, too?"

"Maybe. Do ghosts count?"

"Huh?"

"Never mind. This is . . ." He patted the dog's head. The dog, who was sitting on its haunches beside him, wagged its tail, sending up swirls of dust from what used to be his grandmother's flowerbed. But it wasn't an enthusiastic wag; more like, *Oh yeah, I'm a dog. This what I'm supposed to do.*

"He's sort of an understatement type of dog, isn't he," Laura said.

"You're assuming it's a he. We're new friends, and I haven't been so forward to ask, but it's so gentle I'm assuming it's a girl dog."

"That's you. Always the proper gentleman; you won't use the B-word, even if it's appropriate," she said. "But from where I'm standing it's obvious he's a he."

"Too bad. I was considering naming him Diana."

"Maybe he's gay, and you could still name him Diana? Hey, could I have some water?"

"Sure. No ice, but the water from the outside spigot comes out cool. Here, use my glass."

She looked at the cup with suspicion. She knew about his shortcomings as a housekeeper.

"I washed it just the other week," he said.

Shaking her head, she filled it from the outside tap. She chugged half the glass, then poured the remainder over her head and ran her finger through her dark, black hair to brush wet strands off her forehead.

"Want to tell me about it?" he asked her.

"In a minute. I'm still embarrassed. Why Diana? Girl dog or gay boy dog, it doesn't look like a princess to me."

"Because Diana – the Roman – or was she Greek? Whatever, I'm talking about the goddess, not the British royalty. She was a hunter. This girl –," he patted the dog on the head, "– or rather boy – brought me a fresh March hare. If you'd gotten here a half-hour earlier, we'd have shared our hasenpfeffer, wouldn't we, what's-your-name?"

He patted the dog on the head again.

"Are you sure it's a he?" he said, disappointed.

"Bryan, he has testicles. Really big ones. That's a sure sign in the dog it's a he. I don't think there's such things as transsexual doggies."

"Yeah. I guess I was in denial. You know? It's hard to get past first impressions."

They shared a moment of silence.

"Apollo?" Laura asked after awhile.

"What about Apollo? You mean the god? My mythology is a bit rusty."

"The nature of ancient mythology is to be rusty."

"Maybe we need some new mythology then. Tell me about Apollo."

"He was Diana's brother."

He patted the dog again. His fur was too clean and well groomed for a stray. "Apollo?" The dog just looked at him. "Diana?"

Lacking shoulders, dogs can't shrug, but his body language said, *Sure, why not?*

"Okay, I think I'll just stick with *Dog,* for now. It's a unisex name."

Laura laughed and so did Bryan. It was good to share a laugh again. The gloom-and-doom of the morning lifted for a moment.

"Okay, *Dog* it is until someone claims you."

Laura refilled the glass from the tap and sat down beside him on the concrete step. She smelled of sweat and piney forest. Her eyes were bloodshot. Had she been smoking pot this early?Most likely. Mixed with the sweat he caught a whiff of the distinctive odor.

The cheerful moment dissipated as quickly as it arrived. Bryan could sense that Laura wanted something but was holding back asking. He restrained himself from making an opening for her to ask. Let her suffer for once.

Odd, no, only weeks ago, she had held him completely in thrall. He had felt suicidal when she ditched him. Then he had found Suzanne in the woodpile only a half-mile from here and everything had changed. He should resent the woman sitting next to him now, but they had been through a lot together and had worked out some personal issues in the process, both of them. Besides, he understood part of the reason she had ditched him wasn't that she hadn't cared for him. Because of her history of abuse, she would always have the impulse to run away from those she became close to. And there was the matter of the undead John Wright. If she had been pulled to Wright as irresistibly as he had been drawn to Suzanne, he could understand why she had turned her back on him.

He gave up. "Want to tell me why your car is in a ditch?"

"I saw something big in the sky. It scared me, and I drove into the ditch."

"Was it big and green and sort of sausage shaped?" He laughed without thinking." Like a helicopter, maybe?"

"I know a helicopter when I see it," she said tersely. "It was just my imagination and startled me at first, that's all."

"Startled you, did it?"

"I screamed like a little girl," she said, smiling finally.

"You *are* a little girl."

"And now you're being sexist."

The smile vanished, but he knew her well enough to know she was feigning indignation – well, somewhat feigning it.

Even on a good day, Laura, like everyone else, had hot-button issues. Given the history of her childhood, she had a right to them. And now he was also sure she had been getting stoned lately, probably quite a lot. There would be no right answer at this point. He considered showing her the severed angel hand. Earlier, he had swaddled it in a towel. Like an abandoned baby, the bundle now lay in the ruined flowerbed beside the porch. Was now the right time to show it to her? Maybe he should wait until she came down a little more.

The silence dragged on. Laura made no attempt to restart the conversation. She absent-mindedly scraped patterns in the dirt with the toe of her incredibly filthy sneaker. He waited, knowing when she needed silence.

After about ten minutes, she said, "It was silhouetted by the sun. It was like a negative image of a huge blue man. I could see clouds through him. Don't look at me that way!"

"Calm down. You don't have to convince me. These are crazy times," he said. He had meant to sound supportive, but it came out like an accusation.

The dog got up and gave them a look that said, *You two, poor deluded humans*, then trotted off. Before he disappeared through the gap in the overgrown hedge, he gave them the look again. Laura looked at Bryan, and they both laughed.

"That's a weird dog," she said. "He looked disgusted with us, I swear. Giant blue men, prudish dogs; you're probably thinking I need to stop smoking the local production."

"I saw it too, and I haven't been smoking anything."

"You saw it too?"

"I mean the look the dog gave us." Now he was really worried about her. Hallucinating in broad daylight – then he remembered the apparition he had seen in his living room.

"I think he left out of disgust. Maybe you've lost him," Laura said.

"I think he'll be back, probably bearing gifts."

"Gifts? You mean more wild game?

"That or more body parts."

She looked at him questioningly.

He put the towel at his feet and unrolled it. He expected at least a shocked gasp from Laura as he uncovered the severed hand, but she just stared at it. He hadn't noticed before that the hand, though large, looked feminine. There was still no blood, and the delicate tracing of blue veins lay like lacework under the skin of the back of the hand.

Laura's eyes moistened, and a single tear rolled slowly down her face. He couldn't remember her crying before, not even when John Wright had died for real.

"I think it's May's hand," she said softly. "May Tyre, the angel. Don't ask me how I know, but I do."

✳ ✳ ✳

4.

Hide Their Intent

Major Minor.

Major Karl Minor was discontented even before opened the food travesty called an MRE. What had the Army become? The greatest fighting force in the world was reduced to providing its soldiers with a vegetarian bean-and-rice burrito Meal Ready to Eat. Well, that was just perfect, fucking perfect.

Laughter and music filtered through the woods from the main encampment. At his orders, the troop had moved most of the supplies out of the Chinook and into the woods. The rationale he had given the men for a camp removed from the helicopter was to escape the mosquitoes, which swarmed in large numbers near the lake. But the little blood-suckers were rampant in the woods too. The main reason for the move had really been to mitigate the danger of Plan-B accidently detonating. But on retrospect, anything within a half mile radius would be shredded if Plan-B went off prematurely. On some level, he suspected, he had really wanted to distance himself from the sight of the alien saucer. It was disquieting to them all, maybe him most of all.

The laughter from the camp was accompanied by the smell of wood smoke. They had erected a bivouac tent, complete with a little field kitchen, but the troops had chosen to cook outside. Major Minor had chosen not to join them.

Now he ate by himself at a small tourist campsite another twenty yards or so farther into the woods. It had few amenities: a weatherworn trestle table, a rusty cast-iron cooking grill, and a water faucet. The faucet actually delivered water – it must be a gravity-fed supply from a tower – but the water was brown and smelled like a latrine, so Minor elected to drink from his canteen. Had they brought purification tablets? If not, they would run short of water soon. He made a mental note to have a couple of the more reliable men find a new source of potable water. Stupid how he still found comfort in these mundane day-to-day responsibilities of command.

More laughter came from the main camp. A new song played on a boombox: "Old Man, take a look at my life…" Neil Young; that was about right, though he suspected it was meant as a tongue-in-cheek insult directed at him. He was by no means like they were. They were of another species altogether, and they disgusted him, even more than he disgusted himself.

From the sound of their voices, the men were drinking more than water. Drugs, at least marijuana, were probably on hand, too. Minor had long since given up trying to police these actions, as had today's Army in general. With the federal government in a shambles – it had been a broken-down piece of crap on the verge of anarchy even before the Fall – and no real collective will at the Pentagon, there was little to prevent soldiers from going AWOL. So the command strategy was fewer sticks and more carrots, but with the military-industrial complex in a shambles, even little carrots were in short supply. So the alternative was tolerance, an odd bent for the Army. If enlistees stayed put, they got three meals a day. As for drugs, commanding officers were told to look the other way as much as possible. Hassle the grunts very much, and they would just stagger off into some hole in the wall. Most of the United States was now just a collection of holes in the wall. Court martials were out, as no resources were available to staff them or to even feed the prisoners. As for capital punishment, Army firing squads would accomplish nothing except mass AWOLs or widespread mutiny. So the standing orders were to leave men alone as much as possible and keep them fed. But even the three square meals a day had rounded-off corners these days, as was obvious with this sorry shit MRE – perfect example, even by Army standards.

Still, looking the other way was difficult for him. He wondered if anything harder than pot was being used. Twenty years ago, it was booze. And as the Afghanistan war dragged on and on, opium production climbed, and a lot of soldiers became camouflaged junkies. But since industrialization had come to a virtual standstill and commercial alcohol production with it, and imports dropped to zero, pot had become much more common.

He'd always considered himself strong-willed. He had been able to deal with booze, and pot only made him even more paranoid and depressed. He had fell victim to crack cocaine, but whipped the addiction without help from anyone.

But being the presence of the angel was the most intoxicating experience he'd ever had. This morning, after offering him advice on the dangers of suicide, the angel had flown off, casting an *I'll be back* look over her shoulder as she flew upward. That had been ten hours ago, and that was the real reason he was out here, closer to the edge of the lake. He hoped if he was alone, the fabulous creature might return. It wasn't that she had been the most beautiful woman he'd ever seen — though she had. And it wasn't love — he wasn't sure he knew what the word meant. He was hooked on being in her presence, and the addiction had formed instantly, like the first puff of crack.

Twilight was here, and she still hadn't returned. She'd abandoned him – the story of his life with all women except for perhaps his mother – out-of-sight, out-of-mind.

He spat, disgusted with his sorry-ass self.

Grumbling, he opened the MRE, and laid out the various packets on the table. The burrito was in its own sealed drab-green packet, salsa in another smaller foil pouch, as were a fudge brownie, a plastic fork, and, if the vegetarian burrito wasn't suspect enough, there was also some oozy, orange-colored cheese cream in a clear tube. Thinking the burrito would be best served hot, he salvaged some dry wood from the surrounding woods and started a small fire in the camp grill.

The grill was basically an iron box with a slotted metal lid. It sat about waist-high on a metal pole. The cooking surface was encrusted with something black and caramelized. He hoped the black crud on the grill was only baked-on barbecue sauce and not charred crankcase oil as it appeared to be.

As it cooked without a skillet and oil, the burrito threatened to char with zebra stripes rather than brown all over. He rescued it with the fork, breaking one of the plastic tines in the process. At first taste, it was bland, hot enough to burn his tongue on the outside and lukewarm in the middle. Mental note: Send a couple of the least-stoned men out tomorrow with assault rifles to hunt for game. He didn't really care for venison, but right now he'd eat anything that didn't come in a foil pouch.

Another burst of laughter intruded on his silence. For the briefest of moments, he was tempted to join them at the main camp, but he knew that laughter would end the minute he stepped into their midst. There would be a furtive attempt to hide the contraband. All he'd get would be a few half-hearted sloppy salutes, and some hostile stares. Better he stay here and choke down his burnt burrito.

There was no moon, and the stars were coming out bright. With no artificial light to wash them out, the Milky Way would soon fill the sky. At one time he would have been excited at the chance to see the zodiac light; now it just promised to be another gray, listless night.

He tried to remember exactly when he had lost that sense of joy of just being alive, even of taking interest in being alive. It would be easy blame the loss on his ex-wife, on his being abandoned by his friends, even his children, but here in the quiet darkness, with no distractions to keep him from looking inward, he knew the truth.

His right hand found the wedding band he still wore. He should have taken it off and thrown it away long ago, but he kept it for reasons he couldn't explain. Hope? No. Put on a front for the men? Maybe. Sentimentality? No. He couldn't, wouldn't, shed a tear over a woman who showed him no respect. *Love?* He tried again to understand the term and failed. But he did know the textbook definition of love. The loss of his wife, his friends, and his children's affection had nothing to do with betrayed love. He suspected – *shit, he knew!* – he had brought about their abandonment. Exactly how or why this had played out he wasn't sure, but he was aware of gradually shutting them out, of some dark, rageful creature of in the depths of his subconscious pulling him him, pulling his strings, driving anyone who might care for him away.

He refused to feel sorry for himself. How many times had his mother told him about his father's simpering sentimentality, his inability to listen to reason, his effeminate irrationality? Why couldn't his wife have understood that he had to be strong and immune and suppress such congenital weaknesses?

These unthinking demands had gradually undermined his professional life as well. His career had stalled out, and as a result a vital part of his soul had been lost long ago, leaving him a spiritual husk, for what was a man but the work he did? So of course the other officers had distanced themselves from him, not out of cruelty or indifference, but for self-preservation. True, his family had to bear some of the blame. They had forced him into that corner by their own selfish, childish needs, but he had let them, hadn't he? He should have been stronger, harder, more commanding — more the man.

He still remembered his wife's parting shot as she walked out the door: *You're just a mean little prick – and I do mean little!*

But what had he truly lost? If he looked back at his early life, it was full enough, though filled with what? Desire? The quest to achieve, to rise above the ordinary? Perhaps.

Had it been love? Perhaps he had sought love, but never known how – or even whether – to trust it. He suspected that women would always betray him, that somehow he encouraged the betrayal. He had learned slowly over the years that all women were not whores, as his father had thought they were. (His father would never have said such in front of his mother.) But maybe they would always be whores where he was concerned, creatures of secret intent or simply mad as birds. But other men, less deserving men, were luckier – or stronger.

Why was he worrying about this? He spat on the leaf-littered ground. He was a dog trying to catch his own tail.

The very nature of what had been lost was hard to detail and therefore nearly impossible to put into words. He wished he had some artistic talent – painting, music – then perhaps he could at least define the loss. That was the essence of it. Some unheard, unseen phenomena that imbued life with meaning and purpose: That was what he had lost.

He hadn't realized this until this morning, when he had pulled the lady out of the lake. At that moment, as she stood before him and spread her wings in the morning sun, that sense of wonderment about life had returned. He had been high for hours after the brief encounter. He was a statue brought to life. She was the apotheosis of meaning. She was purity in the flesh, as contradictory as that sounded.

If it hadn't been for Warrant Officer Scalzi's description of the angel who had hit the Chinook, Minor would have questioned his own sanity. It didn't matter that the angel he'd pulled from the lake didn't match either of those Scalzi had described. The one Scalzi had seen was red-headed. Another one was blond, he said. The angel of the lake's hair had been coal-black, a natural black stark against her light skin. She had no pubic hair – of course he had looked – but as she turned to fly away he had noticed she had black hair at the base of her spine. Not coarse hair, but a fine downy hair that lay flat against the skin like scanty fur.

Now, as the spotlight of his imagination's eye played over the memory of her body, he felt an erection rising.

More barks of laughter came from the main camp. He didn't care. Let the fools have their fun. For a moment, even the charred burrito tasted zesty. Of its own accord, his hand moved to his crotch. He was definitely turned on, but it wasn't entirely physical. It couldn't be love. It was more like... what was the word? ... living in a dream ... being under a spell, or ...

"Excuse me, sir?"

Minor jumped and banged his knees on the underside of the trestle table. Sergeant Smith stood at the edge of the clearing. Had he seen him fondling himself?

How dare the shit sneak up on him!

Minor cleared his throat and tried to control his anger, but it came out a growl.

"Oh, sorry, sir," Smith said. Evidently misreading the cause of the major's anger as a lapse in military protocol, he saluted. Minor sat back down, afraid the embarrassing bulge in his trousers was obvious. He returned the salute.

"Something wrong, Sergeant?"

"I was sent ... came to report that we captured some intruders."

"Intruders? This is a public park, Smith."

"Well, they were sneaking around, sir."

"Around the bivouac?"

"No, sir. The beach. A man and a woman."

"Maybe they wanted to go for a swim," Minor said, surprising himself with his own ease. He wanted to be left alone with his musings.

Smith must have picked up on this and looked confused. "Sir. I thought we were supposed to secure the area, sir."

Minor decided not to acknowledge that Smith was right. That would show weakness. He smoothed his trousers under the table and stood up. The burrito was a hard lump in his stomach, but his erection had subsided. "Show me these intruders, Smith."

"Yes, sir," Smith said but made no move to return to the main camp.

"What is it, Sergeant?"

"The fire, sir?" He pointed at the grill. The coals were still smoldering.

"What about it?"

"Shouldn't the fire be put out?"

Minor felt his bile rising and again suppressed the urge to chew Smith a new asshole. But the sergeant was right. What was wrong with him? He wasn't thinking clearly. He couldn't get the Lady of the Lake out of his head.

"I only have drinking water here, which is scarce," Minor said. "Send a man back to take care of it. He can use the water from the lake."

"Yes, sir." The sergeant turned and started back to the bivouac.

Minor followed, trying to clear his mind of the vision of the Lady of the Lake. Twilight was giving way to night, and the insect orchestra was tuning up. Minor was cheered despite himself.

His good mood evaporated as he stepped into the large tent the men had erected near the broken-down merry-go-round. The tent was smoky as the men had built a small campfire near the opposite entrance, and a westerly breeze was blowing the smoke inside. This seemed incredibly stupid even for them until he saw one of the privates in the far corner taking a toke on a joint. The smoldering wood fire covered up the smell of pot.

Inside the tent, a couple of dozen sparrows flittered about.

The men had hauled a couple of the wooden trestle picnic tables inside the tent. A young man and a dark-haired woman were seated side by side at one of them. The man was dressed in khaki shorts and a T-shirt with a tiger on it. The woman was in blue jeans and a gray hoodie sweatshirt a size too big for her. He looked frightened. She looked ready to spit nails.

"Civilians," Major Minor said.

"They were launching a john boat, sir," Sergeant Smith said.

"It is a public lake," Minor said.

"They had a rope with a hook on the end," Smith said. "I – we – think they meant to enter the saucer."

"Did you ask them if that's what they were doing?"

"Well, no. Sir. But it was obvious, sir."

It was cool in the tent, but Minor noticed the sergeant's forehead was beaded with sweat. *The man is terrified of me. Good. Fear is the foundation of discipline and order.*

The young woman stood. She had to turn sideways and swing her legs over the bench of the trestle table, and as she did so he saw that her hands had been cruelly tied behind her back with plastic zip-ties. Her hair was deep black and as long as the Lady of the Lake's, but her complexion was darker, Mediterranean, perhaps a Middle Eastern genetic line in there somewhere. Her eyes blazed at him, and he knew she was as crazy, as fucked-up-in-the-head, as he was, someone whose childhood had been something of a nightmare. Takes one to know one.

Get a grip. You can't expect sympathy from this woman. You don't know what she and the punk she was with were up to.

Though her facial resemblance to the angel was shocking, this woman was definitely human. Shorter, of course, wingless, certainly – he inwardly laughed at this thought. His heart fluttered in his chest at the thought of the angel, as perfect and beautiful as a Botticelli painting. This was a real, live woman, and though very attractive, certainly flawed. Despite the baggy clothes she wore, he could tell she had good legs. Her upturned breasts were not completely hidden by the sweatshirt, and as she twisted on the bench, she showed off a tight ass under the blue denim.

What was happening to him? She was just a woman, attractive and damaged in some key way that pushed his buttons, but she was just a woman. Many such women who hung about the base were just as young, just as much the emotional road kill of runaway parenting, and they could be had for the price of a few good meals and a fifth of whiskey.

The man looked like a putz, but a handsome young putz, which made Minor was all too aware the he was not only old, but ugly – cartoonishly ugly. He felt the young woman's eyes crawl across his face as she looked at him. For the first time in a long time he hated his pockmarked face, his age, his palooka nose, his softening middle. Worse, he hated his desire for her, which had verged on obsession for a brief moment. What was he doing, looking at the bitch in that way? She'd spit in his face if she could, like most women would. It must have been her chance resemblance to the Lady of the Lake that confused him.

Laura.

"Stay calm," Bryan told her as the officer came into the tent.

Stay calm? They had been trying to launch the flat-bottomed john boat when the stoned soldiers had come upon them. The soldiers had trussed their hands behind their backs like common criminals.

They were sitting close enough that Bryan could whisper to her, "It's an officer. Don't mouth off to him. Be cool!"

"Be cool? You didn't just have a couple of slime balls try to do a cavity search on you through your clothes!" She had meant to whisper as well, but she was just too pissed off. The soldier guarding them, one of the gropers, was a couple of feet away, and the son-of-a-bitch now gave her a lecherous wink!

As for the officer, she didn't know military rank – the golden thingies on his shirt collar were one clue – but it was his bearing, the way he carried himself, the way the other soldiers deferred to him that was the tell. He was short, bullish, and scowled like a man whose emotional range vacillated from a sour pout to red-faced rage.

He was talking to the sergeant, and the sergeant looked like he was getting chewed out. Good. The sergeant had arrested them, and the sergeant stood by while the soldiers groped her in pretense of a search. If it hadn't been for the soldier with a permanently arched eyebrow, the groping might have turned into a gang rape.

Ignoring Bryan shaking his head, she swung her legs out from under the table and stood up, nearly losing her balance because her hands were bound behind her back with a plastic zip-tie. When the officer turned from the sergeant to look at her, he did an exaggerated double take. He seemed to recognize her. He recovered, but made no attempt to step closer. His mouth was set, the scowl back in place. She held back a laugh. All he needed was a big cigar stuck in his mouth to look like the perfect caricature of a male chauvinist pig. He cleared his throat authoritatively, but this was more bluff and swagger. His eyes gave him away. He was genuinely shocked at seeing her. But she was sure they had never met before.

Since he wasn't coming toward her, she would go to him. She tottered forward. Having her hands tied behind her back caused her hips to sway in a way she hoped wasn't provocative. As she closed the distance between then, his eyes remained locked on hers. It was one of those instances – brief moments really, as only a couple of steps separated them – that time expanded. She became hyper-aware of everything, of the sparrows chittering overhead like happy children, the smell of the men's sweat, beer, and faint whiffs of pot. The classic rock song "Thunderstruck" played faintly somewhere in the background.

She sensed a touch of lust in the officer's look; she felt it as his eyes crawled like cockroaches up her body. *Do I dare work that to my advantage?* She didn't need Bryan to tell her they were in a dangerous situation, but decided toying with the officer's desire was a dangerous game she dared not play.

Maybe her history caused her to even momentarily consider such a ploy.

Will I always be driven to put myself in a position where I'm going to be hurt, abused? The hell with it. It's who I am. She tottered forward, and true to form the officer stepped forward and grabbed her arm to steady her.

His face had softened as he held her arm. The name tag on his uniform said 'Minor.'

"Captain Minor," she guessed.

"*Major* Minor," he replied and made a stiff attempt at a smile, and for a brief moment, his eyes did another of those fast crawls up and down her body. He looked embarrassed. It was a reflex rather than an intentional prolonged leer. He was trying not to ogle her, and this raised her estimation of him a little.

Despite the pain from the plastic-tie strap pinching into her wrists, despite wondering if these frigging military nut stoners would just take her and Bryan out and shoot them, she had to struggle to stifle a laugh.

Instead of laughing at him, she took a breath, cocked a hip (just a bit) and asked, "Why are we here, Major?"

"Good question," the major said. "But I'll rephrase that. What did you think you and your friend were doing here?"

Bryan had risen from the table and now stood behind her. "It's a public park," he said. "We were only going boating."

"Sure you were," Sergeant Smith said.

"Can it, Sergeant," Minor said. "Were they carrying weapons?"

"They had that rope and grappling hook I told you about," the sergeant said.

Major Minor turned to the sergeant. He looked like he was going to give him another ass-chewing, reconsidered, and turned back to Laura.

"Well?" he said.

"I, we . . ." Laura said, stuttering, feeling spacey. She really, really wished now she hadn't smoked all that pot this morning.

"We needed a rope to tow the boat out beyond the shallows," Bryan said.

"I didn't ask you," the major said. "I asked her."

"I brought it," Bryan said. "She just came along to keep me company."

The sergeant took a short baton from a sheath on his belt. He flipped his wrist, and with a metallic clank, the baton telescoped to four times its length. He stepped to one side raised it overhead. "The major said shut the fuck up!" he said.

"Let him speak," the major said.

Laura checked the sergeant's face; it was deadpan. He lowered the baton but held it ready as his side, a threat. *I recognize this now. It's good cop, bad cop. Did they work out this act in advance or is it ad lib?*

She guessed for the sergeant it was mostly an act. But despite his touch of chivalry, she sensed the major was the dangerous one. Like a sick animal, he positively leaked anger, pain, and ill will. She could almost taste his angst in the air between them.

Bryan surprised her by stepping forward, partially shielding her from Smith, like some kind of hero.

"The hook is an old hay-hook," he said. "You jab it in and drag the bales. I use it like an anchor."

Which was a good lie, but the sergeant wasn't buying it. "It's too small, too lightweight to be an anchor," he said.

"You can snag underwater brush with it. There's lots in the lake," he said.

The major was silent for a moment, considering this, deliberately not looking at her. The air became tense and hostile.

"I need to go to bathroom," she announced, as much to break the spell than anything, but she really did need to go.

The major looked at her as if she were from another planet.

"I need to pee. I can't do it with my hands tied behind my back," she said.

This embarrassed the major – he blushed red – but it amused the sergeant.

"I'll make a deal with you," he said. "Both of you."

Laura was instantly angry again. Maybe it was his patronizing tone or just her full bladder or the psychic leakage of resentment from the major, but it was all she could do not to spit at his face. "First tell us what right you have to hold us," she said.

"Mistake," Bryan whispered just to her.

But the major heard him. "Yes, it was a mistake to come here. This area, like the rest of the country, is under martial law," he said matter-of-factly.

"The lake wasn't posted. We've been coming here for years," Bryan said in a small voice.

"Yes, Major," Laura said. "We had a town weenie roast here just a couple weeks ago."

"I could have you shot as insurgents anyway, by provisions of the NDAA, and not even have to fill out any paperwork – purely my call," he said and paused, watching them.

Laura knew NDAA referred to the National Defense Authorization Act, a piece of fascist legislation enacted to counter terrorism after 9/11 that had turned gradually into a Big Brother way to oppress U.S. citizens.

But despite the major being a prick, he wasn't terrorizing them for the pleaure of it. It was just a job for him. The sergeant, on the other hand, was grinning like a happy baboon at the thought of shooting them.

"But that's not going to happen if you cooperate," the major said. He paused again. Was he waiting for them to volunteer information? Or was it just his technique of intimidation?

"What do you want us to do?" Bryan said, his voice betraying his anger. She inched closer to him, hoping to calm him. This got a glare from the major. She didn't know whether to move away or get closer to Bryan. She pretty sure they wouldn't club her, a woman, but they might beat the crap out of Bryan.

"We need some supplies. Most of all, we need a vehicle to haul them."

"I have a truck. A half-ton pickup" Bryan said. "It's at my grandfather's farmhouse."

"How far?" the major asked.

"About two miles."

"Why didn't you drive it here?" the sergeant asked. "Instead of just sneaking into the park?"

"Gasoline is scarce."

"But the truck runs?" the major asked.

"Yeah, if you've got gas to put in it."

"You'd be willing to let us use it to go to town to requisition supplies?"

"If it'll get our hands untied and out of here, sure I would," Bryan said. "I'll sign the title over to you."

"Not necessary. I could commandeer it anyway," the major said, missing the joke. "Here's how it's going to work. You and Smith are going to take a jerry can of our gasoline with you and get the truck. Sergeant, the truck will carry more than our Jeep. I'll hold the young lady here – what's your name?"

"Laura," she said.

"We keep Laura here until you get back with the truck."

"Then you let us go?" Laura said. She didn't like the idea of being left behind with the major and the men.

"Probably, but we'll see. Deal?"

Bryan nodded. "Untie us. We won't run off, will we, sweetheart," he said. "We're engaged, married as soon as I can scrounge up enough money for the ring."

Another lie, but a bit of genius on Bryan's part, Laura thought. The soldiers – and the major – might be more likely to leave her alone if she was spoken for, if she wasn't a *loose* woman. The "sweetheart" bit was good touch, but funny. Bryan wasn't one to use such silly terms of endearment even when they had been lovers.

"Congratulations," the major said, but he sounded disappointed. A man of the old school. The way-old school.

"Sergeant. Cut the young lady's bonds. The man's, too. Have Scalzi and his co-pilot escort her to the camp toilet. Take him . . ." He looked at Bryan questionably.

"Bryan Douglas."

"Take Mr. Douglas to get some gasoline."

She breathed a little easier when she heard the name *Scalzi*. He had been the one who stopped the groping.

The sergeant put away his baton and took a wicked-looking blade from a holster on his belt. He cut her bonds. "Come on, you," he said to Bryan, leaving her with the major.

Bryan looked at her over his shoulder as they walked away. "We'll be back as soon as we can, sweetheart," he said and winked.

Awakening of an Alien God

When they were gone, the major said. "Grow up here?"

"Yes."

"Do you're parents live here?"

"They're both dead," she said.

"Pity," he said, but something remained left unsaid. The major, for all his old-school manners, frightened her. He seemed on the edge of losing it entirely. He had a hint of madness in his eyes. And the way he kept looking at her creeped her out.

Scalzi came and escorted her to the toilet. As they walked out of the tent, she could feel the gelid gaze of the major's cold gray eyes on her back

.

* * *

5.

As I befriend the dead

"We know that reason is the devil's harlot, and can do nothing but slander and harm all that god says and does." - Martin Luther

Marguerite.

She had been able to find many of May's body parts, and a happy song came to her as she flew over the piney woods.

I want to be friends with the dead
I want their heads to loll my way
as I enter the room
I want them to only have their dead eyes
for me.

I want to be friends with the dead
I want their cold skin,
fresh from death,
to give up its secrets
only to me.

Where had this song come from? For weeks after her metamorphosis, she had difficulties in putting two words together. Her mind had been a clouded pool in a dark wood. Memories had flittered in like silver minnows, darting in and out of sight. Reason was even more fleeting, a dark useless lump hibernating in the muddy bottom. But lately, the waters had cleared somewhat, the woods had lightened, and little memories her past life danced in the open spots.. And if perhaps reason had not yet totally returned, then it no longer spent its days and nights hiding in the mud. Best of all, song and poetry, attributes she had no talent for as a human, now came unbidden.

She also had a new self-awareness, and she was be astounded at the absurdity of her actions. She had collected many of her dead friend's body parts, but she had not truly worked out what process she was to follow. However, she knew intuitively that if she could gather all or at least most of the parts, May would be resurrected.

She had yet to find two important parts, a hand and – the most important – the head. A memory from her past life came back, an image of John, her husband, using – what was it called? Never mind; it was a machine he rode on to cut the green grass outside their house. She paused; feelings about John and the house almost surfaced, then were gone. *What was she thinking?* Oh, yes, John had run over a rabbit. Pieces were everywhere. She had been heartbroken (why?) over the dead creature, and had put on her pink rubber dishwashing gloves to pick up the pieces. Sort of like now. But she hadn't been able to find the head, just the floppy bunny ears, and John had said that was because the head had been smashed to bits and joked about not looking for Easter eggs this year, and she had detested his cruel insensitivity.

She could recall the distaste for him, feel it in the center of her stomach, but had anything else been between them? They had been together a long time. Had that feeling been all there was between them? She couldn't remember.

Her mind returned to the problem at hand. What if May's head had not just been lost but shredded into pieces by the huge whirling blade of the helicopter? How would she find the pieces?

She flew lower, skimming over the treetops. Tucking back her wings, she felt their thin skin and fine threadwork of bones fall around the backs of her legs. She became a streamlined cocoon and fell more than flew between the trees. The branches whipped about her face, but her skin was tough as steel. It would take much more, perhaps huge whirling blades of metal, to do more than scratch her. The ground zoomed up, and at the last moment she opened her wings and twisted to land feet-first. The pinecones on the ground were crushed under her feet with the force of her landing. An explosion of dust and powered pinecone swirled around her.

Why here? What had brought her here?

She folded up her wings behind her so they didn't drag through the rubble of leaves, twigs, and pinecones. She didn't know how she did any of this; fly or land or control her wings. A week ago she didn't question the process, but now as her mind cleared, she found it curious. If she tried to do it, thought about it, either nothing happened or the action became clumsy and stillborn. But if she just let it happen, like when hands automatically come up to catch a ball, then everything worked as it should. Maybe that was a clue. She needed to stop trying. To let the fairies in her head take control.

But how?

Now that her mind worked better, thinking of nothing was difficult. She looked up at the heavens for guidance, and smiled to herself. Guidance would not come from above but from inside.

Before her transformation, she had been so screaming-serious religious, always looking upward for salvation, always praying to an invisible man in the sky, someone never heard from but always longed for, like a lost love who had scorned her. She not dared to admit that she doubted the god of love had existed, or if his love was conditional upon her loyalty to him. However, in her more reflective moments, she had privately questioned the existence of anything beyond the material, of anything that she could not see and feel. She had been a closet atheist. Death was the stoppage of a biological machine. Love was likewise a biochemical reaction. But she feared this vision of an empty, mechanical, impersonal universe to core of her hypothetical soul, feared it more than a hell of eternal punishment. So she covered the thoughts in blanket of unquestioning faith, hoping if she continued outward testimony a magical rebirth would come.

She realized she had been walking, looking up at the tall pine trees as they were washed by the wind. Her body, whether by a will of its own or driven by those fairies in her head, had taken her to the edge of the woods. Beyond, across a small, overgrown cow pasture and a hedge, squatted an old two-story farmhouse. Was that where she was supposed to go?

The house looked vaguely familiar. She was sure she had been here before, had known someone here in her previous life as a human being, but the details would not surface.

Before she stepped out of the shadows of the woods, she saw two men, one in shorts and a T-shirt, the other in a khaki uniform, climb into an old red truck. Her angel eyes could hear the door hinges squeak and the hollow metal sound of them slamming. The engine started; she heard the clank of gears, and then the truck was bouncing down the driveway.

A cloud of tiny black flies swirled around her as she stepped out of the woods. The cloud, which was about a foot wide, drew back, then rammed her face and breasts *en masse*, but the individual flies bounced off her like rain.

They're not attacking me; they just can't see me. I'm transparent to them.

She stepped out of the way, and the flies buzzed past her. She held up her hand to the morning sun, and the light did not pass through. She felt substantial enough, but apparently was visible to flies.

She thought about flying the rest of the way to the farmhouse but decided to walk instead. The grass felt cool on her feet. A slight breeze rippled past her legs as she crossed the pasture. The hedge that separated the pasture from the house's backyard was ragged and without an opening, but she leaped over it effortlessly.

Once she was in the yard, she didn't know what she was supposed to next. Was she to go in the house? Search about the porch, maybe look in those crappy-looking flowerbeds? She looked to the sky for patterns in the building clouds. *I used to do this as child.* There, that's a whale, and that's a . . . the touch of metal interrupted her. She looked down to find her hand on the doorknob of the farmhouse's back door. She tried the knob, but was locked. She tried again, harder, and the knob twisted off in her hand. But the door remained stuck fast, so she shoved it with her shoulder. The doorframe creaked. She pushed harder, and it burst inward, wood splinters flying.

Inside, she found herself in the kitchen. More *déjà vu*, this time of walking across the cracked linoleum floor, sitting at the red Formica table. Yes, she had visited her old friend Mattie here when she was dying of breast cancer. She remembered the old lady saying something about *taking life on faith and one day at a time, dear. One day at a time.* This was Mattie's kitchen. But that was a lifetime ago.

One day at a time . . .

She tried to remember the name of Mattie's grandson who was living here now, but couldn't. Maybe that memory would come back in time, too.

She saw something wrapped in a dirty kitchen towel. Without thinking, she flipped over a corner of the towel to find May's missing hand. This was fortunate but disappointing because she had really hoped to find May's head, but Mattie would have told her that it was all right.

One piece at a time, dear . . .

Bryan.

He tried to keep his eyes on the road as he drove, but Sergeant Smith him made him nervous. A beat-up tan Chevy Cavalier passed them going the other way, throwing up a cloud of dust from the dirt road through the open side windows of his truck. He caught a glimpse of long red hair through the dusty windshield. For a second, the driver was Suzanne, and he could feel his heart beating as if it were in his throat. But the vision resolved into a young man, a teenage hypster, his mouth set, his features dominated by deep-set sad eyes and a giant Adam's apple.

"Why are you slowing down?" the sergeant said. It was really a command, not a question. He had his assault rifle between his legs, the barrel pointed at the roof.

"Sorry," Bryan said.

Anger welled up in him, not just at the sergeant, but at Suzanne, too. Why had she chosen to abandon him? The delicate balance of this physical plane and the astral planes may have been broken with the entombment in concrete of Samiazaz, the last archangel, and that may have tipped the scales so that Suzanne was forced to translate to another plane. But by his understanding, that didn't preclude her contacting him from that other plane. Did it?

"Hey, slow down! I said speed up, not drive like a fucking bat out of hell!" the sergeant shouted. "This old piece of crap isn't safe over fifty!"

"Okay, okay. Sorry. Sorry," Bryan said. Unconsciously, he had floored the accelerator pedal. Above forty or so on a rough road, the truck did sound as if it were about to disintegrate into bouncing bolts and flapping sheet metal. But it wouldn't. Bryan slowed down anyway, to humor the sergeant, who maintained a white-knuckled grip on the assault rife even at only thirty-five miles per hour.

The vision of Suzanne overlaid on the stoned hippie persisted. He needed to get his mind off her. "So what's the plan, exactly?" he asked

Sergeant Smith.

"I think the first order of business is to commandeer a better vehicle," Smith said.

"Go for it, as long as our deal is still in place," Bryan said. "But around here, you need to be careful whose vehicle you try to take."

"I've got this as a means of persuasion," he said, patting the rifle. "These farmer hicks will pay attention."

Bryan paused. Ordinarily he'd let the asshole learn his lesson the hard way, but if the sergeant was killed, that might not bid well for Laura. "This is Aryan Nation territory. If you're going to try strongman tactics, you should have brought more men, more guns – a lot more guns."

"I don't think this piece of shit would haul more men. Besides I think this M-16 is more than a match for shotguns and deer rifles."

"Sergeant, there are meth cooks out in these woods who are a lot better armed than you are."

"What about the law in this town we're going to, what's it called?"

"Creedance. And the sheriff is dead."

"The drug dealers?"

"No, he died by his own hand," Bryan said.

"Hrmmh!" the sergeant said and spit out the window. "A coward's way out."

Bryan didn't tell of the circumstances that led the sheriff's suicide, which apparently had to do with his wife, Marguerite, leaving him to be transformed into an angel. Nor did he mention Wright's revival after his suicide – more like a reincarnation – as one of the undead. The sergeant, he suspected, wouldn't believe anything he didn't experience with his own eyes and ears. Besides, no sane man or woman would believe the incredible reality-bending influence of the archangels unless he or she had experienced them firsthand.

"Watch out for that fucking clown!" Smith said.

"What?" Bryan had been lost in thought again. Up ahead, standing by the side of the gravel road, was a short, redheaded clown. Another hallucinatory overlay? No the sergeant had seen it, too. Still it had to be some sort of jape. A clown? Out here in the middle of nowhere? Really?

But as the truck rumbled closer, there was no mistaking the carrot-top hair, the garishly painted face. The clown was smiling at him, waving his – or was it her? – hand, looking straight at him – no, through him. He was paralyzed. Was he totally losing it? But something was wrong about the proportions of the clown's body, something not just absurd but alien about the baggy striped pants and orange blouse. Was it really clown makeup or was that its actual face?

The creature stepped into the middle of the road and, still smiling, put its hands on its hips, a decidedly feminine posture. In one of those expanded moments where time slows to a crawl, he could see the pupils of her eyes, not human pupils at all, but black featureless pools. And the shirt: little Care Bears or Grateful Dead bears, sort of, but not quite – too many arms and legs.

His foot moved as if through heavy syrup to find the brake pedal, and the truck slid sideways on loose gravel. Smith shouted an obscenity while the truck spun in a complete circle, throwing up gravel and dust. He looked for the clown through the window as they came around, for some reason expecting Suzanne to be standing there, but instead saw the trunk of an oak tree rushing up to meet him. He was momentarily aware of his chest hitting the steering wheel, of glass shattering, then a loud buzzing . . .

. . . and he was lying on his back staring at an impossibly red sky and dark green clouds, with no memory of waking or arriving here, wherever *here* was.

There had been an accident. He recalled that much, but it had seemed to have happened just a moment ago. He remembered pain in his chest, the rush of the big tree trunk filling the truck's windshield. Then he was here.

The clouds drifted lazily across the red tapestry of the sky. Mixed in with the clouds, other objects moved. They were golden in the sunlight and so high up as to hide many details about themselves. They were too slow-moving to be aircraft. Saucers? An involuntary shiver traveled down his spine.

The redness of the sky could be attributed to dust; he'd seen pictures of Australian dust storms, but in those, the redness extended down to the ground. Here the air around him was clear – a mystery.

He was surrounded by tall grass that looked at first like something found in western prairies, except the seed heads were little tridents with sharp-looking tips that looked dangerous to the touch. He sat up carefully, expecting pain, but felt nothing wrong; nothing hurt. In fact, he felt terrific, energized.

Sitting, he still couldn't see over the tall grass, so he stood up cautiously. Standing didn't hurt either. Nothing seemed to be broken, for which he was grateful.

If the sky hadn't proved he wasn't in Missouri any longer, the vista he now saw confirmed it. He was on a vast, flat plane of endless grass. And his clothes had changed. Before – what he remembered as *before,* anyway – he had been wearing shorts, a University of Missouri T-shirt and tennis shoes. Now he had on a kind of coverall, a lot like bib overalls, but made of some fuzzy material with a texture between corduroy and heavy felt. His shirt beneath the overalls was coarse denim. His tennis shoes had been replaced by scuffed heavy leather work boots.

So where the hell was he? In the middle of frigging nowhere on an alien planet? He turned around slowly. There! With the sun behind him, he could see a windmill. Maybe a house was next to it. He couldn't be sure.

With nothing else in sight, he began walking toward the windmill. The tall grass grew in sparsely spaced clumps. Though the trident heads looked razor-sharp, a tentative touch found they were actually feather-soft. The day was hot, but the air was dry, and as long as he didn't concern himself too much with how he had gotten here, he could enjoy the walk. Soon he could see a small brown cube of a stucco house sat near the windmill. Small splashes of color moved near the house. Was that the laughter of children he heard drifting across the grass?

Was this an astral plane? Sophia, Uncle Robert's widow, had trained Bryan and others in astral projection, taking them to a plane called Summerland, but it was nothing like this place. Her theory was that the influence of the archangels had caused the boundaries between the planes become so indistinct that humans – living humans as well as those recently deceased – were often confused as to whether they were on an earthly plane or another.

Sophia had taught Bryan and the others some simple signs to look for to determine which plane they were on. And he had borrowed some of Sophia's books on the topic, but he was definitely not an expert, either from experience or intellect.

But did he need those clues? As he walked through alien grass growing under a red sky, he had no doubt that he was not on Earth. Neither did he have any doubt that this body he was in wasn't flesh, blood, and bone. Summerland was – depending on the source of the information – either heaven or merely a pleasant lower astral plane. All said Summertime was Earth- and spring-like, with pretty trees and rolling plains of grass – no thorns or dangerous animals – a landscaped and endless city park, a regular planet-wide Garden of Eden. It was a place where the mind could recreate Earth-like conditions or live out fantasies. But this world with its endless grassland prairie and red sky was unlike any description of Summertime he'd read.

One thing about the experience struck a familiar chord. As a kid, he'd read Edgar Rice Burroughs' Mars books. In the first book, *A Princess of Mars*, John Carter was instantly transported to Mars after a near-death experience.

Burrough's description the process resembled what Bryan now recognized as a transition to another astral plane. This certainly wasn't Mars; it definitely was another planet, there was no question about that.

The question was had he died back on Earth when his truck had crashed into that big oak tree?

Was he a living human on Earth having an out-of-body experience or a recently deceased moving up the astral planes?

He looked up again at the odd objects floating among the clouds. He squinted and shaded his eyes from the sun.

Yes, they were saucers, much like the one sank in Lost Lake back on Earth. The golden tint came trick of the light sun. They were actually silver, he guessed.

He was a bit disappointed they weren't Barsoomian dirigibles and laughed at himself. The wind carried the sound of his laughter over the tall grass. Too bad. He wasn't destined to be a warlord of Mars, but maybe a day laborer on the tall grass prairies of an alien planet.

Which wasn't so bad, now that he thought about it. Was this a place where he could live out his unresolved issues from Earth, a place sprung into being by his own spirit? If so, who or what would he find in the little house under the windmill?

While he was pondering this, a black-and-white dog came bounding through the tall grass.

"Apollo, I mean Dog?" Byran said.

The dog trotted over, all bright eyes and wagging tail, to lick Bryan's hand. Bryan scratched the dog's head. "What are you doing here, boy?"

In way of an answer, the dog licked his hand again, and started trotting toward the little brown house.

✳ ✳ ✳

6.

Delusion Departs

Major Minor.

As he walked toward Lost Lake, Major Minor's thoughts of suicide were washed away by the intense, impressionistic colors of sky and trees. Even the scrub brush and the littering of stray cans and scraps of paper appeared to be made of brighter stuff than ordinary matter. Just as clean and bright in his mind – though harder to describe – was the residual feeling from his meeting with the Lady of the Lake, a persistent amalgamated vision comprised of excitement, wonder, and lust.

The wind, which had picked up by midmorning, brushed the waters of Lost Lake into small white-capped waves. Minor walked as close to the water's edge as he could without getting his boots wet. He had been compelled to once more inspect the course the Chinook had taken across the lake. The water was even more transparent today than it had been yesterday. With its slightly greenish hue, it looked like liquid bleach and the lake bottom was clearly visible.

He could easily see the marks in the shallows of the lakebed where he had dragged out the Lady of the Lake the day before. As intense as that memory was, he still doubted its reality, couldn't help thinking of it as a phantasmagorical-induced misstep of his psyche – except he could see the outline of the angel where she had lain on her back under the water. He could also make out the trail of his stumbling steps in the sand.

More intriguing was the gouge in the mud of the lake bottom made by the Chinook's landing. The gouge cut a straight line from the angel's imprint in the mud and up the beach. That mark led directly to the Chinook now, which sat like a big, green beached whale at the edge of the woods.

In the other direction, toward the center of the lake, if he imagined a straight line from the gouge, the path of the Chinook intersected what appeared to be a chunk of gray rock about thirty meters out. Yesterday he had been able to make out only vague details of the chunk, but now, after the stirred-up silt had settled, he could see it was not rock at all, but more likely concrete. The water was apparently still relatively shallow there, perhaps only a few feet deep, maybe only waist deep. So what was a huge lump of concrete doing in the middle of a lake meant for public boating?

Perhaps it was the remnant of a dock or a diving pier. Whatever, he could see pieces of rebar sticking out from its shattered surface. Apparently, as Chief Scalzi had skimmed the Chinook across the surface of the lake to dissipate speed, the helicopter had grazed the monolith at eighty or ninety miles per hour, warping the steel landing strut and shattering the concrete clump.

Minor rubbed his chin. If Scalzi had brought the Chinook in just a foot lower, the outcome would have been a lot different. Again, he thought of the long crate in the middle of the Chinook's cargo bay and what it contained. It would have been a much different outcome indeed.

But what of the angel? Was there a connection? Had the angel been in the wrong place at the wrong time? Was it just a coincidence that she lay sleeping on the lakebed in line with the skid marks? That would be leaving too much to random chance, wouldn't it? More likely she had been dragged by the broken landing gear from somewhere near the concrete and dropped here in the shallows at the lake's edge. Had she been sitting on the concrete block and been caught unawares in the path of the Chinook? As much as he liked that image, it didn't ring true. Moreover, he couldn't shake the feeling she had been waiting for him, just for him, to show up and pull her from the lake – as delusional as that sounded.

A few yards to his left, the young man's aluminium boat had been pulled up on the gravel beach. He thought about rowing out to investigate the concrete block.

No, not now.

He needed to get his head out of his ass. He had responsibilities. Should he check on the safety of the young woman? What was her name? Laura? Yes, that was it.

Scalzi was supposedly watching her, but he was only one man, outnumbered by drunks and druggies who most of the time resembled a mob more than a platoon.

Actually, he urgently wanted to question her about the angel, but had no idea of how to broach the subject. He had only had the briefest encounter with the angel. Could he be imagining the resemblance to the young woman? What sort of connection could there be? With all the rules of reality broken down, the woman could tell him any mixture of truth and lies, and he would be hard-pressed to sort out the differences. Trying to work out the angles on this thing was like being lost in a maze – or in a dream he couldn't wake up from.

Dream or not, it was better than the empty nightmare he had been stuck in before encountering the angel. Would he have followed through with suicide if he hadn't chanced across her? He wasn't sure. For the last year, he had been shutting himself off from everything and everyone, which was a kind of suicidal action in itself. For as much as he hated to admit, how else does anyone define himself except by the opinions of other humans, whether those opinions involve love or hate. But he was sick of both love and hate and the indifference in between. Was this why some men just gave up home, job, and security and went to live on the street, as way of gradually erasing themselves?

He spat in the water. This was insanity. He turned his back on the lake and walked quickly back to the bivouac. Inside the main tent, he was relieved to find the young woman, apparently unharmed, sitting at one of the trestle tables as he had first seen her, though this time without the young man, of course.

She was sipping from a tin mug and didn't look up when he sat down on the other side of the table. The red marks from the plastic zip-ties were still visible on her wrists. Her steaming cup smelled of hot chocolate. It was instant stuff from one of the MREs, but still a rare commodity. Someone, probably Scalzi, always the gentleman, had made a personal sacrifice to give it to her.

He cleared his throat, and still she didn't look up. He decided to beat her at her own game and said nothing. Let her fill the conversational vacuum. He studied her as she took another sip. Her hair appeared to be naturally ebony, of the shade usually only possessed by Latinos, but her features and skin tone were Caucasian. As she hunched over her cocoa, he could see the pale skin of her scalp where she parted her hair. If her hair was dyed, it was a good job and done very recently. Though she was dressed grunge, she wore a pearl necklace. He didn't claim to be an expert, but the pearls looked real.

Minutes passed. Even without her nervous fidgeting over her cocoa – she made a show of blowing on it to cool it – he could sense her impatience. He settled in and cleared his mind. If the Army had taught him one thing, it was how to wait.

After another minute or so, she looked up. "What do you want?"

"Have you been treated well?" he asked and surprised himself by realizing he was genuinely concerned.

"Where's Bryan?" she asked. Her dark eyes blazed.

"I imagine it's too early for your young man and the sergeant to have completed their mission," he said. "It's only. . ." He looked at his watch only to find it had stopped at 5:30. ". . . well, it's only mid-morning. I wouldn't expect them to be back until this afternoon."

Curious thing about the watch. Maybe it had got wet when he pulled the angel from the lake. That had been about 5:30 yesterday evening. But Rolexes were supposed to be water-resistant a depth of a hundred meters or more.

"You aren't really going to let us go, are you?" she said.

"What makes you think that?"

"That's the way you all work."

He hadn't noticed it before, but she wore a silver nose ring – what was it called? He couldn't remember. It dangled down to her lip and had little balls on the ends. What sort of fashion dictated that lovely young women should mutilate themselves so?

"I think you've watched too many movies, miss."

"Just call me Laura."

He was happy that he had remembered her name, but he got his ballpoint pen and notebook out of his shirt pocket and wrote it down anyway, knowing that doing so would make her even more paranoid and easier to control.

"What's your last name?" he said.

"You want my rank and serial number, too?"

"There's no need to be a smart-ass," he said. "I'll need it for my report."

"Jacobsen," she said. "It's well-known in this town."

"Is that a good thing?"

"Depends on who you talk to. But there's a family ancestor rendered in bronze on the town square."

"Town founder?"

"Yes, and Civil War hero."

"Impressive."

"Not really. The Jacobsen temperament is high-strung. We're bad all the way to the DNA. We're just as likely to produce maniacs as heroes, idiots and madmen as prodigies."

"And which of part of the Jacobsen menagerie do you belong to?"

"The jury is still out, but I may be of the madhatter side of the family." A scowl flew across her face so quickly he almost missed it.

Minor guessed that despite her droll humor, the question of her own sanity was indeed a serious question.

I can relate.

"I see," he said, suddenly seeing not just a very pretty young woman but someone he could relate to as another human being, despite the aboriginal jewelry. She also had personal demons. Maybe those demons were not of the same family, but they were related — of the same tribe. One side of the nose ring drooped lower than the other. He resisted the impulse to tell her to straighten it, as he would tell a man in dress uniform to straighten his tie.

He saw a curious double vision. Here he was talking to a ripe young woman. Her light skin was flawless. Despite the baggy sweatshirt he could see the hint of perky, natural breasts. He bet her stomach was flat, her thighs and butt firm and without cellulite. She might put on weight or undermind her health with drugs in the next ten years, but right now she was perfect.

On impulse, he said, "I met an angel at the lake," and was immediately embarrassed. It wasn't like him to blurt out anything without deliberating the repercussions, much less such craziness.

She looked up over her cocoa and searched his eyes. "Now, did you really?"

He suddenly felt foolish. She must think him as stoned as the enlisted men. "I know it's hard to believe..."

"No, not at all." She didn't exactly smile at him, but the angry set of her mouth relaxed. "Did she tell you her name?"

"How do you know it was a she?"

"Most of the human/angel hybrids are female, but besides that, the look on your face when you thought of her. Well … it was pretty obvious."

His estimation of her intellect went up a bit. She wasn't just smart; she was perceptive. He should be careful around her. "Well, you're right. The angel was a she, but she didn't volunteer her name."

"What did she look like?"

"She looked like…"

"Like what?"

"She had dark hair like yours, very white skin. Her eyes were dark, too." He paused. "You said human/angel hybrids? What does that mean?"

"You really *are* new to the neighborhood, aren't you?" She still didn't smile, but her eyes twinkled with amusement. "It means they used to be human. All the original angels – all but one – merged with human beings.

"Merged? You mean they had sex."

She laughed. He felt his cheeks warm. He was probably blushing.

"Not like what you'd think, Bob."

"My name's not, Bob."

"What is it then?"

"It's Karl, but . . ." Where had he lost control of this interview?

"Well, Karl, it was more like they implanted a seed of themselves at the host's groin area. More like a parasite. Our local doctor called them homunculi.

"Ho-mun-Q-lie: it means 'little people.' At first they looked like tattoos, except their outlines extended slightly out from the skin like welts. The host humans eventually slipped into comas, while the things gradually grew bigger and bigger."

"You saw this happening and did nothing?"

"There was nothing I could do. I tried to cut away one, but even in the early stages it was integrated into the host's nervous and circulatory systems. So I watched the stages of the process while I was captive on the . . ." She looked away, obviously hiding something. "I watched as they consumed the bodies of people I knew. While the homunculi grew, the corresponding archangels withered. I never saw the final changeover. It was like one moment there were three beings: the archangel, the homunculus, and the human host. Then the archangel and the human were gone, and only the hybrid remained. The result looked a lot like a younger version the original human, but with angel characteristics."

"You say the archangels died in the process? Why would they do it, then?"

"The archangels were sick of being immortal. Or at least, that's what they claimed. By merging with humans, they just became merely very long-lived."

"How long-lived?"

"We don't know. The archangels don't have a very good sense of Earth time. And after the transformation, the hybrids became unstable; frigging crazy, really. Like my friend, May, for example," she said and looked down.

Minor sensed that she might start crying, which made him more uncomfortable. She didn't seem like a weepy woman.

"What do you mean, 'frigging crazy'?" he asked, more to get her out of the weepy mode than out of curiosity. There was nothing crazed about the angel he had met at the lake. Alien, yes, but it had been an alien-ness that inspired awe, a sense of power and aloofness from the ordinary affairs of men, a transcendental quality.

"Yes, frigging crazy," she said, and as if reading his mind, "Don't get lost in their physical beauty. They can be like humans one moment, like animals the next, one sex one moment, then the other then next, or purely androgynous. And they're strong enough to tear you limb from limb."

Behind her, Scalzi entered the tent and started toward their table. Minor waved him away. He looked puzzled but stopped, and then turned and left. Minor asked himself what he was doing, listening to a young woman when he should be learning more about the angels firsthand. He was again cognizant that he had been fundamentally changed by his meeting with the Lady of the Lake.

She brushed back her hair with her hands. He watched her as she produced an elastic band from a pocket and tied her hair in a ponytail. With her hair back, the shape of her skull made her look even more like a smaller version of the Lady of the Lake, whose wet hair had been slick against her scalp. But something of the broken little girl remained about this young woman sitting across from him.

"This reminds me of some sort of fairy tale," he said, and a memory surfaced from the lightless depths. He used to read fairy tales to his daughters when they couldn't sleep, and drink hot cocoa with them. The memory was bittersweet because his ex-wife had never approved, saying the cocoa would keep them awake and the grim tales of witches and monsters would give them nightmares.

"I don't believe in fairy tales. When can I get out of here?" the young woman said.

"What?" Coming back to this dismal reality from those storybook times was difficult. He looked up. He had been staring at the table, submerged in the past. "Sorry," he managed to say. "What did you ask?"

"I said when the fuck are you going to let us go?"

She said "fuck" the way a lot of young people did these days, like it was no more profane than "darn" or "drat." He could smell her now, a faint but not disagreeable woman-scent mixed with the acrid odor of fear. She was putting up a good front, smiling at him, being friendly and just short of flirtatious, but behind the façade, she was terrified. Need she be? Had he become some sort of ogre who petrified young women? What harm could she and her boyfriend in an aluminum fishing boat have done to an alien artifact the size of an aircraft carrier?

"Well," she said. "Are you going to answer me or stonewall?"

"We're here to investigate the artifact in the lake," he said.

"The artifact? You mean the angel saucer?"

"Yes, the saucer." The forbidden word: saucer. He would have to be careful, or he would start saying the word in front of the men.

"You say *saucer* like it's a dirty word."

"We still don't know if it's alien."

"You haven't been inside it."

"You have?"

"And angels: You don't believe in them, either?"

"I told you that I've seen one," he said and paused, realizing she had had not answered his question, which meant she had probably been inside the saucer. He decided to let it pass for now. "I've seen one," he said.

"You said that already, but you still don't believe what I told you. I can see that."

"Yes, yesterday evening, in the water at the lake's edge."

"At the edge? Really? In the water? What was it doing there?"

He very badly wanted to describe what he had seen. He needed to. But he could not risk talking to any of the men in his command. Still feeling he was losing control of the situation, he leaned forward and rested his elbows on the table. She surprised him by mirroring him and putting her arms on the table, too. Her face was less than a foot away, a co-conspirator's posture. He could see the strain around her eyes that betrayed her fear, but he felt her interest was genuine, not feigned.

He took another chance and said, "She was submerged a few feet out from shore. I pulled her out."

"It was a she? You're sure of that?"

"I already told you that she was."

"All the equipment was in the right place? Breasts, pubes – all that?"

Minor felt his cheeks grow warm.

"Yes," he said. The memory of the perfection was arousing.

"That's a relief," she said.

"Why?"

She leaned back and crossed her arms. "I'll tell you why – if you'll tell me when you are going to release me."

He nodded. "I'll release you when your fiancé and the sergeant return from Creedance. If I determine that you do *not* pose a risk to my mission."

She considered this, no doubt wondering if she could bargain for more. He would have done the same in her position. He leaned back and crossed his arms too, feeling as if he were in a poker game. He badly wanted her cooperation. Needed it, and it was making him reckless.

"It's a relief because I heard your men talking about the landing," she said. "They said when the helicopter came down it struck a rock in the middle of the lake."

"That's true. But we survived. It could have been much worse."

"Yes, it could have," she said. She uncrossed her arms. "You have to understand there two types of angels, and that one type is more dangerous than the other."

"From your story, I gathered all were a threat."

"Yes, all are dangerous. But the human/angel hybrids are dangerous like half-tamed animals – more unpredictable than anything else. They might tear you apart on a whim or kiss you the next instant. But you could probably stop them if you had a big enough gun. The original archangels are dangerous on a whole different level. I'm not sure any weapon would touch them. They're not completely in this world. They're just some sort of projection from another dimension."

He decided not to question this New Age-sounding tripe for the moment. "So how much harm can they do if they're just ghosts?"

"You don't understand. Even if they don't plug you with the seed of a homunculus, they'll take your mind, your sanity, and your soul."

"I don't believe in the soul."

"They'll take yours anyway."

"I think I might be better off without it," he said. "What does our landing accident have to do with all this?"

"I don't know. The men said you hit an angel in mid-flight."

He nodded.

"That you're all still alive means it was probably a hybrid you hit. There's only one archangel of the original one hundred who came in the saucer, and we entombed it in the lake."

Before he could ask what she meant by *entombed*, she continued:

"The archangels were androgynous, and what you described was female. Bryan told me they change, become male or female, when they decide to implant the homunculus. Did the angel make overtures of any sort? Offer you some sort of deal or promise of sex . . ."

"Sir?" Major Minor jumped. A private was standing behind him. Minor rose and turned to face him. He was scruffy and like old jock strap, but at least he was saluting.

"What is it?"

"It's Warrant Officer Scalzi, sir," he said, his voice quavering.

"So what does he want now?"

"Nothing, sir. He wants nothing now. He's dead! We found him over in the woods, at the latrine! He's been fucking torn apart!"

The pop-pop-pop sound of small-arms fire came from outside.

"That was nearby!" Major Minor said and headed toward the doorway. The private hesitated for a few moments, then followed reluctantly. The few other soldiers in the tent rushed toward the door. A few had drawn their side arms. One stumbled and discharged his pistol in the dirt as he drew it, barely missing his foot. The other men jumped back and looked at him in shock. One laughed. The clumsy soldier, his face visibly red from across the tent, raised his weapon at the laughing man.

"You there. And you," Major Minor yelled. "Put those safeties on, holster your weapons, and stay in the tent!" Then under his breath, but loud enough for Laura to hear him: "Fucking dumb-and-dumber drunks and dopers."

The soldiers looked at him arrogantly. The major drew his side arm, and she could hear an audible click as he thumbed off the safety.

"You'd better come with me," he told her.

She considered resisting; it sounded dangerous outside, as more shots were fired. But having to dodge bullets seemed a lesser threat than being left alone in the tent with the undisciplined soldiers. She left the table to follow him as he strode toward the sounds of the pistol shots.

7.

Love Comes to an Alien Place

Bryan.

The dog bounded ahead, perfectly at ease, occasionally leaping up to see over the tall grass. The dog's unconcern dispelled Bryan's fears that the tall grass might conceal snakes or other dangerous animals.

"Apollo," he shouted, and the dog ignored him.

"Astral?" Same result.

"Okay, Dog?" Bryan called, and the dog hopped up, made a mid-air turn, raced to Bryan's side, and sat, waiting obediently.

"Okay, so much for calling you anything but Dog. You're just a generic dog, that's what you are." He suddenly wished he had a treat for his new friend.

The windmill and the small house were farther away than he first guessed. Some trick of the atmosphere or the flatness of the tall-grass prairie made things look closer than they really were, and it had taken him nearly an hour to reach the hedge that surrounded the homestead.

Now, he doubted it was a homestead at all. It looked too small for a single-family dwelling; it had only one story, and was not more than fifteen-feet square. A large lot to one side had been hidden from his sight until now by the hedge and the lay of the land.

The lot was filled with perhaps a dozen saddled horses, all tethered to hitching posts. Half-again as many horses were harnessed to what looked like racing carts, contraptions that were little more than two large wheels and a framework with small trunks lashed behind the seats. They looked like horse-drawn rickshaws. The horses were all either dun or black. The carts were various shades of blue, green, red, and yellow. The windmill dominated the center of the lot. A large water trough, brim-full, sat at its base. The windmill blades creaked as they turned slowly in the wind.

Dog raced ahead, and Bryan feared he would spook the horses. But at the last moment, Dog veered the other way, keeping in the grass, and circled around behind the house. Was Dog being careful, playful, or stalking something?

The yard in front of the house was paved with large flagstones. Prairie grass had tried to push up between the stones but had been cropped back to stubble. He approached the front entrance door, which was made of rough-hewn lumber with finger-wide cracks between the planks. Sounds and smells leaked through the cracks. He could hear a muted chorus of conversations, interrupted by occasional laughter and accompanied by a poorly played, somewhat out-of-tune piano. The smells resolved into those of roast meat and beer, and he was immediately hungry and thirsty.

A young boy popped out from behind the windmill and scuttled toward Bryan. He looked like he had stepped right out of a Norman Rockwell painting. He was not more than twelve or thirteen and had red hair and freckles, and was dressed in coveralls similar to the ones Bryan wore, except his were faded and frayed at the cuffs.

"Shwet tome and harries, mutter-buck?" the boy said. Or at least that's what it sounded like. The language was guttural, slavic-sounding. But he smiled good-naturally, and Bryan was sure the boy hadn't spewed an obscenity at him, even though that's what it had sounded like. He guessed the boy had just asked an innocent question, so he just nodded.

The boy nodded and rushed in front of him to open the door, then stood waiting, a tattered little gentleman. Through the open door and down a flight of steps, Bryan could see a large tavern, full of patrons, men mostly, sitting trestle tables with mugs of what appeared to dark, frothy ale. The floor that was at least ten feet lower than ground level. An underground tavern.

"Click-cluck, Mutter-buck," the boy said, still waiting, one hand held palm up. The boy's words might be gibberish, but his body language was universal. He expected a tip.

Bryan dug into the pockets of his coveralls, thinking to turn them inside out to show he had no money, but his fingers touched metal. When he pulled his hand out of his pocket, it was filled with silver and gold coins of various sizes. The boy's eyes went wide. It was evidently a lot of money.

"Now the question is, what would be too little or too much," Bryan said aloud.

The boy took a step back.

"Tra-Vo-loor?" The accent was thick, barely understandable, but it sounded like…

"Tra-Vo-loor?" the boy repeated

"Traveler?" Bryan asked, pointing at this own chest.

The boy nodded.

Yes," Bryan answered with another nod. "Yes, I am certainly a traveler a long way from home."

He held out the handful of coins.

"Take whatever," he said to the boy.

The boy looked at him curiously with youth's startling clear blue eyes. He pursed his lips and knitted his brow, then picked out one of the medium-sized silver coins, put it in his pocket, and gave Bryan a curt bow.

"Well, this looks like the start of a good friendship," Bryan said, and the boy laughed softly, clearly understanding his tone voice if not the exact meaning of his words.

Not knowing what else to do, Bryan returned the bow. The boy laughed at this, too.

Then Dog bounded up to Bryan's side from around the corner of the house, and the boy let out a whoop and jumped back, his eyes wide.

Dog jumped back too in response to the boy's whoop, then hid behind Bryan. He poked his head around Bryan's legs and whined plaintively.

The boy took another step back, still frightened.

"What's the matter? Never seen a dog before?" Bryan asked, and patted the animal's head. "And you, Dog: Never seen a boy before?"

Dog licked Bryan's hand with a long pink tongue.

The boy relaxed, and the corners of his mouth lifted in a tentative grin.

Dog came slowly around from behind Bryan and hunkered down on his belly, his head on his outstretched paws. Bryan knelt beside him, patting his head and ruffling his fur.

"Dog," he explained to the boy, and motioned him to come over.

The boy hesitated, but then took a step closer. Dog lifted his head and gave the boy a wet, sad-eyed, puppy-dog look.

The boy took a step closer, still not quite grinning but not looking fearful either – more curious than anything else. Bryan decided his actions did not come from a previous a bad experience with a dog, but because he had actually never seen such an animal before.

"So what kind of world doesn't include dogs for boys to play with?" Bryan said.

The boy came closer and slowly squatted in front of Dog, who whined expectantly. The boy reached out a hand and touched Dog's snout, and the dog in turn gave his fingers a good lick.

"Yah!" the boy shouted and stood up, looking at his wet hand in shock. But he squatted back down again.

A stick leaned was next to the door – it looked like a piece of broken bamboo – and Bryan picked it up.

"Just about the right size," he said, feeling foolish because neither the dog nor the boy could understand a word. "Let's see if you know how to fetch."

The boy looked at him.

"No, not you, the dog," Bryan said, and after letting Dog sniff the stick, he tossed it a couple of yards out into the courtyard. Dog leapt to his feet, nearly knocking the boy down in his rush to get to the stick. Bryan reached out and grabbed the boy by his shoulder as much to reassure as steady him, but neither was necessary. The boy was fascinated with the dog.

In a few seconds Dog was back with the stick, which he dropped in front of Bryan.

"Your turn," Bryan said to the boy, and handed him the stick.

The stick was now covered in dog slobber, but the boy didn't appear to mind. He tossed the stick back out in the courtyard, considerably farther than Bryan had thrown it. Dog took out after it in a flash, and the boy laughed out loud, a sound that warmed Bryan's heart.

As Dog came back with the stick, Bryan patted the boy on the shoulder. How was he to communicate to the boy to watch his dog? He gestured that he was going into the tavern and, feeling lame, pointed at the dog, then to the boy, then back to the dog again. However feeble his attempt at communication, he apparently got something across, because the boy nodded, started to throw the stick again, but stopped and looked at Bryan for approval.

Bryan nodded, and apparently that was enough. The boy tossed the stick again. Away went Dog. The two could probably keep each other busy the rest of the day. As Bryan turned to go into the subterranean tavern, the boy grabbed his arm and tugged until Bryan stepped away from the door. Bryan let himself be towed, curious. The boy took his hand, which still held the clump of coins. He pried Bryan's fingers apart, and selected the larger silver coin, and then motioned for him to put the rest of the coins back in his pocket.

"Second thoughts?" Bryan said. Odd that he hadn't felt the coins jingling while walking across the tall-grass prairie, but this was a waking dream, wasn't it? "That's all right. It's only dream money, anyway."

The boy shook his head, not understanding. Apparently, his English vocabulary was very limited. "Dane-Ger, Vill Rowbin-Sum," he said, nodding toward the tavern, then put the larger silver coin back in Bryan's hand.

Bryan laughed, but he got the message. Flashing a lot of money around the tavern wouldn't be wise. The tenor of the voices from the tavern turned brash, dirty, and dissonant.

"Where'd you learn that? The Will Robinson bit?"

The boy shook his head, not comprehending.

"Well, thank you, anyway," Bryan said. "Too bad you can't be my translator and guide. I guess I'll just have to stumble through this dream alone."

He put the large silver coin in the breast pocket – his new coveralls had pockets everywhere. He stashed the rest of the money in a deep side pocket with a brass snap button. Before fastening it, he dug another medium-size silver coin out and offered it to the boy.

Bryan was pleased when the coin was refused – the boy was obviously uncomfortable in taking what was apparently an excessive tip. Bryan reached down and dropped the coin in the boy's vest pocket anyway, resisting the impulse to pat him on the head. Instead he gave him what he hoped was a reassuring smile.

The boy blushed and smiled back. Bryan gave into the impulse and patted him on the head, and stepped into the tavern. Now he would have to figure out how to order food on his own, but he would have to deal with it. Whether this was a dream or truly an alternate reality didn't matter, his stomach was rumbling.

"Take good care of Dog," he told the boy.

The boy nodded, and threw the stick into the courtyard again.

The spicy smell of roast meat and the tangy fragrance of beer became stronger as Bryan stepped down onto the packed-earth floor. The conversation stilled as the patrons, mostly grisly looking men with a sprinkling of permanently indignant women, turned in unison to examine him. Finding nothing extraordinary about him – maybe because he was dressed much as they were – they turned back to their food and drink and conversation, ignoring him. But Bryan suspected small-town people are the same everywhere, even on an alien planet, and they were most likely already gossiping about him.

Now what?

The room closed in on him, becoming smaller and more crowded, as he worked his way between tables toward the bar. Shelves were placed at odd intervals between the tables. The shelves were made of rough-hewn wood like the door and were about shoulder height and open on both sides. The were stacked with food in large jars, tools, and paper-wrapped bundles. The effect was if someone had rearranged an old-fashioned mercantile store to make room for a dozen dining tables.

A man bumped into Bryan and mumbled something in a language that, though guttural, was distinctly different from the language the boy spoke. "Elohiym, Elohiym!" he said, glancing briefly at Bryan searching for understanding, but finding none, became his face became suspicious. Bryan avoided meeting his eyes. If the man had been as recently translated to this realm as Bryan had, he hadn't been treated to a similar makeover. No coveralls for him. He wore an off-white woolen robe, belted at the waist, and rough-made sandals. He was just over five feet tall, much shorter than any other man in the tavern. His complexion was dark olive, and his hair was nearly black, curly, and shoulder-length. His beard came down to the middle of his chest. He looked like an Old Testament prophet and smelled of sheep. The man stumbled away, wide-eyed, disoriented. He contrasted wildly with rest of the restaurant crowd, most of whom were as fair-skinned as Bryan and just about as tall. None of them paid the prophet any heed, so Bryan moved on.

"Blathe, pthelag?" said a young woman as she squeezed between two tables and came toward him carrying a large tray balanced on her shoulder. She was dressed in slacks and a flowery, long-sleeved shirt. To make room for her to pass, he had to turn to face the shelves. Something in one of the jars on the shelves was yellowish and had smoky-white dead eyes that stared back at him.

As the waitress passed by, he slipped through a space between the shelves and headed toward a long counter. It looked like a bar, sort of, but was of different levels, stair-stepped, with the top level as high as his neck. He would have to stand a chair to be served there. At the far end, the bar's level was low enough for a man the height of the prophet to be served. The middle section was about the right height for him to stand at and drink a beer.

Unlike the rough-hewn tables and the door, the bar was made of finely worked and polished mahogany. The craftsmanship spoke of another time and showed him the room in a different light. The bar was much older than anything else in the tavern. It had been made by a skilled artisan while the newer tables and chairs were roughshod. This was a world in decline. He stepped up to the mid-level area of the bar.

A hand tugged at his sleeve. It was the stable boy who had apparently been shadowing him. A woman with her back to him stood directly across from him on the other side of the bar. She was filling a pitcher with dark ale from a tap in the wall. She wore her red hair in a bun with a lace hairnet over it. She was dressed in black tights, short skirt, peasant blouse, and heavy, leather boots with buckles, like motorcycle boots. Except for the streaks of gray, her hair reminded him of Suzanne's, as did her frame, though she was a little broader at the hips, a little heavier about the shoulders.

"Madre?" the boy called.

The woman turned – and she was Suzanne. No, this woman – though her features were Suzanne's – was at least twenty years older than the Suzanne he had known. She smiled at the boy with genuine love, then gave Bryan a smile reserved for customers, just using her lips, her eyes either tired or sad, he couldn't tell which. As quick as the professional smile came it was replaced by an expression between shock and uncertainty.

"Travellor," the boy said. "A'nah sprock Bleu."

"Ah, a traveler," she said, still looking at him, curious, her words halting, but clear English. "Are you a traveler from another plane?" The words came easier to her lips this time. Her blue eyes were a little bloodshot.

"Yes, I'm from Earth," he said.

"This is Earth, too," she said in perfectly good English with bit of southern twang.

"A different Earth, then," he said.

She nodded. "Another dream," she said, as if that explained everything.

He studied her closer. This Suzanne was at least forty, maybe fifty. Though she had remained trim, the years hadn't been kind to her. Her face was a collage of fine wrinkles, and dark circles underlined her eyes. A long, thin scar traced a line from her left eye to the edge of her mouth. But her eyes, though a little sadder than he remembered, were definitely Suzanne's. Was this a dream or a visit to an astral plane where time flowed at a different rate? Was this his Suzanne – if it could be said she was ever his – or her doppelganger in a parallel universe?

"Maybe a different time, though," he said. He asked the question more to himself than to her. The stable boy ran around the end of the bar and stood by her. He was barely tall enough to peek over the bar at Bryan. Standing next to Suzanne, the resemblance was apparent.

"Your son? I can see a younger you in him."

She looked at Bryan with new interest, putting a hand to her brow to shade her eyes. He hadn't realized until now, but he was standing in the shadow of one the tall shelves, while she was under the glare of lights over the bar. Between the harsh lights overhead and the shadows, she couldn't clearly see his face. He stepped closer to the bar and into the brighter light.

Suzanne's look of uncertainty changed to one of recognition.

"But it's you!" she said. "If you're awake now . . . you're, you're . . . how can it be . . . ?" Her words slowed; she blinked and squinted. She wobbled on her feet and reached for the bar to steady herself, but missed. As her fingers slipped off the edge, she grabbed thin air, and then she was falling. He reached across the bar for her but missed, and she went down hard on the wooden floor. The boy shrieked, and Bryan raced around the bar to help. There he came upon the boy sobbing. His mother had fallen on him, and he struggled to lift her to a sitting position.

"She'll be okay," Bryan said. "She's only fainted, I think."

The boy looked at him uncomprehendingly. Bryan knelt beside them and lifted Suzanne's shoulders. Her head lolled and bumped on the floor when he picked her up. Keeping one hand under the back of her head and the other between her shoulder blades, he managed to lift her enough for the boy to extricate himself. The boy continued his sobbing. Bryan wanted to comfort him, but the boy's agony was contagious. The Suzanne had turned very pale. Was that a usual symptom of fainting? He had no experience with such episodes.

A small white towel lay on the floor beside her. He grabbed the towel and flipped over a corner to make a pad to put under her head. He was conscious of a murmuring crowd gathering around them, but he was too worried about Suzanne to look up. After placing her head on the towel, he searched for a pulse on her carotid artery. He found a throbbing, but it was slow and weak. Was that normal for fainting victims? He cursed his own ignorance, but his intuition told him it was nothing serious, that she had just been shocked when she recognized him, a face from decades in her past.

Then he was struck by the absurdity of this explanation.

The boy had stopped sobbing but stilled looked distressed.

"I really think she's okay," he said, which upset the boy even more. Who knew what *think* or *okay* translated to on this world? The sounds of the crowd stilled, then was followed by a frantic shuffling of feet. The boy looked over Bryan's shoulder, and his expression turned from anxiety to terror as he stepped back.

At once, Bryan's shoulders were clamped in a steel grip, and he was lifted off his feet. His hand was pulled out from under Suzanne's head, and in a frozen moment he could see her eyes flutter beneath their lids like trapped birds. He was turned around in midair, his feet dangling, and he found himself face to face with an angel so huge that his/her white hair brushed the roof of the tavern.

"Impostor," the angel said in clear English. "How did you get here?"

Laura.

Laura trailed behind Major Minor and his entourage as they left the bivouac and moved, guns drawn, toward the woods. She considered falling behind and then making a run for it when no one was looking, but the major kept glancing at her over his shoulder. She probably wouldn't get away, and keeping close to the major seemed a good idea, especially if there was violence. He might have a *major* stick up his ass (her own pun amused her), but unlike most of the other soldiers, he seemed competent. She was beginning to suspect Samiazaz had escaped his concrete sepulcher, and she didn't want to be alone in the woods. She wasn't sure how much good their weapons would be against an archangel, but they would be better than nothing.

The forest to the west of the camp were of blackjack oak instead of loblolly pine. This area was owned by a neighboring farmer and not the state, and had not been cleared for decades. Blackjack woods are not like pine forests, which tend to form a solid overhead canopy that, along with a solid mat of pine needles, choked out the growth of other species and left a natural park-like landscape. Blackjack oak is the redneck of trees, growing scrubby, disordered swathes, especially after being cleared by fire. Trashy brambles and brush swarmed around big and small trees.

A nearly solid hedge of this thorny, snarly mixture blocked the way into the woods from the Army camp. The briar wall had been recently hacked away in one spot. Following the men through this cut, she found herself in a circular clearing maybe twelve or fifteen feet in diameter. Only an hours earlier, Scalzi had taken her to this latrine area and left her alone to do her business.

Major Minor and three soldiers were looking at something but not speaking. As she got closer, she noticed a pair of boots on the ground. A splash of bright red was visible on one toe – fresh blood. A pitiful roll of soggy toilet paper stuck on a waist-high branch was freckled with blood splatter.

"Sir?" one of the soldiers said, nodding toward Laura. He was the same one who had felt her up and talked of strip-searching her, only to be stopped by Scalzi.

Were those really Scalzi's feet lying there in those bloody boots?

She felt an odd conflict of emotions, sadness at losing a protector but glad it was him and not her. If the angel had chanced upon the area a little earlier when she had been using the latrine, it might be her dead body lying there. She realized she had carried her mug of hot chocolate with her, and it had grown cold. She sipped it anyway.

Major Minor turned to look at her and frowned when he saw the cocoa mug. Somehow standing over a man's body, sipping cocoa seemed wrong, so she dumped the chocolate on the ground and let the mug dangle in her hand.

"Come here," Minor commanded. They stood facing each other like actors in a surrealistic Western movie. He held his pistol at his side, relaxed but ready, and she, her empty cocoa mug. She resisted the silly impulse to point the mug at him and say *bang*.

She took a deep breath and let it out, trying to relax her shoulders. She also had to stifle her impulse to tell any man who used that tone of voice with her – even a man with a gun – to go fuck himself. As she came forward, she tried to put a little sway in her hips, disgusted with herself for doing it. But hey, this was a matter of self-preservation. Major Minor and the nodding soldier stepped aside, giving her view of the body.

Having worked as a nurse's aide, she had seen dead bodies before, even those who died violently in car accidents, but she wasn't prepared for this. She was toe-to-toe with the bloody boots. The body had been slit from Adam's apple to crotch, and then opened up like a gutted turkey and cleaned out. Smiling was supposed to repress the gag impulse, but she couldn't manage even a small grin and threw up a little cocoa in her mouth. She turned her head to spit it out before forcing herself to look at the carnage again. She let her eyes scroll upwards to the face. The lower jaw was garbled flesh – was that a tongue poking out through the gore or a torn chunk of lip? The mangled face would not have been unrecognizable if not for the right eyebrow that was cocked up at that odd angle that had given Scalzi a permanent supercilious expression. Now the eyebrow said, *What? I'm dead now? You've got to be fucking kidding me.*

"Crazy angels?" Major Minor said – a question not a statement.

She attempted to answer but the words came out as squeaky croaks. She had to look away from the body before she could actually say, "Maybe." But what she meant was *most probably*, not *maybe*. But saying anything helped her find her voice and remember to breathe. She started babbling everything she knew of human mutilations done by the archangels, and the subsequent killings of cows, dogs, and wildlife done by the human/angel hybrids.

The men listened attentively as she talked, though she knew they normally didn't pay much heed to a woman. Maybe the horror lying at their feet made them more receptive. Her information dump turned slowly into a ramble. *Was she repeating herself?*

Finally, the major saved her with an interruption: "So…" He drew out the word like a Gregorian chant. "Soooooo, only these archangels, you say, attacked human beings? The angels we saw flying that were once humans, they only kill animals."

She nodded. "That's what I heard – its true, as far as I know." Hadn't he been listening? "Uncle Robert. . ." Saying his name made her heart sink a little, for now he was dead. "My Uncle Robert said the human/angel hybrids were just hungry, ravenous, but were still human enough not to eat people."

But how to tell them about the cherubs who *did* attack human beings? If the major and the soldiers could barely accept human/angel hybrids, a merging and corruption of not just DNA but of souls, how could she convince them of the existence of cherubs, those pudgy neuter spawn of the human/angel hybrids? Maybe it was a moot point because the inflated little monstrosities had apparently popped out of existence with the entombment of the last archangel. She hoped so.

"Your Uncle Robert – I think I'd like to talk to him."

"You can't."

"And why not?" The major's voice rose; evidently he didn't like being told no.

"Because he's dead," she said. "A couple of weeks ago." And murdered by the cherubs, but she wasn't going to try to explain this.

"This is total bullshit," one of the men said.

The major's face reddened some more.

"Oh, permission to speak, sir," the man said, his tone verging on the insubordinate. Evidently, the troops were restless and the major exercised only the most tenuous of commands.

"Go ahead, Lieutenant," the major said.

"Flying fucking killer angels! Come on now."

"So what do *you* think happened?"

"Some sort of wild animal surprised Scalzi while he was taking a crap. It bit off his face and then gutted him."

"And you, Private," the major asked the other man. "Is that what you think?"

The man performed a little symphony of nervous tics, blinking, pinching his nose, rubbing his brow, before answering. "I saw something," he said finally. "Big and white, flying off, skimming the trees." He pointed at the ragged treetops. "There was red on it, too, blood maybe. I shot at it."

"That was your firing we heard?" the major said.

"Yeah," he said. "I hadn't seen this mess yet." And he pointed at the corpse.

Laura, avoiding looking at Scalzi's remains , took a step back and nearly tripped over something in the sodden mat of leaves and cut brambles.

"Then why did you shoot at it?" the major asked, his anger taking a higher pitch.

Laura looked down. She had stepped on a pistol half-buried in the wet leaves. Scalzi's?

"Because. . ." the private said, hunching his shoulders, following it by a facial tic.

Laura dropped the cup and knelt to pick up the gun. The sudden movement drew their attention, but instead of looking where she was reaching, they seemed to focus on her butt. Her lately enlarged backside hid the gun from the men. Thank the god of lard for androgen, fried chicken, and the pot munchies.

"Sorry," she said, and turned to face them but didn't stand up, then made a show of wiping the wet leaves off the cup.

The men turned their attention back to each other.

Laura set the cup on the ground. With her right hand, she brushed an errant strand of hair from her eyes, with her other hand, she groped behind her until she found the gun. Her attention wavered for a moment. From this angle, she could see right into the corpse's chest cavity. A piece of esophagus dangled inside like a shredded, pink garden hose.

"Because what?" the major said to the private.

The private looked confused.

"Why did you shoot at it, shithead?" the major said.

"Because it was so fucking big," the private said, and did another tic display.

Laura stood up, still holding her breath, the cup in one hand, the pistol hidden behind her back in the other. Now if she could just slip it under her sweatshirt. She heard a sound behind her. Where other soldiers at the opening to the clearing now? She should have looked behind her before getting the gun. She debated handing it over to the major. But the major was distracted, still pissed with the private. "Did you hit it?" he said.

"I don't think so, sir," the private said. "If I did, it was too fucking big or stupid to notice."

No one is behind you except me, a voice whispered in her ear.

A chill ran up her spine, nearly paralyzing her. The voice was Uncle Robert's. Not looking to see if his ghost was standing behind her, she slipped the gun under the waistband of her jeans in one smooth move. Then she stood up, making the motions of modestly pulling down the sweatshirt with her other hand. The gun was a hard, cold lump nudging the crack of her ass.

"Big as a woman?" the major said. "Didn't you say something about it being female?"

Something dripped off the gun and ran down her leg. When she looked at her hand there was blood on it. Scalzi's, most likely. She wiped it off on the leg of her jeans.

"Maybe. I don't think I said it," the private said, scratching his head. "But it could have been a woman, a big one with wings. Hah! That's what I saw." Now he added a crotch grab to his repertoire of shrugs and tics.

Laura realized she had been holding her breath and let it out.

The men looked at her. She still didn't know for sure if anyone was behind her, but she if she turned to check, the gun might show as a lump under her sweats.

"I could be wrong about the human/angels attacking humans," she said. "They are unstable."

They all stared at her as if *she* were the alien angel. The idiot private blinked and rubbed his crotch again. He was definitely stoned on something in addition to coming from some place where the gene pool was rather shallow.

"You two," the major nodded to a couple of the men. "Take care of the body. I don't want it buried yet, but we'll have to do so soon in this heat. First, I'll want to examine it again. But for now, just get it out of the latrine area."

There was no snap-to, no salute, not even a grumbling *Yes, sir,* from the men. But the lieutenant said to the private, "You stay with the body; I'll get a body bag."

"By myself?"

Awakening of an Alien God

"Just you and your weapon," the lieutenant said.

"Come with me," the major said to Laura.

When she turned to follow, she saw no ghost of Uncle Robert, but she knew it had been his voice she'd heard.

✳ ✳ ✳

8.

To Whisper Dread

Marguerite.

From high above the clearing, Marguerite watched the soldiers and the young woman leave. She was crouched deep in the guts of a large oak tree, inside a charred enclave that lightning had blasted open not long ago.

Below, humans moved about like toy windups as they milled about the body of the soldier. They seemed more intent on establishing a pecking order each other than mourning the dead man.

A memory surfaced: Hands wearing a familiar looking wedding ring were spooning out a big lump of lime Jell-O fruit salad into a little white porcelain serving bowl. The memory was a single frame, a flash-lit still life in vivid color, at first no more connected to her than a glossy magazine ad. But it slowly dawned on her that those were once her hands.

Could her hands ever been so pudgy and soft, made of human flesh that would now show little more resistance to her probing angel fingers than the gelatin? Had she ever been as mortal as the humans below? It didn't seem possible she had ever been housed in such a limited, earth-bound body: fragile fingers and toes, sagging breasts, thickening middle. Now she was nearly immortal, seemingly physically perfect, but something was missing. There was a hole burned out of her soul, as ragged and seered as lightning-carved hole in the middle of this tree.

Her feelings became thick, viscous, as she tried to get to core of this thought, and suddenly she was overcame by trepidation.

The cavity was large and deep, but not deep enough to allow her to completely withdraw into it. Her head and shoulders were outside, and her mind wasn't so thickened as to prevent her from realizing her white skin and brilliant red-orange hair would be visible against the dark bark.

But though the humans were a few hundred yards away and had stared right at her several times, they hadn't see her. She tried very hard to remember what looking through human eyes felt like, but the effort made her nauseous.

Maybe she was invisible. Or perhaps just beyond the range of their human eyes. That was the simpler solution.

Though she might be hidden from human eyes, she stayed put. They had shot at her before, blaming her for the death of the man in the clearing.

She had not been responsible, had she? Or had she?

There was the matter of the blood on her hands. She didn't remember clearly, but she was reasonably certain all she had wanted to do was search the dead man's mind for clues of what had happened to May's head. It had been a successful reading. She had been in time to intercept his passing to another plane, and in that state the soul is like a complete recording of everything ever seen, heard, and felt. The recording passed before her mind's eye like a flickering antique movie. She had retrieved a vision of May's head rolling back into the helicopter's fuselage after being sliced off by the spinning blades.

Marguerite also knew Samiazaz had killed the man below. A well of dread rose in her. Though she couldn't actually be killed in this plane, apparently she could be torn to pieces and thrown to the four winds as May had been. Who knew what that would be like? Would she be conscious at all? Would her consciousness be concentrated in one body part like her head or heart? Or would her awareness be fragmented, distributed in the various parts, fragments of her mind held captive in an arm, a severed finger, a bit of skin? She suspected the latter, as she had been drawn to May's various body parts in a manner similar to the way she sensed the distant locations of other hybrid angels. The signal emitted by the body parts had been weaker, diluted. No matter. When she retrieved May's head and put her friend back together, she would ask her if she had dreamed while in pieces.

She had hidden in the tree more in fear from the murderer, Samiazaz, than anything else. The soldiers might shoot at her again, and she didn't want to that to happen. Though bullets could not actually damage her, they did hurt. But there would be no hiding from the archangel.

Why had Samiazaz killed the soldier? Surely the archangel was aware by now which humans would make a suitable match and which would not. The fact that the soldier below had died from the encounter showed a certain ignorance on Samiazaz's part. The other archangels had chosen a different method of implanting the homunculi since their early attempts with people like May. The latter implants, as with hers, were seductions rather than rape. The first attempts at union had been born of a misunderstanding of the human nature. But perhaps because Samiazaz had lain asleep in the waters of Lost Lake until just recently, he was now having to learn the same lesson on his own.

She waited until the humans on the ground turned away to leave the clearing, then she exploded out of her nest, leaving a trail of falling twigs and dead leaves in her wake.

The cool wind of her passage dissolved the thick gel of sadness, and more memories returned. The name of the woman on the ground was Laura, and her face came to Marguerite as in a framed family picture.

Below, the woman – only Laura, not the men – turned, looked up, and stared right at her. Marguerite saw herself through the woman's eyes for the briefest of moments, saw herself as an alien speck of white far up in the clear blue sky, a swoop of wings, a tiny speck with red hair. Marguerite felt the recognition of herself in Laura's mind, and saw a curious double vision too, of the flying speck of white and red, and of a strange red-headed woman dressed in a full skirt and yellow apron. Laura had something metallic and cold pressing against her backside.

The connection had a curious overlay, a memory not her own of being a troubled small girl eating Jell-O at a table – that Jell-O memory again! – and an angry young woman yelling. Then Laura turned away, and the psychic link was broken.

As a human, Marguerite had never yelled at a child, had never had a child of her own to yell at , for that matter. *Had she?* She was sure she had been childless. Nevertheless, the memories, false or not, carried a sense of deep loss, and she flew higher until the houses below became like tiny, bright-colored playthings.

Higher, and even the links with the other hybrid angels became tenuous, but she still thought of May.

Marguerite burst into a song in the thin air.

Awakening of an Alien God

You may have other friends,
But none will ever love you like I do.
Friend and lover, fellow flier
Of the Immortal Fractured Night

She flew higher toward the delicate clouds that were scattering before the wind. The substance of her body sang in harmony with this wind. She was not made of tendon, muscle, bone, and flesh, but of a sort of angelic putty. As she climbed into the wispy clouds, they disappeared into icy crystal threads. She wanted to feel something, anything, but even the frigid cold was insubstantial. Disappointed, she folded her wings willed herself to drop. She fell wrapped in cocooned her own wings around her body, her red hair streaming out like tendrils, a visage no doubt both beautiful and horrible.

She dropped thousands of feet, ever picking up speed. She had found no limit as to how fast she could fall, and though she had folded up her wings, they really had no effect upon her flying or not flying. The wings were more like collectors, drawing in and condensing energy from an unknown source. Also, her psychic connections with other angels worked better when her wings were unfolded. About the only effect her wings had on her flying was when she used them for stability upon landing or at slow speeds. Then she used them as a tightrope walker uses a pole for counterbalance.

The force of flight originated slightly above her groin, the exact spot where the archangel Azazel had implanted his/her homunculus. Flying was largely an autonomic reflex, and she could no more divine the physics involved than she, as when human, could have explained the forces involved in walking or running. Like those common human activities, she could initiate the effort, but if she thought about it too much, she might stumble and fall.

She was low enough now roads appeared as paths instead of like lines on a map. Below her, perhaps only a hundred feet or so, she could see the V-shaped formation of Canadian geese migrating north, a sure sign of spring. Ravenous now, she dove at them without thinking. Instinctively, she waited until she was almost upon the trailing birds before completely unfurling her wings. Several birds saw her at the last moment and turned to angrily squawk at her in unison. A mistake, for this action only made it easier for her to grab two of the birds by their necks. In an instant, she wrung their necks and bit off their heads.

She landed, birds in hand, to find she had instinctively returned to the house she shared as a human with her husband, John Wright. She tried the front door. It was locked, and though the stainless steel doorknob twisted off when she forced it, the door remained shut. A single kick shattered the frame. The door swung open, hanging askew on only one hinge. She strode to the kitchen, having to duck under the ceiling fan, for, as often happened when she was excited, she had grown more than a foot taller. She had to duck down even more and scrunch her shoulders to go through the door from the living room into the kitchen.

The kitchen table and chairs were all smaller than she remembered, like children's furniture. She sat at the table anyway, the floral curtains and white stove bringing back foggy memories of cooking bacon and sizzling eggs. Though she was prone to attacks intense hunger, she really no longer needed to consume food to survive. But the thought of food, of the simple act of eating, calmed her, and she shrank some more until she was little more than six feet head to toe.

Then she ate both geese raw, feathers, bones and all, and shrank some more until she felt more at home in the kitchen. She turned on a sink faucet, careful not to twist off the handle, and was rewarded with a stream of clear water. She used her cupped hands to douse her face with water, then rinsed the blood and feathers off her bare breasts. The cool water felt good as it trickled over her stomach.

Now what? A plan presented itself in pictures. One picture was of the soldiers shooting at her with large guns. She could see the flashes of the muzzles and fell pain when the bullets struck. She didn't relish a confrontation with the soldiers. The next vision was of her, under the cover of darkness, retrieving May's head from the niche in the helicopter fuselage.

More images, of May's body laid out in the woods, and of dogs trying to drag them off – red eyes, fangs, and drooling mouths in the twilight. Perhaps this house would be a better place to resurrect May, maybe in the living room. She could use the floor to lay out the parts she already had and block the door with the couch while she retrieved the head. That way, she wouldn't have to worry about pieces of May being stolen while she was away. Odd, she hadn't a clue as how the process of reanimation proceeded; she just instinctively knew it would happen. But she had made a plan! Yes, a plan!

Nightfall was hours away. In the meantime, she would go to the place in the woods where she had buried May's body parts and bring them back here.

Bryan.

He found himself in a holding cell with stone walls and floor, and he did not remember how he had come to be there. Sitting on the rough-hewn floor across from him was a bare-breasted young woman who sat quietly, eyes unblinking, staring at him. Sawdust and yellow straw was scattered across the floor. About seven feet up on one wall there was a rectangular opening about the size of a trade paperback book. It was too small to be called a window, but it cut through the thick stone walls and let in enough light to illuminate the room. But something was missing; at first he couldn't put his finger on exactly what. His mind was working very slowly and took a minute or so to realize that the cell had no door. As his mind cleared, he thought that the door might be behind him, that he was leaning against it. After an immense effort, he managed to turn and check, but he found only solid stone.

For a timeless moment he stared at her with the awareness unique to altered consciousness where the observer is not aware of himself observing, but is instead an empty vessel. He felt no judgment, no intellectual analysis, just observation.

She was a light-skinned honey-blonde with large, firm-looking breasts and dark nipples. She wore a pleated skirt reminiscent of a Scottish kilt. If she had worn it normally, the skirt would have reached her knees, but she had pulled it up so the waistband was cinched right under her breasts and the skirt barely covered that dark place between her legs. Her eyes were dark and angry, and they looked right through him.

She sat with her legs outstretched and her arms at her sides like an abandoned doll. The soles of her feet were blackened with grit. The rest of her body appeared clean, though her skin glistened with beads of moisture as if she had just stepped out of a bath. She was lovely, voluptuous but not Rubenesque, with full breasts and feminine curves, but still athletic-looking.

How had she gotten here? How had he gotten here? For that matter, where was here? His last memory was of being lifted off his feet by an eight-foot-tall archangel. He had no memory of being carried from the saloon or of being rendered unconscious. Nor did he remember the moment when he had regained consciousness. It was as if he had been instantly transported from the angel's clutch to here, as when one emgerges into a lucid dream. He did remember the accusation the angel had laid upon him: "Impostor! What are you doing here?" And the next thing he knew he was her, in the cell staring at the woman sitting across from him.

She hadn't moved or so much as blinked while he brooded. Was she even breathing? Her breasts didn't rise and fall. She looked wooden, a ship's figurehead in flesh tones.

Again he wondered if this was a vivid dream rather than a projection to an astral plane. Was he still in the wrecked truck back on Earth, perhaps injured, maybe comatose? If this was a dream, it was unlike any he had before. The woman's stare laid him bare, powerless, and yet he didn't think it was directed at him. He was just in the way. The energy of her anger was almost tangible and seemed to ricochet in the confines of the cell, trying to find a target. The dust motes sparkled between them though the entire cell was without direct light. She finally moved, shifting her weight, pulling her legs under her and putting her hands behind her head. Her breasts rose as she lifted her arms. Her breath steamed in the chill air of the cell.

She kept staring toward him but still not focusing. She stood and began untying the cord that kept the skirt cinched under her breasts. Her breasts swayed and jiggled a little as she struggled with the stubborn knot, and he was aroused despite his situation. Yes, she was beautiful, dirty feet and all, but he was in a life-or-death situation, wasn't he?

As she worked with the knot, he further examined her face. Her features were classic, but her beauty was flawed by anger and despair. The hackneyed expression "rode hard and put away wet" came to mind.

"Skalt!" she said, a foreign word but with a clear-enough meaning.

She silently struggled with the knot until she had it untied. Watching him now, keeping her eyes locked onto his, she slowly worked the skirt down. It wasn't a strip tease or a prelude to sex. *Or was it?* Her eyes were hard to read.

As the skirt came down to her waist, he gasped to see the early stage imprint of a homunculus. That's why she had been wearing the skirt, her only piece of clothing so high on her waist — to conceal homunculus. At this stage of development, the homunculus looked more like a large tattoo instead of a creature with partial awareness.

She let the skirt fall to the floor and walked toward him. She straddled him, still standing, and he could see the homunculus in detail. It stretched from just above her navel to her pubic arch. The homunculus' eyes were closed, and he was right: It was developed just enough to have a texture of its own rather than an overlay of its host's skin. It hadn't yet stretched down to her legs but its toes touched her mons.

He reached up and slid his hand over the homunculus' midsection, careful not to let his hand drop too low. Yes, the surface was slightly raised, but the warmth of the woman's body filtered through it from underneath. He felt a tingle, as of an electric shock, that traveled all the way down his arm. The woman felt the shock too, obviously stronger than he, for she trembled orgasmically at his touch. The homunculus was hardwired into her nervous system all the way to the pleasure centers of her brain, and it reacted too. A contracting wave swept over it, in sync with the spasms of its host's skin. As thin as it was, it had a life of its own. If he hadn't seen an angel homunculus before, Bryan would have thought it was just body art made by using beads put underneath the skin. But this was most certainly the seed of an archangel. If it were like those he had seen on Earth, it would soon consume her.

She squatted, her buttocks resting now on his thighs, and reached down with a ringed finger to spread her labia lips wide open. The ring was huge, heavy, and gold, and set with a bright blue stone. Even though Bryan wasn't all that experienced with women, he thought her labia lips extra large, almost floppy. On impulse, wondering how he dared to do so, he ran a finger across the lips to find homunculus's toes possessed a Braille-like surface there, too. She let out a sigh. When he looked up, her eyes were level with his own but still seemed to be looking through him. He might as well be part of the stone floor. Her angry eyes had softened, though, and large tears streamed down her cheeks. Something about the tears aroused him far more than her physical beauty had. He was afraid and erect at the same time, so much so hard it almost hurt. He reached out and captured one of her tears, then tasted it. She smiled faintly and reached down with one hand to press against his erection. With the other, she began to undo the snaps on the front of his coveralls.

"Sheat my. Lebe mi," she said. Again her words were incomprehensible, but her intentions clear. She smiled at him again, but he knew this act was impersonal for her. He was just here, at the right time, at the right place, with the right body parts. Or it was the wrong time and place, depending upon point of view.

Another snap came undone, and her hands were on his abdomen. He was afraid to look at his own bared belly, afraid of what he might see. She slipped him into her, and he put his hands on her swollen breasts, both repelled and obsessed with the beautiful abomination on her stomach. She began to rise up and down on him, and as his hands slid from her waist to caress her homunculus, she jerked her head to and fro, consumed by orgasms. Her vagina rippled, contracted, gripped him. Everything else about her – face, breasts, arms, even the homunculus – faded, and there was just that – her vagina and his member. In response, his penis seem to become the largest part of his body, bigger than an arm, a leg, his torso, his entire body. His complete consciousness resided there. The experience was not that of a sweet union; no merging of consciousness that comes to a couple in love. It was merely raw, physical need. Her eyes rolled back in her head, and he followed her into an oblivion that swallowed empty space left there by the loss of Suzanne.

✳ ✳ ✳

9.

Things Only Damaged Souls Know

Major Karl Minor.

Major Karl Minor sat atop of the campsite's trestle table watching a gray squirrel stealthily work its way toward a piece of leftover MRE near the cooking grill. The furry little fuck would scurry a couple of feet through the dead leaves and pine needles, then stop dead, jerk its head to and fro, while keeping an eye out for predators. Obviously, the squirrel seemed to think it became invisible if it stopped still. Minor adopted this *invisibility* tact, knowing it worked on the squirrel-brain level. As long as he did not move, the squirrel would not see him.

Minor's foul mood had returned. The world and everything in it, including the squirrel, had become shabby and inherently flawed again, a pale imitation of the real thing. He needed another angel-fix. Lacking that, he was going to have to kill something. He held a baseball-size chunk of concrete he had retrieved from the shore for this very purpose.

He tried to laugh at this, at himself, but it came out chortle. He knew all about addiction, learned it in a military hospital after a near-miss by an IED. But morphine addition was a deep visceral need. The very cells of the body cried out for it. This need was something else. Momentarily he felt a bottomless hole in his soul, a condition he had resigned himself to live in until meeting her, an unfillable emptiness, bottomless. Now he was strung out. He needed to be in her presence, and not being able now caused him far worse withdrawal symptoms than he'd ever had with any chemical addition.

The squirrel made another dash toward the MRE, a particularly nasty entree known as "Airwing Alpo," corned beef hash and meatballs with a barbecue sauce the consistency of heavy motor oil.

For a moment the squirrel was out of sight behind the garbage can, and Minor brought the chunk of concrete up, over his head, ready to throw. The little fucker stuck its head out from behind the barrel, but only its head, careful not to present a good target, and dissed him with a squirt of chittering. This *up-yours* attitude was amusing for a moment. Minor had half a mind to let the squirrel have the MRE just to see if it would actually eat the stuff.

Then he would kill it if the Airwing Alpo didn't.

The squirrel took another hop and froze. Minor froze as well. Would the squirrel notice his change in position? He held his breath. Apparently it didn't notice, but it still wasn't taking any chances. It was smarter than many of the men under his command – idiots who would stick their heads in a meat grinder without thinking.

The squirrel reconnoitered the area again, its dark eyes flitting to and fro. Minor's hand gripped the concrete tighter, readying it, the rough edges biting into his hand. The squirrel moved partway out from behind the garbage can, almost – but not quite – presenting a clear target. More indecision, more nervous chittering, and it skittered out in the clear, then stopped suddenly, actually skidding in the leaves, looked right at him, and raced behind a nearby tree before Minor could react.

Minor stayed frozen, and in seconds the squirrel stuck out its nose from behind the tree. It was closer now, but it sensed a threat. The little critter really wanted the shitty MRE hash.

Minor knew that in the initial stages of addiction, there is a state of mind that can be called acceptance. The newly addicted knows he is becoming addicted, but sees the alternative as no alternative at all, or sees that the dependency is a sort of necessary evil. There are drawbacks, sure, but that's life, isn't it? Everyone has to make compromises to live, to be human rather than a robot driven by programming alone.

Every addict makes the ethical compromises of the demanding need – lying, cheating, stealing, perhaps even murdering – convincing himself that the addiction is a natural state and anything he must do to supply that need is natural, almost an entitlement. That's when he gets careless.

The little squirrel junkie made up its mind. Surely other, less risky food could be found in the woods, but the squirrel had apparently wanted – on a cellular level – the greasy food with all its preservatives. A real little addict.

Love is like that, especially when it's one-way. Everyone thinks he might die when love is taken away, but he doesn't – not always, anyway, and even then, rarely quickly.

Minor spat. *It was all bullshit! He was bullshit. Love was bullshit. Life was bullshit!* His hand found the butt of his holstered pistol. It would be so easy. Then he could rest. An image of his mother came to mind, a remembrance of times past when he was sitting in the living room late at night, drinking whiskey, angry at himself, usually because of some shit he'd had to take from a commanding officer, and his mother would come in, supposedly sleepless herself, to sit across from him on the couch, and she would smoke a cigarette, and he would try not to let his eyes linger on her heavy breasts under that semi-transparent night gown she always wore, and he would be both repelled and aroused, wanting to pluck out his own eyes, as she tried to make conversation.

You're nearly thirty, she would say. Though the subject of the lectures differed, they would always begin in some variation of that phrase. *You're nearly thirty.* (Actually, she had begun to use the phrase when he had been twenty-five or twenty-six; she always rounded up.) *You're nearly thirty* was usually followed by a long maternal diatribe based on one of a few limited themes: *You Should Not Drink So Much* or *You Should Find A Nice Girl* or *You Should Get Yourself Promoted,* but always ending with a variations on another phrase, *That's All Right, Dear,* followed by a recount of how she had suffered being married to his father, and that she hoped her son would be a different kind of man.

He would sit in that thick, sweet atmosphere of her old lady perfume, feeling like a fossilized insect trapped in prehistoric amber, both isolated and miserable but preserved from the ravages of the world.

It wasn't until a year after his mother had died of a stroke in her sleep that he had actually met someone he thought was a nice girl, and married her. Short thereafter, he was promoted. And it was years later when he realized why he had been so late in getting married, why he drank so much, why he avoided going face-to-face with the hardness of the world. His isolation had much to do with that secret conspiracy between him and his mother, a conspiracy anchored on those little midnight conversations of guilt and secret, thick suffocating sympathy.

But what had really been perverse was that as his marriage aged, as his childlike Filipino wife's English improved, she had gradually become ever so much like his mother: smothering and manipulative.

Minor's shoulder muscles began to ache; the chunk of concrete seemed to have doubled in weight, then doubled again. Did the squirrel see his arm trembling?

He had become addicted to living in that smothering syrup. Not just dependent, but addicted. He knew how to kill a man with his bare hands. He knew how to scare enlisted men into risking their lives. He had risked his own life multiple times in three tours in Afghanistan. But he had been a mama's boy all the same. And the men under his command in Afghanistan and those under his command stateside sensed the weakness.

Perhaps love addictions are a natural thing, at least at certain seasons of life. Karl Minor counted himself wise enough to realize that his dependence on his mother into his late twenties was a destructive addiction. When he had been younger, the love was justified. His mother had been the exciting, mysterious force in his life. But as he grew older and the world turned colder toward him, he had indulged a kind of secret pact with her. He would always be her little boy and a stand-in for her recreant husband. She would always be the protective womb to which he could return.

Music drifted through the woods from the mess tent. *"He's a loser, he's not what he appears to be . . ."* The squirrel made it to the MRE. Minor hurled the lump of concrete. The squirrel looked up in time to see it coming but froze instead of dodging, and the concrete slammed into it.

Minor hopped down from the table to stand over his kill.

The squirrel lay still except for a twitching of its tail. It chattered, either in agony or anger, he couldn't tell which.

"You should be grateful," Minor said. "I probably saved you from dying of fatal constipation."

The squirrel stopped chittering and added a leg twitch to the tail twitch. It was trying to run away from death. Its mouth gaped, revealing two large yellowed upper buck teeth. The sound of shouting filtered through the trees from the direction of the big tent.

Most of the men had taken to sleeping in the Chinook after Scalzi's murder. They were crowded in there like cattle in a feed lot, believing the thin metal shell offered more protection and that an enclosed space was more defendable. They were wrong on both accounts, but he didn't give a fuck about cluing them in anymore. One or two of the wiser ones still slept in the tent. And speaking of brave souls, where was the young woman, Laura, sleeping tonight? Originally, they had decided to use the Chinook as a kind of holding cell. But with seven or eight men sleeping in there now, where would they put her? She might have to take her chances and bunk with the men. And now that he thought about it, where were her young man and Sergeant Smith? They should have returned by now. Had they met the same fate as Scalzi?

Minor knew he should attend to these issues, but all he could think of was being in the presence of the Lady of the Lake again.

The squirrel's tail stopped twitching. Fried squirrel might be a good alternative to MRE, but he had no idea how to clean it. But how hard could it be? Something like cleaning a fish, no doubt. He picked up the small body. It was still warm.

A swoosh of wings came from overhead, and he looked up to see an angel gliding over the treetops, the curve of her hips revealing her gender, the hint of bright stars sparkling like sequins through her wings. He thought of his mother and her diaphanous nightgown, of his wife who grew beyond his reach, and at exactly that moment, the squirrel was resurrected in his hand, squirming, thrashing the claws of its hind legs at his shirtsleeve. Before he could let go, it sank its buck teeth deep into his index finger.

He tried to sling it away, but it held on with jaws strong enough crack walnuts. Pain shot up his hand as the teeth sank down to the bone, and finally, with the image of his mother/wife still in his mind, he slammed the squirrel's body against a tree trunk and it let go. Furious, he lifted a foot to stomp the squirrel into the ground, but the angel distracted him again as it flew lower, heading toward the encampment. When he looked back to the ground, the squirrel was gone. Tough little fucker, clinging hard to a ruined life, it must have scampered off into the undergrowth.

He bound his bleeding, aching finger with a piece of the MRE foil wrapper as he traced his way through the woods back to the camp. It was his trigger finger, which he was sure he would need before the night was out. His rage at the squirrel quieted to a still boil. Fuck it! He hoped the squirrel would die a long, painful death tonight.

Marguerite.

As she flew toward the helicopter, she tried to think clearly about what she would do when she got there. The images she had drawn from the pilot's mind served as a three-dimensional map. The mental images were not clear but overlaid by other images, soggy transparent recollections, some from her life as a human, others from totally alien wellsprings. She suspected these alien memories were also a kind of map, like the routes programmed into the brains of migrating birds, but she was frightened as to where such an alien map might lead her. She thought of these images as dreams, but she hadn't really slept since her metamorphosis, so how could she be dreaming? And even as a human, she'd never had dreams, not ones she could remember.

No, that isn't true. We had dreams, sweetheart, but you attributed them to me.

And that was another thing that she didn't remember from before. The voice that whispered in her ear, at times as clear as if someone was flying behind her, inches above her back, wings in perfect sync with her own. Marguerite resisted the urge to look behind to catch a glimpse of this secret sharer. She knew she would find only empty sky behind her, but the voice was so distinct she wanted to turn to it each time it spoke. Had the archangel inserted some sort of psychic radio in her brain at the time of the homunculus implantation? Was this what May heard, but all the time, louder, more irrational? Was she destined to become like May, always perched on the edge of insanity?

You always had dreams. Remember the night terrors?

"Yes, I do remember them," Marguerite said aloud to her unseen companion. Her screams had awakened her husband many times up in the middle of the nights. John had tried to get her to tell him what she dreamed, but she remembered no details, only vague impressions of heavy weights being pressed upon her, of fear of death and something even worse than death. Finally, she had realized the night terrors often came after sex with John, so she had put a stop to that activity. The terrors still came after she had shut John down, but not so often.

Now that she no longer slept, she no longer had those little slices of death and terror. But as an angel, Marguerite did have moments where she rested, times of relative peace of mind, of a stilling of the compulsion to fly. During these times, she was still aware of her surroundings, but the impressions of the world dimmed and her responses slowed. During these times the visions surfaced. They were more than daydreaming reveries but still not full-fledged dreams. Unlike the dreams she had as a human, the visions did not jolt her to screams, but the images they brought were disturbing.

In one vision, she is flying over an unfamiliar landscape. She comes to an ocean broken by white frothy waves. The waves beckon her, but she is frightened to continue. But she sees a storm coming from the mainland, and she cannot turn back. Nor can she bring herself to fly over the ocean. She sees no beach, just a sheer cliff of white rock streaked with red rust. The cliff is an endless monolith stretching far out of sight. Its base is assaulted by the pounding waves. There is a cave in the cliff's face, dark as a corpse's mouth, and she flies to it.

The inside of the cave is a wonderful place, embued with light from an unseen source and the walls covered with paintings by Stone Age artists. The storm outside picks up, and winds force her deeper into the cave, pushing against her wings like sails. As she stumbles forward, the cave turns from a place of light and beauty into a foul, dimly lit sty, the floor littered with piles of feces. In place of cave art, brownish smudges cover the walls, smearings without form or meaning. Moreover, they appear to have been painted in smeared shit, not charcoal or bright pigments. She senses more than sees or hears or smells a huge dark beast lurking in the back of the cave. She is pushed further into the depths of the cave, driven by the hurricane winds, staggering toward the beast, the wet feces squishing under her feet. As she enters the deepest shadows, she can see the glowing eyes of a beast.

"Ahhhhhhhhh," says the beast, in a voice deep enough to make the stone walls tremble. The creature's eyes emit a luminous white light. Though she is still an angel, and stronger than any mortal animal, she is overwhelmed by fear and loathing. She wants desperately to flee the cave, fly far away from the cliffs, but puppet-like she is compelled to move closer to the beast. She is not simply being pushed from behind by the wind, she is being drawn forward magnetically. She takes another step, and another. As the beast lurches toward her, its paws almost like hands, beneath the growling song 'ahhhhhh' is a semi-intelligible word she interpreted as either "atone" or "alone," she isn't sure which.

She always came out of the trance with a jolt, the reverberant 'ahhhhhh' still echoing in her ears.

The same dream has played out numerous times. Each time, she is relieved yet disappointed that she never gets a clear sight of the beast.

Just thinking about the vision was enough to draw her back into its spell. Disoriented, she over-flown the soldiers' camp. She did a banking turn and headed back toward the camp, determined to keep the intruding images at bay and her mind on her goal. A few hundred yards farther and the big helicopter was in sight again, its olive green turned grayish in the starlight.

She landed on the center of the rear rotor and hunkered down, hoping not to be observed. Bullets wouldn't kill her – small arms fire merely bounced off her – but she had never been shot with larger caliber weapons, and she didn't know what their effect might be. Enough of her remained human to fear mutilation. If an eye was destroyed, would it grow back?

She would have liked to have asked the archangels such questions, but that would have probably been impossible even during the early stages of her metamorphosis. When she was still conscious, the archangels' bodies and minds had already begun to deteriorate. But even before the implanting of the homunculi seeds, it had been like talking with an oracle. She held a sort of conversation with Azazel; she would talk, he would respond, but with answers that could be interepreted several ways. Often she felt that no one was there, that she was not speaking to a single individual, but with the whole race of archangels. They had been an enigma, and now she, as part angel/part human, was an enigma unto herself. And for a long foggy time after her metamorphosis, her span of consciousness had been measured in seconds. Thoughts, impressions came and were absorbed like rain on water. Her past life was a brief flickering of images without apparent continuity: pictures of John Wright, (whom she now remembered as being her husband), of riding in a pickup truck, of wearing an armband with a red cross, of crying over a torn flowered dress as a child. Bits of emotion were associated with these images, but the connection was tenuous, faint.

One exchange with Azazel, however, stuck in her mind. It had been right after the angel had implanted the seed. Hers had been a painful experience, but not like May's, whose mind had been permanently ruined and who had nearly bled to death after one of the first implantations. The archangels had collectively learned how fragile humans were from those first disastrous experiences.

In Marguerite's case, moments after being implanted, the homunculus seed had rooted its way throughout her nervous system and into her brain. Azazel had stayed in attendance, curiously watching her during this stage. As the homunculus threads spread throughout her brain, a mental link with Azazel was established, and the archangel had become privy to the years of religious angst that led to her abandoning her human-ness.

"Interesting," the archangel had said, stroking his chin frighteningly like the way her father would before delivering a sin-and-redemption lecture. "You humans may be physically trapped in only three dimensions, fettered by time, but your unconscious mind taps into many other planes of existence."

"Planes? What planes?" she had managed to utter despite feeling like something was dragging her spinal cord out through her navel.

"It's hard to explain," he had said. "I only get the same glimpses that are allowed you from your unconsciousness. You have a male side there, for example, like a complete other personality, though subordinate to your female personality, of which you're not aware."

"Are you saying I'm a man at heart?"

"No, not at all. I think all human women have this male side. And all men, a female side. It's some sort of balancing mechanism I do not understand."

She wanted to argue, but the pain from the implantation did not allow her to speak. She had met the archangel in a neighbor's barn. The archangel had arched her over a big round bale of hay to do the deed. All she could do was lie down on the bale with her skirt bunched up around her waist and her panty house pulled down. He hovered over her in midair, like something out of the ceiling of the Sistine Chapel.

Despite the pain, she had no impulse to scream. Instead, being bent backwards over the curve of the big round bale had made her think of her Pilates exercises, which was ridiculous. His words began to echo her unspoken thoughts, the moment sealed into her memory by the pain: "We understand the concept of irony now," he said. "It's some of your more admirable human passions that turn on you to destroy you. Trying to be saints, you deny your dark side, and lacking release, the darkness builds up pressure to control you. And it's the same with trying to deny your shadow sex. But the strangest thing is your fear of death, of oblivion, the very thing we desire. Lacking individual immortality, you try to find it in your children and their children, or you make up imaginary gods and paradises. And we see now why you'll always overbreed, always out-race your world's resources."

"Psychobabble," she said, but still had to smile at him because he was so beautiful. She tried to add that it was God's adversary that made men do evil things, but her faith had failed her – that was what had brought her to make contract with the angels in the first place – and her own words tasted like spoiled, brittle bread on her tongue.

Her remembrances were interrupted by voices below, and Marguerite folded her wings behind her and crouched lower on the big pivot of the helicopter blades. Two men had emerged from the back of the helicopter. They both carried carbines.

"Man, look at those stars," one said.

"Yeah, man. You could almost read a book, they're so bright," the other said.

He passed something to the first man, who put it to his lips. A bright red star appeared in front of his face, and a moment later, he exhaled.

"Yeah, you probably could read a book, man – if you knew how to read."

The smoker laughed, then coughed. Hovering twenty feet above them, Marguerite smelled a skunky-sweet odor.

"Let's go over to the mess tent and see if we can score some food," the other man said.

"No, not with those fucking angels about."

"What's the difference?" the second said, then bent over at the waist as he was overtaken by another stint of coughing. His carbine dropped to the ground beside his feet with a clatter. When he recovered, he said, "This shit is just as likely to kill us. Who the fuck knows what kind of bug spray the growers use."

"Maybe so, maybe so," the other said, rescuing the joint from his friend's fingers. "But at least this gets us high."

"Maybe the angels get you high, too; you know, fly high, then drop your ass."

"You are a fucking idiot, you know that," the other said. "They could be flying above us right now, and what could we do about it?" He pointed a finger skyward for emphasis, and the other followed it, looking up right at Marguerite on her perch.

"What's that?" he said.

Marguerite could see the fear in his face. He knelt to frantically reach for his rifle. The other man started to look up as Marguerite launched herself between them. She swatted away the carbine of the man who was standing, and snatched up both men by the napes of their necks. Before either could call out she drove their heads together and pitched their limp bodies twenty feet away into brush on the other side of the helicopter.

From inside came the muted voices of other men. Someone was snoring. Satisfied that none of the men inside were alarmed, she leapt atop one of the things that looked like jet engines. She still didn't understand how she could be as light as a dust mote one moment and as heavy as a truck next, but it was another mistake, for the airframe shifted under her new weight. Voices inside raised in alarm, followed by mumblings, but she couldn't understand what they were saying. The voices quieted, the men probably listening. One continued snoring.

Now she could see what she had come for. May's head was wedged between the engine fairing and the airframe's fuselage. The head was only inches from her foot. Maybe she could just pry it loose and escape. But before she could get a grip on the head, there were footsteps on the metal ramp that extended from the rear of the craft. Three men came out, two with rifles at the ready, the third with a pistol. They fanned out, the one with the pistol going straight down the ramp, the other two with the carbines jumping off to either side. The men with rifles crouched and checked the space between the fuselage's underbelly and the ground. They hadn't looked up yet, but it was only a matter of time until they did and saw her. She could deal easily enough with three men, but she could not do so without them firing their weapons and thus bringing out more men. This was all going badly, but she couldn't leave May's head behind. The soldiers would search the upper reaches of the aircraft sooner or later. Provided she left any of them alive.

"You men, there! What are you doing?" The two men with rifles stood up and turned toward the gruff voice coming from the shadows of the woods on her side of the helicopter.

"Identify yourself," one of the soldiers said.

"This is Major Karl Minor, you numb-nuts," came the reply, and the man stepped out from the woods into sight. "What do you semen-suckers think you're doing?"

One man giggled, then coughed. The other, the one still on the ramp, said, "There was a noise outside. Sounded like something big bumped against the side of the airframe."

The attention of the man on the ramp was on the major; he still hadn't looked up. Marguerite brought up her legs from around the engine fairing and braced herself to pounce on him. She would have no time for subtlety. No time to be gentle. She'd have to break his neck and be done with it. Her human side told her this was wrong, but the angel part emotionlessly calculated the trajectory and the logistics of killing the other men.

"Who's the ranking officer here?" the major asked.

"Well, you are, sir," the man said.

"Besides me, you idiot?"

"Uh, no one, sir. Lieutenant Baudelaire went outside a while ago with Blake. Now there's no sign of them."

"Did you look in the mess tent?" the major said and pointed toward it. When the men looked where he pointed, the major looked directly at Marguerite and put a single finger on his lips. He didn't say *Shhhh*," but she got his message: *Be still, and I'll distract them.* What she didn't understand was his motive.

"No, sir," the ramp man said. The man with the pistol came from around the other side, and looked toward the tent too.

"I suggest you do so now, but keep your eyes on the woods to either side as you go."

"Sir? What about securing the aircraft."

"Are you questioning my orders, Private?"

"Sir. No, sir, but we did hear something."

"Just now?"

"Yes, sir."

"Well, I've been in the woods here for the last five minutes, taking a piss, and I didn't see anything. If you're concerned about Baudelaire and Blake, check the tent."

"What about the angels, sir?"

"You're more likely to shoot each other than meet up with an angel. Keep calling out as you move toward the tent. Everyone is jumpy."

"Yes, sir."

"Besides, if you encountered one those creatures, your weapons won't be of much use. I've seen them move – they're incredibly fast and strong – she'll – they – will take your guns away and tear you apart. Like *they* did Scalzi."

"Yes, sir."

"She?" the giggler asked. Both the ramp man and the major ignored him.

"Best not interfere with them if you can help it," the major said and stole a glance at Marguerite. "At least until we know more about them."

"Yes, sir." There was a tremble to his voice now.

"*Now get on with your business!*" the major shouted as the three men moved toward the tent. Then he looked at her again, and she understood.

When the men were out of earshot, the major asked in a lower voice, "Did you kill the other two?"

She shook her head no, but didn't really know, and reached down to grab May's head. From the woods, one of the three men called out, "Baudelaire, Blake? Are you there?"

No answer came. She only meant to knock them out, but perhaps she had clapped their heads together too hard.

"Do you plan to kill me?" the major asked.

"I don't want to kill anyone," she said and returned her attention the job at hand. The major carried only a handgun, and she wasn't afraid of such weapons. She gripped May's head with both hands and tugged, but it was wedged so tightly it had made an indentation in the metal fuselage, and she had to give it a second, considerably harder jerk to free it, hoping she didn't damage it further.

She stood upright, balanced on the engine, which was as wide as a horse's back, and looked at May's face. Her blonde hair was dirty, and her face was smudged with grease. Marguerite brushed her thumb across an eyelid, peeling it back. The blue-gray iris was covered with a white, semi-opaque film. There was no May on the other side of the cloudy window staring back. *Where had May gone?* The head was an empty shell. Had May ever been there? Was she herself an empty shell now, albeit a nearly immortal one? But she still had a kind of faith, didn't she? Something residual from her life as an evangelical Christian said could it could not be so. Some things transcend logic. She knew May's body could be not only be reassembled but reanimated.

She didn't know how she knew this, but she did. She couldn't say if this knowledge came from faith or instinct, but she knew the body would heal itself once she gathered all the pieces together. But she wondered if when May was reassembled and reanimated, would the soul of May return to inhabit it? Faith said: Yes, it would.

Marguerite suspected her motivation came more from seeking answers to these questions than from an altruistic desire of returning May to life. Truth be told, May had not been a friend when they were humans – they were from different worlds. May would have called her a Bible-thumper. The human Marguerite would have thought May was a honky-tonk slut, though she would have never spoken that word out loud. But now May was the only company she had as an angel, though admittedly May couldn't be counted on to hold a conversation even before the accident.

Marguerite stood, balancing on the curved canopy by willing herself to be as light as willow leaf, and held out the head at arm's length.

"You're not her," the major said. "You're not the Lady of the Lake. Who the fuck are you?"

"I'm not anyone anymore. I'm just someone's bad dream," she said, surprised by her own words. She launched skyward, May's head under one arm.

"Tell her I need to see her," the major called behind her. "Tell the Lady of the Lake! Goddamn it!"

From the woods, the three soldiers called again, "Baudelaire, Blake?"

Marguerite didn't reply because she had no answer to the major's question. She had no idea whom he was speaking of, but flew on toward her rendezvous with her faith in May's resurrection.

10.

Of Wars on Planes Beyond My Ken

Bryan.

Straddling him, the unknown woman reached orgasm, and in that instant her features softened, becoming truly beautiful. Better than the sex, a hint of personal connection passed between them, a fleeting feeling of simpatico. Then another orgasm, and she arched her back, her inner thighs trembled, and her hands and her fingers, like talons, dug hard into his shoulder muscles. More orgasms followed, fierce spasms now. A low moan escaped from her throat.

He would have been proud for bringing her numerous orgasms(to his none), but he was sure her multiple orgasms had more to do with her terrible physical transformation than anything he had done. He had had the weird experience that the toes of the homonculus, which extended down to her labia lips, had been gripping him as much as her vagina.

As quickly as she had mounted him, she withdrew and stood up. Apparently, he was little more than a dildo, a convenience.

Her skin was flushed, which made the dark colors of the homonculus stand out more. He tried to catch her eye, but she was again looking through not at him. What did he expect? A kiss on the forehead as one might do to a child?

Nothing was there, though. He had been caught up in her experience. To delay his own orgasm as long as possible, he had used that Tantric technique Laura had taught him, holding his breath with his mouth open, and now he was left erect, batteries still charged. By Tantric rules he was winning, having brought his partner to orgasm while holding back his own, but he felt deprived.

Awakening of an Alien God

Despite the intensity of the experience, orgasm or not, it paled with sex when his partner was either Suzanne or Laura. With Suzanne the lust had been secondary to the feeling of being loved, compassionately, unconditionally, and that had been the most powerful aphrodisiac he had ever experienced. With Laura, sex had been an intense drama. He had a sense of fated connection with Laura, not the soul-mate thing he had felt, however briefly, with Suzanne in that other life, in that other world, but a simple twist of fate that entangled their lives.

He hadn't felt that sense of connection with this stranger, nothing of the spiritual part of sex, but the act hadn't been merely physical either. They had been more than just fuck buddies, more like survivors, the way two people lost at sea might cling to each other.

He was obviously a hopeless romantic.

The sexual encounter had been his first since losing Suzanne. Laura had sent him a few half-hearted signals, but he pretended he hadn't decoded them. The traditional wisdom among men was that to get over a lost love, find another lover. It was said any kind of sex, good, bad, or even ugly, was the first step to curing the sense of failure and loss. But the adage had never held true for him, except maybe at the moment of orgasm. Then despair would return, worse than before.

The mystery woman squatted a few feet away, then rolled over with her back on the stone floor. The experience had been so intense and so immediate, only after they were actually fucking, as she had rose up and down on him, had he realized she was in some sort of trance, like a sleepwalker.

He got to his feet and pulled up his coveralls and wished he had something to clean himself with. Her orgasm had been liquid, and her juices dribbled down his leg. The only thing available to clean himself with was her skirt, which lay crumpled on the floor. He picked it up and shook out the straw, then hesitated. Using it as a towel didn't seem appropriate. *Yeah, like fucking someone who was in a trance was appropriate.* He rationalized that he had been drawn into her dream, physically and mentally. He shook the sawdust off the skirt and turned to drape her with it, only to find himself alone in the cell. He did a quick survey of the space. There was no place for her to hide. The cell was too small. In a panic, he looked up, halfway expecting her to be creeping along the high ceiling like some sort of B-movie vampire, but of course she wasn't there.

And the paperback book-size window was too small for her head to pass through, much less her body. Besides, her disappearance had been too quick. One second she had been lying there. The next she wasn't.

Had it been real? Of course it had. He was still wet with her juices, he still held her left-behind skirt, and a faint imprint remained in wood shavings and sawdust on the floor where she had been lying. Once more he scanned the room for signs of her, as if, chameleon-like, she had blended into the stone walls, or if like a lost set of keys, she was right before him, filtered out in the blind spot of his mind's eye. She had to be here somewhere.

Then he felt he was being watched.

He tried to dismiss the feeling as false and almost succeeded until he noticed one thing: Though not the slightest wind breezed through the cell, motes of dust danced in the light from the small window. He held as still as he could, but something continued to stir the dust in the air. He looked up and this time noticed the seams of a small rectangle centered exactly in the middle of the ceiling. A trapdoor. The shape and size was about right, and it would explain the disappearence of the woman, though her exit must have been incredibly swift.

A single drop of sweat trickled down his brow and stung the corner of his eye, but he didn't wipe it away, holding as still as he could, waiting for the dust motes to settle.

"You're here somewhere," he said. "I can sense you."

But who – or what – did he sense? He remembered a session in the Jacobsen mansion, when the angel Asbel, invisible but sensed, had invaded their planning session. He had felt a presence like this one, unseen but real and almost tangible all the same. This was what he felt now.

What had Sophia Blackstone said to make the archangel to make itself known?

"Reveal yourself!" he shouted and immediately felt like an idiot. But before he could chastise himself, the air in front of him began to shimmer. Bits of sawdust swirled upward from the floor to outline something man-height. The outlined form became taller. The room cooled. Streams of leaden gray with bits of deep blue-green filled the outline as it coalesced into a semi-solid, chimerical form. Yellow swirls formed into large lumps within the thinner liquid.

Awakening of an Alien God

The color and form was different than the manifestation of Asbel. The dominant colors of Asbel had been purple and black, angry colors, culminating in an explosion that threw small objects around the room.

But this transubstantiation was different. The yellow globs gradually lightened, then merged with the thinner liquid. The leaden gray and blue-green did not seem angry but full of fear and deceit. And instead the bits of sawdust and other detritus from the floor being ejected as projectiles, everything simply oozed out from the congealing ectoplasm. One moment all this swirled in as a shimmering amorphous mass, and in the next the angel became visible, the same one who had abducted him in Suzanne's bar.

His/her/its – whatever – face was pale as marble, and its hair was albino white, just as Bryan remembered. What he hadn't noticed at the time – or perhaps it had changed – was that the angel's hands and feet were bright blue. Moreover, its feet weren't human-like at all; they were more like huge bird feet, taloned and scaled. One blue hand held a brown ceramic jug.

The creature looked distracted, then it sighed and sang:

"Human love! What is this thing, this sorry thing
That drags you across worlds, spans divides sans wings?
Not just some biological urgency, more than lust
Promises happiness, but more often crumbles as dust."

The creature reeked of alcohol. Towering over him, it held out the jug. It was drunk.

"Want some? A little swig of mead? Or do you prefer instead some weed?"

"You have that here? Weed? Marijuana, I mean?" The singsong cadence of the angel's speech was contagious.

"I could find you some, as it grows wild hereabout. But right now, I'm not sure I could fly so well."

Its eyes lost focus, and the creature paused, wobbling a bit. Bryan waited for it to sing another drinking song, but evidently it was finished.

"Sure, I'll try the mead. Why the hell not?" Bryan said and nearly dropped the jug the angel handed to him. It looked like a small moonshine jug in the angel's giant hands, but was nearly the size of a five-gallon bucket and weighed thirty or forty pounds. The liquid swished about inside as he tried to lift it to his mouth. Obligingly, the angel put a dinner-plate-sized hand under the bottom of the jug and helped tilt it. Bryan managed to get it to his mouth without knocking out any teeth, but nearly choked as a gout of sweetness gushed into his throat. He'd read about but had never sampled mead before. It tasted like pinot grigio with a lot of honey mixed in. The angel gave the jug a little boost, sloshing more mead into Bryan's mouth. The angel, like all drunks, yearned for – craved – the company of another drunk.

"Enough, enough for now," Bryan managed to sputter before the angel drowned him in the sticky liqueur.

"I fucking mean it," the drunken angel said. "We don't do it."

"You mean you don't fuck?"

"Love is what I mean. Sex is easy. Love is hard. We don't understand it." It wobbled about some more and tipped the jug to its own mouth; its wings fluttered like a stunned pigeon Bryan had once seen try to fly through a plate glass window. Exactly like that, in fact, except this angel had two sets of wings – or was it four? Bryan found focusing difficult already, and wondered if the mead contained something besides alcohol.

The angel tottered about. Bryan would have thought it was doing pantomime, an ethereal imitation of a loudmouth drunk, but the moonshine jug in its blue hand and the reek of alcohol on its breath was a 'tell,' as poker players say. If it was doing an imitation of a drunk, it was a damn convincing one. Bryan tried to imagine why the angel might want him to believe it was shit-faced, but he came up blank. Even the concept that an angel could get drunk was hard to accept. Weren't they supposed transcend the material: sex, hunger, mortality, and, yes, inebriation? He moved aside to avoid being stepped on by the seven-foot-tall being as it stumbled about on the sawdust-covered floor of the small cell. If it fell on him, the it would most certainly crush him.

Without prelude, it sat down, placed the jug of mead between its legs, and patted the stone floor, an invitation for Bryan to sit beside it. He debated not doing so, but decided if he sat down, maybe the angel wouldn't get back up and stagger around some more. So he plopped down, sitting at an angle to the wall so he could keep an eye on the huge creature. But as he sat, he found the angel's head was at his own level. It was now his size. Though he'd seen the archangels' ability to instantly change height, the process was still disconcerting.

"Did you enjoy it? The physical intersect?" the angel asked. Its breath was as sweet and fruity as a diabetic's.

"Enjoy what?" he said.

"The love-making you just had?"

"It wasn't love-making."

The angel's perplexed look was all too human.

"It was sex, not love. There's a difference."

"I thought I said that, but whatever, whomever, does it matter?" The angel stared through him, its eyes unfocused, staring into infinity.

"What happened to your singing in verse?"

"Singing in what?" The angel took another deep swig from the jug. Though it had shrunk to human-size, the jug had not, but the angel had no problem tipping it. It still had a giant-sized thirst. The jug gurgled. Where did it put all that mead? A hollow leg? Into another astral plane?

"Never mind," Bryan said. The angel's white hair now had a hint of color. "Tell me something."

"Anything, my love."

Bryan just stared at it, speechless. His perplexity must have been as clear to the angel as it was to him, for the angel explained, "Maybe that's not the right expression. I feel we've bonded."

"Well, maybe *my friend* would be more appropriate than *my love*," Byran said.

"That's sthumthing you need to explain to me, mutst explain to me," the angel slurred.

"Okay, if I can, though some humans struggle with the difference all their lives," Bryan said.

Me, for example.

"But first, tell me, what is this place, how did I get here?"

"Easy. I brought you here," the angel said and pointed upward to the trapdoor.

"That's not what I meant. How did I come to be on this world?"

"Easy again. You've always been here. You know that. Have another drink."

"No, no thanks." He pushed away the offered jug. The angel shrugged and took another gulp. It was smaller still, and though Bryan had been looking at it the entire time they had been sitting, he couldn't pinpoint the shrinking process. Had it shrunk between his eye blinks? Or had the dwindling occurred so gradually and subtly that he hadn't noticed? What he found more troubling was that the creature's hair was now a brownish-blonde and its features were more feminine.

She smiled at him – he now had to think of the angel as *she* rather than *it* – and said, "What was the question again? Or was it the answer I was waiting for?"

"The answer, I guess, is a question. Or leads to one. You said that I've always been here. But I haven't ever been here – at least as far as I remember."

"That's it. That's the ticket to consciousness. Remembrance," the angel said. She was clearly in her cups now. "Let's lower our consciousness now and forget!" She thrust the jug up at arm's length as if it were a trophy. Her hair had further darkened to nearly black. And her features had mutated as well. The hair on the back of his neck tingled as an unwelcome thought occurred to him. He remembered a day in Creedance, when an archangel who was a sexual ambiguous being as this one had turned into a female in midflight. The transformation had been disturbing enough – the sudden appearance of breasts, the smooth skin, the womanly curves. But the angel had not diminished in size. It had remained larger than an Amazon. The experience had been of being held in womanly arms with steel-hard muscles. It had made him feel like a child, but in a perverse way, like a fat, grown, middle-age man still living with mummy. And then that angel, whose name had been Envy, had treated him to a vision of God that had shaken him to his very core.

This was a different experience – disturbing as were all encounters with angels – but not soul-shaking, he hoped. The angel had further shrunk to woman-size, perhaps girl-size. And where he had been absolutely in that other angel's power, now this creature was so small that he almost felt big-brotherly toward her.

He was determined now to catch the transformation. Could he just not blink? She must be metamorphosing in those milliseconds of darkness. Did he really want to see? Could he stand to know what he suspected?

"So assuming that I've always been here, what about the life I remember back on Earth?"

"Oh, that was a dream, a reality built by a consensus – a partial consensus." She took another swig from the jug. "The trouble with alcohol is that I need so much of it," she said.

Wondering if engaging in lengthy dialectics with an angel was wise, even if the angel was drunk, Bryan asked, "So, that was the dream and this . . ." – he patted the stone floor – ". . . is the reality?"

"No, silly. They're both dreams. We are being dreamed by the Dreaming God. But being the dream of the Dreaming God, there are multitudes of dreams in which we are players, and . . ." she winked at him as if sharing a private joke " . . . and the dreamers at the same time."

"Well, if this all is being dreamed by someone, I hope he's enjoying it," Bryan said.

"That was a joke, wasn't it?" She brought up her knees, and the robe slipped down, showing more leg.

Fine, white, downy hair glistened on her thigh in the light from the window.

"Sort of. Tell me, what did you mean in the saloon when you called me an 'imposter'? That was you, wasn't it?"

"Yes," she said and grabbed his wrist to lay his hand on her thigh. The skin was certainly feminine, but he was suddenly afraid she would turn into the woman he had just had sex with. He tried to pull his hand away, but she held it firm.

"If that was you, then who are you now?" he said. "Is your God dreaming you in a different form?"

"Maybe it is you who is dreaming me." She let go of his hand. "I'm sorry I called you an impostor. I was out of order, sir." Her tone told him she was not sorry, but fearful, which didn't compute.

"Would you like to see the Dreaming God? This is the basement of one of his houses. I could take you up upstairs for a little visity-wishy."

"You're either drunk or messing with me or both," Bryan said, but when she looked confused, he realized the archangel was absolutely serious. God, the ultimate, transcendental God of the Israelites and Bedouin, God with a capital G, could either be a sky god or a transcendental entity. There were no other choices he knew of. But the creator fuck-up god of the Gnostics might very well be like a modern day Olympian and have a penthouse suite. Perhaps even a Jacuzzi and a wet bar. The question was, what would he – or she – be like? Would he be the vengeful, jealous god of the Old Testament, whose followers' only option was to cower? Or would he be like a buddy Jesus, a celestial good ol' boy, just-us-folks god, but the first one to invent eternal hell and damnation? Or would he be something entirely alien, a god of a million faces and uncountable eyes, like the god in his early vision when he was first taken into the angels' saucer?

In college, he had read Sarte and was taken by his comments about a "God-shaped hole" in the human consciousness. Sarte's atheism had been harmonic with his own at that time, and like the famous existentialist, Bryan believed that even if a loving, just god existed, then his very existence negated liberty.

Later, he rejected atheism because he decided it was a faith-based system too. Evangelicals argued that God must exist because no one could prove that he didn't. Atheists had faith that God didn't exist because no one could prove he did. Either belief system required a sort of faith. So he had perched on the fence as an agnostic.

Then the archangels had come to Creedance. Thinking of them as merely preternatural and not supernatural was convenient. He still clung to this belief, hating to think he was under the thumb of some cruel god who, like a drunken father, would sadistically torment someone who didn't show love and respect. Now, though, he didn't know what to believe, but the thought of a personal god was still too much to swallow.

"Why would a supreme being want to see me?" he said.

"He . . . ?"

"So God is a he?"

"No, we're not sure. He may be – or may be not. The Dreaming God appears to be male, but it could be an illusion – that's why we just say *Dreaming God*."

"How about 'Yo'?"

The angel looked at him curiously. Bryan realized he was as drunk too. He should shut up, but he couldn't stop himself. "It's a relatively new word. It can mean either male or female or whatever. As in, 'yo ready to party?'" Was he grinning like a fool as he said this? If so, the angel didn't appear to have noted. She – or rather *yo* – didn't appear to have gotten the joke.

"Very well, then. Yo won't see you, for Yo is asleep and dreaming, dreaming us and dreaming a war between some of our ex-numbers – I'm sure you're aware this rebellion . . ."

"The hundred?"

"Yes."

"I see. But if Yo is sleeping," Bryan suppressed a chuckle, "what's the point of me seeing him?"

"We think . . ."

"Who's *we*?"

"We, the angelic host, of course. We have decided you are somehow pivotal in this conflict. Think of it as a kind of experiment. We want to bring you into his – Yo's – presence to see if it changes the dream and therefore this reality. We think you'll understand once you see Yo."

Bryan considered this for a moment, now truly regretting having drunk so much mead. The Yo-joke was getting old, too. The angel was offering him an opportunity to meet this bogeyman of theirs, and he remembered the gut-wrenching experience of meeting the god in his dream. Could he refuse?

"Do I have a choice?" Bryan asked.

"Of course. That's what everything is about, choices," the angel said and stood. Bryan got to his feet, too, brushing the straw and dust off his trousers and wondering whether he was dressed properly to meet a god. He should at least fasten the front of his coveralls. Would God smell the sex of the young woman on him? Had that been some sort of sin-test?

When he looked back to the angel, she was an *it* again, towering nearly two feet taller above his head.

"I'm relieved," he said to it.

"About what?" The voice was no longer feminine but not masculine either, as deep as if coming from a barrel.

"I feared you were going to metamorphose into the young woman I had sex with."

"Oh, that. Hah! You suspected I might be your seducer?"

Bryan nodded, afraid of the answer.

"No, she was human, at least for now. Her last request before going to the hatchery was to be loved by a young man, a stranger. You were convenient."

Bryan didn't want to ask what the hatchery was. He feared he already knew.

11.

And Times Forgotten by God

Marguerite.

Marguerite squatted at the edge of Lost Lake under the silver light of the moon and washed the oil and grit from May's face. She had developed the habit of bringing the pieces of May – torso, arms, and legs – here to rinse them in the clear green water, and she felt it would be bad luck to break that baptismal pattern.

She – the *she* of her past life – had been baptized twice, first sprinkled as an infant, and a second time as a teen a big, a human-size aquarium. The second baptism occurred in large font was normally hidden behind purple curtains that formed a backdrop for the pulpit of the First Baptist Church of Creedance.

As the congregation waited, the curtains opened to reveal the white-frocked minister and the one-born-in-sin, the twelve-year-old Marguerite.

She scanned the congregation, deathly afraid she would see someone there who knew her father. The fact she had even stepped foot in a Baptist church would have infuriated him. If he found she had been baptized in a rival faith, she didn't know what he'd do. She had been baptized at birth in the Calvin tradition, and that was supposed to be enough for eternity. But as her crisis of faith deepened, she had looked to her Baptist friends from school for help. They had encouraged and secretly sponsored her for this ceremony, and she'd held high hopes it would *magically* fix her faith.

Seeing no one she knew but her Baptist friends, she let herself be led into the font. She was dressed in a flimsy gown, slit up the side, barely covering her Capris pants and flowery blouse. The minister stood beside her. She intently studied his face, having never been so close to him before. Up close, his face was florid, and his nose showed little tracings of broken blood vessels. One rough hand – he also farmed to make ends meet – gripped her shoulder. His other hand rested on the delicate curve of her lower back.

Steps led down into the font. The tiled steps were cold under her bare feet. She noticed he wore old beat-up black and white tennies. He dipped her three times, in a kind of formal dance, and she thought not of Jesus or John the Baptist, but of ballroom dancing. There was a one dip in the name of the Father, one in the name of the Son, and then one in the name of the Holy Ghost. The minister had gone about the task methodically, his big red hands gentle, fatherly but firm, as if he were assisting the birth of a calf instead of the rebirth of a human soul.

Later, in perspective, it had been worse than if he had copped a feel. His *for-your-own-good-poor-sinner* hands had laid a heavy burden on her, heavier than if he had fondle her in the rectory. Like abuse, the concepts associated with baptism was a weight she had carried into her adult human life. She had sought a rebirth and been scammed, spiritually abused, delivered into a kind of mundane slavery of original sin and misogyny where everything physically human was denigrated. That had been a crime as bad as any sexual abuse – an abuse of the spirit. And that feeling of needing a rebirth of the spirit remained. For all her good intentions and the minister's good will, she had felt cheated.

Her rebirth as an angel had come with strings attached, too, but at least it had been a true rebirth where the world is changed because she had been rebuilt physically and mentally.

And now, that need for rebirth, for experiencing it again however vicariously, drove Marguerite to carefully rinse May's head in Lost Lake. Her angel hands were strong, stronger than the minister's had ever been, so strong she that if he were alive and standing in front of her now, she could crush his huge paws like egg shells.

She sighed. The grease from the engine would not come off May's hair and forehead. Later, back at the farmhouse, maybe she could shampoo her hair and wash her skin clean with strong soap, as she had the other body parts.

She was exposed here, in plain sight of anyone coming down to the beach. She could hear soldiers talking not far away, near the helicopter. She had access to other areas of Lost Lake where she could reach the water and have some concealment. So why did she do this here? Because this ritual washing was more than a symbolic gesture as her baptism had been. She could feel May's hea was taking vital essence from the water – a true baptism of spirit. She felt this in her hands as she rolled the head around, but she didn't know why. Did it have something to do with the saucer immersed in the lake, a transference of energy through the water? She didn't know; she just felt in the very fiber of her being that this washing was worth the risk of being shot by one of the soldiers.

This area had been a children's wading pool at one time. A small, narrow, stone-lined channel fed water from the lake to the rectangular pool. It was, Marguerite now realized, about the same dimensions and depth as the baptismal font from a lifetime ago. She vaguely remembered coming here as a child – the memory came bright and strong and faded just as quickly. She, baby Marguerite, had been wading in the pool and wanting to be an angel, all clean and pure.

Was that a false memory? It seemed too convenient to be true.

Now she was a fallen angel or a sort of child of one, at least. The old Marguerite – that calico creature who for so long had wanted to know without question what was right and what wrong, who secretly feared she was damned for all time – would have considered what she was doing now with May's head a satanic ritual. Moreover, the old Marguerite, if transported in time from even a few months before the angels arrived, would have declared her own reborn form demonic. No question about it. Marguerite the angel found this insight at once hilarious and terrifying.

But some intuition told her the question of what she was doing with May's head wasn't a matter of good or evil; no more than were eating, singing, or flying evil. Like a bird building a nest or a dog chasing a squirrel, it was just what she did. But why? The only ultimate truth appeared to be death. Why was she driven to live, to bring poor, tortured May back to life? If there was a god who had the answer, he/she/it was either dead or asleep.

She lifted the head out of the water and turned it sideways. Water drained from the downside ear and out of the nostrils. The neck looked odd. The helicopter rotor had sliced through May's neck at an angle, and the cut was elliptical rather and circular, but she saw no anatomical details within the cut – no sliced vertebrae, no signs of severed muscle or tendons, veins, or arteries. The cut was pale pink and hard and smooth to the touch. It might have been the sawed-off head of a solid plastic mannequin.

A bird wading in the nearby shallows distracted her from further examining the neck. The bird had brown feathers tinged with iridescent blue, like oil on muddy water, and a long, skinny, down-curved beak nearly as long as its body. The curve of the beak reminded her of the thin crescent moon.

Then she was airborne again, with no memory of taking off. Luckily, she hadn't absentmindedly left May's head behind. It was tucked under her arm, its wet hair cool against her bare skin.

A minute later, she landed on the concrete patio at her old house. The door was as she had left it, hanging by one hinge on its shattered frame. She flipped the light switch at the side of the door, and miracle of miracles, the ceiling fixture came on.

Inside, under the glaring light of the bare bulb, she found the other parts of May as she had left them, laid out like a disassembled doll atop the large dining room table she had dragged into the kitchen. She found a Blue Willow-patterned turkey platter in the cabinet. Marguerite the human had been a collector – a flash of memory came back to her, another snapshot of her previous life, when she had sat in this very room talking about this china pattern with the sweet old neighbor woman. The kitchen had been clean and well-lit, all sunbeams and cheeriness despite death being near.

Now it was a dungeon. Leaves had blown in through the shattered door, and some small furry animal scurried away in the litter. But the Blue Willow turkey platter was still in the cabinet and just the right size to hold May's head, just deep enough to prevent it from rolling off the table.

Working instinctively, Marguerite arranged the body parts on the table. As with the laceration that had severed May's head, the cross-section of all the wounds showed no internal details. The entire body appeared to be made of a solid homogenous material — angel putty. The slices were smooth and flat, and lining up the pieces was easy, leaving only a thin space where an arm had been severed from the shoulder or the legs at mid-thigh.

And then there was the problem of the wings.

She had never found May's sheared-off wings. But she dismissed this apparent problem. In life – if angels could truly said to be either alive or dead – the wings could be retracted into the upper torso, leaving only large bulges that looked like over-sized shoulder blades. These bulges were there now, so Marguerite guessed May would sprout new wings if the resurrection was successful.

She moved the pieces so the shoulders and the part of the neck that remained attached to the torso extended beyond the edge of the table. The legs, which had been sliced off at mid-thigh, were cantilevered precariously over the other end of the table, but the table gave just enough support they didn't topple off. Without thinking further, she took the head to the sink and washed it with green dish detergent.

The washing cleaned the grease smears off May's face, but her hair remained dingy brown with diesel fuel and there were clots of some residue from the helicopter's engines, but Marguerite supposed that if the reanimation succeeded, May could better bathe herself. Marguerite just sensed the surfaces of the wounds needed to be clean and pressed together. She didn't *know* this, but let herself be driven purely by instinct.

The legs were another problem. They dangled off the edge of the table and gravity turned the feet outward. Marguerite couldn't line up the cuts correctly. If she reanimated now would May be permanently duck-footed?

Rummaging through the kitchen cabinets for twine, she found something better: a large roll of silver duct tape.

Attaching the arms was simple because they had been severed at the shoulder joints. She simply aligned the lacerations and used a single, long band of tape around the shoulders and across the chest. The legs were a different matter – the tape didn't want to stick to May's skin, and she could devise no way to make a band, sticking tape to tape, as she had with the arms and shoulders. After wasting several feet of tape, she settled for using long pieces strapped under the heels like stirrups, and pulling the legs in place by wrapping the other ends of the tape to legs of the table.

The result made May look as if she were on a gynecologist's examining table, her legs spread wide and her feet elevated.

The torso had enough inertia that it didn't try to slide away with the legs pressed against it by the tension of the tape.

She stood back, surveyed her handiwork, and deemed it good. But though God might rest after creation, she couldn't. She used a none-too-clean dishtowel to pat dry the laceration on the head's part of the neck. Without further preamble and holding the head with her hands against the ears, she pressed the lacerated neck stump against its matching stump at the shoulder.

Nothing happened.

Well, nothing dramatic, anyway; no glowing light, no sound effects, no vibrations, but the separation gradually faded away as if the neck had never been severed. Marguerite let go, and the head lolled to one side but did not fall off. She checked the legs, and finding they had magically welded back too, she removed the tape. May's feet splayed, not duck-footed but without life. And the arms? They were likewise welded back on the shoulders without any scar to show they had ever been severed. May's hands dangled, palms up, off the edge of the table. Marguerite lifted up an arm and dropped it. The arm fell like a limp rag. Flexibility had returned to the body, but not animation. Something was still missing.

She returned to examine the head, and stared into May's lifeless blue-gray eyes. The eyelids were open, the outer ones, anyway; the nictitating eyelids were half-open, but they were made of a material so clear as to be nearly invisible. Before, the eyeballs had been coated with a semi-opaque white film. Now that the head was reattached, the cloudiness had cleared, but no consciousness remained behind the bright blue irises. The eyeballs might as well been made of plastic.

Marguerite rubbed her chin. What had she forgotten?

"Wake up! Wake up, May," she shouted and shook the reattached shoulders.

Nothing.

She considered slapping the limp face. Would the head fall off again if she did? Doubtful; but it was equally doubtful a slap would do any good.

Though she wasn't sure whether she or any other angel breathed, Marguerite checked the nostrils to find them clear. The little groove above the upper lip caught Marguerite's attention. A memory came from her human life: Her grandmother telling a teenage Marguerite that the groove was where an angel touched the unborn baby to make it forget its life in heaven. Marguerite the angel smiled at the irony of this memory, and without thinking, touched May there, her finger fitting the grove perfectly.

And as if the groove hid a magic button, May's mouth fell open and she gave a long sigh.

Ahhhhhhhhhhhhhhhhhhhhh.

The sigh was subdued at first, a forlorn-sounding yawn from a drowsy sleep. But the tone rose, the volume increased and warbled, stretching, climbing in pitch like a guitar string being tuned too tight.

Ahhhhhhhhhhhhhhhhhhhhhhhhh.

Marguerite jumped back, frightened for the first time since her re-birth as an angel. The sigh's intensity built until it filled the room, filled the house, filled the outdoors, filled the whole world.

Ahhhhhhhhhhhhhhhhhhhhhhhhh.

The sound hurt Marguerite's head, and she clapped her hands over her ears and let out a banshee screech of pain.

But her hands couldn't shut out the sigh. On and on it went, crowding everything else in the room, even the light.

A sparkling snowflake drifted down from the ceiling. A Tinkerbell, sparkling fairy light burning intolerably bright.

Ahhhhhhhhhhhhhhhhhhhhhhhhhhh.

Wings sprang from the lumps on May's back like a popped open umbrella, pushing her body up on the table and spreading out so wide as to push Marguerite back against the wall. A breeze brushed Marguerite's hair and caressed her face. The wind came from May, or rather went into her. Dust motes danced in the air, marking a path toward May's mouth. The ever-loudening sigh was the corpse's indrawn breath drawing May's soul back to some hungry inner space.

Ahhhhhhhhhhhhhhhhhhhhhhhhhhhh.

Marguerite thought of her vision of the beast in the cave, its *ahhhhhh*.

Ahhhhhhhhhhhhhhhhhhhhhhhhhhh.

Marguerite wanted to reach over and push May's mouth closed, but the fully extended wings kept her from getting close.

Ahhhhhhhhhhhhhhhhhhhhhhhhhhhh.

And the tiny sparkling snowflake fled into the mouth. The ahhhh-hhhhh ceased just as suddenly as it began. The body on the table took a deep gasp and sat up, eyes now open. May's soul, the essence of May, now stared out through those eyes with astonishment.

Her mouth opened and closed without sound, and Marguerite steeled herself for an encore of the inward rushing ahhhh- pneuma, but the now-animated angel on the table screamed.

"Too large! Too goddamn big! You're tearing me apart!"

A profusion of expressions rapidly played across May's face. Terror was followed by pain, followed by resignation, then anger, then terror again, then a recapitulation of each with more subtle signatures. May's face gradually calmed. She looked down at her abdomen, bare and clean with a feminine hint of six-pack abs that she had probably never had as a human. Her hands ran over the muscles and the alabaster skin. She began stripping away all the duct tape. Marguerite helped her.

"It's not there. I dreamt this horrible thing was attached to me, but it's not there," she said. "And then I was in this strange room. There was a huge, blue man sleeping. He looked familiar, but he was so large."

May stretched her arms as if she'd been sitting on a bed and had just woken up. Her wings partially unfolded behind her. She went on in a rapid, speedy voice: "And there were all these angels standing around him, pretty faces but they all had claws on their feet and blue hands like they stuck them down in the airplane's toilet bowl, ya' know, and I was standing with them, and I looked down at my feet, and. . . " May paused, her mouth open, her eyes focusing on Marguerite for the first time.

Something different was visible in this May's eyes, something Marguerite hadn't seen during all the time they had been flying together: a sense of self.

All the angel/human hybrids were unstable at times. Marguerite recognized this instability in herself, but felt the periods of disorientation had become less frequent lately. Still, sometimes her awareness was too intense and overloaded her emotions and rationality. Part of the overload was due, she believed, to the magnified senses that came with being an angel. But she had new instincts too, and perhaps perceptions that were native to the archangels caused the human mind to swoon.

After an initial period of adjustment, most of the other hybrids dealt with these alien thoughts and impulses as if they were nearly neuroses, with long periods of relative sanity occasionally punctuated by fixated or obsessive moments. Some angels were better at this than others. Some, like May, had been the reverse: in a constantly addled state, occasionally punctuated by lucid moments.

Now as May stared back at her, Marguerite could see the old May, the human May, the small-town-waitress May, not the brightest crayon in the box, but still part of the set.

May's eyes ran up and down her friend's body, hesitating on Marguerite's face, then flicking back and forth to her wings, which Marguerite had partially spread in shock at the violent awakening.

"Oh," May said, like a little girl admiring a new dress as she turned her head to check out her own now-extended wings.

"Ohhhhhhhhhhhhhh," she moaned, and that was it; then her eyes became confused, then panicked, then crazed. May-the-waitress was crowded out by May-the-deranged.

Marguerite felt her own wings relax. May-the-demented was a known. She and May-the-waitress had not really known each other in their respective human incarnations. Besides, wasn't dementia a more fitting response to this world than sanity was? She ran her hand across her own iron-hard stomach and down to her mons. This body was hers – or was it? Was she even real? Could this be some sort of dream test by God? As she watched May's expressions flicker rapidly from amazement to wonder to pain to joy and back to wonderment, Marguerite became envious. She wished that time of her angel rebirth would return, a time ruled by joy, worship, ecstasy, and forgetfulness, a time where all emotions changed so quickly, every moment was a surety in its eternal immediacy and eternal newness, where there had been no past, no future, just an eternal now.

Laura.

Back in the tent, sitting at the trestle table, Laura felt the hard steely presence of the pistol lodged in her jeans at the small of her back. She smelled it too, machine-oil and burnt powder.

She hoped the odor wouldn't give her away. Why was the gunpowder smell so strong? It smelled stronger than pot. Had Scalzi managed to discharge the gun before the angel ripped him apart?

She was instantly saddened by her mental image of his death. Did he remain conscious as his arms were ripped off, his internal organs scooped out? Scalzi had been a good guy among many creeps. He had a emitted a protective vibe and treated her like a wayward daughter, reminding her a bit of her Uncle Robert.

Who was left to keep the soldier goons off her? Major Minor? He represented order, but his control over the men was obviously tenuous. His self-control didn't seem too solid, either. The way he looked at her was unnerving, like a snake ready to strike. The man's soul was obviously diseased, and she didn't want to be left alone with him. Nor did she relish being left with the enlisted men. The trick was, she thought, to somehow keep the tension between the major and the men balanced. With the major, she would have to play a game of tit-tease. It would be a dangerous game. He was obviously attracted to her, but she wasn't prepared to screw an old man to get out of this situation.

Even if it meant saving her life? It was only sex and not really a fate worse than death, was it?

She flashbacked to when she was about thirteen and had decided to stand her ground against her father's sexual threats. With that act of defiance had defined herself, became more than a doormat. Giving in now to sexual extortion would be an act of self-betrayal.

Besides, if she read him right, once they had sex, he might turn on her anyway, abandon her to the men or even kill her himself. Toxic rage seemed to ooze from his very pores. But could she lead him on, make him possessively protect her, without it going too far?

And then there was a matter of the stolen pistol. Why exactly had she taken it? For protection? That was the obvious motive, but in truth, she hated guns and knew nothing about them. Guns were demon-possessed as far as she was concerned, always jamming or going off at the wrong time.

Worse, she suspected that now she that had introduced the gun into her life, it would surely, in Chekhovian fashion, lead to a tragic scene, either for her or for someone she cared about. No good could possibly come of it.

She had been fleetingly aware of all these factors when she saw the pistol laying there in the clearing, but she felt driven to grab it, as though her hands had been controlled by someone else. She had been trapped in a dream, watching dream-self do something stupid, but powerless to stop it.

She had her head down, staring at those errant hands resting on the trestle table. From the corner of her eye she saw someone moving toward her: the private, the one with the tic or wink. She didn't which.

"Ma'am," he said as he stepped near, with a kind of sneer. His body odor gagged her from three feet away – a mixture of sweat, motor oil, and shit, with emphasis on the shit. But he wouldn't be likely to smell the pistol over his own stink, would he? So maybe it was all good.

"What is it?" she asked.

"The major, he uh, he uh, said . . ." and the tic-wink was followed by a leer.

If he hadn't stunk so, she would have gotten up and smacked him. *Out with it, man! Out with it!*

The tic-wink creeped her out more than the malicious look. Was it congenital or acquired, maybe through drug use – or was he just some sort of pervert, trying to wink at her? She suspected the latter, but she waited, trying not to breathe.

"He said to take you back to the chopper," he said. No stutter this time. No tic-wink. Just the leer, so she now suspected the tic was not a nervous disorder.

"Why?" she asked.

Another leer, then a nod, followed by that creepozoid tic. "Don't know, safer maybe." Tic-wink, tic-wink, tic-wink, then the leer. "More private, maybe." Tic-wink, tic-wink, tic-wink. Or was he even conscious of his own tic?

He must have read her expression, for the leer disappeared, and a mixture of guilt and fear played across his face. No, he was too dense to be so sensitive. She could imagine the major telling him that if he laid a hand on her, he would be shot.

"So you coming . . . ma'am?"

"Do I have a choice?"

"Just obeying orders, ma'am. Don't make things hard for me."

"Okay, but here's the deal," she said.

He waited. A single tic-wink, then a shrug but no leer.

"Don't walk behind me. You creep me out watching me from behind, and I remember you grabbing my ass. Lead, and I'll walk behind. I won't try to run," she said. "Try to grab my ass again, and if I don't kick your balls up into your throat, the major will."

She waited while he considered. He was not stoned jusy mentally very slow, she decided. Worse, he was too stupid to know he was stupid, which was the most dangerous stupidity of all.

Finally, he said, "How do I know you ain't goin' ta' try to run off if I can't see you?"

"I'll keep talking or whistling or something so you'll know I'm behind you."

This amused him. He shrugged again. No tic-wink. "Okay."

She followed him to the helicopter, a distance of about a hundred yards. She hummed a bad rendition of *Onward Christian Soldiers* all the way.

She gagged on his smell each time she had drawn in air, but with him in front, he couldn't see the lump of the pistol, which kept threatening to slip down.

When they were about halfway there, the pistol squirmed down again, hard and heavy, into the deep cleft of her ass. She clenched her butt cheeks to hold it back. The soldier kept looking over his shoulder to make sure she was keeping up, so she had to keep walking. Clenching her buttocks to hold the gun in place made her swish and sway. She was glad she was wearing the hoodie. It was a men's extra-large and was like wearing a short skirt. It came halfway down her hips and covered, she hoped, the lump of the gun in her pants.

She must have fallen back a bit, for he turned, walking backwards, his gaze following the sway of her hips.

"I really need to use the toilet," she said, almost losing the cheek-clench on the gun as she spoke.

He laughed, projecting a fumigating fetor of tooth decay from six feet away. She really wanted to take out the pistol and shoot him right then and there, but he saved himself by saying, "You'll have to squat in the brush. I'm not going back to the latrine. You know that's where Scalzi got his."

When she stopped walking, rather than closing the distance between them, he turned, nearly tripping on a half-buried tree root.

He let her have a little privacy behind a thorny bush near the helicopter. She found she really did need to pee. She had nothing to wipe with, so had to use her sleeve. She hoped she would have the chance to trade the sweatshirt for something cleaner when they got to the helicopter.

The bush was only about waist-high, so she had to squat as she readjusted the placement of the pistol. As she stood, she held her breath, hoping the pistol wouldn't drop out of her waistband. It held – at least for now.

When they got to helicopter, they found the big ramp at the rear had been closed, so she had to enter at the front, up a little ladder and through a door to the cockpit. Taped to the front control panel was a snapshot of bald-headed Scalzi holding a redheaded baby girl. Except for the eyebrow thing, he looked like Daddy Warbucks hold a tiny Orphan Annie.

She felt sorrow for him and the little redhead girl.

The soilder led her back to the main cargo hold, which was big enough to hold a pickup truck – or two. A long skinny wooden crate stretched along most of the length of the cargo bay. Cots had been set up beside it. He pointed to one.

"Yours," he said.

She sat on it, grateful. The pistol had slipped down and poked into her left butt cheek. She crossed her legs and leaned on one arm to take the pressure off that cheek. This must have seemed a provocative position to the private, because he started tic-winking and leering again.

"Get the fuck out, you cretin!" she said, affecting what she hoped was a Bride-of-Frankenstein glare. It must have worked. He jumped up and left before she had to threaten to call the major.

She could hear the cockpit door slamming and wondered if it was locked or if a guard was posted outside. She found a hiding place for the pistol under one of the bunks; she hoped it wasn't too obvious. She also found a small, portable, chemical toilet, campsite-sized, near the back. It smelled but not nearly as bad as the private. He had probably known about it, but made her squat in the brush anyway.

She didn't remember falling asleep or even lying down, but she woke from a dream of finding John Wright on the porch of a huge blue Victorian house in a sea of tall grass. Only something was wrong with him – he was too large and shiny. He recognized her, but instead of smiling and greeting her, escaped inside the house through enormous doors. He didn't even wave. She followed, but inside was a maze of rooms within rooms, dead-end halls and bricked-up windows. One door led to an enormous hall with curved wooden beams that twisted and turned grotesquely and reminded her of the H.R. Gegersets in the first Aliens movie.

I'm in the belly of the Beast, but it's a mahogany beast.

Anti-climatically, a small dollhouse-size replica of the house sat on a low stage in the center of the hall. A miniature John Wright sat on that tiny porch and, just like the life-size John did before, he rushed inside the tiny house as she entered the hall. She peered in one window but saw no sign of him. Unlike Alice, she found no bottle marked "Drink Me," so she couldn't follow.

She woke in a cold sweat, trying to examine the details of the fading dream, but recollections raced away down some rabbit hole of her unconsciousness. She tried to at least recall the feelings the dream had elicited. The technique had worked before, allowing her to face many suppressed real-life memories – abuse by her father, abandonment by her mother, the impossibility of forming meaningful, lasting relationships – but this dream was different. In seconds, the only emotion she could access was a sense of loss – that and the knowledge that the dream had been about John Wright.

She fell asleep again, but fitfully. She was haunted with the sense of being on the threshold of a dream but not able to cross over.

12.

While Illusions Pass as Clouds

Bryan.

The door, twenty feet above the floor of the cell, was wide enough for the angel to pass through, but not wide enough for it to carry Bryan in its arms as it did.

So it flipped open the door with a shove of an outstretched arm while Bryan dangled below, holding on to those scaly bird feet with both hands.

Escaping prison on the heels of an angel? This has got to be some sort of religious metaphor, but I know not what.

Still unsure of the angel's gender, Bryan sneaked a peek up the angel's robes to look for a hint of genitalia. But the creature, as modest as a churchwoman, held its legs together as it flew, and Bryan, in his precarious position, only had a moment to peek. As the angel cleared the door, it did an odd sideways kick that made Bryan lose his grip. Such was the speed of the angel's brief flight, however, that Bryan's inertia carried him the rest of the way upward through the door. Bryan felt a moment of weightlessness, his feet suspended above the twenty-foot drop to the stone floor below, the angel caught him with one arm and slammed the trap door with the toe of a blue foot. It was all done in a blur of speed that seemed choreographed.

Only after they were through the door did Bryan wonder how he had been transported into the cell. He was happy to be out of confinement, though, and decided to let the matter rest.

"Where are we?" Bryan said, breathless, his voice no longer slurred from the mead. His heart was racing. The adrenaline rush from the flight had sobered him.

"We're in an anteroom of the Dreaming God's house," the angel said in a deep but androgynous voice. It was sexless again but still not much taller than it had been when about to metamorphose into a woman.

To Bryan, this "anteroom" looked like a storage warehouse. Plank shelving held various sized of boxes made of various shades of wood, all rough-hewn, all of various colors from terra cotta to light tan. They all looked like shipping crates. Were the crates packed with relics the archangels brought back from lost horizons and far-removed astral planes, or merely day-to-day goods like canned beans?

He guessed the latter. The room was at once alien and mundane. The steam pipes running along one wall looked like steam pipes anywhere, clad in white, toxic-looking, flaking insulation. Instead of connecting to a cast-iron radiator, however, the pipes joined to a stainless steel box that had a bank of colored lights and chrome grill. The box emitted faint clicking sounds: a cross between a refrigerator and a computer? *A steampunk world with angels, giant silver saucers, horses, and steam-powered Babbage machines?* Bryan had been a fan of science fiction in his teens, but this was ridiculous. But the idea of his being here at all, on his way to see a demiurge who dreamed universes into existence, was in itself even more absurd.

Light from the red sun beamed down through a skylight and illuminated, but didn't tint, the angel. Bryan held out his hand into the light, and it appeared red. Evidently the nature of light depended upon whom or what it fell on.

"Now?" he asked.

"Now we visit the Dreaming God, and you'll see why we wonder if we should kill you or worship you," the angel said, and gave him a good ol' boy grin as if he were talking about a choice of barbecue sauce.

This was the first mention of his being killed, though Bryan had always considered it a possibility given the unpredictable nature of the archangels.

"Is there a third choice?" Bryan asked.

The angel shrugged. Then without another word, it turned and gestured for Bryan to follow. They left the anteroom – if that's what it was – through a human-size door. The angel, now huge again, had to bend over, pull in its wings, and scrunch its shoulders to pass through the doorway. They emerged into a vaulted hallway paneled in varnished wood. The wooden beams looked like ribs, and he felt like he was in the gut of a leviathan.

The hallway ended in a blank wall, and Bryan thought they had come to a dead end, but the angel ran its hand along the paneling and pressed a hidden release. A door slid back into the wall with a whisper and a puff of steam.

Through this door, they entered into a large ballroom with a raised stage. The stage was empty except for a six-foot-tall blue dollhouse centered on a little stage. A tiny figure on the porch scurried into the house. Had it been a wind-up doll? It's movements seemed to fluid to be mechanical. Before Bryan could get a second look, the angel imposed its body between Bryan and the house.

"Ignore as many of the details of this house as you can," it said. "As we near the Dreaming God, reality becomes convoluted, illusionary, too complex and misleading for the human mind." It stroked its chin thoughtfully. "And perhaps for the angel mind as well. There are dead ends galore here, and the architectural features have been known to shift when the back is turned. Both humans and angels have become lost for days in this house. Some humans died of dehydration before they were found, which is curious, as there are water toilets everywhere. But still, wandering off by yourself wouldn't be wise."

"So how do you keep from getting lost?" Bryan asked.

"I sense the way," the angel said.

"Sense?"

"The closest thing I can compare it is the human sense of smell, which we don't have, by the way. I don't exactly know the way or have the words to describe how I sense it, but something has always led me from whatever part of the house I find myself to the chambers of the Dreaming God. Now come. Enough talk or I'll think too much about how I do it and we will both get lost."

As they left the ballroom, Bryan felt he was being watched from the dollhouse. He wanted a closer look, but he dared not ask the angel.

From the ballroom, they passed through another hallway lined with many doors like a hotel. But instead of numbers, these doors were labeled with symbols, hybrids of occidental ideograms and runes. Partway down the hall, the flooring changed from polished hardwood to rough-hewn planks that groaned under their steps.

They came to another doorway, this one arched. The angel paused and turned, one hand on the door knob. It laid its other hand on Bryan's shoulder, the oversized thumb pressing at the base of his throat, the chilling alabaster fingers wrapped the back of his neck.

"You are to be quiet in the Dreaming God's chamber. Perfectly quiet," it said. "Understand? I will stop you from even inadvertently accidently waking the Dreaming God. Do you catch my meaning?"

Bryan nodded the best he could under of the angel's grip. The angel's intent was clear: One sound, and it would wring his neck like a chicken's.

The angel released its grip and carefully, silently, turned the knob. It was about to open the door, when it looked down at Bryan's boot-clad feet. Bryan understood, and he squatted and removed them, setting them beside the door.

Satisfied, the angel gently opened the door, moving in slow motion, an inch at a time, which gave Bryan time to reflect. Keeping his mouth shut wouldn't be a problem. But what if his stomach growled? He couldn't remember when he'd last eaten. And for that matter, when was the last time he'd had a piss? Did humans need to attend to such bodily functions in this realm? He considered asking to be left outside, but curiosity as to what or whom the angels had hidden in this monstrosity of a house got the better of him. The angel glided inside, its china-blue feet soundless on an ornate woven rug. Bryan tip-toed behind.

The room was domed and dimly lit, with a little light coming in from small triangular windows in the upper reaches of the cupola. Peeking around the angel, Bryan could see only the foot of a large banister bed. A rumpled blue blanket dangled over the end. His view of the rest of the bed was blocked by hushed, reverent angels of various sizes who stood with their arms at their sides, their wings relaxed.

For minutes no one moved. Then one shifted its feet. Another put its hands behind its back, against its diaphanous wings. Only its thumbs were blue. It twiddled them. Another took a deep, tired breath and let it out silently. They were all dawdling, waiting for something.

His guiding angel stepped quietly forward and touched a particularly large angel on the shoulder. Without turning its head, the huge figure stepped to the side, giving Bryan his first glimpse of the figure asleep on the large bed and a woman sitting beside it.

After a moment of incomprehension, Bryan recognized the sleeping figure and the small, redhead woman sitting on a stool beside the bed, reading from a large red book. Only the fear of his neck being snapped kept him from gasping out loud.

Major Minor.

Major Minor awoke feeling like he'd just been on the granddaddy of all benders. For a moment he forgot he had bunked down last night in a curtained-off section of the tent. Rank still had its privileges, and while the rest of the men slept in the common, open space of the tent, he'd had this little corner cordoned off with blankets for privacy.

The 9-mm Beretta was an arm's-reach away, and as the thought of facing another day dribbled into his mind – and as he had the fifth or sixth time in the last day – he thought how easy it would be to pick it up, stick the barrel in his mouth, and pull the trigger. The safety was off. He could see it. Redemption and atonement lay a foot away. As he reached for the gun, he thought of something the Lady of the Lake had said. Her beautiful face had been framed in an oval aura. *You have to be careful with suicide around here. It doesn't always take in these parts.*

At the time, her warning hadn't registered. He had been hypnotized by her perfection, stunned by her mysterious nature.

He swung his feet off the cot, sat up, picked up the pistol and thumbed on the safety. He'd always said life was about choices. Today he would choose to live, perhaps miserably, perhaps without meaning or purpose, but he would live, at least for another day. But why? He wasn't sure why he bothered, except for those brief moments of wonderment wrought by the Lady of the Lake. And if he was to be honest with himself, the over-powering lust he felt for her was also a factor, maybe even the strongest influence.

Which was incredibly stupid. He'd never been good enough for a normal woman, neither an accomplished enough lover nor spiritual enough nor wealthy enough nor even there enough. What hope did he have with a winged goddess? In this life, he had never gotten what he wanted, much less what he needed—or loved.

The pistol was heavy in his hand. He thumbed the safety on and off, on and off.

He was distracted by the scrapping of metal plates on the mess table from the other side of the blanket. Oddly, the sound made him feel nostalgic for what he now thought as the 'good old days.' Disposable plates and utensils were a thing of the past because many factories had been indefinitely out of production since the Fall. Nostaligic for paper plates and plastic forks? How pitiful.

The smell of coffee drifted in from the common area, as did the voices of the men. He'd heard coffee was being brought in from South America on old merchant marine ships – a priority of the government to counter the increased use of cheap Mexican meth. The world may have technologically slipped back into the early 1900s, but the drug traffickers' distribution network was evidently still in place. Morbidly amused by this thought, he set the pistol back on the plastic bucket that served as his bedside table, grabbed his trousers off the floor of the tent, and stepped into them. The cuffs were dark with mud – and perhaps Scalzi's blood, too – but that couldn't be helped. There was no way to do laundry here, not yet. What they needed was to commandeer a farmhouse with laundry facilities. And as for commandeering, what had happened to Smith and the young man, Bryan what's-his-name?

As if in answer this unspoken question, a familiar voice, muffled by the hung blankets, said, "Sir?"

"Come in, Smith," Minor said as he cinched his holster belt.

The sergeant pushed through an opening between the blankets. His holstered sidearm snagged on loose thread, and he cursed. After untangling himself, he gave the Minor a sloppy salute. The major only nodded as he finished dressing. Smith's forehead sported a dirty gauze bandage with a blood spot in the center.

"Report."

Minor knew it wasn't going to be good from the look on his face.

"What did you find in town?"

The sergeant cleared his throat, a throaty phlegmatic ahem, and said, "We didn't make it to town, sir." And he launched into a detailed moment-to-moment account, starting with leaving the bivouac, continuing to retrieving a dilapidated pickup at a farmhouse and ending right the moment the truck slid into a ditch. He did everything but give the reading on the truck's odometer or the texture of the seat upholstery. He even included conjecture on the truck's make, model, and year, which led Minor to suspect the sergeant, though by nature a detail man, might be one of those using meth instead of coffee these days. But the bottom line of Smith's overly-detailed account gradually sank in: No resources could be commandeered from the town of Creedance, at least not soon. They were stuck here until they could scrounge up enough gas to get the Jeep back to Fort Leonard Wood for supplies. Either that, or they could all hike back the hundred miles or so to the base.

Minor buckled his belt and sat on his unmade bunk to put on his boots. His personal discipline was slipping as well. He usually made his bunk upon awakening, priding himself on the sharp corners. Now it looked like a teenager's bed.

Minor's mind wandered as Smith went into further detail. A vision of Minor's ex-wife, her face, her figure, the conversations they'd had – or tried to have – came to mind, and it was all wrong. She hadn't been his physical type, except for the fair skin and big rack. She had been heavy about the waist and had thick ankles. Trying to hold an intelligent conversation with her had been like speaking to the Sphinx. She just hadn't been an abstract thinker. Yet he had loved her. He hated that word, *love*, for all its illogicalness, but that was the only way to describe it. And he hated himself now for letting his thoughts wander while he should be paying attention to Smith's report.

Another throat clearing by Smith jolted him out of his unpleasant reverie.

"Sergeant."

Smith kept talking, on a roll or perhaps unable to stop himself.

Minor stood up. "SERGEANT!"

Smith stopped talking, but with difficulty. "Sir?"

"You never told me what happened to the civilian."

The sergeant cleared his throat again, and Minor suddenly wanted to strangle him.

"The weirdest thing . . . "

Minor waited, but Smith stuttered something incomprehensible. The major felt the old black-dog rage rising in him.

"You'll think I'm crazy," Smith managed to say.

"I already think you're deranged or on drugs, so out with it, man!"

"He just disappeared, sir."

"Disappeared? You mean ran off into the woods or something."

"No, sir. I was looking right at him, and he just . . . blinked out." Smith rubbed the bandage on his head, and when he took his hand away the blood spot had turned into large blossom. Minor stared at it.

"I know what you're thinking, sir."

"What am I thinking, Sergeant? Tell me, please." The 'please' was supposed be sarcastic in tone, instead it came out as a snarl. This was going to be an especially bad day, and someone was going to pay. Not the sergeant though, because with Scalzi gone, Smith was the only noncom he had. He wasn't sure he could control the squad without him.

"You're thinking I got knocked out in the crash, that I hallucinated," Smith said. "But we didn't crash that hard, and I caught myself with my hands against the dash."

"And the bump on your head?"

"That happened afterwards, as I was hiking back here. I got lost, and something – I think it was one of those damned angels or whatever they are – beaned me from above with a giant pinecone."

Minor tried not to laugh, not at Smith's sad-sack, fuck-up face, but because he believed the sergeant. In this fucked up world, who knew? Maybe Bryan Douglas had simply evaporated.

13.

To Haunt the Dreaming God

Bryan.

Bryan awoke sprawled on the floor. When he managed to sit up, he found he was on the other side of the heavy oak door that opened into the Dreaming God's bedroom.

He didn't recall leaving the bedroom, but he remembered seeing the Dreaming God's face.

The Dreaming God was even larger than the towering archangels – and had been so real, so extra-mundane, that everything, including the archangels and him, had seemed like tiny plastic figures.

There, beside the Dreaming God, had been Suzanne – or her facsimile – sitting on a small stool, reading from a large red book. Both Suzanne and the book appeared to be the same that he had seen in his Earthly farmhouse only a few days ago. (What seemed to him only a few days ago, he reminded himself.)

She was dressed as he had seen her then, in a gauzy dress cinched with a thin red ribbon. But in the farmhouse she had been nearly transparent; here beside the Dreaming God she had been opaque, solid – not as super-real as the Dreaming God, but not a phantom, either.

He could hear her voice as she read aloud, a faintly melodious mix of country twang and sophistication: "'For,' said Tom Brangwen, and the company was listening to the conundrum, 'an Angel can't be less than a human being. And if it was only the soul of a man minus the man, then it would again be less than a human being.'"[1]

She was at once his lover from Earth, still in her early twenties – perky

---

1   Suzanne was reading from *The Rainbow* by D.H. Lawrence

breasts and slim waist, all feminine white freckled skin, hair full and flame red – and Suzanne the barmaid, with thinning hair, and tired face.

She was not his old undead lover and yet, she was.

She was everything in between all at once. Ghosts of Suzanne overlay other ghosts of Suzanne. The ghost images weren't identical; they documented the progression of her life, from youth to the undead blue-jean baby-queen lover he had on Earth to the middle-aged, stressed, and graying woman he had seen in the bar. And if he looked, he saw a series of even younger Suzannes and older Suzannes stretching in all directions of time, but that was too much to take in. Everything was too much to take in.

The Suzannes, all the un-countable Suzannes, looked up from the book and straight at him. He had seen no love in their faces, but maybe the glimmer of recognition in some.

This was not the way the story was supposed to play out. Love was supposed to win out over fate. Love was supposed to win again and again.

Logic and experience told him that heartbreak, like a physical wound, eventually either heals or kills, and the only rational course was to seek a cure or ignore the pain. But his anger was overwhelming, a hot, burning diamond grating against some undefined part of him And part of that anger – more than a small fraction – was completely selfish. He was angry at her for growing older; it was a childish anger on his part. No more young breasts, firm thighs, and tight vagina. Her youth and sensuality were gone, leaving a woman old enough to be his mother. He felt he had been cuckolded by destiny, an unfair event to which Suzanne, though unwillingly, had been an accomplice. Even worse: She no longer appeared to give a damn.

Will that be my favorite lies of all that you told me, that you loved me?

The anger surged. The hell with you, Suzanne, for un-dying on Earth or whatever it was you did to leave.

The anger was good; It washed away the pain until he felt nothing, neither heartbreak nor love, and a clear, unadulterated memory of the Dreaming God to whom Suzanne had been reading came back. His mind reeled, and he grasped for something to hold onto, anything, heartache, fear, rage, that would block his mental image of the Dreaming God. To look at it might destroy him, but he had to look, and when he did, he became everything.

Awakening of an Alien God

Creation spun, spun, spun. Everything was senseless, meaningless, chaos, and yet everything fit together in a grand plan; there was order, and it was good and it was bad too, for the order was in interruption of the grand chaos. He was free of everything, even romantic love. He was everything, including love and hate. Eternity contracted to the space inside a single thought. At once, the room encompassed an incomprehensibly huge space – and a space as small as a point without width, height, or depth – and he was split in two.

The next thing he knew was looking up in the angel's face, but he felt as if he were staring through a kaleidoscope. He tried to speak but had no words, just pictures. He felt a million, million years old. The angel who had brought him here ran a huge hand across Bryan's forehead, wiping away a sheen of sweat. The angel's skin was silky smooth but cold and the hand huge. He felt like a child being comforted by an adult.

"Don't try to speak," the angel said, and the kaleidoscopic distortion subsided, but his face remained ringed by a dirty blue aura.

Was the huge angel kneeling beside him the same one who had led him through this monstrous mansion? Now he wasn't sure.

"What is it?" the angel asked, sounding even more concerned.

"Nothing," he said. "Nothing at all. Leave me alone. I'm okay."

"You can speak again. That's a good sign."

And it was, Bryan realized. His brain was thinking actively, and words that were connected to those questions.

"The universe of the Dreaming God is like an onion," the angel said, still stroking Bryan's forehead. "This world, as well the one you call Earth, are different layers of that onion."

Though his life might hang in the balance, his mind refused to take this metaphor seriously; he thought: *So they have onions in this angel realm too? For sure, they have lame homilies. But onions? Why not pomegranates?*

The angel continued speaking very slowly and deliberately. "There are uncountable outer layers. Uncountable inner layers. However, it is our perception that there is only one center, and the layers emanate outward from that center. At that center is perfect unity. Or *once* there was a perfect unity, for the Dreaming God wanted to look upon its own image, and to do so him had to create a secondary image of itself, a reflection. But because it was the One, everything, he had to make a space of nothing within himself for the reflection. When his reflection looked upon himself, a multitude of secondary images were made. Everything we think of as real, including all the planes of existence and all life, including human planes and angel plane, are echoes of that action."

The angel paused, looking for understanding in his eyes. Bryan's mind still spun. The angel's thumb curled around his neck and rested on his Adam's apple.

Was the angel soothing him or preparing to snap his neck? If he died here, would he also die on Earth? Was there a version of himself back on Earth? If so, was he dreaming himself as Bryan or was that avatar dreaming him?

The thought of another version of himself, still plodding along in mundane old Creedance, while this version of himself lived or died, seemed poignant. He wanted to close his eyes and go to sleep and wake up as another one of his avatars, one who led a simpler, safer life.

"And that's why we don't know what to do with you," the angel said as it brushed Bryan's sweat-soaked hair back from his forehead. "For you are a perfect reflection in miniature of that dreamer, as you now know."

"I don't know what I saw," Bryan said.

"Acknowledging ignorance is the first step of wisdom," the angel said in that hateful, phony guru tone they sometimes used. "But you need a symbol, a mental shorthand to deal with what you saw. Symbols are the union of the rational and the irrational. The problem is you don't have the right symbols to deal with this level of reality."

"Screw that bullshit!" Bryan snapped, but he knew that the angel was right. His mind just wasn't prepared to deal with such conundrums. Not yet. He really did need some kind of metaphysical shorthand.

The angel smiled, encouraging Bryan to continue. "I thought I saw . . ."

What exactly had he seen? The memory was there, but his mind jerked away from it. He couldn't study it any longer, no more than he could hold his hand in a flame. To do so was madness, torture. He understood now what the phrase "the mind reeled" meant.

"You need something to bring you back to your body. I don't know what," the angel said. "Maybe the reader will know." It stood. "I'll be back. She gets a break soon. I'll ask her then."

The angel walked away. Bryan heard the enormous bedroom door open, then quietly close. He tried not to think about what he had seen on the other side of the door. But his mind was irresistibly drawn to the memory.

He closed his eyes and tried not to think anymore. A second later, something warm and slimy washed across his cheek. He opened his eyes to find the border collie staring back at him.

The dog licked him again, in a sort of reserved fashion for a dog. The dog's blue eyes were sympathetic.

He ran his hand through Dog's fur. He still needed a proper name.

"If I were the hero in this story, I'd name you after Odysseus' faithful, flea-ridden mutt, what was its name? Argos?"

The dog yelped encouragingly.

"Or as this may be some dream of an afterlife, Anubis?"

The dog yipped again.

"So I can call you anything, as long as I call you to dinner, right? So I guess we're back to Dog."

Dog sat down beside Bryan, waiting. Bryan wondered how Dog navigated the maze of this house. He doubted that an angel had let Dog in.

His mind returned to Suzanne and the scene with the angel, and the room began to reel again.

"Woof!"

"Yeah, I'm back. I'm back." He concentrated on the dog. "Dog, I don't suppose since you got in, you know a way out of here?"

Dog got up and trotted down the hallway. Bryan was about to follow when the bedroom door behind him opened. He turned and saw the older incarnation of Suzanne, and his heart did a little backbeat. She smiled nervously. He tried to return the smile but it felt wrong, tight. Her appearance was so radically different from how she had looked at the bar he was paralyzed. She was barefoot, her toenails painted black, and was dressed in that all-white, ankle-length gauzy gown with a cherry-red sash.

As she closed the space between them, he saw she wasn't the older Suzanne after all. Her face was years younger than the Suzanne he had met in the tavern. She had been in her early twenties when they were lovers on Earth, and she didn't look much different now – no bags under her eyes, no pooching stomach. And no scar that he could see. Was she wearing makeup?

"You're looking at me as if I was a bug under a magnifying glass," she said.

"Are you the same woman who fainted in the tavern?"

"Tavern?"

Something was tugging at his left sleeve. He looked down to find the dog had its teeth on his shirt cuff. Its eyes were pleading: *Forget her. Let's go.*

"You didn't recognize me before, and you were . . ." He started to say *older,* but she interrupted.

"Before? What?"

Now that she was closer, he realized she wasn't wearing makeup at all. She appeared to be in her mid-twenties, only a few years older than when he had known her on Earth.

"Before, in the saloon?"

She shook her head. "I don't know what you mean."

When he didn't answer, she went on, "You speak one of the angel tongues." She had stopped about a yard from him and made no attempt to get closer. "Amazing! You're so much smaller, and not blue, but otherwise a perfect reflection of the Dreaming God."

"Suzanne . . ." He knew what she spoke of, but he had to keep the the memory of what he'd seen at arm's length or he would pass out. There was a trick to it, like not looking at the needle when a nurse gave you a shot. He knew in the back of his mind what had happened, but if he dwelled on it he would be lost.

"And you speak my name," she said, brushing a stray wisp of hair from her face. She wore a ring, made with gold and a big blue stone that might be lapus lazuli. It looked like the ring the succubus in the dungeon had worn. He wondered it if were some kind of wedding ring.

She noticed his looking at the ring and began turning it on her finger, with her other hand. She kept adjusting the ring a bit too long for it to be anything other than a semaphore: *I'm taken; I'm off-limits.*

He was about to point out that being married hadn't mattered that much to her back on Earth, but that wasn't exactly true. He recalled to the vision of the Dreaming God. Maybe if he directed his mind's eye away from the face . . . and then he was reeling on the edge of a precipice, staring in to a bottomless endless spiraling darkness. At the center of the dark mass was a point of light. As he stared into it, his vision zoomed, focused, and found a face, a huge, blue face with liquid, sleepy eyes. His recognition of the face was more visceral than intellectual, a magnetic force, and he pitched forward into the abyss.

"Hey! Come back here! Don't fog out on me," the Suzanne doppelganger said. She had a firm grip on his forearm, fingers digging painfully into the muscles.

"I'm not sure who – what – who I am," he managed to say. He had a long time lag between thinking and speaking. His mind was remote, as if he were pulling his own strings from far, far away.

"You're confusing me, whoever you are," she said, shaking his arm, then letting it drop to his side. "Don't misinterpret my touching you, sir. I was just trying to keep you from falling." Her left hand came up again to brush an invisible strand of hair from her face, flashing the wedding ring again.

I get it. I get it. You're married – and not just in name. But he was grateful for the physical contact. Her touch had pulled him back from falling into a place where his mind could not go and remain conscious.

The dog again tugged on his sleeve. Suzanne's entrance had made him forget Dog was by his side. The dog was probably wiser than he was. He should forget this Suzanne, just walk away. But she was a clue as to why he was here, a magnet that drew him to this plane and no other. Or maybe Suzanne-doppelgangers existed on multiple planes, each living more or less unique lives.

If he could pick one plane where she was free, could he live a normal life there with her?

"The angels sent me to talk to you," the Suzanne said. "They didn't say about what. They must see the resemblance to the Dreaming God, as I do, but I gather they can't decide exactly what you are."

"I get that alot, but I can assure you I'm no god," Bryan said before thinking. *Maybe he should claim to be a local god, considering the alternative.*

"I know that now," Suzanne said. "Gods don't get dizzy. At least I don't think they do."

"Are you going to report back to them anything, everything, I tell you?"

"Do you really think I have a choice?" she asked.

He wanted to remind her of a conversation they once had, that in an existential sense, there was always a choice, but he suspected this Suzanne would neither remember nor understand.

"Maybe you don't have a choice," he said. "But I'll tell you anyway if you go with me to wherever Dog wants to take us."

"Dawg? Is that what the animal is called?"

14.

In the dark night of the soul

Marguerite.

Marguerite flew beneath the vanilla clouds, only inches above the treetops. The newly resurrected May flew with her. She flitted here and there, skimming down and brushing leaves with her fingertips, veering suddenly right or left without apparent motive, a dustmote on the wind. Marguerite flew straight and level. She was wary of May's childlike hyperactivity, ready to intervene, as she would with a child in busy street.

This is the kind of behavior that had led to your dismemberment by helicopter blades, young lady.

But a lot of good such admonishments would do for May.

May looked up at Marguerite, smiled, and pointed to an open field below. A young Holstein heifer grazed on the newly greened-up grass. May banked and drew in her wings so they draped along her legs, then swooped down to land on the back of the cow.

SMACK!

The sound of the impact echoed in the still air, and the cow's surprised cry was cut off in mid-moo. Marguerite landed a few feet away. May stood over the cold-cocked cow, grinning triumphantly. The cow's knobby spine was bent at an oblique angle. The animal wasn't dead yet, but its back was broken and its lifespan was now measured in minutes. The poor thing turned its head to look mournfully at Marguerite. Its big black-irised eye was wet and pleading. A single vein in the white of the eyeball had hemorrhaged from the impact. It cried out again, a low, stretched-out mournful moo of pain, and tried to stand, but its hindquarters wouldn't obey, and it managed only to partially prop itself on its front legs.

May wasn't in great shape either. Angels' muscles were as tough as carbon composite, and their bones were as hard as steel, but when they impacted large, solid objects at high speed – whether a spinning helicopter blade or a thousand-pound dairy cow – even their otherworldly bodies bent, broke, or tore. May was luckier with the cow than she had been with the helicopter. Her newly reattached limbs hadn't come undone, but one arm jutted from her shoulder at an odd angle.

Unconscious of her injury, May leered and giggled at the dying cow. Then she tried to reach down for the head and seemed confused when one of her hands wouldn't obey her will. A human being would be howling in pain from such a severely dislocated shoulder, but May was only upset that her arm didn't work as she wanted. Without thinking, Marguerite placed one hand on May's shoulder and the other on her forearm. Red Cross training from her former life came to mind. She bent May's elbow upward at a ninety-degree angle and placed her pale-white forearm across her bare abdomen. Then she slowly but forcefully turned he forearm outward. A satisfying POP sounded as the shoulder went back into place.

Why had it made a ball-and-socket 'pop' when there weren't bones inside but only angel putty?

As with many angel mysteries, there was no logical answer to this question. She looked in May's eyes for gratitude and found none. Did she see recognition? Yes, she saw it, but it was faint and distracted.

Marguerite let go, and May rotated her arm, gave her a lop-sided shrug, then put a bare foot on the cow's back, pressing it down in the soft mat of ryegrass. Then she grabbed the cow's head with both hands and ripped it off without as much as a grunt. The cow's googly-eye swiveled back and forth mechanically, and blood spewed from the neck stump onto May's bare feet. May held up the cow's head over her own and chewed on the neck stump with noisy relish. Bits of shredded flesh rained down on her face and breasts, and blood ran in rivulets over her stomach.

Marguerite had stepped back to avoid the blood spray. She became more and more repelled as she watched.

A series of black-and-white visions played across her mind like a slide show. CLICK: Burying her own hands in the gapping wound of a large animal.

CLICK: Bringing up the bloody coiled mash – chocolate-colored in the black-and-white memory – to mouth.

CLICK: Chewing on a limb stripped of fur, just tendons and exposed bone, as if it where a huge ear of corn on the cob.

CLICK: Nibbling down the length of the limb to find a human hand at one end, a wrinkled lump of flesh with a large diamond wedding ring on one finger.

CLICK: Stripping off the ring to work at the tender, aged flesh.

No! That the ring had to be a false memory! It had to be some animal part she remembered gnawing on. But weren't the body proportions all wrong for any four-legged animal? What had she been feeding on?

She didn't dare think about it. Someone screamed; it was herself. Then she was airborne, leaving the gruesome spectacle of May's feeding far below. But she had no way to escape her own interior horror movie as she flew toward the clouds. She wished for oblivion. Would alcohol work on an angel metabolism? Had May dreamt after being dismembered by the helicopter blades? Was her mind a blank until it was reassembled, or had her sleep been tortured, beset by clownish toads, guilt from shadow memories, the whispers of lost redemption? Later she would ask May. Now she just wanted to get away from the disgusting thing her friend had become – and forget the monster she herself had been transformed into.

Something tickled her face as she flew. When she brushed at her cheek her hand came away wet. She thought it was rain at first or some high altitude effect, but slowly she realized that she was crying, an uncommon thing for an angel to do. She had become lost between the worlds of angel and human. Now she was entirely alone. She flew lower, heading toward some uncharted rendezvous bound to a part of herself she had wanted to banish.

Major Minor.

You should really just get this over with, Major Minor told himself. He had toyed with the pistol all morning, once putting it into his mouth. The taste had been surprisingly bland, just a hint of metal and some salty grit from the holster. He had put a pistol in his mouth before, and it had stirred a vaguely homophobic experience, yet given him a sense of primal power over his own fate. The pistol now sat on the trestle table, the barrel pointing at him, taunting him. *Do it, you wuss, you fucking nobody.*

Was this the time? The unfocused rage he felt had no place to go but inward. In the Middle East, he had fought a clearly defined enemy.

Here he had no such enemy, and the venom turned back on himself, an intense and torturous rotting away from the inside-out. This suffering had been coming to a head for some time, so why had he not followed through? He wasn't afraid of death, but a feeling of injustice, of someone, some outside agency, had pushed him into this corner. He felt mutilated, handicapped. Unclean.

He slammed a fist on the edge of the trestle table, wanting pain, but the rotten wood disintegrated in dust and splinters. He had been a fool to ever think that his personal fate was a product of his own will.

He picked up the pistol again, wishing it were a revolver instead of an automatic. Russian roulette would relieve him of the responsibility of suicide.

His encounter with the Lady of the Lake had offered only a temporary remedy to this state of apostasy. Even before she flew away, he had realized that she transcended the physics of the natural world. *Damn it all to hell that he had ever encountered the angel!* He had been so close to pulling the trigger that day on Lost Lake beach. The inevitable failure of the mission after the helicopter crash had been a awake-up call. His military career had once been all that he had to live for, and he didn't even have that any more.

True, the loss of the helicopter had not been his fault – but even if it had been, that probably would not have gotten him cashiered. But the crash had made him realize what a tenuous hold he had on life. The thought that he had been even momentarily panic-stricken at the idea of losing the privilege of command over drunks, potheads, and meth-addicts made him realize what a total washout he was of an officer and a human being.

Shit! Who the fuck was he trying to fool? He didn't know what he felt. He just wanted it all to end. He was sick of his lack of control. But he could at least have control over whether he lived or died, couldn't he?

He picked up the pistol and flipped off the safety. He'd already checked to make sure a round was chambered. But he didn't put the gun to his mouth. Instead he nestled it under his chin, pushing the cold barrel againtst his sagging dewlap. His finger tightened on the trigger, tighter, tighter . . . and he tilted back his head for a last look at the sky. There was movement above, something large, and his resolve dissolved as he looked up, hoping for a glimpse of the Lady of the Lake, hoping for salvation from above.

Would her appearance, her slightest touch, save him now as it had before? Where was she? Had it been a trick of the eye?

The flier – two fliers – flew lower but were still only visible because they were silhouetted against those peculiar light-yellow clouds. They were certainly angels, but not the Lady of the Lake – maybe a pair of the other angels Laura had told him about. He lowered the gun, squinting. Most certainly, they were angels. He couldn't tell how far away they were or how big.

Without prelude, one of the fliers dove toward the ground at high speed. One disappeared behind treetops. The other stopped in mid-flight and poised there, without moving her wings, as if suspended on invisible wires. Then she followed the path of the other, though slower now.

He stood up without being conscious of doing so. He still held the pistol, but his arm now dangled at his side. He relaxed the pressure on the trigger. Funny, he wasn't so afraid of blowing out his brains as shooting himself in the foot. Then again, his foot didn't cause him anguish, but his mind did.

But at the sight of the angels, the feeling of anger and hopelessness lifted, at least temporarily. Should he go investigate? He weighed doing so against finishing the task he had started moments ago. *No, fuck it!*

He brought up the gun, this time lodging the barrel under his chin, careful to angle it backward so he would blow out his brains rather than only shatter his face. Should he close his eyes or keep them open? Close them, he decided.

He paused again. A squirrel, possibly the same one that had tried to bite off his finger, chattered from a tree. Then the world was still, peaceful. His terrible, unfocused rage went away. Ironically, the rage had taken the pain with it, but he feared if he lowered the gun the anger and the misery would return. Only in this moment, posed on the brink of death, did he get any relief.

He felt someone's presence behind him. Had that person been waiting for him to kill himself without intervening? He was instantly furious and sprang to his feet and turned, ready to shoot.

The Lady of the Lake stood there, beautiful, pale flawless skin, eyes deep pools, emanating a presence that made the rest of the world seem a pale imitation. But then he noticed the creature's face was different.

Though reminiscent of the Lady of the Lake's, the face was blockier. And the angel had no breasts. He scanned its body, feeling abashed. It was completely naked, and *it* was indeed an *IT*, for it had no genitalia, neither male nor female, between its legs. *What sort of sick, fucking joke was being played on him?*

He pointed the pistol at its smiling face, but before he could pull the trigger the gun was yanked from his hand, and the angel was holding it, looking at it with amused curiosity. Somehow, without moving from ten feet away, it had reached out and snatched the pistol, as if the space between them had folded in for a moment, then unfolded back. Minor looked at his hand. His index finger was scraped and bleeding, probably from the trigger guard jerking away so rapidly. He was lucky his finger was still attached to his hand.

Minor didn't know whether to run away or charge the angel. As fast as the angel moved, to attack it would suicidal. *But wasn't it sweet death that he wanted?*

"What...?" he started to ask, but the angel was standing right in front of him, again as if the space between them had immediately shrunk. Before he could move, the angel put a cold finger to Minor's lips to silence him.

"Wait," it whispered. "Abide."

He could hear the muted crunch of a twig and the swish of a branch. Someone was coming through the woods.

Laura.
She hadn't meant to break the helicopter.

She had awoken from a nap and decided to explore the craft to take her mind off of disturbing dreams.

From the cargo bay where she had been sitting, she had found the door to the cockpit open. The large acrylic windows up front had promised an expansive view, but were now fogged over. She had been leaning against the side door, wiping away the condensation with an old towel, and put her weight on a large horizontal bar, thinking it was a hand rest. She had not really noticed it was painted yellow with black stripes. It had popped out with a metallic CLUNK. Startled, she had stepped back, but hadn't let go of the bar, and then the whole frigging window, door and all, fell outward, pulling her with it.

Luckily, she and the door had landed in heavy brush. She got painfully to her feet and took stock. She hadn't broken a leg or an arm, but she was going to be black and blue the next day. Scarier, someone had driven a machete into a nearby stump so that the pointy end of the blade stuck up at an angle. Even if she had landed on the stump and missed the machete, she would have broken ribs. If she had landed on the machete, she would have been skewered. Something dribbled down her chin. When she wiped at it, her hand came away bloody. She knelt down to catch a reflection of herself in the window. A red rivulet trickled from one nostril, but her nose didn't look or feel broken to the touch.

Another bit of good news: She saw no sign of anyone guarding her now, though she could hear voices far off. A flicker of movement overhead caught her eye. Though the figures were only specks against the clouds, she was sure they were angels. What had made her look up? Her aunt Sophia had said that the angels emitted some sort of psychic field that she could sense from a great distance.

One of the angels suddenly dove downward. She fell so fast Laura expected to hear a 'whoosh' sound or the shriek of an artillery shell, but there was nothing. Again, she reminded herself angels weren't bound by the laws of physics. They could fly at supersonic speeds without making so much as a whisper.

Sadly, she was bound to those mundane natural laws, particularly the law of gravity, which she was painfully aware of as she climbed back into the helicopter. She'd had apparently done something ugly to her shoulder in the fall, and it hurt as she pulled herself back up. Scrambling through the cockpit into the cargo hold, she retrieved some old pages from a technical manual near the child-size portable toilet. Evidently, toilet paper was as scarce in the Army as it was in the civilian world. The paper was coarse but clean, and she wadded up a piece and stuck it up her nose to stop the dripping blood. She retrieved the pistol from its hiding place and made her way back to the cockpit, following the little drops of blood she'd left behind like bread crumbs.

She peered cautiously out the open cockpit, expecting to find the guard had returned, but the coast remained clear. She scanned the nearby woods – no one in sight there, either. Maybe the guard had never been on duty. Maybe he just locked her in and went back to camp to get high with his buddies. She climbed down, her shoulder still complaining. From her short medical career as a nursing aide, she diagnosed it as not dislocated, just jammed. She sprinted across the beach and into the neighboring woods, waiting for a shout – or a shot. But the only sound she heard was the crunch of her sneakers on twigs and leaves as she entered the woods.

The space between the blackjack oaks was mostly chocked with briar and stunted cedar. But she found a path, wider and more beaten down, little more than a rabbit run through the undergrowth. Maybe it had once been a cleared walking trail, but after the fall of the alien saucer and the breakdown of civilization, the park service employees had gone home on survival mode, and the brush and wild blackberry quickly taken over.

After about forty feet the path took a sharp right turn, and she emerged into a small clearing to find a tableau of an unmoving angel and a uniformed soldier. The angel had a finger to the man's lips. The soldier's face was disfigured with misery and rage. A blue-steel pistol hung from his limp hand. She stopped in mid-stride, hoping to back out of the clearing and back into the brush without being seen. But both figures turned toward her before she could escape. Recognition slowly dawned: Major Minor and the archangel Samiazaz.

The archangel was in its neuter form. Laura had only seen Samiazaz in his male manifestation before, but there was no mistaking the creature's face in any form. As she watched, Samiazaz became female, shrank to under six feet tall, and became a stunningly beautiful woman.

As if reading her mind, Samiazaz said, "Don't run away. Your destiny is here." And the creature stepped away from the major.

Major Minor raised the pistol and pointed it at her. The Major Minor she had met earlier had been an angry man, but controlled, disciplined, a tight fist of pent-up angst. The face of this major was crimson, fierce, with deep, dark circles under the eyes. He looked like a sunburned zombie. "You!" he said, and in that one word was years of betrayal, lies, frustration, and mistrust: *You!*

"Drop the gun!" he ordered

She had forgotten she carried the pistol, and brought up her hand to look at it in surprise.

And he fired his weapon, which was incredibly loud in the small clearing.

Laura was stunned for a moment, thinking the major must have missed her because she hadn't felt an impact. Then she felt a trickle down her leg. Had she peed in her pants? It felt more sticky than wet.

She had no doubt that she was about to be shot at a second time, and this time he wouldn't miss. She tried to drop the pistol, but her hand was leaden and wouldn't obey her. Then the panic departed, and she was calm.

If death is certain, why struggle?

She thought of Uncle Robert. Would she see him again? And John or even Bryan? Like a vision, a few unconnected, random memories skittered across her mind: a particularly beautiful spring morning years ago, a wild deer coming into her back yard, and silly enough, the smell of brand new tennis shoes.

The major steadied the pistol with both hands, but Samiazaz stepped forward, partially blocking his aim.

"You have a choice," Samiazaz said to her. "You can die here, a victim of this sick human, a scapegoat for his fury at himself, at his mother, at his ex-wife, at everything."

"Or?" Her voice sounded as if she were in a well.

"Or you can merge with me, live a thousand years, as you were meant to."

Her body was paralyzed and seemed to be vibrating, but her mind still functioned. "If I was always meant to merge with you, where's the free will?"

"I never said anything about free will – that's a human illusion – I said you have a choice to make," Samiazaz said and glimmered into maleness.

Laura laughed. "Bullshit! Double-talk!" she said, "I'd rather take my chances with death than become a crazed version of you, you lying spawn of a whore."

"So be it," Samiazaz said, turning to face her fully. His/her face was split, male on one side facing her, female on the other. The creature stepped back, clearing a path for the major to shoot.

"Doesn't the major have a choice, too?" Laura asked. "Don't you, Major?"

"Certainly," Samiazaz said, becoming fully female again. To the major, "One of you, either you or this young woman, can be with me forever, but not both of you."

Spittle trickled from the corner of the Major's mouth. Laura fought the impulse to close her eyes.

"So be it," the major said in a trembling voice. His hand shook, and when the shot rang out, she braced for the impact, but instead heard the bullet zinging through the brush behind her.

She thought to run, but Samiazaz's hand was on her shoulder, hold her firm. The pistol was a dead weight in her hands. She would have been better off with the machete.

"Take your time, Major, finish the job," Samiazaz said.

The major took heed and brought up his other hand to steady the gun.

Shit, this is it, this is really it, Laura thought. She let out her last breath. Samiazaz stepped aside again. The major aimed at her chest.

And then an angel with pale skin and red hair dropped out of the sky to land in front of Minor.

Marguerite!

The third shot fired, but the bullet slapped into Marguerite not Laura.

Marguerite, apparently unaffected by the impact of the bullet, took a step forward and backhanded the major to the ground.

"Why do you interfere?" Samiazaz demanded. "I should have my chance at mortality!"

"The man still lives, and he wants you, wants to be more than human," Marguerite said. "Why should this woman have to die?"

"Because that is the way," Samiazaz said, but the creature's voice betrayed its doubt.

"That may be the way where you are from, but here we – I – don't kill innocents," Marguerite said, her voice suddenly strong and terrible. Before Samiazaz could answer, Marguerite swooped up Laura in her arms. Then they were airborne, high above the pine trees. Below, Laura watched Samiazaz turn to face the major. The angel was rubbing its chin, an uncommonly human gesture, as if pondering what to do next.

Still holding her like a babe-in-arms, Marguerite zoomed up over the trees, then swooped down, flying low over Lost Lake, and Laura's vision blurred.

✳ ✳ ✳

15.

And Call the Return of the Dead

Laura.

"Stay with me a little longer," Marguerite told Laura as they moved over the waters of Lost Lake. They flew so low that the water was within reach.

Stay with her? Where was she going to go while hurtling over deep water?

Marguerite's arms, though slender, were as hard as steel. Her wings glistened in the sunlight.

Laura twisted to look at Marguerite's face only to be overcome with vertigo. She thought she was going to throw up, then the whirling dizziness passed, but her ears continued to ring and there was a dull ache in her chest – she must have hurt herself worse than she thought when she fell out of the helicopter.

She turned her head again, slowly this time, to study the face of her angel rescuer. The angelic face was lean and majestic, with smooth and flawless skin, no wrinkles or blemishes or pores. Underlying this countenance was the face of the Marguerite who used to babysit Laura, a Marguerite whose features then were already beginning to give way to the softness of middle age. Where had that shy, sweet, dowdy creature gone? Was there anything left of the Bible-belt lady who believed women should remain humble, quiet, and obedient to their husbands, no matter what? Where was the calico-clad Marguerite who would have been mortified to show even a hint of cleavage or leg above mid-thigh?

If not for the pain in her chest, Laura would have liked to skim her fingers across the still waters. She wanted to ask where they were going, but the flight had taken her breath away and she couldn't find her voice. She should just be grateful that she had escaped the madman, Major Minor.

What had turned him into a monster? Before, he had seemed just a miserable, angry man, a one-sided personality intent on keeping every-thing under control, deeply frustrated that the center would not hold. She had sensed he was crazy but didn't think he would start shooting in-nocent people. Had the psychosis been a result of Samiazaz's influence, or had the major anger blossomed like a flower of evil of its own accord

In seconds they were flying through the blackened gash stretching along the length of the saucer. A barrier, now visible as a soft neon glow, prevented lake water from gushing into the saucer, but slowed of her and Marguerite's passage. As before, when they passed through that zone of darkness, her stomach – and mind – turned inside out for a moment. Then they were inside the saucer, which wasn't an *inside* at all. Rather it was a Dadaistic world that the saucer was merely a portal to. Laura was still amazed and mystified by the very idea of it, though she had been here several times. She wondered if Marguerite was taking her back to the birthing place, the Army surplus, circus-size tent the archangels had set up as a refuge for the final stages of transformation of human hosts.

She became very tired and yearned to just lie down and sleep. Now that she thought about it, she wouldn't complain even if she was taken back to the stinking tent and put on a canvas cot.

"Stay awake," Marguerite said. "Not much farther now."

They were flying over the crystalline desert, an arid landscape popu-lated with things that were neither earth nor fire, mineral nor water, but alchemical hybrids of several elements.

They passed a couple of low hills and then descended into a wide, shallow caldera, a place Laura recognized. She'd been here before with Uncle Robert's ghost, or, more accurately, his astral body. She thought of it for some reason as the *Valley of Lost Souls*. Detritus from Lost Lake – beer cans, a rusted-up old washing machine, orphaned car tires – littered the land, but since her last visit the stream that had carried water from Lost Lake had slowed to a trickle. A lone figure stood near the bottom of the depression. Snowy beard, gray tweed coat, blue jeans, and old black and white Converse sneakers – Laura recognized him from a hundred feet away: Uncle Robert. Somehow, she had expected to find him there.

Marguerite pulled up and landed softly, just a few feet from the old man. She made no move to set down her passenger, which was good, because Laura still felt so weak. Instead, the angel squatted to sit cross-legged on the desert floor and cradled Laura in her lap.

"Hello, kid," Uncle Robert said.

"Hi," Laura managed to say. The word came out as a gurgling croak. *What was wrong with her?*

"Remember this place?" he said, as he squatted on the desert floor.

She nodded. This was where Uncle Robert had revealed to her that he was dead – rather that his mortal body on the Earthly plane had died. He had been drowned in Lost Lake by what they had dubbed *cherubs*, though the perverse spawn of angels bore little resemblance to those baby-faced creatures. Uncle Robert had been so real then – solid – as he was now, and only by showing her his own corpse, which had washed into the basin when Lost Lake was still flooding through the gash, had he been able to convince her of his Earthly body's death.

He took her hand. "Do you remember, kiddo, the training Sophia and I gave you on how to go into a light trance state and project your astral body?"

So tired. So very tired. All she wanted to do was sleep, but she managed a nod.

"Good," he said, squeezing her hand. His hand was firm and warm – for a phantom. She couldn't help thinking of him that way since she had touched the dead body of his other version.

"I want you to try that now," he continued.

"I don't think I can. Let me sleep first," she said.

"You can sleep later. Now do as I ask," he said. "It's much easier to do here. Just let your body relax and keep your mind awake. You know the drill."

She really wanted to go to sleep, but if this was so important to Uncle Robert, she ought to try to humor him. She owed him that much, at least.

The thing was, the technique needed her mind to be fully awake, and everything was foggy.

Uncle Robert moved closer and stroked her forehead. Instantly, her mind cleared. He held a beaker of something foul-smelling that he placed to her lips. It smelled terrible and tasted worse, like a mix of putrid cream, whiskey, and prune juice. Gagging, she sputtered and tried to push it away, but Uncle Robert continued to force it on her.

"Spirit medicine," he said. "You MUST swallow it, and now!"

She couldn't remember him ever ordering her to do anything, and thought about resisting, but was so tired that she acquiesced. She gagged on it, but got it down. In seconds, her mind cleared.

"What the fuck?"

"I think of it as ayahusca, but it isn't really. Nothing is real here, including our bodies."

"Well, your body may not be real, but don't include me."

He gave her a sad look. "Everything is an astral analog, but it works. Even better, unlike the real thing, it works instantly," he said.

"I guess it's the thought that counts," she said. The drug might be only smoke and mirrors on this astral plance, but she felt like she was going to throw up.

"Exactly," he said.

Swirls of color rushed out of nowhere, obliterating her vision. She felt herself teetering.

"Just let go," he said. "Don't get hung up on the colors, go through them."

He took her hand and added, "I love you."

This declaration surprised her more than anything else today. She had never doubted his love for her, but he had never blurted out his feelings before.

Marguerite gently set her down on the warm sand, with Uncle Robert continuing to hold her hand. Laura closed her eyes and relaxed. Her mind had become crystal clear, and her body was almost numb. And Uncle Robert was right; releasing her astral body was so much easier here. In only seconds, she felt the curious mild electric tingling that started in her toes and finger tips and srpead through her body. paralysis set in and then came the falling sensation, which she knew wasn't falling at all, but her energy body's double projecting from her real-time body.

She opened her eyes and found she was sitting up – or rather her energy body was. She could see her energy body's legs hovering slightly over those of her physical body. She no longer felt exhausted. Uncle Robert took the hand of her energy body in his ghostly hand, which would have been impossible on Earth but not here. His hand was warm and firm. He pulled her up to him; she heard a slight popping sound as her energy double completely separated from her physical body. Then she was standing in front of Uncle Robert.

In many ways this was standard procedure for separation from the material body, but there was a subtle difference. She felt energized and lighter. Before she could ask him about this, he said, "It's going to be all right now. It'll be a bit disorienting for a while, a bit of a shock, but trust me, it'll be okay."

She felt great. "You keep saying that like I'm going to freak out," she said. "I've astral projected before, just not here, on this other plane."

Uncle Robert placed his on her shoulder. "You still might freak out, but remember, I survived."

"What? Now you're scaring me," There was a strange feeling in her stomach, a tingling, empty feeling.

"I was slow to realize the projective experience here, within whatever piece of the universe is confined within the saucer, is essentially different from when you traveled out-of-body on Earth."

"Different? How so?" Behind, she could hear the rustle of Marguerite's wings. Was her angel rescuer about to fly away again? She started to turn to thank her, but Uncle Robert's firm hand restrained her.

"This is important," Uncle Robert said. "Don't worry about Marguerite. What I want to tell you is more conjecture than anything else, but it's the only theory I have, and it's important I tell you now."

He paused, looking up as if meditating, then continued. "The Earthly plane is a lower base-level plane. When you travel out-of-body from there, you're mainly projecting your energy body, or more accurately, a copy of your energy body, because your physical body cannot live if completely disconnected from the energy body. When you project into real time, the same plane as the physical level, your soul stays anchored with your physical body. If the soul didn't stay behind, again your physical body would die.

"The astral body itself is something else entirely. Some occultists consider it a subtle body in its own right, not just a shadow or a reflection of the energy body. Others say – and here's what I used to doubt but now believe from experience – it's the other way around. That the bodies we considered our real bodies, those things of fragile flesh and blood on Earth, are really a projection of the immortal astral body from one of these higher planes."

R. Douglas Burns

"Like in Plato's Poetics?" she said.

"Hmmm?"

"You ought to know this, you tutored me in it," she said. "Like his theory of forms. Objects in the Earthly world are merely approximations, flawed ones, of the ideal forms in the true reality."

"Yes, that sort of jives with what the occultists say; at least what some of them say. But I think it's more than that. It's that matter is dependent upon consciousness, is projected by consciousness, rather than consciousness being a product of biology. I'm not explaining this well. I know it might sound like horseshit to you."

"I thought you were an occultist."

"Well, not really. Philosopher and fellow traveler of the radically weird would have been more like it, at least when I had a physical body on the Earthly plane."

"Weird is about right," she said. "I don't know if I comprehend all this, but this seems like an ordinary projection." She looked down and saw the translucent, silvery umbilical cord, the diameter of a thick fishing line, emerging from her sweatshirt and snaking down between her legs, no doubt connecting to her physical body.

"See?" she said, holding up the cord for Uncle Robert. "It all looks like standard operating procedure." But the cord in her hand felt different: colder, harder than she remembered from previous projections.

"The concept of these multiple bodies is hard to get the mind around, even for those who report to seeing auras and such."

"So what happened to you, when you, you know – ?"

"Died? Can't say the D-word, huh?" he said.

"Hah! Yeah, I guess so." The sudden urge to hug him came upon her, and she did. He hugged her back. It was good. He felt just as solid as she was.

Still holding her, he said, "Well, for one thing, I believe my soul escaped my old physical body and returned to the source. What this body is made of, I have no idea. Certainly not flesh and blood, but I think it takes it form mostly from habit. This –" he slapped his chest. "– is how I picture myself."

"It seems real enough," she said. "And if it is solid, how do you know it's not flesh? Have you tried cutting yourself? Banging your head against a rock?"

He laughed again, the laugh that returned warm childhood memories to her, but his eyes were still sad.

"I have done just that," he said. "And I bled, for a while. Then while I looked away and thought about something else, the cut closed like it never had been in the first place." He held up a hand as if that would prove it to her.

"We are all such stuff as dreams are made of," she said.

"Yes, but you have to be careful here, even careful with your quotes. Thoughts can manifest themselves in as solid, physical reality here."

"So I have censor my thoughts, while projecting here or maybe the Bard will show up and sue me for plagiarism? I don't think I'll like that."

"Not so much censor yourself, as to be careful not to get stuck in them. The advantage is that here you don't have to put a physical body in a trance state before translating to another plane, even back to Earth," he said. "I visited your aunt Sophia not long ago. I was insubstantial there, a ghost to her, but she wasn't surprised at all. Ragged at me, in fact, for taking so long to get around to visiting her."

"So are all ghosts on Earth merely projections from another astral plane?"

"I don't know the answer to that question," he said, releasing the hug and stepping back. "I do know the Earthly appears to be one of the lower, more mundane planes. It's not the most base, but not the best place, either. Several planes are below the Earthly plane, and they all are like a kind of hell, where perceptions and freedoms are severely limited compared to here or on Earth."

She wanted to ask what plane John had translated to, but found her throat tightening.

"You look like you're about to cry," Uncle Robert said. "Take a deep breath and look at those mountains."

She did as he instructed and was surprised at how clean and fresh the air tasted, almost sweet. When she had been here before, in her physical body, she didn't remember the air having a taste at all. Or the desert landscape looking so pretty.

Nor had it seemed so friendly when she was here in her Earthly body, tending to the implanted humans. Of course, she had been dressed in only baggy panties and an old Army blanket and had been freezing her ass off.

"The mountains are beautiful, too," he said. "Want to travel there?"

"How?"

"We can just think ourselves there. Thought is action – remember?"

"Just like that? Leave my body behind? I don't know if I can trust Marguerite to guard it. She's still kind of flighty, you know what I mean?"

Uncle Robert just gave her one of those sad smiles of his. "Was that a pun?"

"Sorry, Marguerite. No offense," she said and turned to find the angel had gone. But her physical body was still there, laying on its back on a patch of smooth sand. A small flat stone had been placed under the head and the eyes – her eyes – were wide open, staring blankly at the sky. A large red bloom of blood – like a giant rose – blossomed on the front of sweatshirt.

"I don't think you have to worry about the safety of your physical body anymore," he said.

Sadness overwhelmed her as her fingers sought the umbilical cord. She had noticed something odd about it before. Now she knew what was wrong. In her previous projection experiences, the cord had shone with a diffused inner light and had vibrated with a life of its own. Now it was dead. More than dead. Desiccated. It began to crumble in her hand as she walked toward her body.

She didn't have to stare into the vacant eyes of her body to know that it was dead too.

It took a moment for the emotional reality to sink in. Here she was, standing over a lump of dead meat shaped like Laura Jacobsen.

Uncle Robert came and stood beside her. Big tears were streaming down his cheeks and disappearing into his Santa Claus beard.

"I should be crying, not you, Uncle," she told him. But she wasn't sad. Disturbed, yes, but she felt very little identification with the golem at her feet.

Uncle Robert wiped away his tears with the back of his hand.

"The major didn't miss with that first shot, did he?"

"I don't know who the major is, but apparently not," he said. "You didn't realize you were shot?"

"I didn't feel it. I thought the shot went wide."

"You may have felt it at first, then went into a kind of denial or forgetfulness as death approached. I remember it being like that when I was drowning. I sort of had to reconstruct the memory afterwards."

He knelt and closed the eyes of her corpse. She stepped closer. It smelled of blood and shit.

"They may pop back open," she said.

He looked at her curiously.

"The eyes. I used to work in a nursing home, remember?" she said.

"You're calmer about this than I was when I discovered my own corpse."

"You didn't have a family ghost as a welcoming committee."

"No, but I was nearing my own end of days on Earth anyway – my ticker was winding down, missing ticks – and that made it a little easier to accept my death. But it was still overwhelming at first."

"You never told anyone, did you, about the bad heart?"

"You miss the point. I'd lived my life. Built and explored my own majestic castles of self-absorption. Worked out a lot of issues along the way, hid others in the battlements, and I had become comfortable with my own fears and insecurities. That makes things a lot easier here on this plane. Am I rambling?"

She nodded. "Yes, Uncle, but I'm following you – sort of following – like always."

"I told you about the lower planes, lower than Earth?"

She nodded again.

"There are souls there who believe themselves in hell. And because they believe themselves in hell, they are. It's just a hell of their own imagining. That was what I was trying to warn you of."

"Are you saying I might get trapped in one of those places? I don't think so. I don't even believe in hell."

"Some of those trapped there may not either. But they are in their own private hells, nonetheless, and those hells are peopled with demons of their own psyches."

"I don't think I'll fall for that trap. I think I know my mind – soul – whatever – better than that."

"Another's another way to get lost there. If you have a strong connection with someone there, you can sometimes hear them calling you. Don't go. Don't give in to the urge to even visit to give comfort before you talk to me first. Until you learn what you're doing, there's danger you could find yourself trapped in a lower plane with them – a true ghost."

"There was a movie about that, Robin Williams . . ." she said, trying to remember.

"Forget movies. Forget fantasy. This is a real danger; it may be the most important thing I've ever told you. It's a dark void that will suck in your soul."

He held out his hands as if holding an invisible black hole. His hands trembled.

"You look like you want to say something," he said.

She took a deep breath and started to ask him about John Wright, if he was on a higher plane or a lower one, but she held back, afraid of his answer.

16.

From the Fire and Blood of their Collision

Man knows the fear of mystery everywhere,
And peeps with trembling glances overhead – Baudelaire

"The other Gods died of their temporality, yet the supreme meaning never dies, it turns into meaning and then into absurdity, and out of the fire and blood of their collision the supreme meaning rises up rejuvenated anew." – Carl Gustave Jung, *The Red Book*

Major Minor.
The angel was of him and not of him, close enough to touch and a universe away, cold as a dark sky in winter, warm and real as his own flesh.

"You were not my first choice," she said, folding her wings around him, "but you'll have to do."

Major Minor's soul cried out in relief. He had never been first in anything, in work, in love, in life, so being a second choice was a comfortable, familiar place to be. He knew how to feel, angry yet resigned.

The vacuum, the horrible emptiness, was filled for a moment with pain, an intense fire that spread from his navel to every nerve-ending in his body. The torture was so astonishingly intense it became a kind of ecstasy. For a timeless moment, he looked not up at the face of the Lady of the Lake, but directly into her eyes. The pain intensified, a quantum increase of torture a fraction of a second earlier that he would not have thought possible, and he loved her, loved him, loved it, for the angel was the embodiment of all that had been denied him all his life. The outrage at his pitiful existence was exorcised, and the potential of life, the glorious potential of awareness, pain and chaos, bloomed like an evil flower. All the other ways he had tried to fill the chasm in his soul with had failed. Family? He had infected them with his own needs; he had silently raged at them because of the sacrifice they required. Work, duty, career? He was no noble hero selflessly giving himself to his county. He had been in the thick of things because it was convenient outlet for his rage.

Ironic that he was set free to live now that he was dying.

"You're not dying," the Lady of the Lake said, knowing his thoughts as if they were her own, which perhaps they now were. "You are being reborn. *We* are being reborn. I will pass, your human body will pass, and together, as one creature, we will become the collision of the finite and the infinite."

None of what she said made much sense, but the wings that wrapped around him became a silken blanket, as soft as baby flesh and as strong as Kevlar. The angel glanced down, and Minor's gaze was pulled by invisible strings to where she looked. His shirt and trousers had been shredded, explosively blown back from his torso. A veteran of violet conflict, he gasped, expecting to see his own dangling entrails, but saw only a thick, short, crystalline rope joining his navel to the Lady of the Lake.

The cord did not connect to her navel. She didn't have one. Instead, it was attached to a prismatic structure centered about where her vulva would be if she were human. The prism had millions of surfaces and colors. His head throbbed when he looked at it, so he concentrated on the umbilical cord instead, which also pulsed with energy but of a more benign nature. Was the cord solid matter or a will-o'-the-wisp? He wanted to touch it, stroke it, but held back.

The Lady of the Lake released him from the shroud of her wings and stepped away. The crystal rope extended between them without stretching. Through a haze of marvelous pain, he realized he no longer hungered for that unknown and unnamed thing – it was here, he was one with it at last. He sighed with relief as the pain threatened to explode away his genitals and sear a hole into his stomach.

An fear more frightening than the apparent mutilation of his body popped into his head. He dared touched the cord now, to slide his hand along its length. The feel reminded him of his penis when semi-flaccid except this thing was infused with a mechanical hum.

Was this a hallucination? That would mean the angel was a projection of his diseased unconsciousness. If that were true, then he should ask her – it – questions and perhaps derive some inkling of where this self-torment sprang from. But he was instinctively repelled from the idea of exploring this part of himself, and he let go of the cord.

A part of his mind withdrew, fearing nothing would be left of his old self if that hidden part of him was brought to light.

Too late; the damage was done. He was crumbling and dissolving – not only his physical body and his identity but his ego too, the little self, and something else deeply hidden within him. He caught a glimpse of this shadow before it dissolved.

Now there is no me, no you. There is only a point in a wave, a disturbance in an otherwise quantum vacuum, that you mistakenly call consciousness. We are both wave-forms in the vacuum, and now our individual waves will superimpose to form a new wave of different frequency and amplitude.

The huge creature standing before him was no longer male or female; it was neither, it was both. His lust for it was gone. In place of the physical need was a sense of purpose. Peace. And Chaos. Wonderful disorder.

The creature picked him up as if he were a child. He *was* a child, or that is, he was soon to be reborn. Then they were airborne, and he dreamed as a child would dream, half-awake, half-asleep. He knew he was soon to become something else, something not a man, and he would leave childish human ways behind.

Minor thought that, though this moment might a dream and his life a joke, he might decipher meaning from it. He decided to ask the angel a question that had been bothering him for some time.

"Is there a God of all this?"

"Yes and no," the angel said, and strangely this answer satisfied Minor.

They swooped up and over the loblolly pines, then down toward the lake. He thought he heard one of his men call out in alarm, but it was inconsequential. The pain in his groin subsided, to be replaced with a pulsing hum that spread throughout his body. He saw, in his mind, a blood-red flash of microscopic angels, millions of them, no larger than spermatozoa, pulsing through his lymphatic system. Like little Army Corps engineers, they were tearing down things, rebuilding him from the inside out.

The beach passed in a flash below. From twenty feet he could distinguish the individual sand particles. The angel flew lower until they were running parallel to the still surface of the lake. The angel – he really didn't care if it was male or female at this point – still held him as if he were a small child, and his booted feet dangled. He stretched a toe and skimmed it across the water, sending up an fine mist.

He looked at the angel's face. She was female again, but not the same one he had found submerged in the water only a day ago. Her classic features were withered now, traced with deep lines, but not wrinkles, more like peeling veneer.

"I'm sorry," she said. "But I must hurry the metamorphosis. It will be uncomfortable for both us, but we have met with opposition."

"Rapid mobilization," he heard himself say. His voice wasn't quite his own.

"Yes. I lay dreaming too long in deep water."

They dashed across the lake toward the saucer, toward the gash, then straight into it. A faint green light shimmered across the opening. Though the gash continued beneath the surface of the lake, water was not flowing into the abyss. The green light was some sort of barrier, he guessed.

"A patch," the angel said, reading his mind.

The angel twisted in flight so that its feet encountered the shimmering first. Time slowed, and they oozed rather than flew through the barrier. Minor felt as though he were drowning in syrup. Then they passed through and were in clear, dry air.

He had reflexively closed his eyes as they passed through the barrier. He opened them to find they were not inside an enclosed space at all, but hundreds of feet over a desert plain under an emerald-green sky. The horizon was broken by low, dark basaltic mountains with glowing olive veins tracing paths down their sides. He couldn't tell if the veins were made of a reflective stone that mirrored the sky or were green in their own right. Boulders, large and small, lay strewn across the desert floor. He saw other objects that at first appeared to be cacti that sparkled like prisms. He strained to see better, and as if to comply, the angel flew lower until they were only a dozen feet above the plane.

The prismatic objects did indeed look much like cacti, but as he and the angel flew over them, neon ideographs scrolled on their surfaces like alien advertising logos.

Miles away a shadow passed over the desert. He was sure it was a shadow – he could even identify the cloud that caused it – but it was white, a shadow in negative.

"We're almost there," the angel said, laughing at some private joke.

"What's so funny?" he asked.

"Time, almost or otherwise. You humans bring it with you to this place where time would otherwise have no meaning."

He didn't understand this either, but he let it pass.

The angel pulled into a vertical flying position, feet down.

They landed in front of a set of familiar structures, and it was Minor's turn to laugh, which startled both the angel and himself, for his laugher was high-pitched, lilting, like that of a child or woman.

"Why do you laugh?" the angel asked.

Spread before him was a large Army general purpose tent. He knew the structures well, had carried a similar tent in the Chinook, and they had deployed it in the piney woods.

"I laugh because the tents are out of place here," he said.

"But so are you, and if it be known, so am I," the angel said.

Minor also laughed because though this was a desert, the tent was not desert tan, but camouflage green, which still worked because the emerald sky gave even the sand a green cast.

But mainly he laughed because of the irony of finding the tents here.

Last year a Fort Leonard Wood depot had been broken into and looted. The locked ground-level doors had been left intact, but a section of the tin roof had been peeled off as if it were a huge sardine can. Part of the lost inventory a large GP tent – most likely this very same tent, he was sure.

He had been in charge of the investigation. Unable to discern how anyone could have taken everything out through the hole in the roof even with a helicopter, his investigation had concluded that the cause must have been some sort of freak weather event, like a small tornado. This explanation had left him unsatisfied as each tent bundle weighed hundreds of pounds, but he'd been unable to offer anything better.

The camp officer – that dyke bitch! – had been more than just unsatisfied with his theory. His failure to come up with a more logical explanation had contributed to his getting this shit assignment to investigate "rumors" of a UFO at Lost Lake. She had called him "lazy and incompetent," and since he was given to "flights of imagination," then he was "suited to investigate this one."

He laughed again. The truth had been more fantastic than anything he could have guessed: that archangels had burglarized the depot and taken the tent to another dimension.

He laughed again, which hurt his chest. He felt his chest to find – what? Two mounds!

"What the fuck?" he said.

"Time to rest," the angel said, grabbing Minor under his arms and whisking him into one of the tents.

17.

Rises the Shade of a New Demiurge

Bryan.

Dog's paws made soft clicks on the hardwood floors as he led them through the maze of the mansion to a door. Suzanne – maybe not his Suzanne but an exact facsimile – had reluctantly tagged along, and now she fidgeted with her hair as Bryan yanked at the door.

Finally, it subbornly opened.

They walked out onto a boardwalk circling a town square. He had expected something familiar, either the entrance to the underground tavern or the rickshaw-cart corral, but saw nothing but dusty streets and storefronts.

A few horses were tied to hitching rails, but he saw no carts like those at the tavern. The storefronts were covered with clapboard made nearly colorless by wind and sun. The bleached wood, dirt street – all reminded him of an old black-and-white movie version of a western town. He looked at the sky, which was still red even though the town was a bleached-out gray.

Behind them, the door they had just come through closed of its own accord and looked like the outer doors the other storefronts. Dog had not come out on the street with them. He had been shut inside when the door closed. Bryan looked for a doorknob or handle, but didn't find one, and the door didn't open when he to grip the edges of a molding strip and pull it open to no avail. Just in case it swung both ways, he put his shoulder against it and shoved, but that didn't work either.

"Where are we?" the Suzanne asked.

"You don't know?"

"I think this may be a new part of the dream," she said.

"What the fuck does that mean, Suzanne? – if you really are Suzanne." He was surprised by his own anger. She took a startled step back.

"The angels have spoken of it happening, but they say we humans –" She stopped talking, looking behind him, her eyes wide.

The door had changed. Instead of the bare and rough-hewn wood, now it was nearly covered in tile-size chunks of broken mirror with only bits of weathered wood showing between. He hadn't noticed any transition. Suzaane was freaked.

"It's changed, but it's still just a door, a but things do that on this place, so what's the problem?" he said.

But Suzanne wasn't staring at the fractured reflections on the door. Her gaze was focusing on the lintel. Distracted by the mirrors, he hadn't noticed, but mounted on the lintel was a well-rendered Janus face, also of wood. One of the two faces was young, the other old. Both were familiar, but he needed a few moments before he recognized his own features in the younger one.

When he turned back to Suzanne, he saw tears in her eyes and felt guilty.

"I'm sorry I yelled," he said. "I wasn't yelling at you, I'm just frustrated by all this bullshit."

"It's not that," she said.

He reached over to her and rubbed away a tear with his thumb. She smiled at him, but an emotional gulf stretched had opened between them. Something had been lost.

"What is that freakish thing?" she asked.

"It's sort of like Janus. He was the god of beginnings and transitions. One face looks into the future, the other into the past. Historically, people commonly put him over doors, like here, with one face pointed east, the other west."

"But this one looks like you. What does that mean?"

"I don't know. You started to say something about what the angels told you. What was it?"

She nodded, but didn't speak. Her face was an unreadable stew of emotions, but fear was clearly part of the recipe.

"Tell me, Suzanne, now!" He raised his voice more than he meant, and immediately felt as if he were bullying her.

"They said that they weren't sure if the Dreaming God was dreaming you, as he is the rest of us, or if you were dreaming him."

She looked away, but he could see she was on the verge of tears.

"I really don't know what that means. I'm dreaming the Dreaming God who's dreaming everything else, including you, the angels, everything, including myself?"

She nodded. "That's what they suspect. They don't know. I thought they were mistaken until we stepped out here. This place shouldn't be. Or it shouldn't be what we found when we went through that door."

She looked at him with suspicion. *Did you dream this up?*

"That's so arbitrary. I mean, if this is an astral plane, then thought is action here, isn't it?"

"It's more complex than that. This world is an illusion; all worlds are, really – that's what the archangels teach – but each one is like a big quilting bee, with everyone contributing a stitch here and there," she said.

"Like a consensus, you mean? A shared reality?"

"Something like that," she said uncertainly. If she wasn't the Suzanne he had known on Earth, she was a good facsimile. That Suzanne had been well-read, but with curious gaps in her education because she'd been largely self-taught, a high-school dropout who had spent a lot of time at the local library.

"So where does this Dreaming God come in? If you're all thinking or dreaming this world, why do you need him?"

"I'm not sure. You'll have to ask the archangels, but I know everything gets filtered somehow by the Dreaming God. He balances things. Otherwise, everything would be changing constantly as individual wills jockeyed for dominance. People would think others out of existence, that kind of thing."

"Even if I accept that, I still don't see where I fit in. Am I some sort of projection of this big blue Dreaming God?"

She shook her head again. "That's what I'm trying to tell you; the archangels fear it might be the other way around, that the Dreaming God might be a projection of *your* dream." She stumbled over the concept of projection, as if she were not certain it was the right word.

"Okay, let's say, just for the sake of argument, that I'm dreaming all this," he said. "It's like the dragon eating its own tail, an infinite recursive thing."

"What?"

"Never mind. I got confused."

"Yes," she said, smiling at him, but her eyes still betrayed her fear.

"What I was just trying to say, if this is all my dream, including this body, then what happens when I go to sleep? Do I dream a dream within a dream?"

So was he immersed in some sort of artificial reality? He had once read that a computer would have to be the size of a galaxy to generate the world of the Matrix movie, but at least the movie had given credit to the human unconscious filling in the gaps with expectations and desires. Maybe that's what was happening here – often – a dream state with some part of his mind doing all the grunt work. He had dreamt the first Suzanne as middle-aged with lots of mileage. Now here was Suzanne as he remembered her on Earth, though not undead but apparently one-hundred percent alive and young.

"Have you?" she said, jarring him out of his musing.

"Have I what?"

"Slept or dreamed since you got here? It doesn't matter if you think this –" she waved her hands expansively at the town, the sky "– is a dream, or if I am real, either. But have you slept and dreamed since you arrived here?"

He started to say that of course he had, for he'd been here for a couple of days, at least subjectively. But had he? Had he slept and had he dreamed? He had been rendered unconscious – in a kind of fugue state – as the enforcer archangel whisked him away from the saloon. But he hadn't slept, had he? If he had slept, he had no recollection of dreaming.

"Well, have you or haven't you?" she asked.

"No, I guess not," he said, but in truth he did not know. Had he dreamed but forgotten doing so? How could he be sure of anything? He shook his head. He hated this solipsism; it seemed simpleminded. He looked down the street. No tumbleweeds were rolling across the street, but it was still a ghost town-ish scene. He turned back to the door. Wherever they were, there was no going back in the way they came out. He resisted the urge to knock on the door.

"I wonder if the angels will follow us," he said.

"I think they're going to come for you, especially if they find that you can alter this reality," she said.

"Why?"

"I heard them talking."

"Them?"

"Purah, the one who carried you away from the Hovel."

"The Hovel?"

"You know, the saloon, where I bar-tend. Anyway, Purah and two others, I don't know their names."

"What'd they say? Wait a minute? That really was you back at the bar?"

"Didn't you recognize me? I remembered you."

"Yes, but you were much older. Like middle-aged. Now you're how I remember you from Earth. Wait a minute you said earlier you didn't know what I was talking about."

"I guess I should thank you," she said, ignoring this inconsistency. "I'm younger than that now."

She smiled at some private joke and stomped a foot on the street, raising a little cloud of dust. "Seems real enough, doesn't it?"

"What do you mean, thank you?"

"The angels noticed me changing, of course. I told them I knew you from another reality, but I'd come to think of that as a dream and this as real. I don't think I should have told them that. It changed everything. They hadn't noticed I was young again until I told them that. Several of them had a little conference and decided your secondary dream-mind had revised me. I wasn't supposed to tell you this."

"Revised? Secondary dream-mind? What does that mean?"

"That's the word they used, 'revised' and 'dream-mind.' Do you think I'm making this up?"

The world began to spin. Dizzy, suddenly weak, he had to sit down. The boardwalk rested on cinderblocks that lifted it above the street. He sat on the edge of the wooden planks, one leg folded under the other, and dangled down a hand to let his fingers brush the ground. This should have been a solid position, like the Earth-touching Buddha, but instead of feeling rooted, he was moved by tidal forces beyond his control.

He closed his eyes and saw a vision of a huge rotating wheel. More accurately, a series of wheels within wheels that all turned independently. A mandala, a mecha-mandala.

The wheels turned slowly. Cyrillic-looking letters inscribed on these wheels would light up and enlarge when he tried to focus on one. Different colors were associated with different letters, a pattern of meaning just beyond his reach. It was a trite comparison, but it made him think of a cosmic roulette wheel.

He felt he stared at the mecha-mandala for a piece of eternity, but when he opened his eyes, the sun was in the same spot, and Suzanne was still standing in the street. She wasn't looking at him. Instead she was looking down the street. He followed her gaze and saw three archangels, all in their giant, muscular, masculine avatars. Their faces were set with determination. All three swaggered as they walked, their arms akimbo, their fists clenched, their wings clutched in tight, tense wads of flesh high on their backs. They were headed straight toward him, and he suspected their mission was to harm him. He had no escape, could do nothing other than close his eyes and wait. He wished this Suzanne would at least sit beside him while it happened, but she was probably wise to keep her distance.

It was a nice dream while it lasted, but we all die alone.

The street looked as though he was seeing it though as through an ultra-thin, varnish-tinted vellum of the mecha-mandala. The apparatus continued to turn, it was still transparent overlay of everything, but now he had his eyes open.

The angels were still in the street, still looking like cowhands come to town for a fight – but frozen in mid-stride. A three-dimensional tableau vivant. The sky swam above them.

He opened his eyes. He didn't remember moving, but he was now on his back on the boardwalk. Suzanne was still an immobile statue. A strand of her hair curled in mid-air, blown by an unfelt breeze, her mouth was frozen into a kind of smirk. Above her, the clouds still drifted across the red sky – or did they drift? Were they frozen in time, too? Maybe, but they might be moving on him in the next instant. Would they tear him apart when they got to him? Most likely.

He closed his eyes again and was back in the world of the mecha-mandala.

Upon closer examination, he found concentric wheels within the wheels, each turning at a slightly different speed. The scripts, which he had first thought looked like Cyrillic, now looked more Phoenician. He knew the characters were separated from modern Earth language by an even vaster abyss of time and space than a few thousand miles and years.

In an epiphany, he realized his survival depended on not just deciphering the script, but manipulating it. He relaxed further, not trying to force out thoughts of the world by letting them slide by like waves on the side of a boat. He had no sense of trying to control the waves of thought, but rather of a deep symbiosis, a mutual dependency. He willed himself into becoming the script. He *was* the script, or rather the script was a deeper strata of his consciousness, the underlying reality.

Either that, or he was completely schizoid and delusional.

He mentally shrugged off the self-doubt and focused his attention on a particularly appealing string of characters. The change in the wheel and its motions was so subtle it was almost unnoticeable, but one of the archangels on the street blinked out of existence. *Had he done that?* He touched another bit of one circle, and the remaining two angels became unfrozen. At first they didn't notice their companion was missing, but he gave the cosmic wheel another nudge, and they turned to each other in fear. He granted them a moment of decision, though he found the sense of absolute power he had over them distasteful. Tossing the creatures into the chaos of rebirth would be so easy, but he restrained himself.

Another touch of the wheel, and normal time was restored. Give the angels credit for having courage. Faced with being blinked out existence for their rebellion, they could have turned and run away. That would have been the sensible thing to do. That's what Bryan would have done if he were in their position. Instead, they looked at each other, reached an unspoken agreement, and began walking toward him. Their posture was different now. Their shoulders drooped, their wings hung like the robes of fallen kings. They were the picture of dejection, of grim resolution, and doomed failure. More confident now, he waited until they were only a half-dozen paces away before accessing the mecha-mandala.

He froze them again in mid-stride but did not erase them from existence. He wasn't sure why he was merciful Perhaps he felt some odd connection to them. For all their powers, they were fellow creatures, like him they were caught up in forces beyond their understanding.

He sat up. Suzanne was still standing, frozen, a mannequin.

And standing beside her, smiling at him, was Laura.

She leaned down and, without his asking, extended a hand and helped him up.

He stood up slowly, his legs weak. Laura just stood and smiled. She was still wearing the same baggy sweatshirt and jeans – dirtier now – that she had been wearing when he'd last seen her at the military bivouac on Earth. But her face! Her entire countenance shone with an inner light. Even those grass stains on her jeans looked luminous.

"Well, College Boy, aren't you even going to say hello?"

"I'm not sure if you're real – if any of this is real." The truth was he wanted to grab her, hug her or something, which he wouldn't have a problem with on Earth. But something was different about this Laura. Like Suzanne, she had changed in some fundamental way. But unlike Suzanne, he was certain this really was Laura, the Laura he had known since college and not some clone on this astral plane.

"Reality is greatly overrated; reality as we used to know it, that is." And she closed the space between them and hugged him, then stepped back, reached up and tousled his hair as an older sister would.

She turned and touched a finger to Suzanne's cheek to brush away a big tear. "She's still pretty and apparently alive and breathing in this plane. Why is she crying?"

"That's not the question, right now."

"What is the question then?"

"I have several. One is: Did this Suzanne misled me, set me up, play her cards on the angels winning this showdown here at the O.K. Corral? Another is what is this Matrix crap? But I guess the first one I want you to answer is why do you have blood stains on the back of the sweatshirt?"

She twisted at the waist to look at the back of her shirt. She couldn't turn far enough. "Blood, you say? I can't see it. I cleaned the front, here. . ." She poked a finger in the front of the shirt where the U of University was. ". . .but I guess I forgot about the back. How about you change me into something more presentable?"

"Me? What are you talking about?"

"Well, you are the local demiurge, you know. Or do you? By now you should realize that you're not the ordinary college drop-out, particularly after banishing that archangel into nowhere-land."

"I don't know how I did that."

"Figured as much. That's what I'm here to help you work out, I guess. Funny, me being a spirit guide to anyone. Now remember me in something cleaner, less grungy. Whatever first comes to mind."

"I don't know how I did the thing with the angel."

"What did you do first?"

"Closed my eyes and emptied my mind."

"Well, do that now."

Obediently, he closed his eyes, and she said, "Remember me when we first met."

He was staring through translucent eyelids again. The wheel now was off to the left, cranking away.

She twirled on her heel, a flash of motion. "At the Student Union, remember?"

And he did, just for a moment, remember that time, a universe away, and when Laura stopped spinning, she was dressed in a mid-thigh black skirt and white blouse.

She looked down and laughed. "All right. You even got the tennis shoes right and – oh, shit! Even the panty hose." She ran a hand over her stomach. "I think you took off ten pounds while you were at it. What do I owe you?"

"No charge. Dreams and memories are free." Her happiness was contagious, and for a moment he forgot how weird all this was.

She kissed him on the cheek. The kiss felt real. "Too bad we never worked out together when I was alive, you know," she said.

"We're dead?"

"Yes, well I am, and on Earth, anyway. Shot through a lung by that crazy fucker, Major Minor," she said. "I bled out on the saucer, but thanks to Marguerite, I'm still walking and talking because death on that intermediate plane is a conscious transition. But if she hadn't rescued me, who knows what happened to my physical body. It could still be walking around undead, a soulless zombie like your old Suzanne, or. . ." She paused. ". . . John Wright."

He studied her face but couldn't tell if she was serious.

"I sort of doubt that. I was pretty sure Suzanne wasn't some kind of soulless zombie," he said. "I'm pretty sure you know that Wright was something else. If they weren't real, then the love I felt wasn't real either, and I can't accept that. I rather forget it happened at all."

"Careful there, Bryan," she said. "Your thoughts actually are reality on this plane. Remember, you're the local god here. If you think too hard at me, all I'll be is a reflection of your memory."

"I'm not sure that you aren't already."

18.

As a Shared Delusion

Major Minor/Samiazaz.

The entity who had once been the human, Major Karl Minor, re-covered consciousness lying on his back on a cot, staring up at the olive camouflage fabric of an Army bivouac tent. It all seemed comfortingly familiar. Then Minor remembered his encounter with Samiazaz, the pain, the flight from camp to here — but where was here? Wherever here was, it was not Missouri. Everything might look like U.S. Army issue, but he wasn't even sure if it were real.

Minor lifted his head. A blanket covered his body from the neck down. It was also olive green and Army issue. The coarse wool was scratchy against his bare skin. As he shifted his weight on the canvas cot, he could feel the individual fibers, millions of them, brushing against his body. His feet stuck out from underneath the blanket. His? They didn't look right. His legs were too long. For a second, he had the crazy feeling that someone else was under the blanket with him, an Amazonian ballerina cuddled up between his unfeeling legs, her nearly superhuman, female feet poking out from the end of the blanket.

What a ridiculous thought.

He tried wiggling his toes – success! If some giant woman was un-derneath the blanket with him, her feet and toes obeyed his will.

He pulled a hand from under the blanket and pounded on the side strut of the cot. The strut shattered and the cot leaned, almost pitching him out. He felt the force of the blow, but his hand was unharmed. His hand? It was pale without a hint of hair, the fingers elegantly slender and strong.

He knew he had been changed by Samiazaz, knew the change was bone-deep – deeper even, down to the shadows of his being. As the Lady of the Lake was carrying him across the waters, organs and bone were shifting under his skin. This transformation had continued as she had transported him through the rift of the saucer and into the alien world inside. The pain had been indescribable, but that was expected with rebirth, as with birth. He shouldn't be surprised that he would be physically changed, but this wasn't what he expected.

He sat up, holding the blanket to his chest, and only then noticed the desiccated archangel corpse on the cot next to him. Little remained of the Lady of the Lake, but he knew it was her corpse, knew it at a visceral level. A gust of wind raced into the tent and whisked away whatever substance had formed the archangel's flesh. What was left looked like dead coral.

When he dropped his blanket, he wasn't surprised to find he had breasts and was no longer male. He and the Lady of the Lake were now one, and the female warrior form she had taken at the moment of their merging now apparently dominated.

Yet quite a bit of Major Minor remained. As this new creature examined its human memories, it found huge censored spaces. But one thing remained, one thing that inhabited this dark human space: rage – glorious, powerful rage.

Minor's new wings sprang forth and she burst upward through the tent's ceiling. The heavy canvas offered no more resistance than tissue paper. The desert flashed by in a few heartbeats, and then Minor was through the riff in the saucer's skin.

Minor zoomed over lost lake toward the encampment and landed near the Chinook. A soldier was sleeping on the ramp. When Minor touched his shoulder, he opened his eyes, staring uncomprehendingly.

"What the hell!" he started to say as he came fully awake, but before he could get the another word out, Minor swatted the head off the soldier's shoulders. The head bounced on the ramp, and Minor moved in a blur to catch it on the second bounce. He held up the head by one jug ear. One eye was wide open, and it focused on Minor for a moment. The other was half-closed, the eyelid possessed with spasmodic tic.

"You won't fall asleep on watch again, soldier," Minor said, and tossed the head into the bowels of the Chinook. The bouncing head made a sound like a dropped cantaloupe. Shouts of surprise from the soldiers came from within, followed by silence. Minor considered going in but decided to wait for the inevitable.

Awakening of an Alien God

Voices, tiny voices, came from within: two soldiers whispering from deep within the belly of the Chinook. Minor the human wouldn't have been able to hear them, but Minor the angel could – and clearly. They had heard the bumping sound on the floor of the Chinook but didn't know that it was made from a decapitated head. They were on alert though.

Two men had evidently been caught with their pants down. One had been sodomizing the other, or at least that's what the whispers implied. Someone laughed. Another told him to "shut the fuck up."

Aroused, Minor let his hand stray downward, forgetting that he/she/it was no longer male. Minor felt a moment of panic as the hand found pudenda and not a man's package. Before, being female hadn't been an issue; now Minor felt mutilated, demonically changed into another form. And somehow all this had been done to him because he had done his duty, killing an escapee, that Laura woman. But life was more often than not unjust. How had he forgotten this?

Minor gave this further thought as the men inside scuttled noisily about, trying to get organized. The old Karl Minor had not been murdered, but rather had been submerged, wrapped inside this woman-angel suit.

Minor checked a second time. His dick and balls were only a phantom package, like an amputated limb.

"Shit!" came from inside the Chinook. Someone had finally found the tic-wink soldier's head. Before they had been alarmed at the thump of some foreign object tossed inside the cargo bay. Now they knew what that object was, and he could smell their terror.

Minor could sense as well the tension building within the Chinook. A metallic clatter was instantly recognizable as a clip being removed, checked, then reinserted in a carbine. Minor waited, knowing what was going to come next.

He/she didn't have long to wait. Like the snout of a frightened animal, a carbine barrel hesitantly poked out of the cargo hold. It wavered, trembled a bit, then advanced. A man's shoulder followed, then the whole man.

The man – Minor could not think of him as a soldier – stared with his eyes wide open. His back was hunched, and his face ashen – he looked as if he knew he was deadman, which was disappointing. What pleasure would there be in killing him if he had already resigned himself to death? The second man emerged from the other side of the open hold, but he held his weapon at waist level in a stupid, Rambo-like fashion, more testimony to lack of training.

With barely a thought, without being conscious of traversing the intervening physical space, Minor was no longer standing in the shadows but behind the gray leech soldier. The man obviously was not aware of Minor crossing the space, for he kept scanning the undergrowth. A mishmash of smells, a stew of body bacteria, sweat, unwashed orifices, semen, and fear created an aura that expanded outward for yards.

The Rambo-wannabe also scanned the brush, then turned, M-16 still held low, to nod at his compatriot. His eyes popped wide open, comically, as he saw Minor standing behind the gray leech.

Before either could react, Minor slammed his hands against the leech's back. As if hit by a speeding car, the soldier hurled forward, caroming off a support bracket, then colliding with the other solider with a loud, wet, slapping sound.

Again without being conscious of crossing the space, Minor was standing over the bodies of the two men. The leech was obviously dead; his neck broken upon the impact. The break was extreme; the neck had bent in a U-shape so that the head was facing backwards, the face upside-down, but the grayness was gone, the complexion now almost rosy. The face was left unscathed without even a scratch, the eyes wide open, with the expression a mixture of surprise and serenity.

Leech, death becomes you. I did you a favor.

The other man moaned and tried to push off the corpse. But one of his arms was bent at an unnatural angle, and all he managed to do was shift the dead mass enough to make the head loll back and forth.

"Mother, Mother, where are you? I love you," the man said, looking up at Minor. A thin trickle of blood ran from his nose.

Minor was taken aback, but only for a moment.

"Fool, I'm not your mother. She didn't love you, and I abhor you," Minor said and stuck a finger through the his eye and into his brain.

The man's feet drummed on the steel ramp, a toppled toy wind-up soldier, still marching. Spasms rolled over his body, and the wind-up soldier slowly wound down as Minor pulled his finger slowly out.

Brain tissue dripped from the tip of his/her finger, and the ruined eyeball rode halfway up the finger like a ring. Minor sucked the gore off his finger, momentarily sated. The killing had been an orgasmic experience, better than any sex he had ever had.

But the sated feeling was already fading.

He rubbed his crotch, her crotch, still finding a woman's pudenda where a man's package should be. The Laura woman had said something about angels being able to change sexes, hadn't she? But how was it done? A matter of will? An incantation? An unconscious manifestation?

What to do next? Or rather, what or whom to kill next?

The remaining soldiers would be armed and ready now. Should he/she take care of them before they had time to group? As fierce as this new body was, Minor didn't know if it could sustain high explosives or sustained small-arms fire. The blonde angel, after all, had been decapitated by the Chinook's rotor blades.

He heard a stirring in the underbrush, followed by the clink of a gun bolt being pulled back and released. Rounds pinged into the metal ramp of the Chinook, but Minor was already airborne, high above the towering pines. The choice had been made. Shots followed, but these were not trained soldiers, only paid thugs. Minor's blood was up. She/he flew between the thick branches, both exhilarated and deeply saddened. It was an easy matter to loop up over the treetops and dive down toward the bivouac tent. She/he tore through the heavy canvas and caught the panicked men by surprise.

Only a few had time to fire their weapons, and most of the shots went wild.

Bryan.

"You look real enough," Bryan said.

Laura had just kissed him on the cheek. He could smell her scent, light lilac mixed with something else he couldn't identify but was relaxing. She was still holding his hand in a sisterly fashion.

"Even if I believed in gods, which I don't, how could I be one? How can I be creating this universe? I couldn't even finish college," he said.

He meant this to be a joke, but she wasn't laughing.

"Who says you're God?"

"Well, Suzanne, for one," he said.

Laura let go of his hand and stepped over to Suzanne, who was still frozen in time and place. Laura pinched her cheek, not hard, just enough to distend the skin a bit. Laura let go, and the pinched skin stayed distended.

"Will that leave a permanent mark?"

"You're trying to sound flippant," Laura said. "But you're really concerned, aren't you?" She touched Suzanne's cheek again, smoothing out the puckered area she had made with the pinch. "If you looked closely – and had a lot more patience than I think you possess – you would have seen the skin gradually returning to normal."

"I don't get it," he said. He took a step closer to Suzanne. She had a hand up one side of her face, frozen in the act of brushing away a strand of hair. He leaned forward to touch her but stopped when the noticed the strand of hair was ever so slowly moving of its own accord.

"I can't believe that I'm doing this," he said.

"Doing what?"

"That I'm even giving the weight of a mosquito's ass to the argument for a god, a big Kahuna, much less thinking of myself as one."

"Uncle Robert would say . . . well, wait, let him tell you himself."

"How do we arrange that?" But he saw a shimmering of colors to Laura's right, like oil on water, and in one instant there was Uncle Robert.

"From one god to another, that was quite an understated entrance, don't you think?" Uncle Robert said, grinning under his beard. He was dressed as Bryan remembered him in life: bib overalls, dirty red Converse All-Stars sneakers that looked as if they dated back to the Big Bang, and a brown wool herringbone jacket. Becoming transcendental hadn't helped the old man's fashion sense.

"I've seen better CGI effects, even on TV," Bryan said.

"Yes, but this is better than 3D, don't you think? Sort of holographic. Puts you right where the action is."

"You're not going to metamorphose into some sort of monster right now, just to show off, are you, Uncle?" Laura asked.

Uncle Robert scratched his beard, as if considering. "I suppose I could, though my residual body image is pretty strong. By the way, I saw that movie too – *The Matrix*. That's where I learned the term, 'residual body image.'"

"So, you're saying this is a sort of construct? Like the one where Warren Fishburne trained Neo in after he was decanted?" Bryan said.

"Laurence," Laura said.

"What?"

"The actor's name is Laurence Fishburne, not Warren," she said.

"Whatever."

"Maybe in Uncle Robert's alternate reality he's named Warren," Bryan said, not quite believing he was taking part in a movie-trivia conversation under these circumstances. He laughed anyway.

Uncle Robert rolled his eyes.

"You expect me to take this seriously?" Bryan said.

"I'm getting there, to the point, I mean," Uncle Robert said. "Have patience with an old man." He paused, and Bryan realized he was waiting for some sort of acknowledgement. A nod did the trick.

"There's a bench over there," Laura said. "Let's go sit down."

What bench? Bryan started to say, but saw a kind of church pew-like bench a couple of feet away. He wondered if it had been there all along and he just hadn't noticed it, or if it had sprung into existence at Laura's suggestion. *Then again, what did it matter?*

He followed Laura and Uncle Robert over to the bench. The two sat down, leaving a space for him in between. He chose instead to lean on one of the hitching rails so he could see their faces. The two looked at each other, and an understanding passed between them. They both gave him patronizing smiles. *It was a bit maddening, this rapport they had.*

"Okay, where do I start?" Uncle Robert said.

"At the beginning?" Laura suggested.

"No, that won't do, as there is no beginning, no ending, at least as far as I understand. Which means there's no middle either, only an ongoing phenomenon. Am I making any sense?"

"No Big Bang, so no Big Chill?" Bryan asked.

"Something like that. But only in regards to consciousness," he said. "I can see by your expression that you're finding this hard to accept."

"Pretty much impossible. I was not just an agnostic. I was an atheist. No sitting on the fence for me, you know."

"Well, as I was an atheist in my previous life, I found this hard to accept, too," Uncle Robert said. "Oh, Sophia, you know, had shown me how to astral-project, but before this happened, before I was convinced of the death of my Earth-bound body, I still secretly entertained the conviction that it was more a journey to the inner dimensions of the human consciousness than an exploration of other realities."

"How do you know that's not still the case?"

"More to the point," Uncle Robert said, stroking his beard. "How do *you*, Bryan, know anything?"

"I don't," Bryan said, hoping they weren't about to delve in solipsism again.

"Well, suspend your disbelief just for awhile. Will you?"

"I'll try," he said, but honestly, he was afraid to.

"Super. Remember, I'm having trouble accepting this new existence, too, but I'm going to try to make the case that there can be a reality that includes a transcendental consciousness that doesn't involve a big alpha-monkey, tribal chiefdom god, like that total jerk of Abraham's. Will you bear with me?"

"Like I said, I'll try," Bryan said, relaxing a bit.

"First point," Uncle Robert said. "Consider the possibility that Earth – the consensus reality that you and I shared – was a kind of incubator of consciousness."

"Consensus?"

"All reality is a consensus. We agree upon what is real and what is an illusion – did I just quote someone?"

"Suzanne said a similar thing about this place."

"Her?" Uncle Robert pointed toward the immobile Suzanne. "I wouldn't give her too much credence."

"Why not?" Bryan was immediately angry, even though he doubted the authenticity of this Suzanne himself. His anger must have been obvious.

"Whoa, cool your jets, boy," Uncle Robert said. "I didn't mean to insult your lost love."

"She's not – wasn't – my lost love."

Laura rolled her eyes, but didn't say anything.

"Whatever. I spoke out of line. I'm sorry. Tell me what she told you. Please."

"Yeah, yeah," Bryan mumbled, but couldn't help to check to see if this Suzanne had moved or if her expression had changed. He was being an asshole, he knew, but he couldn't stop himself. He took a deep breath and let it out slowly, then continued: "Yes. The theory is that there's a god whose dreams stabilize things. Otherwise reality would be shifting, mutating constantly as one person after another tried to gain dominance. People would dream others out of existence, and so on."

"You mean, just anyone, like a woodcutter for example, could try to be the god of this realm?"

"Hah! Exactly. Maybe they'd do this without trying?"

"You're still not convinced you're actually here, are you?" Laura interjected.

"It's hard to ignore my senses. This is nothing like a dream. No tunnel vision, no sudden leaps of time and place . . ."

"That can be done, though," Uncle Robert said. "Leaping in time, I mean, not the tunneling of vision. But you know, now that I think of it, you could have tunnel vision if you wanted to. Thought is action on this plane, you . . ."

"You're getting off track, Uncle," Laura interjected.

"You're right. Where was I?"

"Earth was an incubator of consciousness."

"Yes. I don't know about you, but I think the tendency of all us here – you, me, my niece – is to think of our experience on Earth as Reality with a capital R, and of everything else as a kind of secondary reality or even an illusion.

"But the more time I spend on these planes, especially now that my Earthly body is dead, the more I come to think of the Earth experience as the illusion, and this, even though it's mutable by consciousness, as something more authentic."

Laura was nodding. "Me, too. I was just thinking of a famous quote by Einstein: 'Reality is merely an illusion, albeit a very persistent one.'"

"I'm not sure what that has to do with anything here," Uncle Robert said.

"Maybe not, but it's a really good quote," she said.

Bryan laughed, the sound echoing down the empty street. "I think I know what you're getting at," he said. Laura was beaming at him so he continued, though where he wasn't sure. "We live in our own little virtual constructs of reality all the time. We assume that the reality we experience is essentially the same as everyone else's, but for all we know it all could be some sort of personal delusion, maybe even a manufactured one ."

Laura, still beaming at him, said: "You know, Bryan, that was always the hottest thing about you – your intellectual paranoid brain."

He started to reply it wasn't the area between his ears she had seem so interested in, then he realized that there might a clue to her dumping him in her joke. After the angel had kidnapped him from the town square in Creedance, he had been nearly schizophrenic, and that's when Laura had been attracted to him again.

Uncle Robert was still talking, drawing him away from these speculations. ". . . you see, something happened about forty-thousand years ago. I'm talking Earth time, millennium before our last lives there in the early 21st century."

It made a kind of upside-down psychological sense. Her father had been schizophrenic; you always are attracted to what you know, and so on. But what did that say about his being obsessed about an undead goth redhead with a borderline personality disorder?

"Son, are you listening to me?"

"Oh, yeah, Uncle Robert. Sorry. Just kind of drifted off into a regressive conjecture."

"Well, you need to be careful of that here. Thought is . . ."

"Yes, yes, I get it already. Go on."

Uncle Robert cleared his throat. Not quite a *harrumph*, but close. "You know what I'm talking about when I say quantum theory of consciousness – yes?"

Uncle Robert looked at Laura. She shook her head. "Sort of . . . not really."

"It's something to do with quantum entanglement," Bryan said.

Where was this going?

"That's right," Uncle Robert said. "Let's see, where do I start?"

"Maybe you could explain to me how this isn't solipsism," Bryan said.

"That would be some trick for me to convince you that you, only this you here now, exist."

"What?"

"Just joking. Are we talking metaphysical, epistemological, or methodological solipsism?" Uncle Robert said.

When Bryan shook his head, Uncle Robert said, "Shit, I miss Wikipedia. But I'll try to explain. Methodological solipsism is the line of logic Decartes struggled with. It's also the skepticism that the Wachowski brothers – geniuses by the way – toyed with in *The Matrix*."

"Are we getting off the narrative track?" Laura said.

"No. Well, maybe we're on a side rail, but we'll still get there eventually," Uncle Robert said.

"Bear with him, and he'll probably prove we're all just fictional characters," Laura said.

Uncle Robert glared at her as if she had just made a bad smell, but went on. "Anyway, what Descartes asked as a kind of exercise, and the Wachowski brothers made movies about, is that there's no way of being sure of objective reality. We could all just be brains in vats, being fed false scripts via some evil demon, deluded into thinking we have *real* experiences.

"Epistemological solipsists are on the fence. You can only believe what your senses tell you, but it could be that there's an external world, or that only the Self exists, but it's impossible to say with any certainty which is true.

"Metaphysical solipsism says that the Self – your Self in this case – is the only existing reality. Like Renee said, '*I think therefore I am*,' and in fact, that all I think is all I can be sure of. All other realities, including the external world and other people, are representations of that Self and have no independent existence. Myself, I call this *metaphysical narcissism*. A lot of my fellow brains in vats might argue with this term, but fuck them."

"Hah," Laura said and tugged the old man's beard. "That's how I know this isn't just my dream when my dear uncle surprises me with asinine philosophical jokes. I couldn't dream this stuff up."

"What's all this got to do with quantum consciousness?" Byran asked.

"Now we're getting complex," Uncle Robert said. "I'm ill-equipped to explain this well. You need someone like Amit Goswami, but here goes."

"I think I've read part of one of his books, something about the universe being aware," Bryan said.

"Yes, he wasn't the first to make the connection between quantum mechanic theory and Hindi philosophy, but he was the first classically trained physicist to really build a coherent cosmology with – I think, he was the first, that is."

"I don't think anyone hereabouts is going to challenge you philo-

R. Douglas Burns

sophically," Laura said.

"Well, the archangels have a metaphysical mind bent, but they don't seem inclined to speak up right now," Uncle Robert said. "What about it, boys?" He looked toward the archangels. "Care to contribute?"

The back of Bryan's scalp tingled, but when he looked at the archangels, they were still immobile mannequins. As for Suzanne, her eyelids were now half-closed in the middle of a blink. They'd been wide open before – so was everything frozen or just moving in extremely slow motion? Would the angels eventually close the distance to him? He tried to will the mecha-mandala back into existence and failed. Had that been a one-time experience?

"Are you okay, young man?" Uncle Robert said. "You look a bit peaked."

"Yeah, yeah, go on."

"So. . ." Uncle Robert continued. "You understand the general theory, that quantum mechanics says that, among other things, that the whole universe is connected, that space, time, particles *communicate* with each other instantly across the vast expanses of time.

"That much is science. Goswami went further and said that consciousness, human consciousness, is based on that quantum wave-front collapse. Do you know what that is, either of you?"

When they didn't answer, he cleared his throat and went on: "You know that thought experiment called Schrödinger's cat, the cruel one with a randomly tripped poison gas vial. The thing is whether the cat in the box is neither alive and dead until someone opens the box. The cat's existence is a metaphor for a waveform. Once observed the cat's indeterminate state becomes determinate. That's called, I believe, a wave-front collapse."

"Poor cat," Laura said. "Who's to say the cat isn't the prime observer? Why does he, the physicist, opening the box get to decide what is real and what is an illusion?"

"The point is that neither is an illusion, that both are real. Or maybe Schrödinger didn't like cats. But that's quantum mechanics for you. There's no such thing as an objective observation. It's science telling us that there's another, deeper structure to reality than just Newtonian or Einsteinian matter and energy.

"Goswami said that to get around these seeming paradoxes of what the science was telling us, that we merely to have put aside the concept of objective reality being independent of consciousness. More to the point, he said our consciousness creates matter and is very similar to what mystics have called God with the capital G."

"You're saying we create this material universe by thinking of it?" Bryan said.

"Yes, though like all things metaphysical, it's not that simple, at least not on most planes of existence. There are local and subtle forms of consciousness. But Goswami did say that the human mind or consciousness isn't dependent upon a few pounds of gray matter between our ears. Rather, it's the other way around. That the brain is an organ formed by consciousness. It means we're all tapped into the God-consciousness." The old man stroked his beard again, looking a bit puzzled. "What was the question again, by the way?"

"There was more than one question," Bryan said, wishing he had his own beard to stroke. "How did we get here? Is this *here* real or not? Are you two real or not? If this is real, if I am somehow connected to this Dreaming God, why should it be me and not some other consciousness? As Laura said, why me instead of the cat or for that matter, Suzanne or those?" He gestured toward the angels.

"Maybe it's a matter of being chosen rather than choosing," Uncle Robert said.

At this moment the world woke up. Suzanne screamed, put her hands up to her face, and the archangels were close enough to lay their dinner-plate sized hands on him.

19.

Unravels the Universe

Minor/Samiazaz.

The creature who once had been Major Karl Minor and the angel Samiazaz landed in the Creedance town square with enough force to crack the concrete sidewalk.

He – despite being technically female, the creature who was once Major Minor had decided to think of itself as *he* for simplicity's sake – sniffed the air. His senses were greatly enhanced when compared to a human's, several orders of magnitude even more sensitive than a dog's.

Human smells filled the air. Rage and disgust washed over him.

The cooking and body odors were bad enough. But he was also aware of humans on a metaphysical level, a non-physical perception that registered as ugly waves disturbing a still, pristine pool.

In the center of the town square, a moldy bronze soldier sat on a horse with his saber upraised. He glared down at Minor. A memory surfaced slowly like a waterlogged corpse: the conversation with the young woman named Laura before he had killed her. *There's a family ancestor rendered in bronze on the town square.*

Emotions, alien ones, were associated with the vision, a combination of lust, paternal protectiveness, and something remote and incomprehensible, smothering and dark.

Had he really intended to murder her? Or had he merely acting upon Samiazaz's will?

Minor slowly levitated ten feet above the ground and slapped the statue's head. The bronze casting shattered at its neck. The head flew in a clean arc over the un-mown grass and bounced with a hollow gong on the pothole-ridden street.

Still suspended in front of the statue, Minor punched it in the chest, caving in a fist-size hole. Rancid black liquid gushed out of the hole. How could a statue bleed? Then he realized water had somehow been leaking into the hollow casting for years, perhaps decades, until flowing free now.

The souls of humans were likewise trapped in their artificial shells. His mandate was to set them free, too.

So many lives, in all directions. Minor descended, unsure of where to start.

"Why did you break the statue?" A small voice came from behind. Minor turned to find a tiny redheaded creature, perhaps seven or eight years old, dressed in a dirty white and blue pinafore. Her tennis shoes were dirty too, as was her face. Her knees were black with grime. To complete her ensemble, a redheaded Raggedy Ann doll, equally filthy, dangled from one hand.

Minor knelt in front of her.

"Are you a daddy angel or a mommy angel?" the ragamuffin said.

"Today I am a woman, but I'll never be a mommy. Never!" Minor said, almost choking on the word.

"I don't have a mommy anymore," the urchin said. "Not a live one." A thin line of snot ran from one nostril to her upper lip, and she licked it away.

"You don't sound like a *woe-man*," she continued. Her mouth twisted on the unfamiliar word – or maybe it was the taste of the snot.

The girl's scent, a mixture of dirt, ketchup, and fecal matter, was perfectly nauseating. Minor raised a steel-hard finger and pressed it against the bib of her pinafore. Through the dirty muslin and the boney sternum, he could feel the child's heartbeat, as fast as a bird's. He paused, relishing the moment, then said in a falsetto, "And why is that, dear?"

"You have boobies, but you also have that *thing*," she said and pointed between his legs.

Minor looked down and found a set of male genitals there. They were as bald as a porn star's, but much larger than his human ones had been.

"Oh!" the urchin said, but Minor didn't look up, for an erection was arising. Some remnant of his past persona was disgusted by this. But when he looked up to apologize to the child, he found her mouth gaped and her eyes little empty dark pools. The thin line of snot had been replaced by a trickle of blood. Her feet were several inches off the ground because

Minor's finger had skewered through her boney chest and into her heart. Her body now dangled from his finger as weightless as a deflated baloon.

He was relieved that the girl had probably died before seeing his erection. He stood up, and the little corpse slid off his finger with a sucking sound. She fell in a heap on the scrubby grass next to her Raggedy Ann doll. A pool of blood welled up through the hole in her chest and spread like a rose across the off-white of her pinafore. Minor leaned over and wiped his bloody finger on the front of the Raggedy Ann. Now the two matched. Two dirty, abandoned dolls. A sense of release washed over him, more intensely orgasmic than he had ever felt as a human.

Was he really a *he* now? Minor reached down to check between this body's legs. Nothing. Now there was only a mound, but no vulva, no penis, no scrotum – nothing. Everything had magically disappeared. Had it been a delusion? No, the little girl had noticed.

A memory trickled into his angel mind, shadowy, indistinct, as if piped into his brain through a long, dark tube. A little girl, his daughter, calmly burning the stomach of a slick, pink, naked Barbie with one of his smoldering cigars. *Stop that!* A shout. And the girl dropped both the doll and the cigarette on the carpet. Fear in her eyes and an accusation: *You did the same to mommy.*

Humans, bad monkeys who imagined themselves to be more than meme-infested meat. How glad he was to be no longer human!

"I have become death, the destroyer!" Minor shouted to the empty street. Somewhere a door slammed, an insult to his authority.

Enough that was human was left in the creature to momentarily doubt its right to destroy something it had not created, enough to feel revulsion at its own evil. Exorcizing the doubt from its mind, Minor soared above the street, leaving the bloody dolls behind. It had more purging to be done, and *he* would start with whoever slammed that fucking door!

Marguerite.

Her old bedroom was smaller than Marguerite remembered it. The door from the hallway was so narrow she could barely squeeze her wings through. Entering the adjoining bathroom was even more difficult. She had to duck her head and slither sideways through the door, and still her wings caught. Impatiently, she tore off a piece of the molding and punched out the underlying two-by-four framing. The rest of the doorframe sagged and the ceiling joists creaked alarmingly, but the remains of the wall held.

Inside the bathroom, her Zoloft was in the medicine cabinet, just where she had left it a past life ago.

The fact that she could remember such details proved the insanity that had nearly completely clouded her mind after her transformation was evaporating. Not only could she now remember specific details of her life as a human, those memories were more complete, more sharply enhanced with smells, sights, and sounds, than they had been when she was human. She could remember her childhood, moments in the crib, the smell and taste of her mother's milk. And John, the feelings of falling in and out of love with him were as powerful as when they had happened.

So what was she doing here with the Zoloft bottle in her hand? The answer came slowly as her mental facilities returned.

It had seemed such a grand bargain – not one made in heaven but promising salvation nonetheless. Azazel got oblivion, if not the complete erasure he craved. (She could sense his presence in the back of her mind, like a reptile hiding hibernating in cold mud.) In exchange, she was spared the inevitable decay of flesh and mind that all living beings face. To her, growing old had been a kind of horror movie in slow motion, a fate she had thought was the cause of her unbearable sadness. Now she was beyond all the weaknesses of flesh; she didn't even need to eat. The cravings had disappeared. She was beautiful, almost frighteningly so, and she feared almost nothing. But the horrible feeling of emptiness and spiritual malaise that had tortured her before her metamorphosis had returned.

She emptied the bottle into her palm. At least twenty yellowish tablets, each stamped with the numeral one-hundred, nestled there. Her toothbrush glass was on the rim of the sink. She dumped out the brush – along with a large squirming water bug – into the basin, filled the glass with water, put all the tablets in her mouth, and washed them down.

Now what? She went in the bedroom and sat on the bed. The window to the backyard had been broken out – no, broken inward, for glass shards and a mixture of leaves spread over the floor. The glass crackled under her bare feet but could not cut them. As she waited to find out if the pills would have any effect, she absentmindedly brushed leaves and glass off her old bed. Strewn across the bed was a pair of pantyhose and an orange waitress uniform with a plastic name tag safety-pinned to the lapel: *Hi! I'm Laura*. Blood splattered the uniform, which confused Marguerite for a moment. The blood stains were old and brownish. *Wasn't it only yesterday that she had transported the mortally wounded Laura to the saucer?*

Yes, she was sure of that. The uniform must testify to some earlier drama, one that involved pain and blood, and by association with the house, her undead husband. She knew that Laura and John had been drawn together in some sort of karmic linkage, but for some reason the thought of him bringing her here felt like a betrayal, and she couldn't stand to be in the house anymore.

She left by the front door and ascended slowly over the giant oak tree in the yard, letting her toes just barely brush the leaves of the top branches.

She had meant to visit town, but once she was in the air, the smell of human blood was strong in her nostrils and drew her toward Lost Lake and the military encampment. She landed near the big helicopter to find May squatting over human body parts. May looked at her with that vacant gaze she'd had since her transformation. Dark blood covered her arms and breasts.

Oh, May, what have you done?

Her crazed friend was sorting the parts out into separate heaps, trying to match arms, legs and heads to torsos. Two torsos, one with legs still attached and one without, lay at her feet.

"I didn't do it, but I'm going to make it right," May said, which was a surprise in itself, because May hadn't said much of anything since a few minutes after being reassembled, and when she had, she had rarely formed complete sentences.

May studied the shoulder joint of an arm, turning it one way, then the other, to see which torso it might fit. She reached a decision after a moment and placed the arm with the legless torso, then changed her mind and moved it to the torso with legs.

"May, what are you doing?" Marguerite asked, not expecting an answer.

"I'll get blamed for this," May said. "Help me fix it." Another complete sentence. Two, actually. She used a bloody hand to sweep away an errant strand of blonde hair and left a red streak across her forehead.

"There's no fixing this, May."

"They're all dead," she said, pointing toward the large bivouac tent.

"All the soldiers?"

May nodded, looking abashed.

"I don't think you can reassemble them like I did you."

"Why not?" May said.

A question, even! This was indeed a new May. Addled maybe, perhaps not entirely rational, but conversant. Marguerite felt her depression lifting. She had been lonely without May to talk to. Mabye her friend's mind had returned. Then May looked up at the sky, and her eyes glazed over. She let out a screech and launched upward without even a goodbye, leaving Marguerite alone with the scattered body parts.

In her human life, Marguerite had been a volunteer at the Creedance Care Center. Patients in the early stages of Alzheimer's had been like May – lucid for a moment, rational, but falling into dementia the next. There was probably no hope she would ever get better, only worse.

Had May killed the soldiers? Marguerite didn't think so. Not that May as an angel hadn't killed other things. That recent killing of a cow, for instance, came to mind. But killing meat animals was one thing, murdering humans another.

She and the other angel/human hybrids didn't kill and eat humans, did they?

But if May had descended into deeper madness, who knew what she might do?

Deciding to walk instead of fly, May set off through the woods toward the big tent. Within fifty yards of the camp, she could smell more blood and knew what she'd find there. She didn't want to see, but perhaps she would find a clue as to the perpetrator. She desperately wanted to believe that it wasn't May.

Within minutes she was at the tent and not surprised at what she found. The sulphuric odor of guns having been fired was strong. The soldiers had put up a fierce gunfight, though apparently a losing one. A couple of bodies had been torn limb from limb, but most were intact. Their killer must have been in a murderous rage. Heads were turned backwards on bodies, faces shattered, chests torn open. Weapons were scattered about, some with barrels bent double. The firefight must have been intense. Dust sparkled in beams of light from bullet holes sprayed through the roof and walls of the tent.

Marguerite's restored mind brought her a childhood memory of her mother telling her the dust motes in sunbeams were tiny guardian angels; the dust motes in moonlight, however, were little devils.

Marguerite had grown up in a sin-and-redemption household. Most of her adult life had been an effort to reconcile the popular image of a loving God with the fear, hate, and prejudice she grew up with. These were the real demons of normal human life: the nightmares of guilt and fear bequeathed upon children by deluded parents.

She tried to dismiss the memory, but in a brief epiphany, she realized the recollection had surfaced because of her maternal feelings toward May. May was her ersatz damaged child.

What nightmare of existence had she visited upon her by reanimating her?

But with the certainty of a mother, Marguerite knew May was damaged but not homicidal.

May had been obsessed with men, many men, and Marguerite knew that her bedroom activity had been more about winning approval from men than sex. Some of that compulsion had carried over to May the angel, so her main danger to men was as a succubus. She might accidentally fuck them to death, but she would never tear them apart in rage.

There was movement among a pile of bodies. The body on top was obviously dead because its head was bent backwards until the top rested on the spine. She lifted body and set it atop a nearby trestle table, and turned its head until it faced up. As an afterthought, she straightened the uniform and wiped grime off the face. When she turned back to the body pile, she found a young soldier, watching her with eyes clouded with blood.

Alive.

She knelt by him. He had a resigned, peaceful look.

It's over; I might as well relax.

She laid a hand on his cheek. He couldn't be more than twenty-something. "Who did this to you?" she asked.

"You, you," he replied.

"No, no, it wasn't me," she said.

"You angels. It was him, then it was her." He tried to shake his head, but the bones in his neck crackled, and he grimaced in pain. "Thirsty."

"I'll get you some water."

"No, don't leave me," he said and laid a hand on the bare skin of her inner thigh. "Finish me. I'm done anyway."

"Maybe not."

As if to prove her wrong, he coughed up a mouthful of blood. She held both his cheeks in her hands and gently turned his head to let the blood drain out of his mouth.

"Who?" she repeated kindly, she hoped. "Tell me, and I'll give you what you want."

"A kiss," the soldier said, his hand snaking up her thigh.

Amazing! Dying, broken inside, he lusted for her.

"Okay, a kiss before dying it is."

He whispered, but so low she could barely hear, even with her enhanced hearing. She leaned closer, and he reached up, put a hand on the back of her neck and tried to draw her face to his. She could have easily pulled his arm out the socket, but she let him draw her face close.

"The major," he said in a monotone. "Horrible bitch, not a man anymore, but it was the major. Bullets wouldn't stop him. Nothing would stop him."

His eyes told her he was telling the truth, and she realized Samiazaz had at last found a host.

She leaned over and kissed his bloody lips. He sighed – a long drawn-out sigh, almost orgasmic.

"Now kill me," he said.

"That wasn't our agreement."

"Yes, it was."

"No. It wasn't. You'll have to die on your own." She almost added 'sweetheart,' as if she were instructing a mischievous child. *You have to eat your vegetables. You have to be a big boy and die on your own.*

Without taking his eyes off hers, he pulled up his blood-soused shirt. A shattered rib poked through his chest. A thick stream of blood streamed from the wound, snaking down his side and around the small of his back. His eyes were full of tears.

"It hurts like a son-of-a-bitch. Stop it. Stop the pain. I'm dying anyway. Do that for me. I want to stare into something beautiful as I pass. Please."

She studied him. He didn't look nobly stoic. His nose had been broken long ago, a crude jailhouse tattoo of a tear labeled one cheekbone, and he reeked of alcohol and corrupt flesh.

Maybe dying would purify him.

Without further speculation, she grabbed the top of his head as if it were large jar lid and turned it halfway around. This took more strength than movies depicted, but as an angel she was much stronger than ordinary humans. Bone gritted on bone. He had time for a single quick gasp but that was all. When she turned his head back around his eyes were empty, staring at the sky.

Bryan.

One moment he was in that little western town, the archangels were reaching for him, Suzanne was screaming . . . and then he was standing in another street, in another little town. He was disoriented but only for a moment. He was in the Creedance town square, in the little grassy park-like area where the Jacobsen war hero statue stood.

The bronze statue had been beheaded, and a hole had been punched in its chest.

Compared to the hundred-foot wide streets of the frontier town on the Red Sky planet, the main street of Creedance looked like a cowpath. Already the experience with the archangels, the manfestation of the mecha-mandala, the pseudo Suzanne, and the conversation with the spirit bodies of Uncle Robert and Laura, seemed as insubstantial as a dream.

How had he come back here to Creedance? Had days elapsed? Had he been wandering around in a trance since wrecking his pickup truck? He did an personal inventory and found he was still wearing the dorky coveralls from the Red Sky planet. So at least that much hadn't been a dream.

Not knowing what else to do, he checked out the vandalized statue. What appeared at first to be a bundle of rags lay at the base of the statue, near the fallen bronze head. He prodded the bundle with the toe of his boot and choked off a cry as it rolled over. It wasn't a bundle of rags at all, but the body of a child in a shabby, sad, little calico dress. The child was obviously dead. She lay on her back, her eyes staring blankly at the sky, a surprised expression on her face. Blood had crusted around a hole in her chest. The wound went all the way through her tiny body, and he could see the blood-smeared grass underneath.

He touched one of her small hands. The spring air was cool, but her skin was still warm. She hadn't been dead long.

Alarmed now, he searched for the murderer. He didn't have to look far. A scream came from across the street at Boucher's Cafe. Through the café's large plate glass front window, he could see running figures. A body thumped against the inside of the window. The plate glass jiggled but did not break. A gunshot sounded from inside. The door slammed open and several Creedance residents burst out into the street and scattered off in different directions like cockroaches. Another body hit the window, shattering it this time. Large shards of glass – and an obviously dead body – fell on the sidewalk. Bryan recognized the dead man as Salman, the owner of the cafe, his head flattened grotesquely on one side. Salman clutched a aluminum baseball bat to his chest in a deadman's grip.

An angel stepped through the shattered opening, and Bryan almost choked on his fear. He had been threatened by archangels and kidnapped by human/angel hybrids, and both had been terrifying. but in the impersonal way a wild animal, a runaway machine or a force of nature. This creature was purposefully malevolent. It stomped out in the street, caught a fleeing woman by her arm, and threw her against the building's brick wall next to the window. She hit the bricks with a meaty slap and fell on her face onto the sidewalk.

People were running down the street in both directions, and the angel vacillated. Bryan gasped. He recognized the angel's face now. Major Karl Minor had been transformed not as the other hybrids had been – bigger, perfect versions of themselves – but changed in gender too, for the major now had breasts. A hairless something nestled between his legs. Bryan couldn't be sure from this distance, but it looked like a penis. But the most unsettling thing about the creature was the pure murderous hatred that clouded its face. Bryan wanted to crawl into his own boots to hide, but he was paralyzed. If he ran or moved in any manner, he would draw the creature's attention. His own heart beat insanely in his ears, so loud the angel must be able to hear it across the street. All he could do was stand perfectly still, hoping the angel would go away.

Smoke began rolling out of the broken window, and the smell of burnt meat filled the air. Byran hoped it was hamburgers on the grill and not human meat he smelled.

The angel appeared to make a decision and turned toward the peo-

R. Douglas Burns

ple fleeing eastward. Then it apparently changed its mind and looked at those fleeing westward. Major Minor – it, he, she, whatever – spread out its wings and looked ready to launch after them, then stopped and turned slowly to look directly at Bryan. It smiled, and an unspoken understanding passed between them. Bryan realized the angel had been aware of his presence from the moment it had stepped through the window, but had affected indecision to give him false hope. The thing was not just murderous, but sadistic.

A young woman stumbled out the smoke-filled door. Blinded by the smoke, she hadn't seen the angel at first, and now it was too late. The major grabbed her around the waist and pulled her close. She didn't scream or fight in any way. Instead she went limp, paralyzed with terror. As she slipped down in Major Minor's grip, her skirt to hiked up to show pink panties. The angel noticed the frilly panties, and keeping its eyes on Bryan, reached down to stroke between her legs.

The major laughed a shrill, gurgling laugh of dominance.

I can do anything I want to her or to you, the laugh said.

Bryan tried to will himself back to the Red Sky planet – he preferred being killed by the archangels instead of by this monstrosity – but nothing happened. He was still standing in the shadow of a beheaded courthouse statue, with a tiny, tragic corpse at his feet, facing a psychopathic superbeing who would most likely soon tear him limb from limb.

20.

And Unfolds a Revelation

Marguerite.

Guilt-stricken, Marguerite stumbled out of the bivouac tent and into the littered forest. She had abandoned part of her soul when she had snapped the dying soldier's neck. She couldn't name what she lost, but it was connected to the last remnants of her humanity.

How far she had come in little over a year! Compared to her spiritual change, her physical metamorphosis was trivial. Less than a year ago, good and evil were like black and white, simple concepts of God and Satan. Now everything, every thought and action was measured in shades of gray.

As a Calvinist, she had been taught that God had already decided who was to be saved and who was not, and neither she nor anyone else could do anything to change that. Some were filled with the Holy Spirit at birth. Others were not. Moreover, and more relevant, no matter how sinful a saved believer became, she would still not go to Hell. Once saved, always saved: true cradle-to-grave-and-beyond security.

A memory came from month ago: She had made a last-gasp effort to recover her faith by giving testimony. She had accosted Uncle Robert in the clinic parking lot, brochures in hand, determined to save his immortal soul. But what she had really been trying to do was save herself. Her heart had been empty, dead, and the church's teachings offered no respite. Her depression actually had gnawed at her heart.

The episode with Uncle Robert had reminded her of predestination. Everything clicked. She had not known it, while standing on the hot asphalt among the abandoned cars, trying to force religious brochures on Uncle Robert, but she had been fated even then to meet and merge with Azazel.

And there was that moment of choice later as she listened to Azazels' offer. She was once-saved, forever saved, so she could escape the unbearable sterility of her life by accepting Azazel's offer and still avoid God's wrath, even if she did evil things as an angel – right?

But shouldn't there be limits to what she could do and remained saved? Hadn't she just crossed some line in the willful act of killing the dying soldier?

She had another revelation. Azazel and she were two beings in the same body. Was her will still her own? Had it *ever* been her own since Azazel planted his homunculus in her? Had she just imagined she had free will?

Also as a Calvinist, she had been taught to believe in demons and demonic possession. By the faith, the demon was the enemy within, but it was on a kind of time-share basis. The demons had billions of souls to corrupt, and their numbers were limited. In fact, that was exactly the term preachers had used: time-sharing.

But if Azazel had been a demon, he was a demon who was with her always, no time-sharing, but a full-time resident with whom she shared skin and bone, blood and brain, gristle and nerves. She knew this as a certainty. Felt it in every fiber of her angel being.

And the truth was, despite his admitting to being a fallen angel, Azazel could never be a demon to her. He had been too beautiful to be truly evil. More, he exuded love and peace – not the lust, greed, and hatred she had been taught were the hallmarks of Satan. And then there was his description of the entity he and his fellows had revolted against. She thought that the archangels seemed to be revolting against a powerful being who had more in common with Satan than with God, and were not in league with him.

Had she been wrong? She tried to focus on that moment when she stared into the face of the broken soldier and had chosen to give him what he wanted, a quick exit. Had that been her or Azazel who made the choice of life or death for another? Had she taken pleasure from it? Had the Azazel part of her relished killing, even though it was a mercy killing?

Had she?

She believed – felt – the answers to all these self-doubts was: No. Snapping the soldier's neck had felt like the decent thing to do. She had ended his pain when it was obvious he was soon to die anyway. But it had gone against all the religious training she had received as a human.

She had granted him a gift. Or had that been the Azazel part of her rationalizing? How could she ever know who was actually in charge, and whether she was doing right or wrong? Such choices had been so simple when spelled out in black and white. Now each choice required examination, a balancing act, a weighing of possibilities. This was the true loss of innocence: the realization that nothing was simple.

And there was Major Minor/Samiazaz. Had the major, a sick soul by any definition, become a serial killer? Or was it Samiazaz's influence? Azazel would know if Samiazaz was predisposed such evil, but he was silent within her.

On impulse, she willed herself into the sky, up, up, through the towering pines, and toward Creedance. She would confront the major/Samiazaz creature. If she could divine its nature, learn what part of the human and what part of the angel were in control, maybe she could understand her own nature.

Bryan.

The angel who had once been Major Karl Minor crossed the street arm-in-arm with his sobbing hostage as if he were escorting her to the prom. Bryan fought the urge to run. He was resigned to his fate, which apparently was to be a gruesome death at the hands of the major. From what Uncle Robert and Laura told him, after he died here, he would simply translate to another level of existence. Not heaven or hell, just another astral plane.

So it wasn't fear that made him want to run, but outright disgust. All the archangel/human hybrids he had met before had been beautiful – though often crazed – but were deveopmentally as innocent as children at times and looked like works of art. They exuded an aura of unworldliness, of being above the flesh.

But this creature moving toward him emanated evilness that registered on some level so putrid as to make Bryan want to vomit.

The poor woman in Minor's clutches must have also felt the diseased nature of his soul. She doubled up and dry-heaved as Major Minor stepped over the curb and into the small grassy area around the beheaded Jacobsen statue.

Though she dressed like a teenager, as the two drew closer, Bryan could see the major's hostage was in her late twenties or early thirties. She was panting, her mouth open, and she had the black stubby teeth of a meth head. She was terrified, but she was also obviously strung out. He wondered where meth cooks found the ingredients to make their poison these days. Even aspirin was hard to find two months after the Fall.

"Look what I brought you," the major said.

The major's breasts were as large and hard as a silicon-enhanced stripper's. His facial features were now more feminine. The heavy brow ridge was gone, and the jaw line was sharper. He didn't have an Adam's apple. But the maleness between the creature's legs belied the feminine upper body. Before the Fall, Bryan had seen online pictures of transexuals in various stages of their reassignments. But the creature who stood before Bryan now did not resemble any of those photos. It was a parody of any kind of human sexuality.

Bryan doubted that the new Army would condone sex changes or breast implants, so obviously these physical changes must have happened with the metamorphosis. Maybe the changes signaled something about the major's sexual identity issues as a human. And which archangel had the major merged with? With all but the hundred archangels already merged with Creedance citizens, which one had it been? Then it struck him: The fool had recovered the concrete sepulcher from Lost Lake and freed the archangel Samiazaz and merged with it. A big mistake.

"You look surprised to see me," the major said.

"What happened to you?" Bryan stammered.

"I upgraded," the angel said and let go of his female hostage. She sank to her knees, began sobbing, and started to crawl away. The major grinned manically, but *his* eyes remained dead, like a blue-eyed shark. He put a dirty bare foot on the small of her back. "Stay put. And if you don't stop crying, I'll stomp you into the earth."

She looked up at him. For a moment, she seemed defiant. Was she aware of how close she was to being murdered? Bryan looked at her and shook his head. Whether she heeded his silent counsel or some had some residual common sense, he didn't know, but she put her hands over her eyes and curled into a fetal position.

"Upgraded, you say? Bullshit," Bryan said. "When you were human, I don't think you killed the young and helpless."

Major Minor reddened under the marble-like skin and grew in breadth and height to tower over Bryan. "This thing, this drug whore –" It nodded at the woman. "– is hardly young or helpless. She's an abomination."

"She's only human. She's made mistakes, big ones. Like we all have."

Like you have, major.

Other than a few more moments of life, he had nothing to lose by confronting the creature. Maybe he had a slim chance to save the woman, though he wasn't sure why he cared. As a meth addict, she was already the walking dead.

The major watched, grinning broadly, his eyes manic, while Bryan mulled over his next action.

Beyond the physical ambiguity, a sense of extreme maleness encased the creature who had been the major. Back when Bryan had been enrolled in the university – several lifetimes ago – weightlifters in the school gym had *juiced* – used anabolic steroids to enhance their muscle growth. As a result, they had suffered episodes of rage, paranoia, and manic delusions.

"You disgust me. You're all sewage slime, monkey-shits of the Earth. I see it now!" The major's voice deepened and became more masculine, a sermon from an angry pulpit.

"You've murdered people, not monkeys," Bryan said.

"It was a cleansing," the major said. "There's something different about you."

"I am who I am," Bryan said without thinking.

Silence fell, broken only by the woman's attempts to stifle her sobs. Shouts in the distance were too faint to intrude in a space defined by the small grassy town square.

"And this child?" Bryan nodded toward the small corpse. "Was that a cleansing too?'

"An accident. No, a reflex, but not a loss. Look at the thing. See how trivial and distorted it is."

"I see only a child. Someone's daughter. She could have been yours," Bryan said, remembering a wedding band on the major's hand when he had been human.

The Major-thing looked down at the body. When he looked back up, it was eye-to-eye with Bryan again.

A voice from behind and to Bryan's right said, "That was a smooth move. A leap of faith in the basics of human commonality, I'm guessing."

Not wanting to take his eyes off the major long, Bryan turned his head slightly. He wasn't surprised to see both Uncle Robert and Laura standing there, looking solid and real.

"*The major can't see or hear us,*" Laura said. "*You know what that means.*"

Yes, that I'm completely bat-shit crazy.

Bryan didn't say this aloud, but Laura, answered him anyway.

"*Well, yes, that goes without saying, but we really are here.*"

"*You know, he could be right,*" Uncle Robert said. "*We could be archetypical projections. I just realized this. I'm the Archetypical Wise Old Man.*"

"*Word! What does that make me? Wisdom?*" Laura said.

"*Shhh! Beatrice, you're not. Wise, maybe, as in wise-ass,*" Uncle Robert said.

"Jokes," Bryan said. "Don't you two realize how serious this is?"

"What? What are you talking about?" Major Minor said. Bryan had spoken aloud to the visitations.

"Nothing. Just thinking aloud." But the major was looking around. Was he squinting at the place where Laura was standing? She should be invisible to him, as this she probably just some dissociative delusion on his own part.

"*Dissociation. That's the ticket,*" Uncle Robert said. "*Stop thinking of him as an evil angel, but as a mentally ill human with superhuman powers who is projecting the repressed, unconscious aspects of his personality on others – those parts of himself that he hates.*"

"*Spiritually sick,*" Laura said.

"*That too,*" Uncle Robert agreed.

"*You should probably play up the conflict the major is having. What did he fear most as a human? What does he fear the most now?*" Laura said.

"*That's the key to this behavior. He's projecting his fear, his hatred of his own shadow, upon the world at large,*" Uncle Robert said.

"*Are you still subscribing to that bogus Jungian stuff?*" she said.

Bryan tried to ignore them. If his hallucinations were going to argue, he'd have to play this conflict out by logic and reason. But the fear angle seemed as good as any. He wondered how someone as macho as the human major had been could now deal with having female characteristics.

"You didn't have breasts last time I saw you, Major," Bryan said. "Was that a choice you made?"

"I'll ask the questions here," the major said. "Tell me what happened to that slut you were with, that Laura, or I'll kill this one." He grabbed the young woman by the hair and pulled her to her feet. The woman had stopped crying, but mascara streaked down her face. Her eyes were blank. She had given up hope, maybe so even before becoming the major's hostage.

"She moved on. You killed her, but she moved onto another plane where you can't reach her."

"Bullshit," the major said, grabbing the woman's neck. "You're toying with this one's life." The woman made a gurgling sound, and her complexion blanched. The major was slowly strangling her. Bryan felt impotent. He was standing within arm's reach of tragedy and was powerless to stop it. More than anything right now, more than anything he had ever wanted before in his life, Bryan wanted a weapon that would kill the monstrosity standing before him.

A crunching sound came from above, and Bryan the major looked up. There, perched upon the shoulders of the headless horseman, was Marguerite. She had broken off the statue's hand holding the bronze saber.

In a blur she was on the ground, saber held high, truly the image of a vengeful angel. Without preamble, she swung the saber and severed the major's arm at the elbow. The woman collapsed, but the hand of the severed arm still clutched her neck.

21.

Of the way to the Threshold

"You are doing it all wrong! You can't be sure if all things are made of atoms—it's an assumption. Suppose all things, including atoms, are made of consciousness, instead." -- Amit Goswami, Ph.D, "The Self-Aware Universe"

Bryan.

Marguerite's saber had shattered as it severed the Major's arm, but it had done the job. The major stared blankly at his arm, which now ended just below the elbow. No blood flowed from the stump. It wasn't even red; it ended in a smooth, undifferentiated flat ovoid, like a geometry textbook illustration.

Marguerite stepped back, looking uncertain. Bryan stood his ground, braced for the major to shatter his skull with one swipe of his good arm. Instead, the major picked up his severed arm by its wrist. But the dismembered hand stubbornly kept its grip on the young woman's throat, so tightly her face was turning blue. The major tried to retrieve his arm with his other hand, but it stubbornly held on.

"Let the fuck go!" the major ordered to the hand.

As if listening, the hand did as ordered. The woman fell to the ground, gasping.

The major cocked his head to one side as he examined his severed limb. Marguerite took advantage of the moment of confusion and punched him in the head. Angel striking angel made a sound like an elephant belly-flopping on concrete. The major took a short step back, hardly even a stagger, then enlarged and morphed. The breasts changed, becoming flattened and slab-like. His marble-like skin turned florid red. His jaw became boxy square, his cheekbones bulged and his brow ridges exaggerated until they shadowe his piggy blue eyes.

Bryan stepped back, worried for Marguerite but feeling powerless. He could help the pitiful meth girl, though. He grabbed her by her ankle and began dragging her away from the battle, past the poor little murdered Pippi Longstockings. Meth girl remained curled up, her arms wrapped around her head as he dragged her over the grass.

The major made a sound that changed from a snort to a growl, and swung his severed arm at Marguerite like a club. She brought up a wing and an arm to block the blow, but the major was now nearly eight feet tall and as massive as a tank. The arm struck with herculean force. She was apparently made of frailer angel stuff than the major, and her wing and arm snapped with a crunch. She staggered to one side, toppling over and landing on Bryan. The impact knocked the wind out of him, and he lost his grip on the meth girl's ankle.

Though severely injured, Marguerite was instantly back on her feet as if launched from a trampoline. Meanwhile, the major fitted his severed arm back onto its stump, twisting it to and fro as if trying to screw it on. His efforts seemed futile, but at once the arm, which had been corpse gray, reddened, matching its owner's new livid color, leaving no seam to show it had ever been severed.

The major gave another arrogant, animalistic chortle, and advanced on Marguerite. She stood her ground, her shoulders hunched, her wings bunched up behind her. She had picked up a stone and held it to her side. The tendons in her arms and shoulders strained beneath the white flesh.

Still stunned, Bryan rolled over on his hands and knees, grabbed the meth girl's ankle, and resumed trying to drag her to safety. She kept her hands clasped over her face but sneaked a glimpse with teacup-size pupils between spread fingers.

The major moved toward Marguerite like a boxer, grinning insanely. Marguerite let out a screech that rattled Bryan's ears and attacked first, swinging the stone at the major's head in a wide arc.

The major blocked the punch karate-style, and Marguerite's wrist snapped. Her hand flopped backwards until the backs of her fingers touched her forearm. Bryan grimaced in empathy, but Marguerite showed no sign of pain. She swung at the major with her other hand, but he deflected it as well, breaking it at the wrist too, then advanced to grab her throat. Marguerite's wrists flopped back and forth like wet dishrags as she tried to defend herself. Then the broken wrists straightened and healed in mid-shake, and she brought up both hands to gouge at the major's eyeballs.

But it was no use. Marguerite may have been super-strong compared to a human being, but the major was stronger – and more vicious. He let go of her throat and thrust both hands up between her arms and sprung them outward, another karate move. In a flash, he brought both fists down on her head. Marguerite bounced off the park statue's pedestal and fell like a rock, the top of her skull flattened. The Major put a bare foot between her breasts, grabbed her head with both hands and pulled it off with a pop. As with his arm, no blood flowed from the stump. Her head came off as if she were a life-size Barbie doll.

The major let out a war whoop that was a mixture of triumph and the howl of a rapid animal, and pitched the head into a pile of leaves near the statue.

The battle had lasted but a few seconds, giving Bryan only enough time to move back a couple of steps. Dragging meth girl away had proven nearly impossible because she was either too terrified or too strung out to help herself. But in any case he would not have been able to get far enough away to be safe. Now the monster that had been Major Minor turned to him, grinning.

"She can't help you any more," the major said, nodding at Marguerite's headless body. "Who knows why she tried in the first place."

"Maybe because she retained some vestige of her humanity," Bryan said.

The major casually backhanded Bryan, knocked him to the ground next to meth girl, whose bony ankle he still gripped.

The major loomed over him. His complexion, even redder than before, clashing with the cloudless blue sky. "You tried this ploy of appealing to my humanity before," he said. "It didn't work then, and it won't work now. There's nothing left of my humanity. It's been burned to ashes and reborn into this." He pounded on his chest between the unlikely looking breasts.

The world spun behind the major, an effect Bryan first attributed to dizziness from the blow, and he waited for the spinning to stop or for the major to finish him off. But the spinning didn't stop and the major's drawn-back arm froze in mid-pose.

Awakening of an Alien God

Bryan knew what was coming. The huge rotating wheel was first only a wisp of the mecha-mandala he had seen on the Red Sky world. Now as then, its substance thickened, and it coalesced into something more substantial, all but blocking out the blue sky, stretching from behind the two-story buildings of Creedence on one side and loblolly pine forests on the other. The wheels within wheels turned slowly as before. The Cyrillic-looking runes were also identical.

He asked himself the same question he had at its first appearance: Was the mecha-mandala merely a pattern of stimulation on the neurons of his visual cortex or a physical manifestation? If it was a physical reality, was it actually hundreds of miles in diameter?

He had never quite accepted the Red Sky plane to be as real as this Earthly plane his home reality. Now he was back in Creedance, not far from his grandfather's farmhouse where he had lived for more than a year.

Without thinking, he let go of the meth girl's ankle and reached tentatively upwards, finger outstretched, toward the mecha-mandala. The major remained frozen. The meth girl's raised foot stayed where Bryan had let it go.

The mecha-mandala now overlay everything – the buildings, the park, the grass, Major Minor, meth girl, even the body of the slain child.

Bryan focused on Major Minor. A specific part of the mecha-mandala seemed dedicated to the major, a small series of scripted cams rotated around an unseen center. The motion of the cams had a unique sequence, Bryan realized, but it was long and complex. What he needed to understand was at the center, the pivot about which all the parts that were the major. The pivot point represented the major's inner essence, a kind of keystone of his personality.

Bryan's outstretched arm pointed toward this network of encrypted cams. The mecha-mandala appeared to be the roof of the world. His arm stretched impossibly far to reach it, just as the archangels defeated ordinary time and space. At his touch, the cam-complex unfolded like an incredibly intricate Chinese puzzle cube. And it unfolded not just in three dimensions but four, five, six – too many for his mind to take in. But he didn't need to completely fathom all the multifaceted layers. He could see there – yes, there – at the precise center of the complex was the key to what made the entity known as Major Karl Minor into the sick creature he was. It was a tiny construct that was at once gooey and slimy, something broken, something vulnerable.

Bryan had a choice. A flick of his finger at one precise point and Major Minor would cease to exist on this astral plane, not as an angel, not as a human or anything else. He would be translated to another plane, probably not a very pleasant one, considering how sick his soul was. That was the fate of the archangels on the Red Sky world. He hadn't obliterated them completely – that was impossible because of the universal law of conservation of consciousness, which was just as universal as the law of conservation of mass and energy. He had just re-tuned them so they couldn't exist on the Red Sky planet plane any longer. His manipulation of the mecha-mandala had been intuitive at that time – and it still largely was. He had no quick-start guide. He was guieded only by a mystical sense of tapping into knowledge outside himself and beyond rational understanding.

But it wasn't a god or gods speaking to him; he was not that delusional. Rather, it was as if the force that resisted the chaos of mindless cruelty was acting through him. He couldn't call that god – though maybe some people would. To him, the force felt impersonal, beyond good and evil, but he knew that the outcome would be favorable in some way.

Without further thought, Bryan poked the slimy, hard thing at the major's mecha-mandala core and was flooded by feelings of abandonment, self-loathing, and pure, red-hot rage. Disgusted, he pinched hard on the thing to pull it out. It resisted. The rotten bit was really lodged there hard, like a barbed hook. The complex of cams and gears of the mecha-mandala ground against it, trying but failing to turn in their habitual manner. But Bryan's persistence won. With a high-pitched squeak the fetid thing came dislodged and squirmed in his grasp. Not wanting to touch it any longer than he had to, Bryan tossed it away, where it landed on a fast-moving section of the mecha-mandala and spun out of sight. He immediately regretted discarding the thing, for it might infect someone else, but he had felt defiled just touching it for a split second, and expelling it back into the mecha-mandala had been reflexive. Besides, what else was he to do with it? Eat it?

The major showed no immediate visual effect, but Bryan felt some critical change. The major, the town, everything but the mecha-mandala, was still frozen. Again without knowing how he did it, Bryan released the time freeze. The mecha-mandala faded, receding from this reality but not disappearing completely. The major's arm, which had been drawn back for a death punch, now sped forward toward its target: Bryan's face.

Bryan didn't have time to flinch – and didn't need to. The major deflated in mid-punch – literally. He instantly shrank in size by at least a third, and the punch fell short. Teetered, his wings fluttering, he fell to his knees. His breasts disappeared. His face's lividity faded to the pearlescent tones shared by most human-angel hybrids and the archangels. The exaggerated jaws and cheeks warped back to something of normal human proportions. As Bryan watched, his features became those of a man in his prime. Before his features had become distorted by too much booze and self-loathing, the major had been evidently been a handsome man. Now he was no longer an ogre angel on super steroids but just another human/angel hybrid.

Bryan got to his feet as the meth girl scrambled away toward the street. "Anywhere but here," she mumbled.

Bryan didn't interfere with her escape and checked to see if the major was going to go after her.

He found the major crouched with his knees up to his chest and his head down and face hidden. He was sobbing like a small boy.

So, now what? The major was emasculated, even though he was less sexually ambivalent now than he had been before the manipulation of the mecha-mandala. With the malevolent major, Bryan hadn't had to think about long-term strategies. His goal had been merely to survive. Now what? He was back in the same kind of limbo he'd been in on the Red Sky world.

He needed to talk to Uncle Robert and Laura, but they were gone – if they had ever really been there in the first place. Again, he wondered if this was a delusion, a complex and vivid hallucination. If it *was* just some sort of alternate reality or a dream all his own, the other characters – including those he thought he knew well – were merely stage dressing. Could something so detailed and sustained be either a dream or a hallucination?

But just as unbelievable was the idea that his karma included supernatural power over other's destinies. *Him, a god?* Hell, he couldn't even manage a normal human relationship. His one outstanding love affair had been with a married dead woman and had really only lasted about a week. And he had spent all his time since pining over something that was lost forever and never should have happened in the first place.

Did he have any qualifications that allowed him to feel superior to the rest of humanity? The answer was painfully obvious: none whatsoever.

The major struggled to his feet. His face was still wet with tears, but he had stopped sobbing. Bryan braced for another onslaught, but the major avoided even looking at him. He must know, somehow, that Bryan had affected the change on him. Fear in his face, and something else, too.

It was shame.

The major looked past him, spying the meth girl who was no longer crawling on all fours but up and running away. She glanced over her shoulder and saw the major watching her, and looked confused for a moment – the major's appearance had changed dramatically in seconds. Recognition gradually registered on her face to be replaced by terror. Bryan wondered if he was going to have to intervene again, but the major was too consumed by his own inner demons to torment anyone now. He looked up at the clouds, then ascended into the sky without a word. The meth girl watched him fly off, then scurried into a shadowy alley.

Which left Bryan alone in the square with the dead child and the beheaded Marguerite. He could do nothing for either –or could he? Marguerite's disembodied head lay on its side, facing him. The open eyes shocked Bryan when they blinked. His imagination? No, the mouth was working too. Was the head trying to speak?

Impossible!

But how many impossible things had happened to him already? He knelt by Marguerite's head, not daring to touch it but feeling he should do something. He had fond memories of her when she had been human. His grandfather had told him that she had made frequent visits when his grandmother, Mattie, was dying of breast cancer. He had been visiting his grandparents on one of those occasions, before the Fall. Even in the late 1990s, Marguerite had favored frilly dresses and sensible black shoes and looked like a time traveler from the 1950s. Though an evangelical or something like it, Marguerite hadn't preached or made Mattie pray. Instead, she had brought comfort food and just sat with her. Mattie had been unable to eat because of the chemotherapy, but that wasn't the point.

Marguerite appeared to genuinely care.

More immediately, Marguerite appeared to have been defending him when she attacked the major. So Bryan forced himself to pick up her head with both hands. It was heavier than he expected. This close, he was staring directly into her violet-blue eyes and got the definite impression they were still possessed of awareness. Her mouth continued work as if forming words, and Bryan held it closer to his ear, hoping to hear something. But there was no sound. Evidently, even angels were subject to some laws of physics: Without lungs to drive air through the vocal chords, Marguerite couldn't make a sound.

Now that he was over his initial revulsion of holding a decapitated head, he examined it more closely. Before pulling off Marguerite's head, the major had slammed it with both his fists, flattening the top. But Marguerite's skull had already recovered and was normally shaped. He lifted the head higher to examine the bottom of the neck. *Crap! It must weigh forty pounds!* He saw no gore, no dripping liquids or dangling sinews and veins. The bottom was sheared off as cleanly as the major's arm had been.

Marguerite was flicking her eyes to one side then back, further creeping him out. Evidently she still had full control of her facial muscles. Bryan said, "I don't understand," and she rolled her eyes, but then continued quick glances to the left.

Bryan realized she was trying to direct his attention to her body, which lay only a few feet away. The body had slumped over on its side. The neck stump of the torso showed the same cut as the bottom of the neck. Bryan couldn't get the Barbie doll comparison out of his mind. He half expected a plastic knob on the top of the shoulders for the head to fit onto, but it was just a clean, smooth, flat stump.

Bryan looked at Marguerite's head again. She continued to make odd movements with her eyes.

"I know what you want me to do, Marguerite. Yeah, I saw the major reattached his arm. But isn't your head seems a different matter."

Marguerite winked at him and tried to speak again. This time he thought he could read her lips: *Yes, you can.*

Bryan shrugged and set her head on the base of the park statue for safe keeping. Then he wrestled with the body, trying to get it into a sitting-up position. Like the head, the body was much heavier than it should have been. Moving it was like trying to push a car, and the wings kept snagging on the corner of the statue base. Finally, he put his shoulder on it. His shoulder joint popped, but he managed to get the body sitting upright.

He picked up the head and slowly lowered it onto the neck stump. He glanced at Marguerite's face, and her eyes told him this was the right thing to do. Because of the head's weight, his arms trembled a bit as he tried to match up the cuts exactly. He worried that if he didn't align it perfectly, Marguerite's head would sit askew on her body. At the last moment he slipped, and the bottom of the neck plopped down a good half-inch off to one side. But before he could say, "Shit!" the head aligned itself perfectly and the seam disappeared. Marguerite's eyes closed, her lips pursed and the body still. Without thinking why, he touched the little groove underneath her nose and pushed it like it was a computer's reset button. With his touch, Marguerite's eyes popped open, and she stretched out her arms out like a small child wanting to be picked up.

She started to get up, and Bryan, from a lifelong conditioning of how to behave around women, took her hand to help her. She held onto his hand, though obviously she didn't need the help. She didn't stand up so as elevated, and then she was standing before him.

She smile at hime, and for a moment she was the human Marguerite again, dowdy and eyes haunted by personal loss. Then she was Marguerite the angel again, more beautiful than ever before.

Bryan caught his breath. All archangels and human hybrids he'd ever seen – except the major – had been physically beautiful. But he still couldn't get over how Marguerite had been transformed into a goddess. Her hair was so bright it looked aflame. Her skin glowed. Her eyes burned through him. He was both aroused and awed.

But her eyes were still sad.

Without preamble she put both hands on his shoulders and kissed him on the lips, stunning him with lust. Before he could collect his wits, she stepped back.

"What are you?" he stuttered.

"We are such stuff as dreams are made of — as are you," she said.

Before he could absorb this, she embraced him again, carrying him up into the clear blue sky. Looking down as they ascended, he thought of his first encounter with the angel, Eloaios/Envy, not that long ago in this very park. As before, they were inside a bubble where Newton's laws were invalid. He still felt the breeze of the flight on his skin, smelled the change in air as they passed the edge of town and glided over the hickory and oak forest, but they were immune to what must be fabulous forces of acceleration. He knew without asking they were headed to the saucer.

22.

Where Lies the Self

Bryan.

Marguerite flew him over the desert landscape inside the saucer. In seconds they arrived at a large gaping tear inside a bivouac tent.

Bryan was confused at first. As Marguerite flew through a large gapping tear in the tent's roof, it was if he had been transported back to the major's camp near Lost Lake. Then he remembered Laura's description of the birthing camp in the saucer, complete with purloined Army cots and wool blankets.

She had described everything as new when she was there, and that had been only about a month ago when she had helped the Dr. Jenkins attend to those humans implanted with the archangel homunculi. This tent and its contents looked like they had been rotting in this alien desert for decades. He put a foot on a cot to test it, and the wooden struts crumbled to dust.

Time must run at an accelerated rate here. Could he spend a month here and only minutes would pass in the Earth plane?

Did it really matter?

As they landed on the tent floor, he wasn't surprised to find Uncle Robert, Laura and Dog from the Red Sky planet apparently waiting for them. But he was taken aback find Suzanne there too. The memory of her possible portrayal on the Red Sky planet – as well as the thought that she might be only a simulacrum of the Suzanne he had once known – kept him from going to her.

But could this be *his* Suzanne? She sat on the floor, reading what looked like the same huge red book he had seen her with when she was an apparition in his grandparents' living room – which for him had been only a couple of days ago.

She wasn't looking at him but only at the book. If it was real and bound in leather and with heavy parchment as it appeared to be, it must weigh a hundred pounds. Yet she held it open in her lap without straining.

Uncle Robert, who had been standing with Laura in the middle of the tent, walked over to sit on one of the nearby rotting cots, which should have collapsed under his weight but didn't. Evidently the old man's astral body, though it appeared solid, obeyed different laws of physics. Maybe the book did too. Uncle Robert was dressed in his usual outfit – a frayed professorial tweed jacket over a T-shirt and faded denim bib overalls with red, snarly looking sneakers.

Laura, on the other hand, was dressed as he had never seen her before. She wore a top that was a can-can dancer-inspired Mexican peasant blouse over clownish-looking barber pole-striped tights. The overall effect was of a very sexy clown.

Her outfit wasn't the only change about her. She was calmer and radiated happiness in way he'd never seen before.

"I guess you're looking for some pat answers," Uncle Robert said.

"I suspect you're going to tell me there are no such things."

Uncle Robert's eyes gleamed with amused good will, and he shook his head. Bryan, irritated, suddenly wanted to go shake him. Instead, he growled, "How about a few ambiguous clues, then?"

"No reason for you to take a nasty tone, boy," Uncle Robert said. "In many ways I'm just as much of pawn in this game as you feel you are."

"So you say. Others believe I'm somehow in charge."

"Do you believe it?"

"Are you using the heuristic method again?"

"No, it was an honest question. If someone actually claimed to be in charge, who knows; I might follow her."

"Bullshit, Uncle Robert," Laura said. "You're an iconoclast through and through. You challenge any authority reflexively. You never follow anyone."

Suddenly tired and filled with ennui, Bryan found a relatively clean spot on the tent floor and sat down with his legs crossed. Laura followed, sitting next to him and giving him a comradely pat on the shoulder. Her hand felt solid, not at all ghostly. She practically oozed happiness. Death really did become her.

The woman who looked like Suzanne – Bryan still wondered if she was the Suzanne he had known – flipped a large page of her book and continued reading, completely absorbed, ignoring them all.

"Hello, Suzanne," Bryan said. She made no sign of recognition.

"Career girl, I guess. Work comes first," said Uncle Robert.

"That's sexist," Laura said, but she smiled at Uncle Robert.

"I don't know why rude, goal-obsessive behavior in a woman should be tolerated anymore than it is in a man. Why . . ."

"Enough, enough, Uncle Robert. We're getting sidetracked," Laura said. "Bryan, do you believe you're somehow in charge of this reality?"

"Well, I've only had one semester of abnormal psychology – the one I took with you, by the way – but this seems too involved and convoluted to be some sort of delusion. More likely it's some sort of magical thinking on my part."

"I've been told I resemble an aging Jean Piaget," Uncle Robert said. Bryan had no idea what he was talking about, but Laura nodded in understanding.

"Maybe if you shaved once in a while and wore suits instead of bib overalls," she said. "Get serious, Uncle."

"Okay, I will," Uncle Robert said. "If you two will entertain the idea, even if just for a minute, that consciousness isn't a side effect of a material body – or the material world, for that matter – but that the material world is an affect of consciousness."

Bryan sighed. *Was this going to be the same convoluted line of reasoning he'd used before?*

When neither Laura nor Bryan spoke, he continued, "That thing is not just some New Age mantra. You know what I'm talking about? *I'm not a human having a spiritual experience, but I'm a spiritual being having a human experience.* It sounds overly simplistic, I know, but what I'm trying to convey is that consciousness is permanent, universal, and independent of the impermanent material realms."

He paused again and waited, expectant. "Haven't I said this before?"

"Not exactly, but it sounds like something you told me once, but more poetically this time," Laura said.

He shook his head.

"Thought is action on this astral plane," she said. "Remember? Out in the dessert when Marguerite brought me into the realm of the saucer after the major shot me dead?"

"Yeah, I guess that's something like what I said. But I think this is something more astounding. We keep thinking on terms of the Earthly plane."

Bryan shook his head. "This all sounds like some sort of acid trip."

"You can call it an alternate dimension if you're more comfortable with the term. Have you ever taken DMT, by the way?"

"No. I just saw the documentary."

"You're kidding, aren't you?"

"No," Bryan said. "There actually was one: *DMT: The Spirit Molecule.* I streamed it before the Fall. It sounded intriguing. The researcher, a medical doctor specializing in psychiatry, gave volunteers intravenous dosages of DMT – I don't recall what that stands for."

Dimethyltryptamine – Di-Methyl-Trypt-Amine," Uncle Robert said.

"Yeah, that's it. He was interested in DMT because he it was produced by the human pineal gland and had something to do with out-of-body experiences. DMT is found naturally in many, many plant sources, and it has been used as a shamanic sacrament in the Amazon forests for centuries.

"He came to call it the 'spirit molecule,' due to many – most, really – users' claims of contacting alien god-like beings when they were given the higher dosages. Many of the volunteers were professionals and atheists or deists when they went into the study. He reported there were no atheists after a certain dosage"

"So where's all this going?" Laura said. "Are you saying we're just tripping? That's none of this is real?"

"Not at all," Uncle Robert said, picking up where Bryan left off. "Strassman – that was the researcher's name – tried to remain empirical upon hearing the reports of the volunteers, but he came to believe that DMT was a trigger, perhaps acting on the pineal gland, to allow the volunteers to actually visit alien realms. The recorded trip reports had remarkable similarities. Clown-like beings doing healing operations, for example."

"Clowns!" Laura exclaimed. "Really? Clowns?"

"Yes, clowns," Uncle Robert said. "It's hard to imagine we all share a structure in our brains that generates hallucinations of alien clowns, isn't it? But I'm getting off track here, Laura. Remember what I told you when you found your own corpse?"

"Pretty much the New Age thing," she answered, but seem distracted. "It was only my Earth-bound body that had died. No sweat, you said, because it's not the material world that's real. Only consciousness is real."

Bryan considered this for a moment. Uncle Robert waited.

"So," Byran said. "Whose consciousness is creating this reality? Mine or Laura's or yours?"

"Now that's the sixty-four gazillion dollar question, isn't it?" Uncle Robert said.

Laura said, "You know that you could just accept this and the other planes we visited as real, or at least as real as the Earthly plane we all shared."

Bryan shook his head. "I don't know. That way lies madness, I think."

"Or that way lies clowns, maybe," she said, shaking her head. "Well, one way is to follow Uncle Robert's suggestion, that only consciousness is real, and it creates material constructs as sort of nurseries for the growth of awareness. It's not that Earth isn't real; more like it is a primitive nursery for consciousness. There consciousness has to have a material anchor. But it's not the only reality. None of us are anchored to a single reality now."

The air shimmered for a moment, and Bryan felt a shiver run down his spine.

She paused and looked at Uncle Robert. "Did you feel that?"

"Yes," he said. "Something has changed. Or rather, I think the major has come to a decision."

"The major?" Laura said, but Uncle Robert didn't explain.

"None of this explains me being cast as the Dreaming God," Bryan said.

But no one answered him. They all felt it now: Energy building in the air as before a violent thunderstorm.

Marguerite:

Everything had changed, Marguerite realized as she glided down to land beside May.

May hadn't been hard find; some kind of radar-like connection linked them, stronger than that between her and the other angel/human hybrids.

The world had changed. Colors looked brighter; the edges of everything were crystal sharp. At the same time, the boundary between her and the world was indistinct. As her feet touched down, she couldn't tell where her flesh ended and the grass began.

May was sitting on the stump of a large oak tree outside her old house trailer, her wings folded behind her, watching an emaciated horse in a weedy pasture on the other side of a barbed-wire fence. The horse's ribs showed prominently. It watched May watch it. Both she and the horse looked miserable and confused.

The stump May sat on was the remains of a hundred-year-old oak tree that years ago had been hit by lightning. The fallen tree had been harvested as firewood, but never used, and was stacked in rotting cords near by.

There was plenty of room for Marguerite to sit beside her friend on the tree stump, but what to say? The two hadn't talked since Marguerite had come up on her trying to reassemble the dead soldiers. Really, they hadn't talked much at all since Marguerite had reassembled her.

"How are you?" she said

"Elvis is sick," May replied.

It took Marguerite a second to remember that Elvis was May's horse, the one on the other side of the fence.

"He just looks hungry to me," Marguerite said. "Maybe you should feed him."

"Everything I touch dies," May said with a whimper. She wrapped her arms around herself, a self-hugging posture reminding Marguerite of a person in a straitjacket.

"Nonsense. Feeding Elvis won't kill him. Not this Elvis, anyway."

At the sound of their voices, the horse came to the fence and gave a plaintive, slobbering nay.

"There's a hay barn over there," Marguerite said, nodding toward a tin-roof building in a nearby field. "I bet there's hay inside. Come on, I'll help you bring a few bales back to Elvis."

May looked at her, a rare moment of eye contact. "I can't even cry. I wished you hadn't put me back together."

Despair washed over Marguerite, but while May was lucid she needed to ask a question she had wanted answered since the accident with the helicopter.

"When you – before I reassembled you – were you aware?"

May looked at her questioningly.

"I mean, did you dream or anything? Did you know you had been chopped up?"

May shook her head. "I don't remember – but then I don't remember a lot before the helicopter. I just remembered Elvis today."

"Think back." Marguerite was surprised to hear pleading in her own voice.

Why was this so important to her?

"Think back," she repeated, "to the time when I woke you up last."

May looked thoughtful for a moment, then said, "A blue man. I remember big room with no walls and no ceiling. It was huge. I couldn't see where the walls ended. A blue man, dreaming a smaller blue man, who was dreaming a smaller blue man – that went on forever."

May's account was similar to what she had said moments after being reannimated. But Marguerite wondered why hadn't seen this blue dreaming man when the major had torn off her head? Was there a time lapse? She remembered watching the confrontation between the major and Bryan Douglas, but she hadn't seen anything but a faint aura surrounding Bryan when he had finally picked up her head to reattach it. Had that aura been blue? She didn't remember. A more important question was if her consciousness would have faded to black if she had been left decapitated long enough?

"Was it peaceful there?" Asking her if she had been happy was too much. May had never been happy, either as a human or an angel.

"I just was," May said. "I wasn't me." She patted her breasts. "I wasn't anything. I wasn't tits. I wasn't just ass. I wasn't just a dumb waitress. Or an angel. I was just there, but I wasn't anything." The sadness left her face to be replaced by serenity, but flickers of madness rippled the peacefulness.

Marguerite wanted to shake her, slap her, anything to bring her out of the trance. Instead, she took May's elbow, brought them both to their feet, and said, "Come on, let's see if we can find some hay for Elvis."

"I want to go back, go back home," May said, but Marguerite knew she didn't mean the ratty, faded trailer.

"I wish I could go back home, too," she said. "But the barn is just a hop away. Let's go."

Inside they found some big round bales of hay. Though a single bale weighed a thousand pounds or more, together they had no problem carrying it out of the barn, over the fence, and to the scrubby pasture where Elvis resided.

They unrolled the bale so Elvis would have plenty to eat for some time. Then at Marguerite's encouragement, May tore out a section of barbed wire fence so Elvis could roam free if he wanted.

While May sat watching Elvis munch his hay, Marguerite went back and retrieved a scythe. It was an antique tool, predating mechanical hay harvesters. A three-foot scimitar-like blade was mounted on a six-foot-long curved wooden handle. It looked like something a cartoon dipiction of Death would carry.

She ran her thumb across the edge of the blade. It was razor-sharp – someone had honed and oiled it before the Fall.

She returned to May. Standing behind her, she lifted the scythe and considered the elegant curve of May's neck.

✸ ✸ ✸

23.

That Knows Life is but a Tale

"*What happens when the spirit molecule pulls an pushes us beyond the physical and emotional levels of awareness? We enter into invisible realms, ones we cannot normally sense and whose presence we can scarcely imagine. Even more surprisingly, these realms appear to be inhabited.*" -- Rick Strassman, M.D., *DMT: The Spirit Molecule.*

In the sky there is nobody asleep. Nobody, nobody.
Nobody is asleep.
The creatures of the moon sniff and prowl about their cabins.
The living iguanas will come and bite the men who do not dream,
and the man who rushes out with his spirit broken will meet on the
            street corner
the unbelievable alligator quiet beneath the tender protest of the
            stars. -- *from "The City That Does Not Sleep" by Federico Garcia* Lorca

Laura.

It was the troupe of outlandishly unreal, orange, alien clowns that finally convinced Laura she really was not dreaming, that her Earthly body was dead, and that this traipsing between planes was not just as real *as* anything in her previous existence but *more* real.

What was less likely to be a phantasmagoric projection of her disturbed unconsciousness than orange clowns with big red noses and size-twelve blue jackboots?

She had translated here – wherever *here* was – immediately after Bryan had disappeared from the Western town under the red sky. One moment he was there, the archangels were advancing, and the next he just blinked out. She must have blinked out too, though she didn't remember consciously doing so.

But what would take her to a world inhabited by clowns?

They were so tangible, so imbued with life. And she should have been terrified of them, but didn't feel they were out to get her. She was the visitor here, and they were obviously at home in this plane, a place of contradictions. She was completely within their province, under their limitless alien power, and she wasn't frightened. She didn't know how or why she came to this place.

Upon her arrival, the clowns smiled and danced about, grinning foolishly, whooping and holding big placards covered with hieroglyphics that communicated something to her though she had never seen the symbols before.

At first, the cards reminded her of those chartered limousine drivers held up at airports to identify themselves to their passengers. Maybe they said, *Laura Jacobsen. Welcome to Clownsville.*

Whatever, as the clowns continued laughing, jumping, and flashing those cards, she had been deeply touched. The cards spoke to some deep, hidden part of her that had been damaged in her childhood, touching gently a wound that no amount of Earthly therapy had ever reached. They had been waiting all along to do this for her, their laughs said. Why had she taken so long getting here?

That initial setting had been circus-like, with many flashing lights and huge strange rotating objects rising over multicolored tents. Though reminiscent of Ferris wheels, the turning wheels were not rides or huge ornaments or anything within her experience. Energy focii maybe, but she wasn't sure.

She had been saddened that Uncle Robert hadn't been transported with her. During the transition she had seen beautiful colors and patterns, like those of Tibetan sand paintings, but more hypnogogic, dissolving, reforming before her eyes. She would have like to asked her uncle what they meant. Then she was here, the visions fading, and the pack of clowns had surrounded her in a flash.

As a child she had *coulrophobia*, fear of clowns, and when she had arrived on this plane she had screamed, a whoop of panic the clowns immediately imitated, which amused her despite her phobia. They had mistaken her outcry for language and were trying to communicate.

They began fluttering their hands near her face and groin. Their multi-coloring was not clown makeup, but the actual color and markings of their skin. Their mimicking of her scream had calmed her somewhat, but she still half-expecting them to sprout fangs and take bites out of her. They came closer and closer, their oversized white hands nearly touching her, and she felt their love and acceptance of her.

Then the encircling crowd of clowns parted to admit a larger figure to come closer. She thought of this one as the Jester Clown because its head diverged into three large floppy parts like a court fool's three-pointed hat. She couldn't tell if the three floppy parts were flesh or dense Rastafari braided hair, but like a court jester's, they came to points that ended in small brass bells.

But this being radiated nothing of the fool. Its bearing was regal and its presence overwhelming. She nearly swooned except for the clowns then grasping her arms and supporting her.

The Jester towered over her, but mixed with its power was a sense of benevolence. But there was no mistaking the fact it ruled here.

Having issues with parental abuse in her childhood, she should have been terrified by a huge, commanding figure towering over her, but the Jester emanated something more than just kindheartedness. It was eternal, at once parental and transcendental, and it truly loved her.

While she had focused on the Jester, they had all been transported somewhere else. The carnival landscape had disappeared, and she, the clown troupe, and the Jester were now on the front porch of an expansive adobe hacienda. Although she had seen only a dozen or so clowns at first, they were either multiplying or arriving unseen. As large as the porch was, the clown troupe overflowed into the large courtyard in front. The courtyard was enclosed by high, thick, adobe walls, and atop these walls sat huge iguana-like lizards. She was reminded of a Lorca poem, something about dreaming, and iguanas and snakes, but the complete verse escaped her.

And another minor detail: She was naked now. She had arrived at the carnival place in the college outfit that Bryan had conjured up for her on the planet of red skies, but those clothes had been left behind when she came here. Neither the clowns nor the Jester – and certainly not the iguanas – seemed to care she was naked.

She could feel the desert wind patting her breasts, slipping gently between her bare thighs, and caressing the small of her back. Also, the attending clowns' hands continued to flutter about her, not quite touching her skin, a therapeutic, spiritual massage. Their ministrations were not sexual but very friendly and platonic. Hugs without touching. They led her to a wooden stool in the middle of the porch. The Jester loomed over her, his arms and body bending without show of joints, like a Claymation figure. Dinner plate-size hands each with three fingers and a thumb reached forward gently. The three fingers elongnated until they were as thin and delicate as a concert pianist's.

His fingers touched her forehead – and opened a door there.

This didn't seem surprising at all, though she hadn't been aware of a door in her head. This door was a real, actual, physical door, not a metaphoric door. It was at least as real as this place and her astral body. Rectangular, about three inches tall, it swung open smoothly at the Jester's touch. Looking up, she could see the door's bottom edge, which was about a half-inch thick and made of something organic, but not skin and bone. She had no doubt it was an integral part of her. Of course, she could not see what lay behind the door inside her head.

The Jester made an uh-huh sound, and pulled something out of her skull doorway that didn't want to come. He pulled harder and put his other hand on her forehead to hold her head steady. A long, thin, slimy thread stretched out through the doorway, and she felt a stinging pain, not unlike the twinge that comes when plucking off a particularly stubborn wood tick. At once the thread snapped out of her head like a rubber band.

The Jester said, *"Ahhhhh,"* and held up the thing for her and the clowns to see. It looked like a slimy clump of rotting hair she might find in the bathroom sink drain, not something that belonged in her head.

The clowns started cheering and pulling grapefruit-looking objects out of their pockets. Holding them over their heads like castanets, they began squeezing the balls, which emitted squeaky bicycle-horn honk-honks. They were clearly overjoyed and began colliding with each other, knocking one another down in their exuberance. Then they began tossing the balls back and forth between them, raising the honker-din to a higher level. The iguanas turned their heads to watch, not with alarm but in expectation.

Laura found herself laughing and crying: laughing at the clowns' antics and at the cartoonish iguanas, but consumed by a sense of well-being she had never experienced before, even when she was on opiates.

She had been instantly healed in some way she couldn't explain, some way that years of psychotherapy had never accomplished. All therapy had done was remind her to recognize that she was damaged and to adjust her life accordingly. Somehow the dancing clowns and their cryptic placards had cured her. Those broken pieces of herself, which she had pictured as sharp-edged shards like from a broken mirror, had naturally come back together. She could see an image of herself in those melded pieces, a whole person without cracks.

The Jester closed the little door in her forehead and patted her on the head. She should have found his smile grotesque. His lipless mouth looked like a wound from ear to ear, his teeth like broken twigs, and his tongue lolled out one corner. Yet she found his face beautific and she loved him for it.

Still chuckling and tossing the honker balls back and forth, the clowns began to drift away. Laura half-expected a tiny car to arrive, and the two or three dozen clowns all pile into it and drive away. But no, they left without fanfare, simply walking out into the desert, juggling the honker balls, laughing.

The Jester stayed on the porch for a few moments, still smiling at her, then turned to follow the clowns into the desert. She wanted to follow but understood she was not to. But that was okay too.

A hand-hewn wooden chair sat next to the front door. On it was a pile of clothes. She wasn't surprised to find they fit her perfectly, including the knee-high soft leather boots. Everything was frilly and feminine – at least a clown's idea of frilly and feminine. She felt like a chic, sexy Ms. Bozo when she finished dressing.

Laughing at herself but still basking in the feeling of being loved and protected, she opened the screen door and stepped into — not the hacienda, but into a very familiar place, the Army tent on the desert of the Archangel's saucer. Uncle Robert was there, as was the undead woman, Suzanne, Bryan's former lover. But no Bryan.

Uncle Robert smiled at her, then looked toward the large gash in the tent's ceiling, so she looked up too, and saw the angel Marguerite arriving with Bryan in her arms.

Major Minor.
The mechanical gremlins had dismembered Major Minor while making love to him. And it had been making love, not just fucking. They had been waiting for him, expecting him, wanting to repair him, they said. They hadn't spoken aloud, but he knew it all the same. They had smothered him in love and understanding.

It had been the most horrible experience of his life.

One moment, he had been in complete control, standing in the shitty little park in the middle of the redneck, peckerwood town of Creedance. All the good citizens loathed and feared him and for good reason – he had become Death incarnate. He had been standing over that Bryan Douglas punk, in complete control of him, watching him pitifully try to protect the little meth whore, and was about to punch a hole in his chest, when .. , when . . .?

What exactly had happened then?
He remembered what he had seen, but he couldn't make sense of it. The kid had turned blue. Just his skin, not his clothes. A sort of pastel blue. Then rays of light had come out of his eyes – not laser beams exactly, more like someone had opened windows behind his eyes to let floodlights stream out.

As the light struck him, Minor had been swept away to the realm of the gremlins.

The physical dismemberment had been the least shattering facet – as a career military man he had seen horrific wounds in others and had always been expected to undergo them himself someday. The transformation into an angel had surpassed his fears of castration and had left him powerful and fearless. He was prepared to undergo any mutilation and survive.

The gremlin experience had been something entirely different. He had found himself in a kind of operating theatre, on a table, immobilized by invisible straps. The gremlins, scurrying around him like windup toys, waved brightly colored wands. The wands looked innocuous, like things out of a toy store bargain bin. Then the gremlins started using the wands to slice off pieces of him, cutting through whatever his angel body was made of as it were softened butter.

First they removed his angel wings, then his arms and legs. He wanted to look down and see exactly what he had left there, but he couldn't move his head. Then they moved his head for him – they popped it off and set it on a separate table that magically grew out of the floor like a giant mushroom.

He had thought them as gremlins at first, but as he watched them from the little table he soon suspected they were mechanical. And they were more clown-like than anything. Their movements were super-quick, blurringly quick, with abrupt stops between moves.

While he watched from the mushroom table where his head sat, they reattached his limbs to his body, leaving off the wings, and flipped the body – his body – over on its stomach. Then three gremlins began taking turns sodomizing the body. Though his head was still detached, he could feel them entering him from behind with cold, steel-hard penises. Two others came over to his head and began stroking his brow, his ears, and kissing his cheeks with their big inflated red lips.

He could feel their love for him – warm, enveloping, and accepting – and only then did he try to scream. It was a silent scream, for he had become mute when his head was removed.

He didn't remember losing or regaining consciousness or being transported back to Earth, but he found himself back in the woods, at the same campsite where he had shot Laura Jacobsen. He was an angel again, mostly unchanged, though definitely in male form. His head was reattached, as were his wings. And he had male genitals again, though greatly enhanced. His scrotum was as hairless and his penis was as white and shiny as an albino snake.

He should have been ecstatic, but all he wanted was death.

Walking toward the helicopter, he no longer felt at home in this angel body. Although he noticed no lag when he took steps or moved an arm or turned his head, he felt if he were controlling the body from a great distance.

He made his way through the woods to the Chinook where he found feral hogs, bristling with coarse black hair and showing yellow tusks. They were feeding on the rotting corpses of soldiers at the back ramp. One hog, the alpha-boar, weighing perhaps four or five hundred pounds, charged at Major Minor. The animal was blindingly fast but not fast enough, and Minor crushed its skull with one blow. Wild hogs are smart and pragmatic. At the sight of their fallen comrade, the rest ran off into forest, leaving him alone with the soldiers' half-eaten corpses.

Had he murdered these men? He wasn't sure if the killer had been him or Samiazaz or another angel. His memory was fogged. Did it matter? Inside the helicopter cargo bay, he found the large wooden crate still undisturbed.

He pulled the nailed-on lid off the crate with his bare hands. Packed inside, encased in shock-absorbing foam, was the Mark 84, all two-thousand pounds of it. Like the wild hogs, it was a primitive but pragmatic thing.

The Mark 84's design dated back to the Vietnam War, where it had been an unguided dumb bomb. Later the Army had upgraded the weapon with electronic guidance devices, transforming it into an early smart bomb. Now all the smart electronics had been rendered useless, but the 1970s-era time-delay fuses were mechanical and still functioned, and this Mark 84 had been refitted to Vietnam-era dumb-bomb mode.

The Mark 84 looked just a proper bomb should look – a small rocket ship, eighteen inches in diameter and more than twelve feet long. It was pointed at one end and had stubby fins at the other. Half its weight was the high explosive Tritonal. Dropped from a sufficient height, its steel casing could penetrate up to fifteen inches of metal or about 11 feet of concrete before detonation. At the surface, its detonation would make a fifty-foot-wide crater and throw fragmentation four hundred yards in all directions at lethal velocities.

The major had been trained on arming the Mark 84 before leaving Fort Leonard Wood. His orders were provisional. If the saucer rumors proved to be legitimate, and he felt it to be a threat, he had discretion to employ the Mark 84.

Of course, none of his superior officers had considered the saucer to be real – that's why he had been given so much leeway. It was a fool's mission, and he was the fool.

He had no doubt that he could arm the bomb correctly. He needed to determine how to deliver it to the saucer now that the Chinook was grounded and the pilots were dead. Tentatively, he wrapped both arms around the bomb at about its middle. He strained. His angel joints creaked and complained, but he managed to heave it out of the crate. He set it back down as gingerly as he could. Lifting it was one thing. Flying with it was another. He was going to need some help.

It was at this moment the redheaded angel, the one whose head he had torn off in the park, now whole, walked into the cargo bay.

24.

As Told by Clowns and Lovers

Bryan.

"That still doesn't explain me being cast as the Dreaming God," Bryan said again when neither Uncle Robert nor Laura said anything.

The sense of a violent buildup of energy had intensified. They all noticed it, but by an unspoken consensus they waited for whatever was to happen.

"You're a kind of a contradiction," Laura said, nervously looking toward the tent door. "You're basically a decent person, very kind, loving."

"Thank you."

"But you have this buried need to control things. It's fear-based. That's what you have in common with the archangels."

"I take back the thank you."

"You shouldn't. Most of them are ethical creatures, I think. The ones we encountered were rebels, criminals, intent on using humans to their own ends."

"So were the ones on the Red Sky planet. I saw it. They were implanting humans with the homunculi there, too."

"No, you're mistaken," Uncle Robert said. "I spent some time on that plane, too, just watching, listening to conversations. There are some really good bars there, by the way."

"I know what I saw. There was this woman I was put in a dungeon with. She had one of the things attached."

"No, it wasn't attached. It grew there naturally. That's the morphology of the species on the Red Sky planet: zygote, embryo, fetus, human, homunculus, angel. Or I should say, human-like, for what looks like humans there are just an intermediate stage of the archangels' biological development, though the outward resemblance is nearly indistinguishable until the angel metamorphosis, isn't it young lady?"

He directed the last question at the woman who looked like Suzanne. In answer, she shifted the huge book to one hand, reached down to her waist with the other, and undid some invisible snaps on her gown. She pulled the garmet aside, clearly showing the homunculus there.

"I believe that until the metamorphosis takes place, they can have human-like children," Uncle Robert said. "They must be able to do so, because the archangel form is neuter despite their varying appearance as male or female."

The Suzanne simulacrum nodded.

"But you remembered me," Bryan said. "Didn't you?"

"I remembered you from a series of dreams I had," the Suzanne said. "It's not really a past life. I thought so at first, but the Lords – you call them archangels – let me read a copy of my Akashic records." She let the gown fall closed and hefted the book. "It's in here. Sort of. There must be some sort of strong connection between me and your Suzanne, but I'm not her. I think I dreamed being her at times. But I'm not. I'm sorry. The Lords were very frightened by you. They thought I might get the truth from you. They used me."

"More like a spy, then," Bryan said. "You tricked me."

"Yes and no," the Suzanne said. "I felt the connection, and I didn't want to hurt you, but my allegiance is to my own kind, my family and race first. I'm sorry, really. But you triumphed anyway. Now, we hope – I hope – you'll be merciful."

Bryan shook his head. "This is all too confusing."

"Not really. The rebel angels were old, very old," Uncle Robert said. "Immortal and tired. Moreover, only a finite number of them can exist in their realm, so until they could die, there couldn't be any more transformations among people like Suzanne here. The humans didn't transform. They just died early, very human-like deaths. So the hundred archangels felt they were at once ending a long, tiresome life and enabling others of their kind to evolve into archangels – like this woman."

"Yes, that's about right," the Suzanne said as she wiped a stray strand of red hair off her forehead. "But they weren't rebels. They drew lots to see who would go. Imagine their concern when they found a human on

Earth who looked like the Dreaming God."

Bryan thought back to his encounters with the archangels on Earth. Yes, he remembered moments when a couple of archangels had said something about recognizing him. The first time was when he disturbed the archangel as it was going through a metamorphosis in the hollow tree. It had shouted something about a dreaming god before running off into the forest in a panic. But he had thought the creature was simply demented by whatever change it was undergoing. Then the angel Eloaios had mentioned something about a Dreaming God giving it one of his names; then Eloaios mentioned that his "disguise" didn't fool them. He had dismissed this as gibberish as all the archangels talked in riddles.

But the real revelation was a memory he had suppressed until now. After his encounter with the angel in the tree trunk, an experience right out the Golden Bough, he had lapsed into a feverish coma. While thrashing about in that coma, he had dreamed of a conversation with a Zeus-like god, commanding a battlefield so large the legions disappeared into the horizon. That god had been blue, and he felt then the face was familiar but couldn't name it. Now, if he mentally removed the black beard and the conical golden helmet, he recognized the face as an older version of his own.

"Bryan, Bryan!" Laura shouted at him.

"What?"

"You still with us?" she said. "You seemed to sort of turn cyanotic there for a moment."

"I'm just feeling blue," he said and laughed when she looked confused. The Suzanne appeared to be the only one who got the joke.

"People, things, conditions – everything seems to fade in and out of existence here in the saucer world, more so than anywhere else," Uncle Robert said. "Death has no dominion here."

"Is that why John Wright was revived after his suicide," Laura said.

Uncle Robert started to reply, then his eyes widened and he pointed toward a figure just entering the big tent. "Speak of the devil, and the devil appears."

"I'm hardly a devil," the figure said. "At least I don't think I am."

"You!" Laura said, her voice cracking with emotion. Then she brought up both hands, their fingers interwoven, to cover her mouth.

At first, Bryan didn't recognize the man stepping into the tent. He still thought of him – despite his later reincarnation as a younger undead man back on Earth – as an older, somewhat soft-around-the-middle, bigoted man. The person stepping into the tent was backlit by the alien sun and surrounded by a rainbow aura. He was young and extremely handsome. As he stepped into the subdued light where the rest of them stood, he still seemed to glow with supernatural light. It was John Wright, one-time sheriff of Harmon County.

Laura started to run, then checked herself, and walked over to John Wright, holding her arms stiffly at her sides.

He hugged her, completely enveloping her in his arms. At first she didn't respond, but gradually she relaxed, put her head on his shoulder, and hugged him back. They stayed in this embrace for a couple of minutes, a romance-novel moment that held even the Suzanne's attention.

Did this version of Suzanne remember John Wright? He had, after all, cut her doppelgänger quite a bit of slack back on Earth. Were this Red Sky planet woman's dreams of being Bryan's Suzanne been so detailed as to show her Wright looking the other way during her Earthly double's drug escapades?

Wright and Laura walked hand-in-hand like young lovers back to the center of the tent. Wright talked as they strolled.

"I been to so many places – died and been reborn so many times – that I'm not sure who I am. I have a dream of you and me; that is, I remember you and me together in dreams, but I'm not really me – this me." He pounded his chest for emphasis. "I'm just a copy. Those early dreams were punctuated with me holding a gun in my mouth. I remember the feel of the cold metal. I think now my suicide was somehow precipitated by the archangels and the influence of the saucer. That I was just in the wrong place at the wrong time. But it doesn't matter now, I guess. Before I died then, you and I were connected somehow, and afterwards, there was a love so intense it threatened to dissolve me entirely. But it's so damn complicated. All these dreams seem trivial except the parts about you and me together. I think we were a sort of family first, then we were lovers. I know how weird that sounds. I'm sorry if I hurt you, if I crossed some the lines of propriety."

"You never hurt me," Laura said. Big tears were rolling down her cheeks. "Except when you left me alone. And we were never related, except maybe in a karmic sense."

"That's a relief – I think."

"I hate to interrupt this moment," Uncle Robert said. "I sincerely do, as I know how much you two mean to one another, but something is coming to a head, has been for a while. Can't you all sense it?"

The air was charged with the portent of drastic change. As Bryan was wondering what they should do, a deafening thunderclap sounded from outside the tent.

25.

Full of Sound, Fury, and Tears

Major Minor.

"Because we are an abomination under the gods, not just one god but all the gods. We eat, we destroy. That's all we do."

Marguerite had given Major Minor these reasons for helping him carry the Mark 84. Trusting her had been easy. She had spoken his very thoughts. The hard part had been maneuvering the twelve-foot-long bomb out of the helicopter. Arming the bomb was simple. Before the mission to Harmon County began, Minor had asked for a fuse that would self-arm after a big change in inertia, like a sudden stop after a drop. He had argued that the bomb could be fitted with a *ballute*, a small parachute to slow the bomb's fall. This ballute would allow the Chinook time to put some distance between itself and the drop zone.

But even something as electronically simple as an inertia fuse had become unreliable after the Fall, and he was stuck with a time-delay fuse that consisted a little propeller spun by air passing through the front end of the bomb as it fell. Not hard to arm, it could be set for a two- to eighteen-second delay. Using the Chinook, they could have dropped the bomb from an altitude right into the throat of the saucer's gash and still had time to climb to a safe altitude. But the major had no idea how to pilot the Chinook, or even if it were still operational.

That meant the bomb had to be carried by hand to the site, and the timer-setting calculations had to be changed. But the bomb still had to be dropped to set off the delay timer, and Minor doubted that he and the redheaded angel could drop it with much accuracy from a high altitude.

So, they would have to drop it from a low altitude, which meant they would likely be caught in the blast. But though the major didn't care if he survived the blast, the little propeller had to be spun for a set amount of time to detonate the bomb. He'd spin it by hand, but he'd have to partially dismantle the fuse mechanism to do so, and he wasn't sure the detonator would still work after taking it apart. They could not position the bomb on the saucer and set it off remotely.

The major decided to set the timer to as close to two seconds as possible. A wire coming out the tail of the bomb triggered the delay fuse. From there he would ride the bomb down, guiding it to the target.

This was the perfect solution, as the major had decided to go for the two-for-one shot. Before the redheaded angel had shown up to help, he was prepared to sit in the Chinook and try spinning the little propeller by hand, maybe even blow on it like a kid with a pinwheel, until it detonated. He would have preferred to take the saucer out with him, but he would not have been able to haul it over Lost Lake by himself. Now with the redhead's help, he could destroy the saucer and perhaps kill some of the other angel/human hybrids at the same time.

Straddling the Mark 84 as it went off should spread his individual molecules – or whatever putrid crap this angel body was made of – over a few thousand square yards. If that didn't grant him oblivion, nothing would. He tried to imagine what it would feel like to be nothing and failed.

The redheaded angel was tugging on the tip of his wing.

"Now's the time. Come look," she said.

She grabbed his hand and took him up above treetops. Hovering there, she pointed toward the saucer. "Something is happening or is about to happen," she said.

Across the water, the saucer was dotted with clumps of white. His angel vision focused, and the white clumps were resolved into angel/human hybrids, dozens of them, maybe more. They had grouped around the exposed gash in the outer skin of the saucer but made no movement to enter. They were clinging to the nearly vertical metal skin by some unknown means.

He didn't need to ask what brought them to the saucer, for he felt it too: a strong attraction to go there that had been tugging at him all day. Fine, so he was a homing pigeon; he would drop a two-thousand-pound bit of bird doo on the saucer.

The redheaded angel must be under the same spell. Her gaze became unfocused and her outer eyelids half-closed. She tugged at his hand, and he realized he didn't know her name and could only shout, "Wake up, wake up!"

When that didn't work, he grabbed her arm, meaning to shake her out of her trance but wound up pulling her face-to-face. He was conscious of her beauty for the first time. Her full, uplifted breasts were against his chest, and he was male again. Her eyes gradually focused on him and brought up her legs and wrapped them around his waist, bumping her sex against his. Without thinking, he slipped himself inside her, and they coupled as they spun in a widening gyre toward the ground. Legs entangled, they landed hard on a bare patch of ground, hard enough to bounce. But neither of them was damaged by the fall, and they continued to pound their bodies against one another, making very loud slaps of angel flesh against angel flesh, a meaty thump, thump, thump echoing through the woods like helicopter blades beating against the air. His will completely dissolved as they climaxed together. She was atop him, and now, without further preamble, she stood, pulling herself off his still erect member. Again, something had been lost in this impulsive act, though the major would not have thought he had anything left to lose since being sodomized by loving alien mechanical gremlins.

"We must do it now, while we still have the will," she said, avoiding looking him in the eye.

He agreed silently. He set the Mark 84's timer for two seconds. The bomb was heavy, but stradling it at opposite ends, the two of them easily got it aloft. He was at the back, his feet lodged between the fins. She was at the pointed end, legs wrapped around the slick metal as if she were on a kiddy ride. They carried the bomb over the treetops and then higher.

With the timer set at two seconds, the major calculated they only needed to be about sixty feet above the saucer when he yanked the trip wire. Then he would continue to hold onto the fins to stabilize the bomb's fall nose down, which would keep the fuse's propeller spinning.

As they hovered above the saucer, he could make out the individual faces of the human/hybrid angels. He saw at least eighty or ninety of them. Maybe more. Surely they could see what he and the redheaded angel were doing. The thing they carried couldn't be mistaken for anything but what it was, a bomb or missle, but the other angels didn't move from their roosts or try to intervene. Even his angel-enhanced vision could not resolve determine the expressions on their faces, but he sensed they were as placid as sheep. He found himself looking for the Lady of the Lake, but remembered, as in a dream, he and she were the same entity now, and this momentarily broke his will. For no reason he could understand, he now wished he could drop the bomb right down the gash, carry it into the throat of the beast, and destroy once and for all the portal to the other realm. But his fate was sealed, the timer set, and the deal with the redheaded angel fixed.

"What's your name?" he shouted to her.

"Marguerite – I think. Azazel, maybe," she called back from the other end of the bomb.

"Now's the time to let go," he said, surprising himself with a sense of compassion for her. Had it been the sex that changed his attitude? No, that had been just a last animalistic act. This was something else. A sense of camaraderie perhaps, that bond between two soldiers on the edge of death? That's what the sex act had been between them: a little death, a preview of the Big Sleep – he hoped.

She let go of the forward end of the bomb as he pushed the fins up so the bomb was pointed straight down. He gave the trip wire a hard yank. The bomb seemed to hesitate for a moment before falling.

I should have set the timer for three seconds. I could have slowed it down if that was too long. Too late now.

He tucked his wings in and hugged the bomb about midway where it was the thickest. And then Marguerite was on the other side of the missile. She locked her legs around it and him. Her arms were just long enough that she could reach around and grab his shoulders. She peered around the perimeter of the missile and smiled at him. He wasn't sure if he could smile back, but he tried.

The gash in the saucer was just a few feet below when a loud click came from the forward end of the bomb, and eternity swallowed them both into its abyss.

26.

Where Endings become Beginnings

Laura.

After the thunderclap came a moment of silence, then a distant roar was rolling toward them.

"Out of the tent!" Uncle Robert shouted. "Now!"

Something in his voice stopped Laura from questioning his command. Holding John Wright's hand and pulling him with her, she trotted, nearly stumbled and fell, then regained her balance, and ran at full speed out of the tent. Uncle Robert was ahead. She looked over her shoulder to see Bryan talking to the Suzanne simulacrum, urging her to leave, no doubt, but she wasn't budging.

Outside the tent, the roar grew louder, louder, louder until it sounded like a tornado.

Uncle Robert motioned them to the shadow of a large rock outcropping. John Wright had stopped at the edge of the outcropping, staring toward the roar. She could see it now, the source of the sound. A huge a water-like substance, colored red and blue by the alien sun, was pouring across the desert floor. The substance wasn't water, but fire. As the wave of fire rushed over the prismatic cacti, they vaporized into clouds and dissolved in the wind.

Laura kept tugging John's hand to get him to move. He seemed hypnotized by the sight of the wall of flame.

Uncle Robert tried to pull her away from John and deeper into the shadow of the outcropping. *If these bodies weren't material, not in the usual sense, why were they worrying about being burned to death?*

"Because it will hurt!" Uncle Robert shouted above the roar, reading her mind. "And because that kind of violent death may not leave us the choice of where we translate next!"

"You should listen," John said. He held her tighter, his arms hard around her waist. She grabbed at him, wanting to feel his strength, but his arms crumbled, granules sifting through her fingers like coarse cornmeal. She panicked and tried to hold on tighter.

Was the firestorm already here? Was it eroding them both?

No. She wasn't crumbling away, nor was anything else – only John Wright was dissolving. She looked up at his face, and he was still smiling, and he leaned forward to kiss her. She felt his lips on hers, then those too turned to dust and were whisked across her face by the wind.

She didn't have time to mourn as the roar grew louder, and now that she didn't have John to hold onto, Uncle Robert easily pulled her farther back into the shelter of the outcropping. She hadn't realized it was so deep. Inside, they seemed to be in a small grotto. She could see the opening of the tent from where she squatted. Bryan stepped out of the tent and looked toward the roaring firestorm, then turned and looked back into the tent, probably concerned about the Suzanne, if she were only a simulacrum.

Laura waved to him, beckoned. Could he see her in the shadow of the rocks?

Apparently he could, for he started walking toward them – then the firestorm washed over the scene. The tent immediately burst into flames and was blown away as ashes, and Laura heard someone scream, but it was neither Bryan nor the Suzanne – it was she herself who was screaming. She stilled her own outburst, then waited to be burned, more worried about Bryan than herself. She couldn't bear the idea of losing him as she had lost John Wright.

She realized that though she and Uncle Robert were sheltered from the force of the blast, the sides of the grotto were open except for the small enclave where they crouched. The heat should be radiating and broiling them but it wasn't. The air was sucked out of the enclave as the fire passed. It scattered the the pile of dust that had been John Wright, but still she felt no blistering heat, just radiating warmth as if she and Uncle Robert were sitting next to a fireplace.

As the flames began to subside, she could see a large translucent bubble, at least six feet in diameter, squatting in front of the tent's former location. The bubble's outer skin was white. The bubble wasn't completely spherical, but came to a point at the top, making it look like a large onion.

As the flames subsided and the sphere's surface became less opaque, they could see a man-sized shadow inside the hollow bubble.

The firestorm died down entirely, at least locally. The tent had been turned to ash, as had all its contents, including the cots and the odd storage chest here and there. And the Suzanne? Laura saw no sign of her. Had she merely translated to another plane or been incinerated in the inferno? Had she ever really been there?

Beyond where the tent once stood, perhaps a half-mile off, the wall of fire sped on, leaving behind what she least expected. In place of the burned-up prismatic cacti were what looked like completely normal Earth cacti. Some were even sporting yellow flowers.

The boulders and outcroppings had changed too, scraped clean of their alienness. Above, the sky was still emerald green, though. Far off, yet untouched by the firestorm, the basaltic mountains still had glowing olive veins tracing paths down their sides. The wall of fire continued rushing toward those mountains. Would it run up the steppes and wipe off the mountains' alien skin as well?

The figure inside the bubble poked at its outer surface with a finger. It was, of course, Bryan inside the bubble. The bubble had appeared exactly where he had been standing when the firestorm washed over the tent. His first poke bulged the translucent skin but didn't break it. He poked it harder – and again, even harder. For a moment, the skin stretched like a latex glove around his hand, then whole thing popped, leaving nothing behind, not even a scrap.

Bryan met her and Uncle Robert as they emerged from their shelter.

"Don't say it," Uncle Robert said.

"Don't say what?"

"Don't ask what rock we climbed out from under."

Bryan just shook his head. "How you can joke at a time like this I don't know."

"Me neither," Laura said.

"Many here among us think life is but a joke."

Bryan laughed at this. "Are you the jokerman or the thief?"

"Both," Uncle Robert said. "Maybe we're all bozos on this bus."

"Maybe this is where the clowns come in," Laura said. "Life is a fake bouquet of flowers, magically appearing, then disappearing down someone's sleeve."

"I wonder what that firestorm was all about?" Uncle Robert said.

"I know, but I can't explain how I know," Bryan said. "The major dropped a bomb down the hole in the saucer's skin. He wanted to find personal oblivion, and he saw it as a kamikaze mission: He wanted to take as many with him as he could. He killed all the human angels in the process."

"Marguerite, too?"

"Yes. In fact Marguerite helped him. She had a religious disease and wanted to follow him into oblivion. If I'm a god, then I'm a screw-up of a god, because I thought I'd fixed the major's murderous impulse. I guess all I did was turn it inward."

The news of Marguerite's death saddened Laura. Marguerite had saved her from an ignoble death – or rather delivered her into a safe realm after death. She had been a real guardian angel for Laura, a flawed, tormented one, but a kind creature nonetheless. Laura wondered what would have happened if Marguerite had allowed her to die normally back on Earth? Would she still have translated to this plane? Would she still remember her past life?

"But none of that matters, not really, not now," Bryan was saying. He was now surrounded by a faint blue aura. "Let me tell you what happened in the moments just after I stepped out of the tent. I had just given up on coaxing the Suzanne simulacrum to move."

He sighed.

"Go on," Laura said.

"Only moments passed for you two as the flames rolled over this place, but for me, uncountable eons ensued as the time-space bubble enclosed me.

"I was in an unlimited space at first, a boundless white space. But it wasn't really white, it was just totally without form, an emptiness where the blackest black would have still been something. It was empty of even that. And I was it, that emptiness, and it was me, there was no beginning, no ending, not really an *I*.

"And then I was overcome with something akin to loneliness, only, like I said, there was no I. If you're all there is to existence, you can't have individuality. That requires something to compare yourself to. And lone-liness isn't quite the right word, but it's close. I was sleeping, but aware of everything. I know that doesn't make any sense."

"It does. It sounds like Brahman the supreme soul or the Param-Atma," Uncle Robert said.

When Bryan and Laura just looked him, he said, "Hindi terms."

"Whatever," Bryan said. "Anyway, then I divided into many, many copies. All of us were in something that seemed like bubbles in this empty soup. And we were all dreaming, dreaming of each other, for we only existed independently of the white nothingness as long as each and all of us participated in the group dream. It felt like a great experiment."

"Were you dreaming us, too?" Laura said. What she really wanted to ask was if he had dreamed John Wright back into her life and then out again.

"You don't understand. Maybe I'm not explaining it very well. All those bubbles, billions, gazillions, an uncountable number, were all what we would call individuals, us, you, me, Uncle Robert, everyone, and yet they were all me, too. We were all of The One, and we were all individuals, and we were all participating in dreaming each other and the world."

"I think you're trying to cop out of being the Dreaming God," Laura said. "Of taking responsibility for dreaming up universes like the arch-angels said you were."

Bryan scratched his head. "Maybe; maybe not. We were all participating in the group dream experiment, but evidently some – most, really – forgot they were dreaming and got lost in the dream."

"So," Uncle Robert said. "There you were in what sounds like a very good place. Why did you come back here? Or did you have a choice?"

"A choice? Yes and no. I was compelled to come back here and tell you that you can choose your dream. That's what I'm going to do. I've chosen a little piece of the dream I want to live in for a while, and forget about being any sort of god, dreaming or otherwise."

"Are you telling us you're some kind of bodhisattva, come back here to save us?" Laura said. She was suddenly angry at him for reasons she couldn't fathom, and then a whispered message from one of the mystic clowns came back to her, words she couldn't really grasp, and her anger faded. She was still under the benevolent spell of the clowns and Jester, and she hoped she always would be.

"I'm saying that we are all bodhisattvas, and we choose –for reasons that are unclear to us most of the time – to live the dream we live in," Bryan said. "That's all there is to it, really. Sort of an anticlimax, don't you think?

Then he popped out of existence.

Laura stood, stunned. A big desert fly lit on her shoulder, buzzed something in her ear, and was blown away by the wind. In the far distance, the firestorm was rushing up the foothills of the mountains, erasing the olive veins.

"Hah," Uncle Robert said. "I think I know where he went and with whom."

"Where?" Laura said.

"That's not the question you should be asking," he said. "You should be forming an image of the dream you want to live in. I think he gave us the choice."

She thought about this, but the elements of such a dream seemed a jumble in her brain, like a stack of alphabet blocks that wouldn't quite balance. One of those blocks was John Wright, but the other question was: If what Bryan said was true, did he have to share her dream to make it happen?

She was going to find out.

Bryan, the Dreaming God.

Bryan Douglas was resting from cutting wood near Lost Lake when he saw the plane. He had quite a bit of firewood to harvest after the tornado had touched down, tossing loblolly pines around like matchsticks and opening a huge circular space in the forest that looked as if it had been stomped flat by a giant.

The site creeped him out a little and he didn't like working here. He always got an overwhelming sense of portent, not exactly *deja vu*; more like he was someone else, another person with a different history when he was here.

But most of his work had been done for him by the tornado, and he needed to sell as much wood as he could if he wanted to get back in school next semester.

On slow, boring days, he would imagine that an alien saucer had crashed there and expelled creatures from another world. But today, if he wanted to eat this winter and to take classes at the university, he had to stick to reality. A lot of deadwood needed to be cut and loaded – that was the bad news. The good news was it was all free for the taking.

Then he saw the plane, a private two-seater. It came in too low over the treetops. He hadn't heard the plane because its engine wasn't running, but by chance he had looked up as the morning sun reflected off its shiny white wings. The engine stuttered as he watched. The propeller turned idly.

The sight made him catch his breath. For a moment, empathy put him in the cockpit with the pilot, inside a powerless hunk of metal, falling out of the sky.

The engine suddenly sputtered to life and coughed a cloud of white smoke from underneath its cowling. The motor settled into a steady drone, died, and started again. Bryan let out his breath. The propeller turned, then spun into a blur. The plane's wings stopped wobbling, and the craft gained altitude. But at that moment a large white blur of motion exploded from the nearby woods. His eye glasses were sweat-steamed, andBryan had the momentary delusion that two large angels had burst up out of the piney woods. He yanked off his glasses, and, though he was near-sighted, his naked eyes resolved the fliers as a large flock of geese.

The geese were large, heavy birds, and the pilot, swerved to avoid a collision. He missed most of the birds, but one rogue straggler veered into the swirling propeller at the last moment. When the bird hit the blades, Bryan heard a thump-sound, like someone slapping a huge pillow, a red smear appeared on the passenger side of the cockpit, and the windshield shattered.

The plane waggled its wings again and staggered across the sky. The propeller still spun, but its sound was changed in pitch. Amazingly, after all this, the pilot regained control, gained altitude, and cleared the treetops by a few feet. In moments, the craft was out of sight.

Bryan had stood motionless during the entire drama and now felt a bit disappointed. He was sympathetic to the pilot – a nosedive at even fifty miles per hour into the surface of the lake would have killed him. But something perverse about human nature secretly loves other's tragedies, if for no other reason than to allow momentary forgetfulness of the mundaneness of daily life, and some part of him had hoped for a crash.

As the sound of the plane faded into the distance, Bryan knew he would have no disaster to talk about at Boucher's Cafe this evening.

In half hour, he had filled the red Ford pickup with as much split wood as he dared. Time to take the load home. Time for something to eat too. He had skipped breakfast, and his stomach growled.

He lodged the chainsaw and axe in a nook beside the loaded wood. He always held his breath when he turned the ignition key, but the truck started right up.

"Dog," he called, as the truck's idle smoothed out. "Dog."

Dog raced out of the woods, consumed with glee. Riding in the truck was his favorite thing. But then, everything was Dog's favorite thing.

He never regretted adopting the black-and-white dog that had showed up on his back porch a week ago with a rabbit in his mouth. The animal was good company, especially since Bryan's grandfather was on an extended Winnebago vacation since grandma Mattie had died. But after a month, Bryan still hadn't come up with a suitable name for the retriever. So he was still just *Dog*.

He inched out of the work site with Dog in the passenger's seat. He had to drive carefully because the ground was rough and the truck was loaded down on its springs. Then he and Dog were on Old Buffalo Road, heading back to his grandparents' homestead.

About a mile from Lost Lake he came upon a young redheaded woman walking by the roadside. She was trying to pull one of those suitcases with wheels, but wasn't having much luck on the dirt road. She didn't have her thumb out, but when she glanced over her shoulder, he recognized her: Suzanne.

She was a high school dropout who had moved in with John Cartwright, the weird old man who had a ranch down the road from his grandfather's farm. Though Cartwright was thirty or more years older than she was, the arrangement had evidently been good for her, as she had gotten her GED while there and the old man had supported her as she took some college classes. She and Bryan had taken a comparative religion class together at the university. An intense attraction had blossomed between her and Bryan, but nothing had come of it, as she seemed to have some sort of trust-relationship with the old man – which was both creepy and honorable.

They had coffee together once at the student union, and he had found her to be painfully intense, as very bright rebellious young women often are.

Last month, Cartwright had died of a stroke, and she had continued living at the ranch but working part time at Boucher's, apparently to feed herself.

He braked very slowly, the undercarriage and springs squealing from being overloaded, and stopped beside her. When she looked at him through the open window he could see she'd been crying.

He didn't know what to say, but just put the truck in neutral and leaned over across the seat to open the passenger door.

She didn't say anything either. She just smiled and wiped away tears, then struggled to haul up her suitcase onto the load of wood. He watched for a moment, then set the emergency brake, got out of the truck, and helped her get the suitcase up. Whatever she had in the suitcase, it weighed nearly as much as she did.

Obligingly Dog moved over to give her room on the passenger side.

They drove. She occasionally sniffled. An unspoken understanding passed between them. She reached across the space between them and patted his hand as it rested on the gear shift: *a thank-you.*

"They threw me out," she finally said. "John's relatives. Said as we were never actually married, that I was just *the help*, and made me leave."

He wasn't sure what to say. Her touch had been electric, though he told himself she probably hadn't meant it that way.

The world outside the windshield suddenly seemed decrepit, everything living and inanimate seemed old, out-of-date, like a black-and-white dream. Just as suddenly his perception shifted again, and things were *normal*. It was a bright spring day. He had a very pretty damsel in distress riding with him in his truck.

"Are you hungry?" he asked.

She nodded. "I could eat."

"Don't take this wrong," he said, though the truth be known, he was thinking all the wrong thoughts. "We're almost to my grandparents' house. There are some eggs and frozen hash browns in the fridge. You're welcome to join me – my grandparents are gone all month on vacation, and I hate to eat alone."

"I guess," she said and smiled. Despite her puffy eyes, something about her face made it hard for him to pay attention to driving. "But only if you let me cook for you."

Was he imagining it, or was there was promise of more than cooking in that smile?

He wanted to blabber on that he had the DVD version of Joseph Campbell's *The Hero with a Thousand Faces* at home. They had talked intensely about Campbell's hero cycle over coffee at the student union last year. But he managed to restrain himself from blathering.

Dog gave her face a big sloppy lick, and she laughed.

More wrong thoughts. He also had some peach moonshine he could offer her if she wanted to dull the pain of being homeless. Who knew what might happen after that?

Life suddenly seemed dreamy.

The End

R. Douglas Burns

http://magichatbooks.com/

Awakening of an Alien God

R. Douglas Burns

Awakening of an Alien God

www.ingramcontent.com/pod-product-compliance
Lightning Source LLC
Chambersburg PA
CBHW031300170626
46807CB00001B/232